A FIRESIDE BOOK

PUBLISHED BY SIMON & SCHUSTER INC.

NEW YORK · LONDON · TORONTO · SYDNEY · TOKYO

CHAMPIONS

OF THE WORLD

A NOVEL BY

DOUGLAS MINE

Simon and Schuster/Fireside

Simon & Schuster Building
Rockefeller Center
1230 Avenue of the Americas
New York, New York 10020

Simon and Schuster, FIRESIDE and colophons are registered trademarks of Simon & Schuster Inc.

Designed by Snap-Haus Graphics
Manufactured in the United States of America

10 9 8 7 6 5 4 3 2 1
10 9 8 7 6 5 4 3 2 1 Pbk.

Library of Congress Cataloging in Publication Data

Mine, Douglas.
    Champions of the world : a novel / by Douglas Mine
        p. cm.
    "A Fireside book."
    ISBN 0-671-67130-8
    ISBN 0-671-66802-1 Pbk.
    I. Title
PS3563.I4638C5 1988   88-15776
813'.54—DC19   CIP

We gratefully acknowledge A. P. Watt Ltd., Macmillan London Ltd., and Macmillan USA for permission to reprint "The Mask" by William Butler Yeats.

ACKNOWLEDGMENTS

My thanks to Morgan Entrekin for his criticism and encouragement; to
Charles Simpson for blowing wind into my sails; and, especially, to Laura
Yorke for her enthusiasm, sense and eye.

For my brothers

BOOK

O N E

1

9

7

8

CHAPTER 1

THE WIND WATERED HIS EYES AND HE BLINKED AGAINST IT.

Santiago Maglione, his feet sheathed in sheepskin, stood at the terrace rail and faced the wind heralding winter from the south, from the Patagonian steppe. The wind rolled the wide River Plate, shivering the skeletal elms. In September, the lindens' new leaves would glow and their fragrance mingle with a drizzle of jasmine. But spring was a long way off.

Santiago bundled the down jacket across his naked chest and tasted last night's wine in the brassy thickness of his tongue.

He never missed the dawn. He rose according to an intrinsic clock that varied with the seasons, waking him in the still darkness. Now he watched the sun show itself slowly, brazenly in the violet-colored space between earth and sky. The shallow river turned copper. He inhaled deeply, tilting his head back, closed his eyes and pushed the night's staleness out of his chest.

He went through a sliding glass door into the bedroom, into the faint smell of stubbed-out cigarettes, and padded silently down the carpeted hall and stairs to the kitchen. He opened the refrigerator and took out a liter bottle of milk, the butter dish and two eggs. He half filled a large enameled metal cup with milk and set it on the smallest burner of the range. He watched as a ring of gas whooshed orange and blue against the bottom of the cup.

When the milk was warm he cracked the eggs into it, then poured in a reluctant gob of honey and stirred. The tap-tap-tap of the spoon against the cup began the imperceptible erosion of the tranquility he had found in the day's first light.

After Santiago had munched his toast and drunk his potion he went upstairs and knocked lightly on his son's bedroom door. Then he went back downstairs to a room off the garage.

A bench for pressing weights sat in the middle of the room. Barbells and discs of iron were strewn like change over a padded mat on the floor. A heavy bag hung from a hook in the ceiling, a speedbag dangling next to it.

Santiago stripped off the jacket and his pajama trousers. He was wide and tightly wound, the pleated muscle of his abdomen split by a trail of sandy hair from his chest to his groin. He pulled on a jockstrap and a tubular elastic support over each knee and took a pair of baggy blue sweatpants from a peg on the wall. He stepped into the pants and pulled a gray sweatshirt over his head. He was lacing up a battered pair of sneakers when Alejandro entered. The boy yawned then shook himself from head to loins like a dog drying off and hastily replaced his robe with a red and white nylon jogging outfit.

Santiago sat on the bench with his head in his hands and his elbows on his knees. He stared at his feet and wiggled his toes inside the canvas shoes.

"You think if he hasn't called by now he won't call?"

"If he doesn't call today, that's it," said Alejandro. "I just wish I knew one way or the other, so I could get some sleep. I feel like a zombie."

Alejandro looked like his father, or rather as his father had looked when he was Ale's age. Dark blond curls fell across the boy's forehead and over his ears. His eyes were dark and wide.

Santiago had been handsome like his son. But boxing had broken his nose, thickened his brow and conferred on his long face a brutish cast. Santiago, after years of seeing this face in the mirror, had come to believe he was not as smart as he once thought he was.

"How did it go last night?" asked Alejandro.

"Air force officers are not the most stimulating conversationalists. They talked about the Beagle Channel and how we'll kick Chile's ass if they try anything. I'm tired of these *milico* dinners. But your mother enjoys herself. So I sit back, shut up and enjoy the meal." Santiago watched the tendons flex in his son's forearms as Alejandro pulled his shoelaces tight and tied them.

"I hope he calls, son."

There was a note of such fervor in his voice that Alejandro looked up. But Santiago had risen and stood with his back to his son. He was facing a broad leather belt with a big bronze buckle hanging from a nail on the wall. The buckle, dulled by the years, was inscribed: CAMPEÓN ARGENTINO AMATEUR, with the weight class MEDIANO and the year 1964.

Santiago turned around. "Which route?"

"The river road," said Alejandro.

They stepped into the new day and broke side by side like hounds into a lope.

Santiago was a running addict. He ran every day, at least five kilometers and as many as fifteen. It blanked his mind. He lost himself in the rhythm of his breath and heart and the hypnotic tempo of his footfalls.

Sometimes, when winding up a long run, fatigue conjured the image of him spinning the entire earth beneath him with his stride, like a circus lion on a rolling drum.

Alejandro ran with him because he was his father's son and because it helped to keep him in shape. The boy played forward for Boca and was one of the country's rising soccer stars.

During an interview the previous week, César Menotti, the coach of the national team, had mentioned Alejandro as a candidate for summons to the training camp in José C. Paz where Menotti was assembling the squad that would represent Argentina, the host nation, in the World Cup. Ale, though hopeful, did not entertain much of an illusion. Maradona had already been called to the camp, and Alejandro thought Menotti unlikely to recruit two rookies.

The father and son ran with matched footfalls down the road along the river's bend. Two gulls, one chasing the other, darted and whirled above them like the tail of a kite. The birds sailed away out over the muddy water, their squawks dissolving in the bright damp air. They passed an old man burning a pile of leaves by the curb. He leaned on a broom with his eyes closed, inhaling the ribbons of blue smoke that curled around him like vines encasing an ancient trunk.

The suburbs along the River Plate north of Buenos Aires are affluent and peaceful, the streets lined with trees. At this hour, the neighborhood had scarcely begun to stir. Silence was broken only by the barking of guard dogs—spring-limbed Dobermans and implacable Alsatians—moved by the two joggers' footfalls to gallop the length of their link-fenced terrains. Santiago and Alejandro ran past the riverside homes, some of brick—modern and angular—some of stately Tudor fashion. The yapping ceased, the dogs left behind with their caged anxiety. The men were drumming along an empty stretch when a powerful engine closed quickly on them. They veered to the left and a vintage Mercedes sedan whipped by.

"Slow down! *Boludo!*" Santiago shouted after it.

Later, when Alejandro made his statement at the police station, he was amazed that he could recall the scene in such detail. He could still see the fender of the hurtling car strike the blazered schoolboy who, hunched over the handlebars of a ten-speed bike, his tie flapping in the wind, had wheeled headlong out from a side road.

The car screeched and struck. The boy flew and everything else stopped in suspense of his cartwheeling trajectory. He landed and bounced awkwardly, like a rugby ball, before coming to rest in an angular mound.

The driver, a fat man, scrambled out of the car and bounded three steps forward. He stopped and looked toward the boy twenty meters ahead at the curb. He hopped like a hen caught in the middle of a highway, inclining first toward the boy, back toward the car, then back toward the boy. His head snapped around to check the road and he saw two men approaching at a sprint. He leapt with the peculiar and comical celerity of the obese back into the car and, just as Alejandro grabbed the door handle, took off.

Ale jumped onto the Mercedes's abbreviated running board and planted his feet. With both white-knuckled hands wrapped around the door handle he pulled himself against the side of the car. His face pressed against the window. The fat man shifted and accelerated. The driver looked forward, then sideways at the road and at the boy clinging to him like a locust. The man's thick glasses magnified bulging eyes and his face turned redder as the car picked up speed, as if his foot on the pedal were accelerating the flow of blood to his head. Through the window and above the wind Alejandro heard the muffled shout: "Get off!"

The stinging wind coursed over him and he pulled tighter against the door. His biceps knotted. The driver swerved violently in an effort to shake the burr. But Alejandro clung and clenched his teeth against the pain. He heard a screech, then felt and heard his arms pop in his shoulder sockets as the car was wrenched from his grip. He tumbled across the hood to the pavement. When he looked up, he fixed on a black and white metal rectangle. As he focused he read the numbers 373157.

The car sped past and away. Ale shook his head and pushed himself laboriously to his feet. His right knee stung. His sweatpants were torn from thigh to ankle and blood trickled down his shin from the scraped knee. He began running, a limping run, toward the boy two hundred meters back down the road. He repeated the license plate number out loud as he ran. He neared, and shouted to his father leaning over the boy.

"Dad!" he yelled. But Santiago did not hear or was too lost in contemplation of the broken boy to respond. Alejandro hobbled to a halt.

"Dad!" He shook his father by the shoulder. Santiago looked up at him.

"Remember these numbers: 373. Got it? 373. That's the first part of the license plate. I've got the second part."

Santiago's eyes were blank.

"What's the number?" Alejandro tested. Santiago did not answer. The boy cursed and picked up a stone and tried to write the number on the curb, but the stone left no mark.

Alejandro knelt and winced. The fair and freckled schoolboy would have appeared to be sleeping had it not been for the impossible position in which he had come to rest. Buckled over, his head lay on the inside of one thigh. The other leg was twisted backwards and a crooked arm stuck out from beneath him. Alejandro touched his finger to the wrist and felt a pulse.

"Stay right here. Don't do anything," he instructed Santiago and hobbled hastily down the road reciting six digits aloud.

It was noon when they got back home and opened the door to a petulant cry.

"Where the devil have you been?" called Monica, bolting from an overstuffed chair in the living room. She stalked toward the door, but pulled up short when she saw her limping and tattered son.

"Oh my God!" she gasped. "What happened?"

"We were witnesses to a hit and run," answered Alejandro, his arm draped over his father's shoulder.

"Witnesses? You look like the victim!" She lifted Ale's arm and replaced Santiago as the boy's crutch. She walked him to the kitchen and sat him down, making clucking noises as she brushed the hair off his brow.

Santiago followed them into the kitchen and opened the cup-board. "Where's the coffee?"

Monica looked up at him and her red lips curled under to expose brilliant white teeth. "Is that all you can think about? Coffee? We have to get this boy to a doctor."

"The police doctor took care of him. It's just a scrape."

"I can imagine what a hack the police doctor must be. I want to take him to Chavez-Luna, for a look at least."

"I'm okay. Really, Ma," protested Alejandro. "I'd feel it if there was something wrong."

Monica sat down in a chair next to Alejandro. Her right arm rested on the table. She began drumming her thick fingers against the tabletop. Her nails were filed to points and painted red.

Monica's face, the color of cream and enticingly freckled, was surrounded by wavy tresses. People described her as a redhead, but the hue was that of late ripe cherries, reflecting a spectrum from auburn to black, depending on the light. Her eyes, green and brown, shone flatly like glass. She had been a beauty, her aristocratic features more Gallic than Latin. During her youth she had mastered a charming—and disarming—sort of animal simplicity that had so thoroughly masked her faults, her pettiness and spite, that they had been practically invisible.

"Well," she said. "I hope there is nothing too wrong." She looked at Alejandro. She was radiant. "Because you got a phone call."

"Menotti?!" Ale flew out of the chair.

Monica nodded and beamed.

"Holy shit! Holy shit!" Alejandro jumped around the kitchen, oblivious to his injury. "What did he say? Does he want me to call him? Should I go straight there?"

"He wants you to report tomorrow morning," she said, then added, with immense satisfaction, "I knew he would call. Your chart said these days would bring fulfillment of your dearest desires."

Alejandro was slung between two yews in a Paraguayan hammock set up beyond the swimming pool. He was making up for a week of fitful sleep when the television reporter arrived.

Monica was delighted to lead the young woman journalist and her cameraman through the house and across the yard to the hammock. She shook Alejandro gently. He opened his eyes and squinted into the light.

"What the hell?" he demanded, shielding his eyes.

"You're going to be on TV!" squealed his mother.

She hurried back inside and stationed herself—cigarettes, ashtray, Cinzano and ice within easy reach—at the telephone. She would not abandon the post for an hour and a half, until she had called her parents long-distance in Mendoza, her sister, and her friends from the spa. She told them not to miss the evening news.

"What the hell is this?" repeated Alejandro.

"The crash. The hit-and-run," said the chicly attired woman flashing a practiced smile. "You're quite a daring young man."

"How did you find out about it?"

"We call the precinct houses as a matter of routine, for newsworthy murders and car crashes." She surveyed the length of her prostrate subject. Alejandro thought he noticed her eyes pause at his crotch. "Do you want to do the interview from the hammock?"

The predatory appraisal disquieted him. "I'd prefer to sit." He hoisted himself from the hammock and walked stiff-leggedly to a chair at a wrought-iron table beside the pool, empty except for a leafy puddle of rainwater in the deep end.

The videocameraman pointed and began rolling. "Tell us about it in your own words," said the woman into the microphone, then jabbed it in Ale's face.

"In who else's words would I tell it?" he said to himself and then described the morning's incident matter-of-factly.

"What was going through your mind while you were hanging on to the speeding car?" the reporter asked dramatically.

"That if I let go, I'd bust my ass."

The cameraman burst out laughing.

"Erase that!" snapped the woman. Then she turned with an indulgent smile to Alejandro. "This is for television. Could you please rephrase your answer?"

"Sure," said Ale. "I was thinking, 'If I fall off now, I'm fucked.' "

The crewman guffawed and Alejandro smiled broadly at his amusement.

"Cut!" The woman stood. "We're not getting anywhere like this."

"Look, señora . . ." Alejandro called her "señora" even though he had noted the absence of a wedding band and was certain she cringed at being taken for anything but the sensuous and desirable señorita she fancied herself. "There must be more important things to put on the news. But if you want this and my answers don't suit you, why don't you talk to my father. He was there too."

"You're missing the point." Her smile was gone. "You're the boy wonder. We can interview your father too. But we have to get something usable with you first."

So she asked him some inane questions and he provided unobjectionable replies. When they had finished she said, "Now, would you please ask your father to come out?" Her smile was back.

Alejandro rose and went into the house. His mother was gibbering at the telephone, so instead of asking her where Santiago was he went down the hall calling, "Dad? Dad?" There was no answer. But as he neared the garage he heard a rapid-fire thumping. He opened the door to the exercise room.

Santiago stood squarely before the heavy bag, his feet planted. His fists snapped like pistons and the stuffed cylinder rolled stoically with the blows. Grunts punctuated the punches. He battered the bag savagely at torso level. It was his worst enemy and he had him on the ropes. He hopped a small step back and measured in a blink the distance to the imaginary head and dispatched him with a murderous combination. Then he stumbled backward and plunked down, almost fell, on the pressing bench. He panted and cradled his head in red-knuckled hands. He did not notice his son at the door.

"Dad." Santiago looked up, alarmed. "There are some television people outside. They interviewed me and want to talk to you."

"Tell them to go fuck themselves."

That night, the family gathered around the big color set in the living room to watch Alejandro on television. When he appeared, Monica shushed Cristina's giggling and held her own breath, loath to miss a word. Alejandro leaned forward and watched intently, amused at his image and what seemed to him the foreignness of his voice. Santiago sat expressionless until the end of the report.

The newscaster, the same woman who had interviewed Alejandro, closed the segment with praise for the modesty of the young soccer star's publicity-shy father. She said his cool-headed administration of first aid had probably saved the boy's life, then added: "When so many are eager to take credit unduly, such humility is rare and refreshing."

Santiago listened incredulously. When she finished he pushed himself out of his chair. "What a bunch of bullshit," he said, and walked out of the room and out the back door.

Later, before going to bed, Alejandro sat in his bathrobe at the kitchen table sipping a cup of hot chocolate. Santiago appeared in the doorway and crossed the shiny tile floor. He held out his hand.

"Congratulations on the call from Menotti," he said, and shook the boy's hand firmly.

"Thanks, Dad. Even if I don't make the team, it's a great experience."

"Just do your best." There was a moment of silence before Santiago breathed deeply and said, "Son, even more than about the call from Menotti, I want to tell you how proud I am of the way you handled yourself this morning. You're a brave boy, and that's more important than the national team or even the World Cup." He leaned down and kissed Alejandro on the cheek. "Good night," he said, and turned and walked to the door. He stopped in the door frame and stood still with his back to Alejandro. Then he pivoted slowly. His eyes were wide.

"I don't know what happened to me. It was like I was paralyzed. I couldn't move."

"Don't say that, Pa," groaned Ale, flushed with the sudden and startling sensation that he was about to burst into tears. "You did all you could! You stayed with him until the ambulance came then gave your testimony and that will help catch the guy. What more could anyone ask?"

Santiago's head dropped. He turned and went up the stairs.

Alejandro sat for a long time staring at the swirls of chocolate in the bottom of his cup.

Diego Maglione sat in the harsh light of a single bulb, huddled over his kitchen table. It was late and the house was silent and still. His shoulders hunched, Diego studied a package of cigarettes. He unstuck the crackling cellophane from the bottom of the pack. It was meticulous work, like tying sutures. He blinked his arid eyes and tried to focus them on his uncooperative fingers.

He set the package down and held his hands aloft in a plane, flexing them open and closed. He intertwined his fingers and turned his palms outward, extending his arms. Then he pressed his hands together as in prayer, separated them and examined them. He stroked his black beard, scratching the skin beneath the whiskers.

He picked up the pack of Marlboros and opened the red and white package paper, exposing the tips of the tawny barrels. He held the open bottom of the pack to his nostrils and inhaled. The smell revived him somewhat. He pondered the package. It said: "Production authorized by the Philip Morris Company, New York, USA."

The tobacco came from Corrientes province. The paper surrounding it was from trees and mills in Tucuman. The hands that picked the tobacco leaves and cured them and cut them, the hands that felled the timber and processed the pulp into paper and ran the machines that transformed those elements into cigarettes were all Argentine hands.

Because he was so tired, Diego spoke to himself out loud. "What the fuck does New York have to do with these cigarettes?" he asked. His voice was oddly nasal.

He emptied the cigarettes onto the formica tabletop and was briefly distracted by the heads of harpies he devised in the swirling marble motif. At his right hand was a four-page tabloid newspaper weighing the same as twenty king-size cigarettes. The newspaper, *The Socialist Advance*, had been printed on a seventy-year-old press in the basement of the home of a man the same age.

Diego folded the paper four times in half, taking care not to smudge the ink, and inserted it into the open-ended pack. He closed the package with clear glue and examined his work. He balanced the tampered pack against the legitimate pack in his other hand and was satisfied they were indistinguishable.

He got up and walked down the short hall to his son's room, entering quietly and kissing the sleeping boy on the cheek. Then he went across the hall, took off his clothes, tossed them over the back of a chair and slipped into bed beside Ana, who was asleep. He lay still, awash in the narcotic of respite, and marveled that simply lying still could be so physically delightful. Right before he slipped off he decided to stop kissing Daniel before retiring each night. Daniel was almost thirteen and was likely to begin jerking off soon.

Ana got up early and went to the bakery at the corner. She bought a dozen crescent rolls called "half moons"—six made with butter, and six, browner and crispier, made with lard.

When she returned, Diego was up and dressed, standing by the stove pouring the day's first maté. He tipped the burnished kettle to fill the fist-sized gourd and let the water work a minute on the chopped green herb. He brought a filter-tipped metal straw to his lips and sucked up the bitter tea. He stepped to the sink and spit out the first pull, then filled the gourd again, waited and sipped. When it was empty, he refilled it and passed it to Ana. She sipped savoringly, then refilled the vessel and passed it back to him.

She reached over across the counter and pressed a button on a cassette player sitting there. The rewinding tape hummed inside the machine.

"*Oye, chico!* I can't start the day without some salsa, *tu sabes,* because it's so *chévere!*" she said in a thick caricature of a Caribbean accent. The cassette clicked and she punched another button. From the machine burst a chorus of horns. Diego took the kettle from the stove and sat down at the table. Ana stepped sideways across the floor, her hips swinging like a tolling bell.

"I can't stop myself!" she clowned, and danced over to Diego. "*Bailas, morocho?*" she invited through pursed lips and tried to pull him out of the chair, but he anchored his ass to the seat. She tugged but he did not rise and she desisted, too exuberant to lose time in persuasion. He watched her whirl and listened to her sing with Rubén Blades and Willie Colón:

> *No te dejes confundir*
> *Busca el fondo y su razón*
> *Recuerda, se ven las caras*
> *Pero nunca el corazón*

> *Don't let yourself get confused*
> *Look for what's behind, and why*
> *Remember, you see the faces*
> *But never the heart*

The song ended. "*Que chévere, chico,*" she said, grinning.

"What a tiny mouth you have," Diego mocked her lovingly. "Take care not to wet your ears."

"Look who's talking! You stand on the corner and smile and they'll start dropping letters down your throat." Ana turned off the tape player and poured herself a maté.

A sudden seriousness came over Diego. "I have to go to Constitución before we go to my parents," he said, picking up the cigarette packs on the table. "For this."

"*Ufa,*" she said.

"I'll be back soon." He put the two packs in the breast pocket of a blue flannel shirt. He stood up, pulled on a black windbreaker and pulled Ana against him. They touched foreheads and she pressed her pelvis against his loins, then pulled her head away and ground her hips against him. She looked at him through lynx eyes, Indian eyes, the kind that give provincial Argentine girls, the wives of gauchos, the name *china.*

Ana had those eyes and cinnamon skin. But her indigenous ancestors were so remote not even her great grandparents had recalled family members who spoke a language other than Spanish. Ana was simply *criolla,* the mixture of Iberian (mostly Andalusian, thus a good measure of Arab) and Indian that had formed the race of River Plate pioneers.

Diego held her face in his hands and they kissed.

"Come back fast," she said after him as he walked out the door.

He stepped from the house, the same house in which he had been born and raised, onto the streets of La Boca, the dockside neighborhood built by Italian fishermen and stevedores, where the Riachuelo meets the River Plate . . . which is not a river.

El Rio de la Plata is a broad muddy estuary where the Paraná and Uruguay rivers empty into the Atlantic. The Spanish explorer Juan Díaz de Solis called it a "freshwater sea."

Sometimes, after heavy rains in Brazil, the Paraná delta chokes with floating islands of tangled vines carried two thousand kilometers from the tropics. Boatmen ferrying fruits and vegetables to the Tigre market struggle through the snarl and sight an occasional black *macaco* monkey, forlorn and adrift, wondering how he got so far from home.

Summer mugginess and chilling winter humidity belie the name— Santa María del Buen Aire—that Pedro de Mendoza gave the settlement he founded in 1536. the "*argentum* (silver)" that the Spaniards, their avarice whetted by tales of Indians and deluded explorers, believed abundant proved illusory. The colony was for more than two hundred years a brackish backwater, neglected and forsaken. The immense richness of the land was slow to show itself.

On this Sunday idle cranes stood along the malodorous black Riachuelo water thick enough with oil and scum to float a stone. A dredge on overtime whined sermonically. Diego walked down Mendoza Street a block, past the blue and white tugs and rusty barges (the fishing boats were long gone, to Mar del Plata, as the river here poisoned all life). He turned up Rocha between rows of green and yellow and orange corrugated metal houses stacked upon each other like a toddler's blocks. Clothes hung damp and still from lines strung between the dwellings.

He looked up and saw an old woman in a faded pink dress sitting on a wrought-iron balcony, her hand perched on a cane. Her nut-brown face had fallen into a chiseled frown. He walked up the middle of the street over gray and red cobbles splotched with patches of worn asphalt. A boy played with a broomstick along the old pitted and polished trolley tracks. He threw the stick forward like a javelin, only to run after it, pick it up and throw it again.

Diego reached the cantina at the corner of Irala. A woman sang inside as she swabbed the floor, suds spilling out over the stoop. He looked at his watch and saw he would be late if he took the bus, so he hailed a cruising taxi.

The black and yellow cab pulled to the curb. On its rear windshield was a sticker: "We Argentines are human and right."

"Shit," thought Diego. But he was late, so he opened the door and got in.

"Constitución," he instructed.

That sticker, it was everywhere these days. The cops plastered it in shop windows, buses and bars with a portentous wink to the proprietor. To Diego's relief, the driver did not want to talk politics or human rights. He wanted to talk soccer.

"So, which are the teams to beat?" he asked, looking in the rearview mirror at his fare. "Germany? Holland? Brazil looks good, as always."

Diego did not want to talk about soccer. It wasn't that he didn't like the game. He enjoyed it immensely, as did the great majority of Argentina's male population. But he had other things on his mind, so he spoke to the driver in hasty Neapolitan.

"I'm going to the station to meet my wife. She's arriving on the train from Italy. The transatlantic special. I haven't seen her in ten years, so I'm excited and unconcerned with *fútbol*."

The driver, who fortunately was not Neapolitan, muttered, "Oh. Tano, huh?" and drove the rest of the way in silence. (The term is an abbreviation for Napolitano and used to describe Italians—southerners and northerners alike—and their Argentine-born progeny.)

Diego had not lied when he said he was excited. But more than excited he was apprehensive, a little scared. After all the years, he was still not accustomed to the risk. Though the day was cool, a drop of sweat tracked from his armpit down his side. He did something he only did when he was nervous. He put his thumb into his mouth to feel the thick scar tissue inside his upper lip, where the halves had been joined. It looked like he was sucking his thumb. But he was tenderly touching his congenital imperfection, reminding himself of his deformity. His other hand loosened its clutch on the worn and ragged armrest and he settled into the seat. He exhaled profoundly, almost a sigh.

He watched the Sunday morning cityscape slide by and mused on this manner of drawing comfort and something akin to courage from the very thing that marred him; he wondered that strength could reside in debility.

As the taxi approached the eastern entrance to the imposing, centenarian railroad station, a swarm of boys sprang from their common crouch on the steps to dispute the opening of the taxi door. One of the biggest, his bare feet in too-large shoes, grabbed the handle and opened the door in spite of Diego's attempt to let himself out.

The runny-nosed boy held out his hand and looked up, dejected and subservient. Diego started up the steps.

"Cheapskate!" the boy spat after him.

Diego wheeled. "I may be a cheapskate but I'm no beggar and if you have any pride you won't be one either."

The boy released the cab door and shifted his weight to his heels, poised for flight. Perhaps he had insulted a cop. Then the strange, almost feminine quality of the voice pierced his fear and the boy realized, in wonder, that he—skinny, hungry, louse-infested—was better and more blessed than the man opposite him. The boy laughed loudly and his companions laughed with him.

"And if you have any pride . . ." he mimicked in a nasal whine. "What are you so proud of, *pelotudo,* your harelip?"

Diego took a step down toward the boy, then checked himself. His rage consumed itself with a soft pop, like the last bit of gas in a lantern, and he turned and bounded up the stairs by twos. He trotted through the portal and melded with the bustling travelers in the cavernous hall.

He felt capable of anything. He strode past the sandwich and pizza stands and saw his contact, a man he knew only by the pseudonym Emilio. The middle-aged man, wearing khaki work clothes and a corduroy jacket, stood beside the information desk and looked up in a pretense of supplication to the green-caped and gold-crowned wooden statue of the Virgin Mary perched above the door to the stationmaster's office. Flowers flanked her and a goldleaf inscription below her read: VIRGIN OF LUJAN, GRANT US A SAFE JOURNEY.

The transaction was to be synchronized according to a large clock hanging from the center of the vaulted roof. Diego was to go down the stairs to the men's room at the west end of the station at 10:30. He was to leave the cigarette pack with the newspaper on the farthest urinal.

Emilio was to enter at 10:32, pass without acknowledging the exiting Diego and pick up the package.

Diego was walking across the station toward the stairs leading down to the lavatory when he was knocked sprawling by a tremendous blow, like a mule kick between the shoulder blades. As he slid on his belly the station hall swelled with a skull-ringing clap and everything before him tumbled and shone kaleidoscopically. The thunder reverberated off the high stone walls then retreated from them.

(The newspapers would report that the bomb went off near a queue at the window for the General Roca line to the south. Five people died, including the Montonero carrying the bomb. The organization sent a communiqué to the international news agencies with offices in Buenos Aires explaining that the device had been intended for use against a military target, but had detonated prematurely. The Montoneros apologized and offered condolences to the victims and their families.)

Silence flooded the space voided by the blast. It seemed to Diego, stunned on the floor, like a long silence. Then he heard groans, screams. He struggled to his knees and looked around. The air was thick with eddying amber dust. Ten meters away a teenage girl with her right arm severed at the elbow walked rapidly in a tightening gyre, leaning inward as if she were being pulled down a drain. Her mouth gaped blackly but issued no sound. She cupped the stump with her good hand but the blood slipped through her fingers.

Diego pushed himself up and ran to her. He caught her as she fell and he sat on the floor with her draped across him. Blood spurted onto his shirt. He pulled her belt through the loops of her jeans and cinched it tightly around her bicep. He lifted and carried her toward the daylight slicing into the settling, glimmering specks of debris.

He stood for a moment at the top of the steps to the station's main entrance. People streamed toward him from the bus stops across Brasil Street. Sirens cried, tires screeched and a police officer with drawn pistol bolted up the steps. Diego made his way down, toward a patrol car. A stocky officer opened the rear door and Diego sidled in with the unconscious girl on his lap. The policeman flung himself behind the wheel and took off, tires spinning.

Diego did not know how many minutes it took to reach the San Andres hospital twelve blocks away. But he knew exactly how many drops—fifty-five—of blood the girl lost on the way. The stump of her arm was suspended over a rubber mat on the car floor and the vermilion beads fell, ticking against it with a slow but steady beat. Diego did not know if he counted the ticks aloud, but their tally seemed paramount, a matter of life or death.

He and the cop delivered the girl to the emergency ward. Diego identified himself as a physician and stayed to watch the first-aid crew work. When the girl had been dispatched to surgery, he was able to speak with the emergency room chief.

"The tourniquet saved her life," said the gray-haired doctor, handing Diego a faded green physician's smock. Diego shed his windbreaker and took the two packs of cigarettes from the pocket of his blood-soaked shirt and placed them on the counter. He stripped off the shirt and tossed it into a waste bin. He was donning the smock when the cop came back in. He signaled to Diego with a crooked finger.

"Sir, if you'll come with me to the station house to fill out a report . . ." Then he noticed the cigarette packs on the ledge. "Mind if I have one of these?" He had already picked up the top pack and was unwinding the cellophane tab. "I left mine in the car."

Diego grabbed the other doctor's arm as his knees buckled.

The cop peeled off the cellophane, smacked the pack against the countertop to tamp the tobacco, lifted the foil and rapped out a cigarette. He fastened his wet lips on it and drew it out.

"Want one?" He proffered the pack and jutted his chin at the two doctors.

Diego loudly exhaled, then snatched the pack from the extended hand and snapped, "You're offering me my own fucking cigarettes."

The old man crawled slowly down the row of harvested bean and pepper plants, pulling up weeds as he went and tossing them aside in bunches. His baggy trousers were gartered at the knees by the elastic straps of hard leather kneepads, the kind masons use when they float a floor. He paused at intervals to put his nose to the soil and examine a worm or a beetle. He hummed.

Mikhail Maglione pushed himself up from the ground and walked from the garden past a wooden fence draped with laden grapevines, to his carpentry shed. He was barrel-chested and short, but his arms were long and strong and swung as he strode bowleggedly across the yard.

"The moment has arrived. The moment of truth," he said in Neapolitan as he crossed the cluttered shop. He kneeled and opened a hatch and reached down into a hole, a small cellar. He pulled out a five-liter *damajuana* wine bottle.

"*Tre anni.* Three years I have waited for you to grow up, *cara mia.* For your breasts to swell and your hips to curve. Now you are a big girl." He stood and ferreted through a workbench drawer for a corkscrew. He skewered the cork with a twist and pulled it out with a grunt and a pop. He took a glass from the shelf and filled it halfway with the dark wine. He held it aloft and examined the color, inhaling and exhaling exaggeratedly.

"Breathe, *cara mia.* Breathe the good fresh air of the pampa." Then he brought the glass to his lips and sipped. He closed his eyes and held the liquid in his mouth a moment before swallowing.

"Ahhh," he sighed, and set the glass on the workbench. His smile exposed big tobacco-stained teeth the color of old ivory. He tittered like a baby and the back of his left hand snapped up to his forehead. The index finger and pinky—the two middle fingers were missing—stuck into the air like horns.

"*Siamo tutti contenti, siamo tutti cornuti!*" he exclaimed and jigged a quick step.

Mikhail's head was round like a pumpkin and his face was deeply tanned. Creases furrowed his brow and ran down either side of his broad nose. His slightly skewed eyes gleamed from a web of wrinkles. His gray hair was clipped short, almost as short as the salt-and-pepper stubble on his jaw. There was a bald patch, like that of a monk, at the crown of his head.

It did not matter much that Mikhail Maglione had changed his name. No one, except his daughters-in-law, ever called him Mikhail. Acquaintances (his few friends had died) called him El Bizco (Crosseye) when he was out of earshot. When talking with him, they just called him Tano.

That he was rarely called by his proper name did not make Mikhail unique. Along the River Plate, a man is known as Fats or Skinny or Blackie or Red according to his build or complexion. If his grandparents were Arabs, then he is El Turco—even if they were from Lebanon or

Syria. If they were Jews, he is El Ruso, and if they were Spaniards, then he is El Gallego regardless of whether they were from Galicia. Argentines are not prone to call things by their names. Maybe they think names are simply not appropriate.

In any case, it did not matter to Mikhail what he was called, as long as it was not Franco, the name he had been christened with. He had been called that all through his youth, and he had always thought it a fine enough name. But the first thing the haggard carpenter's apprentice did after disembarking back in Naples in 1939 with what was left of his International Brigades contingent was to go to the courthouse and change his name. He had chosen that of his deceased hero, Mikhail Aleksandrovich Bakunin.

Mikhail had lost a brother, many friends and two fingers in Spain. More correctly, he had left a finger and a half behind. Because after they had been snapped off by a bullet he had found one of them—he was never sure if it was the middle finger or the other one—not far away on the ground. He had stripped off the flesh, boiled and dried the phalanx, lacquered it and worn it ever since on a leather thong around his neck. It warded off the *gettatura,* the evil eye, and he touched it whenever a stranger looked at him or when an eerie sensation made him think someone had walked across his brother's grave.

It was in Spain, around crackling campfires and in comrades' *cantinas,* that the young Mikhail had heard the old anarchists speak reverently about Argentina, about *La Patagonia Rebelde* and its martyrs. He had drunk many toasts to their memory. The old men, some of whom had taken part in the episode, had told him and anyone who cared to listen about the vast expanse at the bottom of the New World where, in 1920 and '21, poor immigrants from Spain, Germany, Italy, Poland and Russia banded with Argentine and Chilean ranch hands and *campesinos* to demand decent wages and humane working conditions on the British sheep-raising *estancias,* in the ports and in the hotels where the recent arrivals worked as cooks and waiters. They had made themselves un-derstood to each other in a babel of thick accents and forged a move-ment, Anarcho-Unionism, that they believed would herald a truly New World. The federal government in Buenos Aires, pressured by the tweedy guarantors of the Argentine economy in London, broke the unionists' general strike with infantry and cavalry. The workers fought back and more than a thousand died, most of them summarily executed after surrendering.

So, in 1945, after years of resisting the Fascists, after realizing that Mussolini was defeated but the bourgeoisie was stronger than ever, Mikhail had convinced his wife that they should pack up and go to America, to Argentina. And he and Angela had walked up a gangplank, little Santiago in his father's arms, and sailed away from Europe. (That was Santiago's most distant memory; boarding the ship and watching the port, the squat white buildings shimmering on the hillside, drift farther and farther away, until it was gone.)

Of course, they never made it to Patagonia, to the land of Mikhail's gilded vision. Angela discovered during the voyage that she was pregnant. Upon arrival, they made friends among the Neapolitan community in La Boca, Mikhail found work and Patagonia receded far beyond the horizon. When they finally moved from La Boca, after the children were grown and gone, it was to this small block house on a pasture-bordered half hectare in Longchamps, forty kilometers south of the capital.

Mikhail, after tasting the wine, recorked the bottle, placed it back in the pit, closed the hatch and went back to his gardening. He was carrying uprooted weeds to a mulch heap and loudly singing, "*Che bella cosa, la giornata al sole!*" when Angela came out of the house.

She dried her hands on a yellow apron as she neared the garden. She had been making pasta, and flour dusted her eyelashes and decorated her nose where she had scratched it. She was a big woman and her unlined face fell naturally into a pensive, saddened expression. Surprisingly it could lift into a tender smile with ease and her eyes would crinkle and gleam.

She took a pair of clippers from the pocket of her apron and cut a branch from a small box tree shading the patch where she grew parsley and sweet basil for pesto, and borage for stuffing raviolis. There was also *vira-vira*, which, before her menopause, she had used in a tea to calm menstrual pain. In a stronger solution it brought on sweating and relieved coughs and colds. She bent over and examined the *carqueja*, the *broon*.

"I'm going to make you a stiff tea of this, old man," she said mischievously to Mikhail.

"You want to wear me out. But one must take care of the flute, for the concert is long."

"And what about the piccolo?"

"How would you know if it's *piccolo?* The fingers on my left hand are more than enough to count the ones you've seen."

"That's what you think! I'm no expert but my brothers were stallions in that regard."

"Better small and frolicsome than big and boring, I always say."

Angela pinched off some branches of *broon* and took them and the box branch back into the house. The devout have branches of the box tree, or "Easter bush," blessed by a priest on Good Friday, then keep them in their homes to preserve the family from illness and to ward off lightning. Angela did not practice this Roman Catholicism she had been infused with during her youth, but neither did she reject it adamantly, as did Mikhail.

A little while later, as Mikhail finished setting up the table—a door supported by two sawhorses—beneath the olive tree in the front yard, Santiago, Monica and Cristina appeared at the gate.

Mikhail met them on the walkway. "And the car? And the big boy?" All three kissed Mikhail.

"Alejandro is at training camp with the national team," said Santiago. "If you had a telephone out here in the sticks you would have found out sooner. The car is in the shop, so we took the train."

Angela came across the yard. Cristina ran to her.

"Nona!" cried the girl, wrapping her arms around her grandmother's waist.

Cristina was big for her thirteen years, but Angela lifted her off the ground and sang out, *"Bellezza mia!"*

"We were lucky to have made it," said Monica dramatically as they entered the house. She loved the role of news-bearer, and did not so much inform as bestow her privy knowledge on the rest. "A bomb went off in Constitución this morning and service was interrupted for hours while they cleaned up the mess."

Before Mikhail and Angela had time to assimilate this, their daughter-in-law pronounced her verdict and sentence: "These terrorists must be gotten rid of to the last one."

Everyone stopped. Santiago looked at Monica, then at his father.

"But then the country would be left without an army, navy or air force," said Mikhail, his eyes fixed on Monica.

"Let's not start," said Angela. It was more order than request.

Mikhail took Santiago by the arm and said, "I want to show you something." He led him out through the back door.

At the back of the house, standing like an orphan against the exterior wall, was a small spindly tree planted in a can.

"It's a jacaranda," said Mikhail. "I made some cabinets for a guy who has a nursery, and he gave it to me. I thought it would be happy in your yard."

"Great. Thanks, Pa. I know just where to plant it. Next trip out, when we've got the car, I'll take it back."

They heard the sound of a car pulling up out front and circled around the house. Diego, Ana and Daniel, a soccer ball under his arm, emerged from a blue Fiat.

The brothers embraced. Angela and Monica came out, and everyone hugged and kissed each other.

"I'll go get the wine," said Mikhail ebulliently, and made for the shed.

"Wait, Grandpa!" Daniel tossed the ball across the yard, ran to Mikhail and took his outstretched hand.

Daniel loved the shop. Whenever he came to Mikhail's house he spent time there with his grandfather, who was only too delighted at the boy's interest in his trade. Daniel would perch on a chair and peer intensely over Mikhail's shoulder while he explained each step and had Daniel hand him tools, sand an edge, apply the glue, tighten the vice.

Mikhail knelt to reach into the cellar and Daniel mounted a stool before the workbench. He pulled open a drawer. In it was an old wooden Cuban cigar box with a picture of a grass-skirted, bare-breasted Indian woman on the lid. He lifted the lid and his eyes widened. He closed the box and the drawer then grabbed the handle of the saw set in the miter box on the benchtop.

"What's this for?" he asked as Mikhail pushed himself back to his feet.

"It's for sawing wood at an angle." Mikhail put the straw-wrapped glass jug on the bench and held up his hands so that the two fingers of the left touched those of the right in a peak. "So the corners come out right." He reached down to pick a scrap of wood off the sawdust-covered floor. "Watch." He loosened the nut on the miter and swung the saw to the right, then tightened the nut. Holding the piece of wood against the brace with the heel of his maimed hand, he sawed through it in a few strokes. Then he loosened the nut again, swung the saw to the left, tightened it in place and sawed through at the complementary angle. He held the two pieces up together to show Daniel.

"Perfect," said the boy. "What a good tool."

"All tools are good. Most of these," he gestured to the array of hammers, drills, awls, chisels, saws and files hanging from a pegboard, "are from Italy, older than your father." Mikhail paused to regard the boy, reminder of a remote and wide-eyed studious face in a cracked mirror on a wall in another world. "The tools and the skill are what is important," he said. "Not so much the things you make. Because with the tools and the skill you can make beautiful things without limit."

He ran his hand through Dani's curly black hair and felt a rush of love. "To construct your life you also need good tools."

"Where do you get them?"

"You see them working in the lives of the people around you." Mikhail pushed the sawdust on the benchtop into a small pile and sifted it through his fingers. "But there are only three you really need. You know, like from yellow, blue and red you can make all the colors."

"Which are they?"

"I could tell you, but you can't learn such things that way, just by being told."

"Tell me, *Abu,*" pleaded Daniel. "I'll remember."

Mikhail held up his gapped left fist. He stuck out his thumb and said, "Compassion." He stuck up his index finger and said, "Honesty." He stuck up his pinky and said, "Courage."

"Now let's go eat," said Mikhail. "Afterwards I'll show you how to use the plane."

Daniel climbed down off the stool but hesitated there beside it. Mikhail moved toward the door, then stopped and looked back at the boy. Daniel pulled open the drawer and opened the cigar box. He reached into it and lifted out an old but clean and recently oiled, dully gleaming revolver.

It was a Spanish Orbea, .32-caliber.

"Won't you show me how to use this?" The gun lay across his open hand.

Mikhail walked over to him, took the weapon and put it back in the box. He closed the drawer.

"That's also a tool," he said. "It can be an important one." He took the boy's hand and they stepped together out into the brightness.

It was a fine meal, beneath the olive tree, of agnolottis daubed with Angela's subtly seasoned fileto sauce, roast chicken, homemade bread and Mikhail's hearty vintage.

Daniel sat across from Cristina. He had drunk a half glass of wine mixed with soda water and felt light and happy. He had finished eating and was looking across the table at his cousin when, for the first time, he was struck by her beauty. She had her mother's complexion, smoother though, and glowing. But her eyes were the dark, deep eyes of her father. Her mouth was small, like a fig, and she had a small beauty mark or mole high on her left cheek. Dani was looking right at the mark when she looked up at him. Blood flooded his head and he averted his eyes, hotly ashamed at having been caught. When he dared to look again at her, she gave a glimpse of a smile.

Over coffee, Santiago mentioned that he and Monica were considering the purchase of a small sailboat, a sloop that could sleep four and make the crossing to Uruguay.

Diego had been peculiarly silent throughout the meal. Now he looked up and spoke, his uncharacteristic sarcasm surprising everyone. "I suppose next you'll be joining the Jockey Club and buying a condo in Punta del Este." He chuckled humorlessly and stared at Monica.

"And what would be wrong with that?" She set down her cup and laid her hands flat on the table before her. "If we could afford it, why not? And we may be able to, before long." She placed one hand over Santiago's. He looked across the neighboring field. "Just because your idea of a holiday is coming out here to your parents' *quinta,* that doesn't mean you have to belittle your brother's success."

"Success?" Diego snarled. "Collaborating on fat-budget military projects is success? Don't give me that mound of shit."

Monica pretended offense. She glanced at her daughter and said, "I wish you wouldn't swear in front of Cristina."

"Oh come off it. She's a big girl." Diego looked at Cristina and she raised her eyes to meet his, at the same time raising her napkin to cover her mouth. Diego saw the smile in her eyes.

"There's no use arguing with you," said Monica exasperatedly. "You're totally blind to anything good in the armed forces, which as far as I'm concerned have saved the nation from disintegration."

"General Videla could not have put it any better. But that skull-faced hypocrite is responsible for the abduction and murder of thousands of people. And anyone who has anything to do with him is an accomplice." Diego slammed his fist on the table and the glasses and coffee cups rattled. He got up and stalked away.

Ana and Angela looked at each other. Angela shook her head slowly. Mikhail drained his wineglass and spit a mouthful on the ground. "I shit on the holy· host," he declared, and also left the table.

Daniel slid inconspicuously from his chair and followed his grandfather across the yard toward the shop.

Monica sighed. "It is difficult to believe that an intelligent person like Diego, whatever his political beliefs, can be taken in by the propaganda of the same terrorists who tried to destroy the country. Human rights, human rights. I'm fed up with hearing about it. As far as I'm concerned, we Argentines are human and we're right."

"Very original," said Ana.

Santiago rose and walked over to where Diego was kicking Daniel's soccer ball into the air, then letting it drop down on him so he could kick it aloft again. He was trying hard to concentrate on the ball and its debate with gravity, trying to calm himself. But it was not working.

Santiago neared and Diego spoke, without taking his eyes off the ball. "You can't see anything any more. You stand on your terrace and look out over your big yard and think that because your personal park is tranquil, the country is tranquil too."

· "Would you stop kicking that damn ball and look at me?" Santiago stepped forward and snatched the falling sphere. "I design airplanes. Are you smart enough to tell me how I am going to do that and not have some kind of relationship with the air force? They control the purse strings right now, but it won't be forever."

"Everybody has his justification."

"Diego," said Santiago imploringly. He wanted to end the matter and go back to the table with his arm around his brother's shoulder. "You can't expect everyone to love politics like you do."

"I don't love politics. But it's a fact of life."

"Well," said Santiago, his ire rising, "it's a fact of life that makes me sick. You're just like our old man. You live in a dream world where everyone is everyone else's brother. That's bullshit. Because politics is just words. Flesh and blood are what counts. I've got just one brother, and that's all I'll ever have." He slung the ball with a hard underhanded flip to Diego. "You're so concerned with criticizing, you can't see what's good about this country."

"What? The best beef in the world and the deepest topsoil and Juan Manuel Fangio and the Teatro Colón? That's the line they use to turn out good little patriots. Because of a coincidence of birth we're supposed to shout 'Viva Argentina!' with our dying breath?"

"It's the only country we've got. And it's a goddamn good one. The best, as far as I'm concerned. Our old man came here with a box of tools and a suitcase and you're a doctor and I'm an engineer. Where else could that have happened?"

"So everything is all right then?"

"No, everything is not all right. But what do you want me to do about it?"

"Why don't you just buy a yacht and sail it to Punta and have a grand old time?"

"Vafancul," spat Santiago. "You're gonna change the world, right? Why don't you start by providing for your family? You think getting yourself killed is going to usher in the utopia? Fuck the utopia." His choler subsided, leaving disgust. "You're impossible to talk to." He turned and headed back toward the table.

"You sure haven't worn yourself out trying these past few years," Diego called after him.

The words stabbed Santiago and he stopped. But he did not turn or respond, he walked away.

As soon as he sat down, a mighty bang like a New Year's firecracker rang out from behind the house. Diego, standing with the ball where Santiago had left him, dropped it and ran toward the sound. Santiago jumped up and followed, with the three women and Cristina trailing.

When they turned the far corner of the workshop they saw Daniel steadying a large revolver clasped between his two small hands at the end of his thin, extended arms. Mikhail stood at the boy's back. A can sat on a stump fifteen meters ahead.

"What the devil?" exclaimed Angela, the last to arrive.

Without lowering the weapon, Daniel turned his head to the family, then sighted back down the barrel and squeezed the trigger. The report resounded sharply and the can jumped tumbling high and glinting in the sunlight, end over end, before it landed with a clank.

CHAPTER 2

THE EUCALYPTUS TREES BORDERED THE PLAYING FIELD LIKE SENTINELS IN RENT GARMENTS, IRON-RED BARK PEELING AWAY IN JAGGED SWATCHES, MOTTLED LIME AND FINE WHITE SKIN EXPOSED TO THE BREEZE.

Twenty-six men in gray and red sweatsuits were scattered like beetles over midfield. A loudening buzz made them look up from their stretching and twisting and groaning. A helicopter whirred toward them over the treetops. They stood up one by one and shaded their eyes against the sun and watched the craft settle unhurriedly like a falling leaf. The rotor slowed and a big man in a dark blue uniform emerged and ran stooped over, holding on to his peaked hat, from beneath the spinning blades. Menotti made for the visitor.

"Hello Admiral Massera," he said, extending his hand.

"How's it going, César?" inquired the navy commander and junta member.

"Coming along. We'll be in good shape by the second." Menotti was tall and bony and long-necked like a llama. He always looked tired or hung over.

The two men exchanged small talk for a moment beside the helicopter. Emilio Massera, known to his friends and more familiar subordinates as El Negro, flashed a thin-lipped toothy smile and knitted his huge black eyebrows. Dark eyes darted beneath them from Menotti's face to those of the players, gathered in groups of four or five, talking reservedly and watching the two men.

Menotti extended his arm toward the players in invitation and the admiral strode across the turf. Alejandro was standing with Passarella, Bertoni and Kempes. Massera came toward them and shook each one's hand.

"I'm just one more fan rooting for you. One among twenty-five million," said the admiral, grasping Alejandro's hand in a firm cold mit, looking him directly in the eyes, wrinkling the furry Neanderthal brow. "We're all counting on you. We know you can do it."

The navy commander circulated among the players, encouraging, joking and backslapping like one of the boys. He made a bet with Fillol, the goalie, that he could not stop the admiral's penalty shot and Fillol accepted the challenge good-naturedly. The admiral, in full uniform and shiny black thick-soled oxfords, awkwardly dribbled one of the scattered balls to the near goal's penalty spot. Fillol ambled to his position on the midpoint of the goal-line and stood there leaning forward in relaxed anticipation.

Massera doffed his hat and sailed it to the gallery of players. Luque caught it and placed it on his head. Massera backed off the spot a few paces, studied the goal and approached the ball with short quick steps. His right leg swung down and through, and the ball shot off his instep. It was not at all a bad shot. But the admiral, determined to do himself and the navy proud, had put much into it. He left foot, the one he had shifted all his weight onto, skidded on the grass, swept out from under him up into the air and the bulky dictator hung suspended horizontally a long instant before falling with a heavy thud flat on his back. He landed just as Fillol, lunging like a puma, diverted the ball up over the crossbar.

The entire team, except Menotti, burst out laughing. It was a short explosion of common raucous laughter. As soon as it escaped them, the players realized its impropriety and smothered it, turning their backs and stuffing their fists into their mouths. Fillol and Menotti ran to the fallen commander. Only a second or two passed before the prostrate figure let out a hearty guffaw that freed the constrained laughter and even Menotti, seeing the red delight on Massera's upturned face, tittered. He helped the admiral to his feet amid boisterous howls and brushed the grass off his tunic.

"Good job!" Massera congratulated Fillol when his own cackle subsided. "That's what I want to see in the tournament!"

The sportingness of the admiral endeared him to the team. A few of the players even ventured to slap him on the back. "That's quite a shot you've got there, commander," one complimented. "We could find a spot for you," joked another.

Massera beamed and bragged about his younger days and had to be convinced by the helicopter pilot, a navy captain, that pressing affairs of state demanded his attention. He left after another round of handshakes and encouragement.

This was Friday, May 19, the day of the final cut.

The training camp outside the small town of Jose C. Paz northwest of the capital was run something like a military camp. The candidates for the squad were isolated there, away from family and friends, as part of a program Menotti considered necessary to temper their minds and bodies, and forge the team's common will.

The deadline had arrived for the submission of the final list of the team's twenty-three members to the International Soccer Federation. Menotti had to scratch three more men. He had decided that Bottaniz and Bravo would go, and one of the two kids, either Maglione or the seventeen-year-old Diego Maradona. But he was agonizing over which it would be.

It was obvious Maradona had more raw talent. But Menotti knew that ability is not the only factor, perhaps not even the most important one, in a tournament as emotionally charged as the World Cup. He had decided to choose between the two during this afternoon's scrimmage. He knew they were both aware that their youth made them candidates for the cut, and were feeling the pressure. How they handled it would be demonstrated in the pick-up game.

He put them at midfield on the same squad.

Not long into the game, Maradona took a pass from Tarantini and advanced the ball alone for more than twenty-five meters in a display of footwork and feints that left three defenders in his wake, two on the ground, one in pursuit. Fillol was his last obstacle and Maradona, his short muscular legs pumping and shaggy black curls bouncing, gauged the goalie's advance and lifted the ball—more than a kick, he tossed it with his foot—in a lofty arc. Fillol, sprawling in hopes of blocking the low, hard shot anyone else would have taken, could do nothing more than raise a futile hand and wave at the ball that floated over him like a soap bubble, fell and bounced unimpeded into the goal.

It was a maneuver of splendid finesse. Maradona's teammates, Alejandro included, cheered and gathered around him to clap his back. The young phenomenon grinned and stole a glance toward Menotti to assure himself that the coach had not missed it.

Maradona told himself silently, joyfully: "That was the most important goal I ever scored."

Alejandro played well too. He ran and ran, up and down the field, fashioning offensive thrusts with sharp passes and falling back to corral the advance of his opponents. He was giving his all.

They were playing a single forty-five-minute period. Houseman had tied the game at one-all and time was running out. Alejandro dribbled the ball up the left side of the field. He got around Ardiles and took Olguin deeper toward the corner. He stopped and whirled like a fighting bull around a center of gravity defined by dipping head and shoulder, and passed the ball back toward the center of the field right onto the foot of the advancing Kempes. Ale darted behind Olguin and took the return pass from Kempes. He faked in toward the goal. Passarella moved that way and he skirted him to the outside, planted his heel and turned back in, past Passarella. He looked up at Fillol.

The goalie advanced with only a slim chance of blocking the shot. Alejandro probably would have shot and scored if he hadn't, during the second when he selected his angle, perceived a figure advancing on his right. He knew it was a teammate, so instead of firing a shot he tapped the ball away off the outside of his foot. The ball rolled to Maradona, who had the entire undefended goal yawning before him. He just kicked it in.

When the game ended, Menotti called the players around him.

"I have to deliver the list," he said solemnly. "This moment was inevitable. The decision hurts me and I don't want to say anything more. I hope you'll understand. Those who go are Bravo, Bottaniz and Maradona."

Alejandro was struck dumb. Then, even before joy could well, he was enveloped in the same wrenching and chest-pressing emotion felt by all the men standing there, those whose names had not been called. It was a suffocating empathy for the three, an empathy so strong it was tinged with guilt and even shame. They remained to partake of the glory while the three were banished to a land more barren than any desert, condemned to return to the real world.

All heads were bowed. Maradona knew he was going to cry and did not want his companions to see his tears. He looked down at the ground without seeing the grass or his dirty striped cleats, fallen socks and sweat-streaked calves. He could not see anything but the blur of the tears in his eyes and he stepped tremulously out from among the players. The huddle opened, as if for a prophet or a leper, and he made his way without touching them.

Within two years, Diego Maradona would be universally recognized as the world's best soccer player. Now he was just a shattered seventeen-year-old boy and he walked alone toward a solitary palm tree, choking on his disgrace.

Santiago lay face up in bed, his hands behind his heavy head. He wore pajama bottoms striped like prison pants and his chest was bare. He stared at the white ceiling.

The bedroom was a large suite with an adjacent bathroom. Monica stood before a big mirror in the bathroom with the door open. Her right hand fluttered beneath her chin like the wing of a trapped bird. She patted her gullet with the back of her hand and counted the taps in a low fast voice, "eighty, eighty-one, eighty-two . . ."

When she reached one hundred she stopped. She made a half turn and, lifting her negligee, pushed herself up onto her toes and appraised her buttocks from over her shoulder. She pivoted to get a good look at the other side. Her buttocks were in admirable shape for a woman of thirty-seven years, thanks to determination, aerobics, sauna and massage.

She leaned close to the mirror, placed her fingertips at the corners of her eyes and stretched the skin slightly back toward her small ears.

"Do you think I'd look more exotic with almond eyes?" she asked. "It's a simple operation. A lot of the top models are doing it."

Santiago did not take his eyes off the ceiling. "That might make you look like a *china*," he mused. " 'A pretentious, mate-sucking *china*.' "

They were the words Monica had used earlier that day to describe Ana.

Monica was unstung. It was difficult to sting Monica and even when she was she didn't show it. She went on to another subject, in the same casual tone as before.

"You know, I like your father a lot," she lied. "But I find it disconcerting to talk with him. I don't know which eye to look him in. If I look in his right eye, it seems like he's got the left one focused on me. I switch to the left, and it's like he's got the other one zeroed in."

"Why don't you look at the tip of his nose and really fuck him up?"

"Oh, you're no help." She turned out the bathroom light. She propped a satin-sheathed pillow against the headboard and got into bed with Santiago. She picked up a book, *The Wisdom of the Stars,* from the lamplit nighttable. She found her place and read, but only for a few minutes. Then she sighed tiredly and turned out the light.

"*Buenas noches, querido,*" she said, and rolled onto her side so that her back was to her husband.

Santiago stared at the shadows on the ceiling. He pushed his tongue against the back of his upper lip. After a while, he spoke softly.

"Monica?"

She made no response. But Santiago knew she was awake.

"Would you have married me if I had a harelip?"

Monica lay still as a cornered rodent. The only thing that occurred to her by way of response—her honest response to herself—was, How in the world could he ask such a foolish question?

She lay silent and still.

Santiago did not nudge her or ask again. He too knew the answer. So he went back to his memory.

He was remembering a big-wheeled wooden cart he had made many years go.

As a boy, Santiago was always making things: scooters and wagons from discarded fruit crates, roller-skate wheels and whatever else was available. Almost all the things he made he gave to Diego.

Santiago was thirteen, in his first year of secondary school. Diego was ten and still in primary school. Santiago was big for his age, athletic and rough, while Diego was small and hare-lipped and, to make things worse, smart. Santiago knew Diego's classmates teased him, so when Santiago's classes let out for the day he would walk the five blocks to

Diego's school, which finished later, to wait for his brother. They would walk home together.

That year, Santiago's school began its summer vacation a day before Diego's school. Early on the morning of his first day of vacation, Santiago went to Don Leonardo's grocery store around the corner from his house. He had noticed that Leonardo, a jovial red-haired Calabrian, was nearing the bottom of a forty-kilogram bag of Flor de Lis maté herb. In those days, maté came down from Corrientes pressed into cylindrical canvas bags with a circular wooden slab at each end. The herb was tightly packed and the bag stood on end on the floor. The grocer would lift off the top and scrape the pressed herb with a metal trowel to loosen the requested amount.

When Santiago arrived that morning, he saw that a new bag of maté had been opened.

"And the old bag? Are you going to use it for anything?" He shifted anxiously, scratching the top of one foot with the other.

"Why no, *m'hijo,*" answered Doña Ester, Leonardo's wife. "Have it if you want. It is out back."

Santiago scurried out and dashed down the alley, hoping that no one had beat him to the treasure. And there it was, amid the cartons and crates and the thick smell of discarded fruit and vegetables that hadn't begun to rot but wouldn't last long in the early summer sun. He snatched up the collapsed canvas barrel and hurried home, where he spent the better part of the day getting in his father's way in the shop.

With the two new wheels, two more he had squirreled away and Mikhail's scrap wood, Santiago built a handsome cart. He greased the broomstick axles and the hinge where the handle joined the coach, then went off pulling it down the road. He arrived at Diego's school as the students, their white smocks billowing, streamed out of the building in a high-pitched whirling fervor of release. Euphoric though they were, they stopped shouting and laughing when they came upon Santiago and his cart at the schoolyard gate. They circled mute and awed around the dandy rig. Diego pushed through the press and ran to his brother's side.

Santiago told him to climb in and Diego got aboard. Santiago pulled the cart down the street and he felt like a horse, but not a dumb, hatchet-faced beast. He was the most stately and cherished stallion in the land. He whinnied loudly, his head high and breast risen like a crowing cock's, and both he and Diego laughed deliriously. Diego stood in the cart like Cesar in his chariot, deigning occasionally to acknowledge the curious and amused looks from people on the sidewalk and shop-owners in their doorways. A small parade of Diego's classmates strung out behind the vehicle.

Santiago pulled it slowly and steadily up a gradual incline. When he reached the crest of the little hill, he heard a shout from the far sidewalk.

"Hey, Santiago!"

He stopped and looked across the street. It was Cacho Fontevecchia, a loud and rude boy from Santiago's class who, because he had been held back a year, thought himself king of the eighth grade.

"You won't win any races with that contraption," shouted the boy. "You move like a tortoise!" Then it came to Cacho; the intimation of a witticism, or a vulgar, cruel parody of one. He grinned.

"You're the tortoise and your brother's the hare!"

Santiago dropped the cart handle and ran across the cobbled street at Cacho. But just as he reached the other curb he was pulled up short, violently, like a charging dog at the end of his leash, by Diego's cry. He turned to see the cart rolling down the other side of the hill, gaining speed as it bounced over the paving stones. Diego, rigid and erect, clamped the sides of the wagon with his small white hands. The cart rattled and veered and struck the curb. It flipped forward and launched Diego like a boulder from a catapult. He crashed against the brick front of a hardware store and fell to the sidewalk.

Santiago flew down the hill. By the time he reached the bottom, a crowd was huddled around his motionless brother. Santiago fought his way through and fell across Diego. He started to cry and had to be pulled off, flailing and kicking, by two men.

Diego was taken to the hospital, then home. He had a concussion and was in bed for three days. The first day he was delirious. Santiago was not allowed into the bedroom they had always shared. He spent the endless hours sitting on the front stoop, imagining his flight from home, or his suicide, if Diego did not recover. Then, when Angela told him he could not sleep in his bed that night, that he would have to sleep on the couch, Santiago broke into sobs and clutched himself.

He could not sleep. He lay on the couch, prickled by the horsehair and the guilt, and listened. At intervals he heard Diego groan. After some hours had passed, the house quieted. Santiago waited a while then tiptoed into the bedroom. Angela lay curled sleeping in her housedress and slippers on Santiago's bed. Diego was sleeping too. Santiago stole to the side of the bed and kneeled lightly there and took Diego's hand. He stayed like that for hours. He begged someone, or some power, to make his brother well.

Santiago was regarding Diego's face at the moment, toward dawn, when his eyes opened. Diego looked immediately wide awake. He spoke naturally, as if nothing had happened. He looked at Santiago.

"Santi?" he said.

"*Si,* Dieguito."

"I'm tired of this harelip. Won't you take it for a while? Just for a while."

Santiago fell forward against his brother's breast and placed his head against Diego's and stroked his hair. "Yes, Dieguito. I'll take it. And for more than a while. Forever if you want."

Angela awoke and shushingly admonished her elder son. Diego, as spontaneously as he had awakened, fell back into fast sleep or unconsciousness. Santiago retreated to the couch and lay down. But only a few minutes, long minutes spent probing his shame, passed before he got up and went into the bathroom. He searched through the medicine chest and took out Mikhail's bone-handled straight razor. He opened it and lightly brushed the edge of the gray blade with his thumb. He looked at himself in the mirror and slowly but without hesitation lifted his upper lip and pressed it up and back against his nose. He pressed the razor against it and the pink flesh parted without resistance. He winced and tasted warm blood. He spit out mouthfuls before the flow subsided. Then he went back to the couch. He lay down and watched the light slowly overcome the darkness. Certain that Diego would live and thrive, he touched the slice in his lip with his tongue and swallowed small sips of the faintly sweet mix of blood and saliva.

Now, many years later, he touched with his tongue the silky thread of scar and thought, "Diego, *hermanito,* if you only knew."

The ombu tree, in its enormity, complements the vast pampa. It stands alone in a sea of grass, providing refuge from the sun to a hundred head of cattle.

An ombu grew in the center of Plaza Vicente Lopez. Winding massively around itself, twisting out of the ground, its gnarled lower limbs were so long and heavy they were supported by timbers. They spread over the plaza's paths and benches, over the milling crowd.

The day was not cold, but almost all the women present wore furs; gleaming black nutria, Patagonian fox, the long gray hairs shining blue in the sun. One woman wore a lynx stole. The feline's varnish-clawed paws fastened mockingly over her throat. A very wealthy lady modeled a Russian mink and was the envy of the others.

The people were gathered for the plaza's reinauguration following an extensive renovation for the sake of the many high-ranking military men, cabinet ministers and dignitaries who lived on the adjacent streets.

Sculptures—bathing maidens and naked boys with waterjug founts— had been brought from Europe. Fully grown jacarandas, elms, pines and palms had been delivered on flatbeds, raised with cranes and nurtured in their elegant new environment. A roller-skating rink had been constructed, as well as jungle gyms, swings and sandboxes. The plaza had been transformed into a lush and beautiful pausing place for the neighborhood's adults and a lavishly appointed playground for their progeny.

For the occasion, red carpet adorned the entire three kilometers of paths crisscrossing the square. Officers, distinguished neighbors, the neighborhood's entrepreneurs and their wives stood on the red carpet chatting.

The sound of sirens turned their heads. A black Mercedes limousine arrived amid a swarm of motorcycles mounted by frowning and mustached policemen in black leather. The corpulent gray-haired mayor, Air Force Brigadier Osvaldo Cacciatore, emerged from the vehicle, saluted the assembled military contingent, shook hands with some of the more notable civilians and smiled for the photographers. Cacciatore had eschewed his uniform for a dark gray suit, but his step was eminently martial as he trod the carpet to the podium.

He tapped the microphone, which was turned up too loud, and startled people engrossed in conversation, causing a few drinks to tip. The volume was lowered and he tapped the mike again.

"Ladies and gentlemen," he began in a stentorian tenor. "This is not merely the dedication of a plaza. It is a concrete example of our determination to recover the faded glory of our city, the regal Buenos

Aires of years past that, for its sumptuous boulevards and sublime plazas brought sighs of admiration from Parisians, Milanese and Romans alike. This plaza is a sample of our will to restore our beloved capital to its rightful place in the pantheon of exquisite metropolises.

"The timely completion of this plaza and others like it is also a token of welcome to the thousands of visitors from all over the world who will spend the coming weeks as our guests. We want them to see our city as it really is—civilized, sophisticated, cosmopolitan—and we can only hope that they will enjoy our parks and plazas and stop to sit on the benches to contemplate for a moment the tranquility of their surroundings. In that moment they may realize, we hope they do, that such tranquility, the possibility to relax safe and secure in public spaces, is one of the most tangible results of the eradication of terrorism by the armed forces of the fatherland. We hope our guests will appreciate that, and see through the insidiousness of the international subversive campaign slandering us worldwide.

"Now, ladies and gentlemen, I invite you to enjoy with me this lovely day in these beautiful surroundings. Thank you."

The mayor received a hearty applause. White-jacketed and gloved brown-skinned servants appeared as if lifted on dumbwaiters from below ground. Their trays and carts were laden with champagne and smoked salmon, crab from Tierra del Fuego, imported pâtés, cheeses and elaborate hors d'oeuvres.

"A fine speech, Brigadier," hailed the ramrod-erect, silver-haired military man approaching the mayor. Though they had never met, the mayor recognized the man and clasped his hand.

The officer was Army General Leopoldo Galtieri, commander of the Second Army Corps based in Rosario, three hundred kilometers northwest of the capital. The general, an imposing figure with his bulk and bearing, was the odds-on favorite to take over the capital-based First Army Corps when promotions came at the end of the year. The step after that could well be commander-in-chief, and after that; who knew? Galtieri, ever confident, had purchased a luxury apartment overlooking the refurbished square.

"A fine speech," he repeated, pumping the mayor's hand. "The capital is looking splendid. Your effort will surely create a lasting impression. I congratulate you."

"Thank you, General. Thank you." Cacciatore placed his hand on Galtieri's epauletted shoulder and eased his comrade aside for a private exchange.

The mayor continued in a more confidential tone. "Appearances are very important. Which is the reason for my perpetual headache. Because what good is it if we beautify this plaza and the Plaza San Martín and Plaza Lavalle if right there in Retiro sits a sprawling stinking shanty-town?" He raised his arm in exasperation toward the south, toward the river. "It's like a wart on the nose of a beautiful woman."

"I was under the impression that the shantytowns in the federal capital had been eradicated," replied Galtieri. A cough swelled and broke from the depths of the general. He drained the three fingers of whiskey from his glass and listened intently as Cacciatore went on with his exposition.

"Nearly all of them have been. But a few pockets remain, and the most distressing of them is Retiro. I have to clean it up before the end of May. But a discreet operation there, right in the center of town, is difficult. The journalists will sentimentalize the issue; photographs of pregnant women crying in front of their demolished shacks, all that. And our undercover work indicates there may be some resistance. Nothing to worry about, mind you. Passive resistance, like sitting down all together in front of the bulldozers."

Galtieri laughed. "Well, you could just run them over! I think the fatherland could survive the loss of a few thousand bums."

"I wish it were that simple. It would save us a lot of trouble and money too. We are offering them train fare back to their country or province of origin. Some accept but the majority do not. It's incredible. They tell me about these little Bolivian Indian bastards waving nation-alization papers, claiming they are as Argentine as San Martín."

The two men, whose fathers were both immigrants, exchanged racist jokes before being drawn into separate conversations with admirers and those who would curry favor.

Francisca Otero shivered and closed the collar of her musty man's overcoat and cinched a blue vinyl belt around her waist.

"Now we're really screwed," she said to herself.

Mrs. Saenz-Brown, her erstwhile employer, had this morning, while

Francisca was swabbing the kitchen floor, proposed that she move into the servant's quarters and serve as a live-in maid. Mrs. Saenz-Brown had said she was assured of Francisca's honesty, and she believed the arrangement would benefit all concerned. It was a way out of the shantytown, she had explained; warmth at night in a sturdy clean bed, hot showers, a life of what Francisca must surely consider luxury.

"You know, ma'am, that I live with my husband in Retiro," Francisca had answered as the mop scythed a swath of brightness across the tiles.

"Yes, my dear. It must be a difficult decision." Mrs. Saenz-Brown looked at Francisca over the half-framed reading glasses perched on her pinched face. "But you realize the impracticability of having you both here and, really, you must begin thinking about yourself and your own welfare sometime. I mean, he certainly has not provided for you. True?"

"It is not a difficult decision at all, ma'am." Francisca paused at her chore. "Thank you, but no."

Mrs. Saenz-Brown, who was convinced her life would only be manageable if she had a live-in maid, raised her hand reflexively and touched the stiff curl of her silver-pink teased hair. "Would you be kind enough to tell me why?"

Francisca leaned on the mop and regarded the woman with wonder. Then, calmly but with the curiously compulsive sensation that she was putting in motion something that would end badly, she said, "If you will come with me, I will show you why."

She walked across the gleaming floor in her ragged terrycloth cleaning slippers. Mrs. Saenz-Brown's heels clicked behind her. Francisca led her employer down the hall to the servant's quarters, a windowless but apparently comfortable room furnished with a bed and a night table. She switched on a light in the tiny bathroom.

"How is this bathroom different from the house's other three bathrooms?" she asked.

Mrs. Saenz-Brown was perplexed. She looked at Francisca, then into the bathroom. "It's smaller," she ventured.

"Yes. It's smaller," said Francisca obligingly. "And the other difference is that it is the only bathroom without a bidet." Her tone changed almost imperceptibly. "Did you ever notice that? No, I suppose you never did."

Mrs. Saenz-Brown looked surprised, not so much at what Francisca was saying, but at the fact she was capable of stringing together so many words.

Francisca continued: "I am not pretentious. I will probably never have a bathroom with bidet. But I will be damned if I'll wash the toilets and bidets of the house in which I live so that everyone save me might go around with their delicate asses clean as kittens."

Then Francisca had said good-bye, changed her slippers for a pair of cracked boots and walked out, leaving Mrs. Saenz-Brown to wash her own dirty dishes. Now she trod slowly, as if without destination, along a canyon of glassy apartment buildings and cursed her stubbornness and wondered where the money would come from.

When she reached Libertador Avenue she saw ribbons of smoke from cooking fires rising like a warning from the shantytown that squatted behind the Retiro railroad station, beyond the sidings of rundown rotting freight cars and yellow commuter coaches.

That was the Villa Miseria—"Misery Town"; the concentration of humanity on public land that in other parts of Latin America is called *favela* or "young town" or "new neighborhood." In the late 1940s, when the provincial poor sold their horses and ate their pigs and flocked from the north, the west, the south, from Paraguay and Bolivia and Chile to Buenos Aires, the slums were euphemistically christened "emergency settlements." But the construction of housing never kept pace with the migrations depopulating the countryside. The "emergency" never ended and, by the mid-1970s, more than a quarter million people lived in dozens of shantytowns spread like patches of eczema over the complexion of the capital.

Francisca and her husband, Juan-Cruz, had built a shack in the Retiro *villa* a year ago thinking they would not spend more than a few months there. Juan-Cruz, after unavailingly offering his skill and brawn at every construction site in the federal capital, now presented himself at dawn every morning to the stevedores' day-labor office on the dock behind the *villa*. There he waited with six hundred other men hoping for work. But he rarely got more than one day a week, and Francisca's meager salary had been their sustenance.

She walked down the avenue, then crossed it and passed the bustling entrance of the railway station. A man with a wool cap pulled down over his brow stirred peanuts in a thick sugary broth in a hot copper kettle.

"*Garrapinada! Garrapinada!*" he called.

The dense sweet smell reminded Francisca of her childhood. She reached inside her coat, into the pocket of her dress, for a coin. She stood still in the flow of pedestrians, then stepped to the vendor's cart and bought a cellophane cylinder filled with the crispy red pellets. She continued toward the shantytown. She opened the pack, poured some nuts into her hand and lifted them to her mouth. As she munched them, she was overcome by an urge to cry.

She crossed some weed-covered tracks, the boundary of the slum, and walked down alleys bordered by a foul-smelling narrow trench and heard a Paraguayan harp lilting from a radio.

The houses were precarious combinations of bricks and block, crate wood, corrugated sheets of zinc, and cardboard. Old tires and rocks the size of skulls held down sheet-metal roofs that sometimes, when a tempest blew in off the river, buckled and flung off their anchors to cartwheel in a clanging chorus over the heads of exposed inhabitants. Most of the houses had dirt floors and none had running water. The water came from long-necked spigots that sprouted from the scraped and rutted earth. Every morning a line of women and girls formed at each of the spigots to fill buckets and basins. During the summer, when the rest of the city was using more water and the pressure in the system was low, the women rose at three in the morning to draw water.

The Retiro *villa* had grown according to its own haphazard geometry and harbored more than five thousand people. Almost all the houses had electricity pirated off city lines in a perilous web of wire and bottleneck insulators. Some dwellers had made a semblance of a comfortable life. They did not pay rent or utilities. There were even some television sets. But most of the *villeros* longed to get out, to get a job that paid a decent wage.

Francisca paused on her way home to greet her friend Mrs. Gonzalez, who sat beside her home washing her feet in the suds of a red plastic basin. The old woman looked up from her sponging.

"*Adiós,* Francisca!" she replied.

Francisca was about to speak when, from the next house, she heard a woman shout.

The house belonged to Sebastian Gutierrez, who had set up a rudimentary photographic studio there. Gutierrez, with his thirty-five-millimeter Japanese camera, tripod, second-hand enlarger, and closet-cum-darkroom, produced handsome black-and-white portraits of pious, angelic girls on their First Communions, proud newlyweds and fat-cheeked babies. Unclaimed pictures covered half a wall of his shack.

Francisca reached the open doorway and saw an obese, bleached-blond, dark-skinned woman shrieking at Gutierrez.

"But that looks nothing like me! This was to send to my fiancé, and you made me come out ugly!"

Gutierrez, whose demeanor matched the benevolent tone of his photographs, barely got out a, "Señorita, *por favor,*" before the woman swung her laden shopping purse of woven plastic over the counter and struck the photographer solidly on the side of the head.

"The cunt of the widowed cow!" she raved, and would have continued her assault if Francisca hadn't grabbed her from behind. Three neighbor women rushed in. The fat woman strained against Francisca's strong arms, then quieted. Francisca released her.

"You making trouble again, Pilar?" asked Mrs. Gonzalez, curling her newly dirtied toes against the cold earthen floor. "You've got less sense than noodle water."

"But he made me come out ugly," whimpered Pilar.

Mrs. Gonzalez stepped over to her, shaking her head in exasperation. "But my dear," she said leaning forward, "you are ugly." The household broke into laughter and Pilar stormed out shoving and cursing.

"I guess that means I don't get paid," said Gutierrez, who despite his loss could not repress a chuckle.

Unable to delay any longer, Francisca walked home. When she passed through the crooked doorjamb into the half-light of the shack she found her son, whom she had not seen in a year, stretched on the bed, delirious.

Diego worked in the Retiro *villa*. He tended to patients free of charge in a cinderblock "clinic" in the center of the shantytown four afternoons a week after finishing his shift as a resident pediatrician at the Hospital de Niños. The clinic, funded by the party in the guise of a charity, consisted of a wooden examination table, a cot, a two-burner stove fueled by bottled gas, and a few metal basins. Water was hosed in from a nearby spigot. Diego worked out of his satchel. He stitched cuts, bandaged scrapes and burns, and administered drugs for fever and the children's diarrhea. If he suspected tuberculosis or influenza he had the patient visit him at the hospital. Complications arising from clumsy abortions he referred to sympathetic colleagues.

He was walking through the settlement on his way to the clinic this midday when he paused to watch a children's soccer game in a scarred bald clearing.

The ball of wound rags bounded through a tangle of flapping arms and skinny legs. A puff of dust enveloped the knot of ragged boys and accompanied them back and forth, up and down the field. All eyes were fixed on the elusive ball and excited laughter like the cries of gulls hurried after it. The goals, piles of tattered jackets, were guarded by tentative tenders smaller and more frail than the other boys, the last to be chosen when the sides were formed.

An errant pass bounced off the field to Diego. He sent it back into play with a smart kick. He watched a moment longer, before continuing on.

Diego was immensely appreciated and respected by the shantytown's inhabitants and his passage through it brought repeated calls of "Adiós, Doctor!" and invitations to drink maté. Concerned with staffing the clinic, he generally declined. But today he accepted when José, a wrinkled Catamarqueño with as many gaps as teeth in his grin, hailed him offering tea and "a snack."

Diego had stitched up José three months earlier after the old man received a crack on the head with a blackjack. A skinny hoodlum had insulted his young niece.

"Your little thing must be nice and tight, but I can loosen it up for you," the thug had said.

José had overheard.

"Shut your trap you little two-fisted double-pumper," he warned.

The youth cursed and threatened him.

To which José replied, "You don't scare me, beanpole. What's one more spot on an old leopard?"

José made two cups of tea from one bag and passed the unsweetened brew to Diego, who sat on a plank bench. The shanty was adorned with magazine photos of Argentine boxers. There was Oscar Bonavena in his glory days, before he was murdered by a mobster at a Nevada whorehouse, and next to him Juan Firpo, "the wild bull of the pampas" who, in 1923, knocked Jack Dempsey out of the ring at the Polo Grounds and was robbed of the world heavyweight title when ringside journalists hoisted the dazed champ up to the canvas, where he held on for the round and knocked Firpo out in the next. There were pictures too of the River Plate soccer team of 1947, the one with Alfredo DiStefano, and the current squad, which had five men, including Fillol, Passarella and Luque, on the national team.

"Don't tell me you're a 'chicken,' " said Diego, indicating the River Plate posters. He used the term by which Boca loyalists referred to their archrivals. "You might kick me out for it, but I'm born and raised in La Boca and a lifelong fan. Alejandro Maglione is my nephew."

"You don't say," mused José. "Well, no one is perfect. You know, I've seen every single Boca-River game played during the past twenty years, the ones we played at home, of course. Don't imagine I'm going to go to the Bonbonera to be urinated on from the grandstand."

"All you've heard is slander. I'll take you myself one of these days and you'll see."

"Thanks but no thanks, I'm not about to change sides at this stage of the game. But to show you I still respect you despite your terrible taste in choosing a soccer team, try a piece of this. I prepared it last night according to my own secret recipe." He proffered a plate of small-boned roasted and basted meat. Diego took a portion and tasted it.

"Very good." He savored the morsel. "What is it? Rabbit?"

"Meeooww," purred José, and burst out laughing.

Diego neared the clinic and saw a powerfully built man about fifty years old standing at the door, shifting his weight from foot to foot. With great deference, in a thick provincial accent, the man said, "Excuse me Mr. Doctor sir. My son has suffered an accident and is in need of immediate attention. He cannot be moved, so I ask you to come to my home."

"Lead the way," said Diego, and followed the man off toward the river. A boy defecating in the rubble of an abandoned home looked up sheepishly as they passed. They ran into the numbers racketeer, who asked the brawny man if he wanted to play a number and received a muttered oath in reply.

They reached the house, where in the darkness of the corner lay a man on a bed. Francisca Otero held compresses to her son's forehead.

Diego crouched by the iron bedstead. As his eyes adjusted to the shadowy interior he saw a stocky man, perhaps a few years younger than himself, semi-conscious and pouring with sweat. At intervals he jerked in short convulsions. Francisca pulled back the sheet covering him and lifted a bloody cloth from his groin to expose a coagulated hole in the crease where the thigh joined the trunk.

"He was shot," said Juan-Cruz.

"He must be taken immediately to the hospital."

"He cannot go to the hospital." Juan-Cruz stood motionless, a featureless silhouette of a man against the bright square that was the home's only window.

"He may die if he doesn't."

"He will surely die if he does." Juan-Cruz's nervousness had disappeared. He was not adamant.

"Boil a white towel or a bedsheet," Diego instructed. "I have some bandages, but not enough."

Francisca went to the battered armoire with its cracked and splotchy mirror. She stooped and took a white sheet from the big drawer at the bottom.

Diego took a tweezer from his bag and sterilized it with alcohol.

"Sit at the head of the bed and hold him down," he told Juan-Cruz. Then he took a small flashlight from the satchel and peered into the wound, pressing into it with the implement. The wounded man bucked. He struggled against his father as Diego probed. Francisca, after setting a pot of water to boil, leaned over the foot of the bed and clamped her son's ankles to the mattress. Juan-Cruz's sinewy arms pressed against his shoulders. The struggling suddenly stopped. Diego probed deeper and touched the bullet. The wounded man twitched. Diego grasped the slug with the pincer and drew it out and dropped it onto the packed dirt floor. He took a bottle of disinfectant and a tube of antibiotic salve from his bag and bathed and swabbed the wound.

The man appeared dead, but Diego registered a weak pulse. He bandaged him with the help of Juan-Cruz. Francisca stirred the sheet in the pot. Rising wisps of steam veiled her face.

*   *   *

Juan-Cruz, Francisca and Diego sat at the table before dented metal cups. Roberto Otero slept. Juan-Cruz lifted spilled grains of ground coffee with his fingertips and carried them distractedly to his lips. He bit the grains between his front teeth.

His face was fallen and his voice tired and distant. "It seems to me that the only way to grow old with grace is to continue doing the things that gave you pleasure in your youth." He rolled a grain between thumb and forefinger and stared at it. "As a boy, I would always take a bit of spilled ground coffee from the grocer's counter. I loved to crunch the grains.

"Antonio Piñero lived next to us. He had an apricot tree. The fruit of that tree was so delicious. After his children had grown and moved away, Don Antonio and his wife let the apricots fall and they rotted on the ground. I would take a long stick, cleave the end and reach through the fence to grasp the apricots and pull them to me. One day, I took a bag of apricots to my father and poured them on the table before him.

" 'Where are these from?' he asked. I told him. He took one and bit into and though he tried to disguise his delight he could not. I told him Don Antonio left the fruit to rot on the ground and he said, 'Still, it is not right to take what is not yours.' Then he winked at me and took another bite and we two sat there eating the most delicious apricots in the world."

Diego studied Juan-Cruz's countenance. He had a long nose set between strong cheekbones and a broad chin decorated with sparse black whiskers. His eyes were narrow and black.

"What brought you to the capital?" asked Diego after a while.

"Hopes of work."

"What is your trade?"

"I've worked all my life in construction, a laborer with considerable knowledge of masonry. But construction fell off in the province. So I went to work in the municipal cemetery digging graves." He stopped and looked across the table at Francisca. He returned his eyes to Diego and continued: "One night an army truck pulled up and an officer asked if I wanted to make some money working overtime. 'Sure,' I said. He enlisted some other *compañeros* and told us to dig a broad pit in the section reserved for paupers' burials. When we finished, they backed the truck to the pit and soldiers threw back a tarp and ordered us to unload bodies and stack them in the grave. There were twenty-three men and women, a bullet hole in the head of each one. Some were mutilated. When we had covered them over, the lieutenant called us around him and said, 'You have just contributed to the war against subversion. We are all in this battle, and if you want your country to be a Christian and free land where your children can grow up in liberty, you will be proud to have sweated these hours. I am sure you are all aware of the seriousness of this matter. Be assured that our heritage as a nation is at stake and our lives—your lives—are at stake.'

"I continued working there three months more and we buried more than three hundred people like that. I could not sleep for the nightmares. But I feared quitting would draw suspicion. I was going mad. So we came to this city. Roberto," he gestured toward the bed, "had come in 'seventy-three when Perón returned, and was working in the Ford factory in General Pacheco. Now we live in a shack on the money my wife makes rinsing the toilet bowls of rich people and my son has been shot by the police." He fell silent.

Francisca stood and cleared the cups from the table. To Juan-Cruz she said, "I have never heard you speak so many words as you have just now."

Diego rose and explained that Roberto's fever would likely continue through the night. "I'll be back tomorrow to change the bandage and see how he's doing," he said, and left.

CHAPTER 3

DANI AND BETO STOPPED HALFWAY ACROSS A VACANT LOT AND LET THEIR BOOK SATCHELS SLIDE OFF THEIR SHOULDERS TO THE GROUND.

DANIEL PULLED A PAIR OF LIGHT WOODEN STICKS FROM HIS PACK AND laid them on the ground in a cross. As he knelt over them he opened a pouch of his satchel and took out a piece of thin wire. He wound it around the sticks where they crossed, the shorter one about two-thirds the way up the longer. Then he reached into his bag and took out a scrap of violet fabric.

Beto crouched beside Dani, watching intently. Dani flattened the diamond-shaped fabric over the frame and after unwinding some string from a ball in his satchel, he tied each corner of fabric to the tips of the cross. Then he tied on a tail of knotted cloth and held the kite for examination. The silky fabric ruffled anxiously.

"Great!" cried Beto. Daniel passed the kite and the ball of string to his friend.

"Let's see how she flies."

Beto held the kite so that the wind filled its belly. It tugged against his small hand and he let the string out. The kite wavered and swayed but pulled steadily away, rising toward the pale, almost transparent afternoon moon.

Daniel stood at Beto's elbow and watched excitedly. The wind was steady and strong and the higher the kite rose, the more firmly it tugged Beto. The boy let the string out faster and the reel flipped and tumbled like a just-landed fish at his feet.

"Higher!" Daniel's eyes were locked on the kite darting like a leaf in a storm. The boys moved forward and back, from one side of the field to the other.

The kite dove and Beto shrieked. Daniel reached up and grabbed the line and pulled in two meters hand over hand. The plummeting bird swooped nose up and resumed its climb.

"When it dives like that, you have to pull in hard." Dani relinquished control back to Beto.

The kite was buffeted by a high gust. The tail snapped like a whip and blew off and away, then the stretched scrap of violet went out of control. It plunged like a meteor and Beto's hauling of the line only seemed to make it dive faster. It crashed out of sight on the far side of the wall of an otherwise demolished building bordering the lot.

Daniel ran toward the wall. Beto dropped the slack string and followed. They reached the wall and saw the kite hanging just over its crest, about ten meters high. Daniel ran to where he could grab the string draping down from the top of the wall. He tugged gently to see if he could loosen the kite from its trap, but could not.

Chunks had been knocked off the front of the wall, leaving it like a narrow stairway of tall steps, some of them almost as tall as the boys. Daniel scrambled up the first three meters of the wall and continued upward, picking the best footholds and handholds. He reached the top and stood up straight, extending his arms out from his sides. He walked surely, placing one foot directly in front of the other, along the wall to where the kite was caught. He sat and freed the string from where it had snagged in the crook of a broken block. He pulled the dangling kite up to him and sailed it like a paper airplane down into the lot.

He pushed himself up and turned around and almost lost his balance when he saw Beto sitting facing him, straddling the wall. Beto was leaning forward, clapping the sides of the wall with his thighs and clutching it with both hands. His face was white and his mouth was open. Daniel laughed, but stopped laughing when he saw that Beto was not looking at him, but with terror at the ground.

Daniel walked quickly and sat down opposite Beto. He put his hands on his friend's.

"No!"

"But you came this far. Just turn around and do like you did until you got here."

"I can't," whimpered Beto.

"Why not?"

"I'm scared."

"You're scared because you look down. Don't look down."

"I'm scared."

"We'll go back together." Dani scooted back a bit, leaving a space between himself and Beto. "Lay forward here," he said.

"I can't."

"Yes you can." Daniel stood up. Beto bent forward until his chest was against the top of the wall and Dani took a long step, almost a jump, over him. He pivoted carefully and stood behind Beto. "Now you've got to turn around." He instructed Beto to lift his left leg up and over until he was sitting on the crest of the wall with both legs dangling over the side. Then he coaxed him to lift the right leg up and pivot on his rear, and Beto was facing him. "Now stand up."

"I can't." Beto's voice was a strangled squeak.

"Come on," Daniel said with exasperation. He pivoted again, so that his back was to Beto. Beto whined.

"Come on. Don't be a baby. Grab onto me."

Beto let go his grip on the wall and clamped Dani's leg with his right hand.

"Now the other one." Beto's left hand clutched Daniel's left leg, and he finally pulled himself to his feet and stood trembling behind Daniel, wringing fistfuls of Dani's white school smock.

"Now we're going to go forward. Look at your feet, not at the ground. Just put one in front of the other."

They made their way like that, Daniel's arms stuck out to the sides and Beto's smock fluttering behind him. By the time they reached the edge Beto seemed to have calmed somewhat. They climbed down.

"I'm afraid of heights," Beto admitted ashamedly when they were back on the ground.

"Then why did you climb up?"

"I was just following you. When I remembered I was afraid of heights, I was already up there."

They picked up the kite, wound up the string and walked across the lot toward their satchels.

"That's called a phobia," said Daniel didactically. "It means fear, in Greek I think. Everybody's got one. My grandmother doesn't like to be in closed-in places. That's called claustrophobia."

"What's yours?" Beto stopped walking.

Daniel thought for a moment. "I don't know what it's called. Maybe there's no name for it. But sometimes I wake up in the middle of the night and I'm positive I'm alone in the house. And I'm scared and have to get out of bed and go check and see that my parents are there."

They fetched their satchels and walked together along the sidewalks of LaBoca. They walked along a row of spindly, leafless trees and took turns kicking a can. The can rattled resoundingly across the cobbles.

Daniel suddenly bounded forward and cried, "Here's my cousin Ale against Hungary!" He approached the can with long steps, swung his right leg back and brought it down and through to send the can flying in a low arc.

"Goalll!"

When they reached Beto's house, a one-story rectangular stone building with grapevines carved around the tall narrow windows, they found the entire family—Beto's parents, his older brother and sister as well as two of his aunts—sitting silently around the dining room table. The curtains had been pulled across the windows, and a gauze of cigarette smoke drifted up through a shaft of light coming from a pane above the patio door. Everyone except Beto's father, whose face was cradled in his hands, looked at the two boys. No one said anything. The mother, her eyes bloodshot, got up and encircled Beto in her shawl-draped arms while one of the aunts shepherded Daniel into the kitchen.

"Beto's grandfather died today," the aunt said softly. As soon as she had spoken the words, the house was filled with Beto's cry like that of a wolf pup's at the moon, a drawn-out bay that wrapped around Daniel's throat and clutched back his breath. He moved in the direction of the cry, but was restrained by the woman. The howl trailed off in the heavy silence.

The aunt, whose breath smelled of wine, led Daniel by the hand back into the dining room and told him to go on home. Then Beto's father looked up tiredly and noticed Dani for the first time.

"You don't have to go home if you don't want to, Dani," he said.

"I want to see Beto."

"Then go ahead."

Daniel walked out across the sunlit patio to Beto's bedroom. He stood in the doorway and watched Beto's mother caress the back of her son's head. When she noticed Daniel she signaled to him to come over. She stood up, leaned over and kissed Daniel on the cheek and, without a word, left the room.

Beto's face was buried in the pillow and his shoulders heaved. Daniel lay face down on the bed next to his friend. He put his arm around Beto and cried too, not for the old man he barely knew, but for Beto.

After a while, Beto sat up and wiped his nose on the sleeve of his smock. Daniel did the same.

"He was the best grandfather in the world," sniffled Beto. "He could play 'El Día Que Me Quieras' on the ocarina and blow bubbles off his tongue."

After a minute Daniel asked, "Is he here?"

"He must be. He was sick, in bed."

"Have you ever seen a dead person?"

"No. Have you?"

"No."

"Want to?" asked Beto. The boys' sniffles had stopped. Beto took Daniel's hand and they walked cautiously down the hall. The door to the grandfather's room was ajar and Beto pushed it open slowly. They stood in the doorway looking at the old man in bed, his head propped on pillows. They held their breath and tiptoed to the bedside.

The dead man's face was gray and the skin was drawn tightly over the nose. The mouth turned down cruelly at the corners. A swatch of linen passed under his chin and was tied in a knot on the crown of his head. The blanket was pulled to his breast and his arms rested atop the cover at his sides. Beto reached out and touched his grandfather's hand, then stepped back.

"He looks mean," said Beto. "He doesn't look like that in real life."

"Come on," said Daniel, frightened by the old man's harsh and hardened visage. He nudged Beto and the two left the room silently to go sit on a stone bench on the patio. They sat swinging their legs for a few minutes.

"The only good thing about it," said Beto finally, "is that now he's in heaven with Grandma and God."

"There's no such—" Daniel stopped. He was going to explain to his friend, as his father had explained to him, that God and heaven were stories made up a long time ago so that people would not dwell on the toil and grief of this world.

"What?"

"Nothing," said Daniel. He felt himself strangely hollow and light. He put his arm around Beto's shoulder to anchor himself to the bench because he thought he was about to float away.

Something akin to mourning was to be found that same evening at the Santa Cruz church in the San Cristobal neighborhood of Buenos Aires. It was worse than mourning, in a way, because of the uncertainty and hollowness of spirit. But it was also girded by faith and anger.

A dozen women knelt in the first two pews. In her own way and words, each asked Jesus and Mary to protect her son or daughter, abducted by the military regime. The women also prayed for strength to bear the terrible burden of doubt and for strength to sustain her hope. Because each of them, at some black moment in the middle of a sleepless night of desperation, had said to herself, "If I only knew for sure what I suspect, I could grieve, then get on with my life." And that thought horrified the mothers, because it was unfaithful to their children.

A knot of husbands and fathers and brothers stood at the rear of the church whispering, murmuring secrets they wished, for now, to keep from God. They had gathered to pool money collected for the publication, in the newspapers *La Nación* and *Clarín,* of an announcement calling for "A Christmas without *desaparecidos* or political prisoners."

At the end of one pew knelt Sister Alice Domon, forty years old. In the middle of the other prayed Sister Leonie Duquet, sixty-one. The women belonged the the Toulouse-based Missions Etrangers and both had lived for many years in Argentina teaching among the poor. Both were active in organizations of relatives of disappeared people, providing spiritual and emotional support to the bereaved.

Among those at the rear of the church was a sturdy and handsome young man who nervously surveyed the congregation from beneath a shock of dark blond hair. He had appeared one day a few months previous at the office of the Mothers of the Plaza de Mayo on Uruguay Street. He had introduced himself as Gustavo Niño and said he was trying to locate his brother, whom he feared had been kidnapped by security forces.

Gustavo had walked with the Mothers on Thursday afternoons in the plaza and had become a friend, a sort of darling, to some of the women.

He brushed his hair reflexively off his forehead and looked at his watch. He went to the architect Mastrogiovanni, who was in charge of collecting the money.

"I just realized I don't have any cash on me. I live nearby. I'll be right back," he said.

"That's all right, Gus," the architect assured him. "You can bring it Thursday."

"No, no," insisted the young man. "I'd feel terrible if I didn't put something in the pot. I'll only be a few minutes."

Five Ford Falcons carrying fifteen men sat in a parking lot two blocks away. The driver of the car nearest the exit looked at his watch and started the engine. The drivers of the other cars followed suit. The vehicles crawled onto the street. None of the cars had a license plate.

Gustavo Niño hurried out the door, down the stairs and across the courtyard. He reached the sidewalk just as the lead car pulled to a halt in front of the church. He stepped around to the driver's side of the vehicle and crouched beside it. After a few minutes the family members and the two nuns began filing out. At first, no one noticed the Falcons parked in a row at the curb. But then plainclothes security agents brandishing sawed-off shotguns emerged from the cars and the slamming of doors struck fear into the courtyard congregation.

"Police!" shouted one of the Mothers. Some ran back into the church.

Padre Andrés, a friend of the Mothers, and the two nuns stepped to the front. Some of the agents ran into the church in pursuit of those who had fled.

A tall bald officer with a submachine gun slung over his shoulder approached the group. Behind him was Gustavo Niño.

Niño lifted his arm. "Her . . . and him . . . and her . . . and that guy with the beard."

The Mothers screamed as the officers grabbed them. The burly men wrenched the women's arms behind them and marched them toward the sinister, stationary parade of Falcons.

"The nuns." Niño pointed to Leonie and Alice. The sisters sat down on the ground. Two commandos bent to pick them up and the nuns kicked and flailed with their small fists. Two men from the knot of relatives rushed to their defense and were savagely pistol-whipped. The nuns were bundled off as their would-be defenders supported themselves on trembling hands and knees. They watched thick drops of blood fall from their noses onto the broad black flagstones, without understanding.

Niño pointed to Mastrogiovanni. "He's got the scratch," he said to the officer in charge. The officer approached the architect.

"Cough it up."

"I'm not giving you anything."

"We'll see about that." The officer ordered that the architect be put in the front car.

Some of those being dragged to the Falcons shouted their names to passers-by. The onlookers were transfixed by the bedlam but were prodded to move on by uniformed police who had appeared from nowhere to ring the church courtyard.

"What's going on?" inquired an old wrinkled woman pushing a small grocery cart along the sidewalk.

"Anti-narcotics operation, Grandma," answered a cop. "Keep moving."

Across the ocean, far across the equator, in the subterranean labyrinth of the City of Light, the metro stop named Argentine near Neuilly displayed a billboard depicting scenes from the station's namesake nation. Paid for by the nearby embassy, the space on the platform wall was emblazoned with ARGENTINA '78 in big red letters and the logo of the upcoming World Cup tournament, a soccer ball held aloft in a stylized stadium that also suggested cupped hands in prayer. Photographs of a Patagonian glacier, Iguazu Falls, an Andean trout stream and a colonial church in Salta were affixed around the logo to inform Parisian businessmen that if they took their family to Argentina for the tournament, the trip could be much more than a soccer excursion.

The rubber-wheeled train slithered to a stop. It was past midnight. A handful of people stepped out and headed for the stairs leading up to the rainy street. Three young people, two boys and a girl, remained on the platform. They huddled, lighting cigarettes, and stood around as if waiting for another train.

"*Allons,*" said one of the young men. He and the girl ran to the billboard while the other stood lookout by the stairway. The boy and girl pulled aerosol spray paint cans from their coat pockets and stepped up on the bench below the billboard. Across it they wrote, 25,000 DISPARUS. 7,000 MORTS. VIDELA ASSASSIN.

A man in a beige raincoat appeared on the opposite platform.

"Hey! What are you doing?" he shouted from across the tracks. He moved to the edge of the platform and debated momentarily whether to jump down and cross the rails but decided against it and ran up the stairs. The graffiti painters finished their work and ran for the exit. They were confronted by the descending man.

"What do you think you're doing?" he asked again.

"Who are you?" countered the smaller of the two Frenchmen, a wiry blond with a large crooked nose.

"I am an Argentine diplomat and I am going to see that you are arrested for vandalizing public property."

"That billboard is not public." The girl's eyes lit up.

"The subway station is, and you have profaned it."

"Playing soccer alongside concentration camps is a much greater profanity," she said.

"You obviously have not been to Argentina." The man took a step backward, up toward the street. "*Gendarme! Gendarme!*" he shouted.

The other Frenchman, a swarthy boy in an army trenchcoat, grabbed the diplomat by the lapels of his overcoat and pulled him down to the platform.

"Shut up, you fool, or I'll break your face," he snarled.

"*D'accord. D'accord,*" stammered the Argentine. "Don't get nervous." The Frenchman released him and the diplomat stepped back, reached into his coat and pulled out a 9-mm Beretta automatic pistol. He pointed it at the trio. His upper lip, shaded by a neatly clipped straight-line mustache, twitched.

"I am licensed to carry this weapon and I enjoy diplomatic immunity. I could kill all of you, claim you assaulted me, and even if the French authorities wanted to prosecute me, they could not. I would like to silence a few self-appointed crusaders. But that would only bring us more attention. So you'll get off with a fine for vandalism, if that. Now get moving." He jerked the pistol toward the stairway.

From the moment the gun emerged, the blond boy's eyes had locked on it. His weight rested on the balls of his feet, his legs tensed. The motion of the weapon toward the stairway provided the instant he required and, as the Argentine's hand swung back to level the pistol at his prisoners it was met violently at the wrist by the boy's foot slicing the air. The pistol flew from his hand and skidded across the smooth concrete floor. The girl ran after it.

The diplomat hunched over, his broken wrist clamped in his good hand, both hands pressed between his thighs.

"The cunt of the dirty whore that bore you!" he shouted in Spanish after them as the three bounded up the stairs and away.

The following day, Navy Captain Guillermo Roig, director of Naval Intelligence's "Operation Pilot," made a difficult explanation of his injury and lost firearm to Ambassador Tomás Anchorena. Operation Pilot had been established eight months earlier by junta member Admiral Emillio Massera. The operation gathered information on Argentine exiles, French organizations and individuals that denounced human rights violations in Argentina—among them Socialist Party Secretary François Mitterand, Marseilles Mayor Gaston Deferre, author Julio Cortazar, filmmaker Constantin Costa-Gavras and singer Charles Aznavour.

Anchorena was ill-disposed to listen to Roig. He resented the autonomy of the naval operation, which dealt directly with navy headquarters in Buenos Aires. It was a sort of parallel and undercover consular section that despite its diplomatic status did not respond directly to Anchorena, the head of the mission. Furthermore, the ambassador was occupied today with a pressing matter. So, masking his satisfaction diplomatically, he curtly informed the captain of the arrival that morning of his transfer orders. Roig was being posted back to Buenos Aires.

The officer gripped the arms of his chair and sat forward. "*Qué?*" He had been in Paris less than a year and had expected to be there at least two. He and his family were just beginning to feel comfortable. His wife's French was progressing and his daughter had been accepted into one of the city's most prestigious schools, an academy for the children of diplomats.

"You've been transferred," the ambassador repeated without expression.

Roig began a stammering protestation, but Anchorena curtailed it summarily. "I'm much too busy to discuss this, which, in any case, is out of my hands."

Roig rose and walked to the door, cursing under his breath. When the navy man had exited, Anchorena picked up one of the two telephones on his desk and instructed his secretary to call the Foreign Ministry in Buenos Aires. Anchorena wanted instructions from the foreign minister, General Carlos Washington Pastor, as to the next step he should take in what was developing into a crisis in Franco-Argentine relations.

Because of the abduction of the nuns and the failure of Argentine authorities to adequately respond to the protests and demands lodged by France, the archbishop of Paris, Cardinal Marty, had refused to celebrate a mass in Notre Dame to mark the two hundredth anniversary of the birth of South American revolutionary war hero General José de San Martín.

The Argentine media histrionically lamented the affront, asking indignantly how such an otherwise unimpeachable figure as the archbishop of Paris could be swayed by the subversive propagandists. But no newspaper in Argentina printed this communiqué, issued by the archdiocese of Paris by way of explanation:

"An Argentine-sponsored public ceremony in a church of Paris now would be absolutely out of place. The public opinion of France has been concerned, and with reason, about the fate of some of our compatriots and many others who reside in Argentina. Many unquestionable testimonies about this painful situation have reached us. The commemoration of the birth of General San Martín is, in Argentina, a legitimate popular sentiment. In Paris, it is essentially an initiative of the Argentine authorities. It is precisely from those authorities that French families, like those in other countries, expect explanations about the fates of their missing relatives."

*　　*　　*

Roberto Otero was propped up in bed sipping maté, the kettle like a faithful pet by his side on the floor.

Roberto was a Montonero. He was not a typical member of the Peronist Youth organization that, following Perón's death in 1974, took up arms against the right-wing government of his widow, Isabel. He was atypical in that he was from a poor family. Most of the "authentic" young Peronists, as they styled themselves, were middle-class pedants affected by a romantic image of the revolutionary. After all, Ché was Argentine.

It is difficult to define Montonero ideology. Its origins were nationalist and Roman Catholic. Many of its eventual leaders were molded during the 1960s in a neo-fascist youth organization called Tacuara. Long-tenured teachers at the Colegio Nacional de Buenos Aires recall how Mario Firmenich chafed at being taken for a Jew. Firmenich, who founded and led the Montoneros, would correct his instructors saying, "It's pronounced 'Fir-men-idge' not 'itch,' and its Croat, not Kike."

Firmenich and a few companions spectacularly publicized the formation of the Montoneros in 1970 with the kidnap and assassination of former president General Pedro Aramburu. Aramburu had signed the execution orders for the thirty-two Peronists who faced firing squads following the coup that toppled Perón in 1955. Aramburu also had been held responsible for spiriting out of the country the meticulously embalmed body of Eva Perón, who by means of tenacious will, fiery oratory and charisma had during Perón's first presidency transformed herself into the saint óf the working class.

> Con los huesos de Aramburu
> Haremos una escalera
> Para que baje del cielo

With the bones of Aramburu
We will make a ladder
So that she may descend from heaven

"Evita Montonera!" the guerrillas and their supporters chanted by the thousands to cheer the aging Perón when he returned to be elected to a third presidential term in 1973.

But relations between Perón and the Marxist-influenced Montoneros soon soured. During a speech from the balcony of Government House, "El Viejo" threw them out of the Plaza de Mayo on May Day, 1974, two months before his death. The internal contradictions had become unbearable even for a movement as enigmatic and all-encompassing as Peronism. From the balcony, Perón waved his hand over the Montonero sector of the jammed plaza and passed judgment.

"It appears that some beardless youths want to take credit for everything achieved by those who have struggled for decades," he declared through the loudspeakers.

The Montoneros marched out en masse beneath their black and red banners. When Perón died and "La Chavela" took over, the young Turks went underground and declared war.

Roberto started at a knock on the door. Diego entered, and the convalescent sighed and sat back.

"I saw your mother outside. She told me to go ahead in," Diego said as he carried a straight-backed chair to the bedside. Roberto filled the maté gourd and passed it to Diego, who took it and sipped.

"Well, cannon fodder, how are you feeling today?" There was a note of weary disgust in the question. He passed the gourd and began unwinding the bandage around Roberto's thigh.

"Better than yesterday." Then, after a moment, "Why do you call me that?"

"Because that's what you are."

"What's with you, Doc? Got a bug up your ass?"

"The country's got a big bug up its ass gnawing at its guts. And you're the ones who spread the cheeks to invite it in."

"Good thing I don't get out of bed these days. If I did, maybe I'd get up on the wrong side, like you did today, and maybe I'd show you the same lack of respect you're showing me."

"Respect for what? If you got out of bed, maybe you'd see the newspaper. You know what your buddies did last night? They blew up the apartment building where Admiral Lambruschini lives. But they didn't kill him. They only killed his fifteen-year-old daughter and two old ladies." Lambruschini was in line to replace Massera on the junta.

Roberto set the maté gourd on the floor next to the kettle. He was silent for a moment.

"It's tragic when innocent people die. I'm truly sorry for those people. But that happens in any revolution."

"Revolution," sneered Diego. *"Mierda."* He examined the wound. "You want instant revolution. But revolutions aren't made by a bunch of communiqué-writers playing Robin Hood. They come when the workers see through the rhetoric, and that's a ways off yet here. Look how your revolution turned out. All you did was give the *milicos* the pretext they needed."

"Sometimes it's not a simple question of majority," said Roberto. "Since the coup, the only respectable path is resistance."

"There are many forms of resistance. You can't resist if you're dead. And you can't resist if you're sitting in a café in Mexico or Rome talking revolution with the other big shots who flew the coup with their hides intact, like Firmenich."

"Allá ellos."

Francisca entered with a plastic basin in which she had washed the family's clothes, pressing them over a corrugated board. She kneeled at the head of the bed and took Roberto's hand in her own red, raw, cold hands.

"I have a bad feeling, *m'hijo querido*. I want you to get out of the city. Go back to Cordoba or south as soon as you can walk. You are not safe here."

"Don't worry, Mama. I'll be all right. You always said I was born under a lucky star."

The tune-up sounded like a catfight. Six boys in kilts and tam-o'-shanters stood at the back of the stage huffing and blowing into bagpipes. The air sacks puffed beneath their arms and the dangling, gleaming black pipes stood up straight like soldiers snapping to attention. Then, all at once, the pipes erupted in a swirling reel and kilted girls appeared from the wings. The girls pranced with their hands on their hips, their legs stirring the air. They jigged and flung in a dizzying whirl and even the most staid of the dark-suited fathers in the audience could not resist tapping his foot to the wild strains.

When the music stopped, the dancers threw their tams high and scurried to catch them. The spectators, almost three hundred parents and relatives of the student performers, responded with enthusiastic applause. The dancers and pipers stepped to the edge of the stage holding hands all in a row and bowed deeply.

The "Caledonian"—the pageant put on every year by the students of Highlands School—was a combination of genuineness and improvisation as could only be expected of a Gaelic fest celebrated by children named García and Antonelli alongside a scattered McIntyre or Campbell. Highlands was one of the most prestigious of the dozen British-founded private schools in and around Buenos Aires where the upper class and those who aspired to it sent their children. All the students attended two sessions. In the morning, the classes were in Spanish. After lunch the courses were all in English and the speaking of Castilian was prohibited, punishable by detention.

The performers retreated to the wings and, as the applause waned, two students carried a podium to center stage. The festival's director, Mr. MacLeod, stepped to the podium and announced in thick-brogued English the poetry-reading segment of the program.

The first girl struggled haltingly through a recital of Robert Burns. Then a boy did better justice to a verse by Robert Louis Stevenson.

Santiago took Monica's hand as their daughter approached the podium. Cristina's hair was pulled back in a high ponytail and her cheeks were red. She had been allowed an exception to orthodoxy in that, instead of a work by a true son of the highlands, she had selected a poem by a Celt from across the North Channel.

She took a deep breath and, in a clear strong voice that filled the hall, she said in barely accented English, "The Mask. By William Butler Yeats." She paused, then began:

> *"Put off that mask of burning gold*
> *With emerald eyes."*
> *"Oh no, my dear, you make so bold*
> *To find if hearts be wild and wise,*
> *And yet not cold."*

She had memorized the poem and looked out over the audience as she recited.

> *"I would but find what's there to find,*
> *Love or deceit."*
> *"It was the mask engaged your mind,*
> *And after set your heart to beat,*
> *Not what's behind."*

Her voice faltered at the end of the verse and she stepped back from the podium to look down at the floor. It appeared as if she were looking for something she had dropped. She stepped forward again and, on resuming, her voice cracked.

> *"But lest you are my enemy,*
> *I must enquire."*

She lifted her hands, which through the first verses had been resting assuredly on the podium, and placed them between her legs, out of sight. She leaned forward in some sort of anguish—some of the spectators thought she was merely overdramatizing the recital—and continued, but now through tears.

> *"Oh no, my dear, let all that be . . .*

" 'What matter,' " she cried out loud, and Santiago stood up. He made his way, stepping on feet, excusing himself, to the aisle. Cristina looked at her bloody hands, then held them up, palms out in supplication and sobbed.

> *"So there is but fire*
> *In you, in me?"*

After Cristina had been examined by the school doctor, after the sedative had taken effect and her parents had taken her home to bed, Santiago fumed and paced before Monica, who sat on the sofa in the living room.

"I can't believe it. I can't fucking believe it." Santiago struggled to restrain the volume of his voice. "The girl is thirteen years old and you never spoke to her about menstruation?"

"I was going to have a talk with her soon." Monica sat passively. She did not look at Santiago.

"Well, your 'soon' is too late."

"She's your daughter too, you know."

Santiago stopped in his tracks. "Are you suggesting that I should have spoken with her about this?" His face flushed and he clenched his fists at his sides. "Are you crazy or what?" He took a step toward her, then checked himself. He wheeled and lunged to the wall, to a framed photograph of Monica and himself standing before Iguazu Falls. His right hand drew back past his ear then shot forward and shattered the glass. Monica jumped up and ran from the room. She ran up the stairs and down the hall toward the master bedroom, stopping at the door to Cristina's room to listen for the sound of Santiago's ascent. But he remained in the den rubbing his hand and cursing.

Monica pushed open Cristina's door and stole in. She rummaged through the pile of clothes beside the bed and snatched up the stained white cotton panties. She wound them in a tight ball and rushed to the refuge of her bedroom. After locking the door, she pulled open the drawer of her night table and searched through it until she found a small key. She went into the bathroom and opened the cabinet beneath the sink. Inside was a black lacquered Chinese box inlaid with a mother-of-pearl heron. She took it out, opened it with the key and lifted out a small glass flask.

She opened the faucet so that a thin stream of water came out and then she passed the crotch of Cristina's bloodied underwear beneath the trickle. She opened the bottle and held it beneath the fabric crumpled in her fist and squeezed until a dozen drops of rosy water fell into the flask.

She stoppered the bottle and placed it delicately back in the lacquered box atop a lock of sandy-colored hair.

ANA STEPPED DOWN FROM THE NUMBER 152 BUS AT THE STOP OF PASEO COLÓN JUST BEHIND GOVERNMENT HOUSE. SHE CROSSED THE AVENUE IN THE MORNING KNOT OF OFFICE WORKERS, AND WALKED UP HIPOLITO Yrigoyen, the southern boundary of the Plaza de Mayo. She walked past the Social Welfare Ministry, close to the building and away from the noxious fumes from the buses screeching and snorting at the curb. She was passing in front of La Franco Insurance Company when her eyes met those of a man leaning against a column. The man, about thirty, with pomaded hair and chapped lips, smiled lewdly at her. She looked past him and continued ahead.

"If I got ahold of you baby I'd fill you full of cream," he said as she passed, just loud enough for her and no one else to hear.

Ana stopped and turned. She stepped up to him and pressed herself against his chest and reached a hand around behind to grab his buttock.

"I'm dying for you, big boy," she said throatily in his ear. "I want you to fuck me hard." The man's face contorted in a mask of panic. Cringing, he turned and ran.

"Faggot!" shouted Ana. The men and women on the sidewalk stopped and stared. She looked defiantly at the cow-eyed crowd then strode away thinking with disgust that even the simple act of walking down the street was a struggle. She walked the two blocks to the Colegio Nacional de Buenos Aires, a stately turn-of-the-century school on Bolívar Street, and hurried up the marble staircase to her classroom on the second floor. When she arrived there was a note on her desk. She was to report to the office of Mr. Figueroa, the principal.

She walked down the dim, high-ceilinged hallway and found the grandfatherly Mr. Figueroa sitting like a walrus at his desk.

He looked up from his newspaper. "Oh, Ana. You got my message. Please sit down." He removed his glasses and regarded her with reddened and watery eyes. "I'm going to get right to the point. You have begun teaching García Márquez's *One Hundred Years of Solitude* in your literature course, is that correct?"

"Yes."

"Did you not realize that that title is on the list of unsuitable material?"

Ana squinted and cocked her head, as if she had been addressed in Bulgarian. Then she said, "In all honesty, I did not. I remember seeing the list at the beginning of the year, but I don't remember any work by García Márquez being on it. And it's absurd that it should be."

Mr. Figueroa rubbed the indentations the glasses had left on the bridge of his nose. "The book glorifies insurrection and undermines the idea of allegiance to national government."

"On the contrary. It transpires during an interminable civil war, but one never knows the differences between the two sides, or what anybody is fighting for or against—and in that sense it reflects the stupidity of most warfare."

"That's your opinion and I respect it," said the principal, who replaced his glasses and straightened up in a posture of authority behind his desk. "I don't want to argue with you. But it is my duty to instruct you to cease teaching that book and replace it with something suitable. There are plenty of good books that don't lend themselves to subversive interpretations."

"I can't believe this conversation is taking place," said Ana, her voice rising. "I expected more from you, Mr. Figueroa. I always believed you were genuinely dedicated to the enlightenment of young people."

"Don't be insolent," he said sternly. Then he again removed his glasses and settled before her. His shoulders drooped as he leaned his head forward and looked at her beseechingly. "Don't be harsh with me, Ana. I don't like to do this. I don't make policy. But it is my responsibility to see that it is carried out. I've been a teacher and principal for nearly forty years. I have one more year before retirement and I don't want to spoil things for myself now. Please try to understand."

Ana rose without responding and walked back down the hall. She struggled to repress an urge to shout. She reached the doorway of her room and looked in. She stood just outside the classroom, out of sight of the murmuring and milling students, and looked across the room through the tall windows stretching from waist level nearly to the ceiling. The glass in the windows was old and over the decades had flowed imperceptibly downward, leaving the panes thicker at the bottom than at the top. Her eyes played down the length of the window and the branches of the tall trees outside changed shape, distorted by the varying thickness of the glass.

She entered. Her first class of the day was the same fourth-year literature section that was reading García Márquez. Latecomers filed in as the bell commencing the school day sounded.

Ana stepped up onto the low platform in front of the blackboard. "Today," she said loudly, strongly, "instead of literature we shall discuss ethics. The theme is censorship, and how a person should deal with an attempt to restrict his or her access to elements of culture. What do you think of the idea?"

The students looked at each other bewilderedly. They looked to the door. Then a girl called out, "Good idea!"

"Let's take a concrete example to get started," said Ana. "Mr. Figueroa has just informed me that the book we are reading has been judged subversive by some paranoid bureaucrat or Neanderthal colonel and that I may no longer use it as material in this class. What do you think about that?"

Ana heard the silence over the blood pounding in her ears.

"It sucks!" cried a boy at the back of the class, smacking his hand against the desktop.

"It's the best book I ever read," volunteered a pale girl with braids.

Then another girl shouted, "They're trying to suffocate us! They want us all to be idiots!"

"Nazis!"

A boy sang out: "Se v'acabar!"

Within seconds the disparate exclamations fused in a chant and the chant swelled like the shock wave of an explosion.

> *Se v'acabar! Se v'acabar!*
> *La dictadura militar!*
>
> *The military dictatorship*
> *Is going to end!*

By the third repetition the entire class was shouting the vow. One by one the students stood, as if in ovation. Some pounded the desktops and others stomped their feet and the chorus rattled the windows. Ana stepped down off the platform and opened the door to the hall and looked out. Other doors opened and tentative teachers, like inmates along a row of suddenly and inexplicably unlocked cells, stuck out their heads along the corridor.

Ana saw Mr. Falzarano step out of his physics class and look down the hall at her. A boy stepped out and the teacher tried to push him back into the classroom. But there were others behind the boy backing him up and they surged past the teacher and streamed into the hall.

Students from other classes ran toward Ana's classroom. The chant grew and echoed boomingly as the voices of those in the hall joined in.

The trucks arrived at the Villa Miseria at dawn. A red blur at the edge of the shrouded river began to light the sky. Blue and black buses disgorged hundreds of federal police infantrymen in light blue field uniforms, their fatigue-cut trousers tucked into heavy black boots. They held billy clubs diagonally across their chests and trotted in formation down the shantytown's main artery. Astonished residents appeared in their windows and doorways. An anti-riot squad with teargas launchers and shotguns at the ready formed in front of water

cannon. Dozens of city trucks—dumptrucks and flatbeds and hydrau-
lic compression garbage trucks—ground their gears alarmingly and
negotiated the narrow streets scaring dogs and chickens. Air brakes
hissed like dragons.

The sounds invaded the Otero household as the family breakfasted
with maté. The three immediately concluded that it was an anti-guerrilla
sweep. Roberto bounded to the bed and a pain shot up his side,
reminding him that his wound was not yet healed. He reached under the
pillow and pulled out a large revolver. He stuck it in his belt and covered
it with his sweatshirt.

Juan-Cruz was the first to recover his composure. "Listen son," he
said in a tone that did not admit discussion. "You and I are going to walk
out of here and down the street. Right past them, like nothing. If anyone
asks, we're on our way to the stevedores' bureau. We don't live here and
only came to visit a friend who is ill. Try not to limp."

They donned wool coats. "Give me a kiss, son." Francisca hugged
Roberto tightly. "May the Virgin protect you."

The two men stepped into the muddy street. The settlement
buzzed with recriminations against the police and warnings from them
to be quiet and follow orders. Men and women piled chairs, beds,
cribs, tables, trunks, pots and rope-tied bundles in front of their
dwellings.

The villeros loaded their meager possessions onto the waiting trucks
and climbed aboard. When a row of houses had been evacuated, an
officer made a final check of each shack and signaled to a bulldozer
poised at the end of the line. The massive machine belched and lurched.
The precarious structures buckled and fell, pressed into the mud by the
implacable tread. Women cried and cursed and prayed aloud. Their
children, transfixed by the machine's awesome power, watched with
wide eyes. Men stood silently clenching their jaws and fists as their
homes folded before the blade.

The police were busy with the destruction and did not pay attention
to Juan-Cruz and Roberto making their way down the line. They walked
past the demolition and turned the corner to head for the port.

"I'll go with you as far as the tracks," said Juan-Cruz. "You just keep
going. Your mother and I will salvage what we can. Who knows where

we'll land. Meet me in Constitución on Friday at noon and we'll decide what to do."

They reached another sector of the slum where a bulldozer was plowing under a row of houses. There was a commotion ahead. Juan-Cruz nudged Roberto toward an alley that would lead them to the edge of the settlement.

"Wait, Pa." Roberto continued toward the knot of police and *villeros*. At the center of the crowd was José, the old Catamarqueño. A policeman restrained him from behind. A nightstick pressed against José's throat and stifled the string of curses rising from it.

José stopped struggling against the yoke. The cop made the young man's common mistake of underestimating the physical strength of his elders and stopped choking him with the club. José reached up and grabbed the nightstick with both hands as if it were a chinning bar and in one motion pulled down, bent forward and stuck out his rear so that the cop lifted off the ground and flipped over José's head onto his head in the mud.

With astonishing agility, the old man darted toward the bulldozer that at that instant was biting into his home. His objective was the driver. He jumped onto the slowly advancing tread and scrambled to his feet. He reached toward the driver, side-stepping so as not to be carried forward on the rolling tread. The driver kicked him and José fell. His chin struck the track but he caught himself with his forearms. He searched for a foothold on the wheels turning the track and struggled to pull himself up.

He lifted a leg onto the tread but could not rise up. The sleeve of his coat was caught between its metal plates. He fought to pull free but could not. The tread advanced and the shanty dwellers and police watched in horrified fascination as the old man was carried forward on the track. He reached the edge, like the edge of a waterfall, and went over.

No shout issued from his gasping black mouth. But the crushing of his bones resounded like the snapping of timbers and froze the onlookers where they stood. The frenzied driver flipped a switch and the engine sputtered, coughed and died. The bulldozer sat atop José, the lower half of his body sticking out out from under the tread.

Juan-Cruz tugged his son's sleeve, but Roberto did not budge. His eyes were fixed on the legs of the old man. Some of the *villeros* began screaming and the police, shaking off their gruesome stupor, shoved people outward, away from the machine.

The officer in charge of the grid's demolition stood over José's legs. He ordered the operator to back the rig off the corpse. Roberto moved slowly, like a automaton. He reached under his shirt and drew the pistol from his belt. His father grabbed the hand holding the gun and pressed himself against Roberto to hide the weapon. But Roberto, with a giant heave, hurled his father back and with both hands leveled the revolver at the officer.

"Hey!" he shouted.

The officer turned, saw the gun and reached for his holster. Roberto fired. The bullet pierced the officer's chest and sent him reeling back against the bulldozer. He slumped to a sitting posture on top of José's dead legs.

Roberto had time to fire the single shot. His arms were still extended when a nightstick swung from behind him in a wide, two-fisted arc and crashed into his skull above his right ear. He dropped into the mud.

People ran in all directions. Juan-Cruz knelt next to his son and moved to take the battered head in his hands but was himself knocked out by a hardwood swat.

Ana was suspended without pay. The suspension was summary and indefinite, pending an investigation by the Education Ministry into the flash-in-the-pan student rebellion. Mr. Figueroa had informed Ana of the measure. He had limited himself to reading, without once looking her in the eye, the directive signed by an army colonel attached to the ministry.

The night of her suspension, Ana and Diego lay in bed enveloped in the winter darkness. What seemed to be myriad particles of light from the moon pierced the shade.

"Diego?"

"Yes, *cuore mio.*"

"You have the right to residence in Italy, right? Even Italian citizenship if you wanted?"

"Yes. Why?"

"I'm getting tired."

Diego placed his hand lightly on the side of her head and caressed her. "'You're upset. You'll feel better in a few days."

"It's not the job. I've been thinking about this for weeks; the secrecy, the precautions, the risk. My insides are scrambled. This dictatorship could last ten years. It's no way for Daniel to grow up. How is he going to have any idea of what freedom is if he grows up here? Sometimes I just want to quit everything, pack up and move somewhere where we could live in peace. I don't want to fail my child."

She turned her back to Diego and drew up her knees. He slipped one arm beneath her head and wrapped the other over her, conforming his body to hers.

As they lay still in the silent darkness Diego thought how, even in apparent weakness—in vacillation and doubt—Ana was stronger than himself. Lately he'd been questioning their activity as well. Not its justness, but its effectiveness. He'd pretty much concluded that perhaps their only hope was survival, to be able to pick up later on with some prospect of progress. Because here and now, they were beating their heads against a wall.

But, afraid of appearing weak, he hadn't been able to express his misgivings. Even now that Ana had cleared the way for him he could not reveal them. He spoke, and his words to his own ear sounded faint.

"No one ever said it would be easy. But if we give up, then what hope is there? They will have won completely. Why do you think our flag is red? Because so many workers have shed so much blood. That's the way it is. Our lives are on the line and we have to accept that. Because if we don't—if we're going to give up because they threaten us—then we've lost already."

Ana said nothing. Her breathing slowed and deepened. Diego thought for a moment she had fallen asleep. But after a while she said, "If we're so willing to die for a cause maybe we should never have had a child. Because he is our responsibility too."

"Then who the hell are we trying to change things for?"

They lay awake next to each other silent and disquieted for a long time before falling asleep.

*   *   *

Diego and Ana stepped out onto San Martín Street through the rear exit of Harrod's department store. They looked down Tres Sargentos Street and saw no one. Diego looked at his watch. They meandered from store window to store window, feigning interest in Savile Row suits and Burberry's raincoats far too expensive for them to purchase. After a few minutes, they saw a young couple turn the corner of Reconquista onto Tres Sargentos and walk toward them up the street. Diego and Ana remained at the store window a moment longer, then walked down the street toward the couple. Halfway up the block, the other couple entered the Belo Horizonte, a short-stay hotel. When Diego and Ana reached the door, they too entered.

The other couple stood at the check-in desk. Observing the convention of discretion prevailing in such establishments, Diego and Ana did not go immediately to the desk, but stood looking at lethargic orange fish in a murky aquarium until the others had received their key.

"Number fourteen, 'the drunk.' A fiver on that tonight," said the man out loud as he stepped toward the elevator. (For playing the daily lottery, all numbers from zero to ninety-nine correspond to a word or phrase. If in a dream one is addressed by someone who has died, the number is forty-eight, "the talking dead." If there's blood, it's eighteen, smoke, eighty-six, and so on.)

The old man at the reception desk reached for key number 25, to a room on the second floor.

"We're celebrating our thirteenth anniversary," Diego told him. "Is room thirteen available?"

"Don't get many requests for that one. But suit yourselves." He handed Diego the key.

They went up to the first floor in the elevator and walked down the hall to where the other couple stood at the door of room 14. The man opened the door quickly and all four entered the room.

The man, known to Diego and Ana as Pablo, turned on all the lights, including the red ones. There was a large mirror on the ceiling and a photographic mural of a waterfall at the head of the double bed. Against the wall was a padded piece of furniture, something between a high chaise longue and a gymnastics horse.

"How are you supposed to fuck on this thing?" asked Pablo's companion, Silvia, as she hoisted herself up on it. She reclined and laughed, then flipped over and knelt with her butt stuck high in the air.

"Enough burlesque," said Pablo, sitting down heavily on the bed. He lit a cigarette. The two women joined him on the bed. Diego sat in the room's only chair.

"Let's start with contributions," said Pablo.

Diego took some bills from his trouser pocket. "Two of my contacts have to skip this month. They don't have any money."

"It's important that they contribute something, even if it's less than usual. Once they stop, it's hard to get them started again."

"One lost his job and the other had medical expenses. They're solid *compañeros,* though. They'll give again as soon as they can."

"*Bueno.* Newspapers. How many? Can you handle six this month? We've got to increase circulation. Under these circumstances the paper is our most important task."

"Give us five," said Ana. "I've been talking with a friend. Ex-PC, sick of Stalinism. She's ready to at least read our line. But papers we have no chance of distributing are nothing but a risk."

Pablo pulled up his pantleg and pulled a sheaf of papers from his boot. He counted five papers and handed them to Ana.

Ana noticed Pablo's long slender fingers. She looked up at his face and their eyes met for a second. His were mischievous and sparkling, belying the downward turn of his mouth and the seriousness of purpose in everything he did. Pablo was younger than Diego and Ana but had a long and lauded past in the party. He had rejected his comrades' call to arms in the early seventies and had seen many friends choose the path of the guerrilla. They had gone to Tucuman and joined the Ejercito Revolucionario del Pueblo despite his protestations that it was elitist, isolated from the workers. Now they were all dead or disappeared.

Silvia got up and went into the bathroom.

Amorous moans from the couple in room fifteen filtered through the wall and rose toward a rapturous crescendo.

"Ta, ta, ta, ta . . ." related Ana in a hushed imitation of the play-by-play soccer announcers on the radio. "Gooalllll!"

Diego laughed and Pablo sighed at the prevailing lack of earnestness.

A pounding on a door on another corridor silenced them. They held their breath.

"Federal police. Open up," they heard, far off. There was a long moment of paralyzing and nauseating fear before they bounded from the bed. Pablo snatched the room 13 key from the night table and jumped to the door. He opened it and the bathroom door at the same time.

"Come on," he commanded in a whisper. Silvia looked up from the toilet, surprised and embarrassed, in the middle of inserting a tampon. Diego stood by the side of the bed. Pablo grabbed Ana, who had followed him to the door to see what was happening outside, by the wrist. He stuck his head out, checked up and down and jerked her into the hall. He opened the adjacent door and they entered.

Diego put the newspapers under the mattress. Pablo did the same in the other room.

"Get undressed," Pablo ordered Ana. He flung off his clothes. Ana stripped to her panties and they scrambled under the sheets. They waited for the knock. After a few long minutes, it came.

"Stay in bed. Be a good actress," Pablo whispered, then rose and opened the door.

"Documents," demanded the officer. "Get up, sweetie," he said to Ana. She sat up but kept herself covered with the sheet as she reached for her purse.

The cop, in a blue wool tunic with white cotton sleeve-guards from wrist to elbow, took the proffered documents. He examined the plastic-covered cards. "Let's see here. You're Suarez de Maglione," he said, indicating Ana. "But," he pointed his chin at the wiry naked man, "this isn't Maglione."

"So what? You from the morals division?" asked Pablo.

"Don't get wise. We're making sure the hotels are being used for what they're intended for; for fucking and not for fucking up the country. But apart from that, we have orders to confiscate the document of any married woman found with any man other than her husband. There's no formal accusation, but she has to come with her husband in person to the station, where the chief returns the document and tells the cuckold with great relish where his wife was when she lost it. See, a year ago, in a raid just like this, we found his señora in flagrante with a Portuguese sailor."

"There must be some other way we can work this out." Pablo

reached into his billfold and extended a bill. The cop noted the denomination and dropped all pretense of propriety.

"I don't take tips. Peel some more, *macho.*"

Pablo handed over all he had on him. The policeman jammed the money into his pocket. "Carry on," he said, and walked out the door.

Ana crawled back under the covers and lay there trembling. Pablo pressed his ear against the wall and heard Diego talking. It had better be a different cop, thought Pablo. Because if it were the same one, he would find something suspicious about a man being shacked up with someone in the room right next to the one where his wife was putting the horns on him.

Pablo heard the door to room 14 close. He picked up a heavy glass ashtry from the table and moved to the door. If another knock came, the charade was over. He would try to club the cop and make a break; in his underwear and bare feet.

But no knock came. He returned to the bed where Ana lay huddled.

"I'm cold," she said. He lifted the covers and crawled in next to her. He put his arms around her and pulled her against him. She felt his penis stiffening against her. She felt small and wanted to melt into the torso and loins of the strong, warm body surrounding her.

Neither she nor Pablo moved a muscle. They lay still until the breathing of each settled into the same slow rhythm. The fear and the ardor subsided, their place taken by a soothing, intimate stillness.

"Thank you," whispered Ana. Pablo softly kissed the back of her head, then threw the covers back off them. They got dressed and left.

Night was falling and with it a mist when Diego and Ana walked together out of the hotel and down the street. Diego turned up his collar.

"Did you make love with him?" he asked quietly, looking ahead.

"No. But for a moment I wanted to."

They boarded the bus for La Boca and sat down next to each other. Diego put his hands in his pockets, clenching them into fists, and looked forward, past the backs of heads, through the windshield at the crazy play of streetlights and taillights off the slick black pavement. Diego looked beyond the reflections into the depth of the darkness.

Ana felt strangely sad. Her eyes fell on a father and his young daughter seated across the aisle. The man's face was brown and lined beneath dirty blond hair slicked back with pomade in the fashion of 1940s tango singers. He wore a mended suit coat and from the frayed sleeves emerged thick brown hands like waterworn stone, a mason's hands. His left arm encircled his daughter, who rested her head against his breast. In his right hand, placed open upward in his lap, reposed her small soft pale hand. The man, deep in thought, stared out the window. The girl wrapped her fingers around the base of her father's thumb and squeezed. The father smiled down at her and answered her squeeze with a gentle closing of his paw around her delicate hand.

Menotti was not sleeping well. The bed in his small, monastic apartment at the training camp was too short and the nervousness kept at bay during the day by the immediate concerns of practice assailed him at night. He tried to read but couldn't concentrate. He could not think about anything but the first game, against Hungary, a week away.

He worried about the tradition, a kind of jinx, of poor showings by World Cup host teams in their first game. He went through the list: England, lucky to salvage a scoreless draw against Uruguay in its first game of the 1966 Cup in London; Mexico, incompetent in its 0–0 tie with the Soviet Union in the 1970 opener; West Germany needing a desperate and fortunate goal by Breitner from thirty meters out to win its first game, against Chile, in the '74 tournament.

The coach woke in the predawn darkness of May 25. He sat up on the edge of his bed and looked out through a round window over the peaceful parkgrounds. He looked across to the chalet where the players stayed and hoped they were not as nervous as himself. He chain-smoked dark-tobacco cigarettes, and finally fell back asleep with the first light.

Not long afterward, a man in uniform walked softly into Menotti's room and knocked lightly on the headboard. The coach, lying face up, opened his eyes and sprang upright with a start. A chain of panicked thought—"I'm being kidnapped . . . what did I do? . . . a coup"— flashed through his mind.

The uniformed man saluted. "Chief of security of the area, sir. I wanted to be the first to say good morning to you on the Day of the Fatherland."

"Oh . . . oh," stammered Menotti, regaining his senses. "Good morning to you too."

When the officer left, Menotti shook a cigarette from the pack and struck a match. He needed both trembling hands to guide the flame to the tip.

Argentina's founding fathers had no clear idea of what they wanted the nation to be. The country is confused about its identity. It even has two independence days.

May 25, the Day of the Fatherland, is the date in 1810 when some influential citizens of Buenos Aires stripped the Spanish viceroy of his power. Since Napoleon had occupied Spain and dethroned the Spanish monarch, they reasoned, the mandate of the king's representative was void. Some of the local dignitaries wanted an outright declaration of independence, but they were persuaded by conservatives that the new authorities, a junta, should swear allegiance to the Spanish crown.

A declaration of independence did not come until six years later, on July 9—the second patriotic national holiday. "The Liberator," General José de San Martín, formed the Army of the Andes and battled Spanish forces in a long war that gave birth to Argentina, Chile, Bolivia and— with the aid of Bolívar and Sucre—Peru.

San Martín is the most revered figure in Argentine history. Firm-jawed and patriarchal, he gazes from all denominations of paper currency. The father of independence, after ceding glory and command to Bolívar during their brief meeting in Guayaquil in 1822, went to live in France. Seven years later, he returned to Argentina. But upon being informed of the chaotic state of his homeland embroiled in fratricidal war he declined to disembark. He returned to France and died in Boulogne-sur-Mer, disillusioned and disgusted with what his inheritors had wrought. San Martín's bones were brought home years later and enshrined in the National Cathedral overlooking the Plaza de Mayo.

At the corner of Viamonte and Suipacha Streets in the heart of Buenos Aires is an equestrian statue of Manuel Dorrego. An angel is leading his horse, presumably, to heaven. Dorrego was one of the nation's founders, a statesman, a victorious general in the revolutionary war. He was executed by General Jaun Lavalle, another independence hero, in 1818.

The city's tallest statue is dedicated to Lavalle. It stands atop a column in the middle of Tucumán Street in front of the Teatro Colón. Lavalle was executed on orders from Buenos Aires provincial governor Juan Manuel de Rosas in 1841.

Rosas said: "The spilling of twenty drops of blood opportunely can prevent the spilling of two thousand." The dictator's gangs of red-poncho'd gauchos slit his opponents' throats—they called it "playing the violin"—and took their heads and impaled them on spikes in public places. Rosas is known as "the Restorer of the Law." He is revered by Peronists and conservatives as a great nationalist.

In the training camp cafeteria, the blackboard with the day's schedule carried a special message: VIVA LA PATRIA! Under the legend was chalked a birthday greeting to team captain Daniel Passarella and under that, forward Rene Houseman had written, "and to my mother." There was also a "Viva!" for Argentina's national juvenile squad, the reigning world champs.

Because of the holiday, there was only a morning practice session. The afternoon was taken up with an entertainment program featuring singer Susana Rinaldi, the Zupay folk quartet, rock guitarist Luis Alberto Spinetta and the tango trio of Rubén Juarez on bandoneon, Roberto Grela on guitar and vocalist Raúl Lavie.

A boxing ring had been set up in one of the camp's pavilions. Victor Galindez, the world light-heavyweight champ, and Hugo Corro, the middleweight titleholder, put on an exhibition.

When their friendly bout ended, Corro leaned against the ropes, took out his spit-shiny mouthpiece and, smiling broadly, said to the players at ringside, "Any of you hot shots want to go a few rounds?"

The challenge excited Alejandro. He had not boxed with his father, or anyone, for almost a year. But the ring, the gloves and the chance to see how he measured up, however goodheartedly, to a world champion set his heart thumping. He stood up.

"I will," he said.

His teammates cheered. Galindez relinquished his gloves and head-gear. Substitute goalkeeper Hector Baley jumped into the ring and pantomimed a reach for an imaginary microphone lowered from the roof.

"Ladies and gentlemen!" he blared. "In this corner, the middleweight champion of the world, Hugo 'Two Swans' Corro. Why 'Two Swans'? Because when he was born, he was so ugly the dispatcher of swans sent two to his house; one to make the delivery and another to apologize." Everyone burst into laughter. "And in this corner, the challenger, the 'Italian Stallion' . . ." Baley stopped and walked over to Alejandro. He grabbed the waistband of his sweatpants, pulled the elastic out and peered down. "Correction. Make that the 'Italian Gelding,' Kid Maglione!

"Let's have a clean fight. No biting! To the death!!"

"Ding," yelled Galindez, and the two laughing boxers approached each other and circled tentatively in the center of the ring. Alejandro felt good. His legs were springy. He threw a jab to get the distance and followed it with another that glanced off the champ's padded forehead. Corro retreated. Alejandro bore in and feinted a jab with his left and delivered a cross with his strong hand. The punch landed solidly on the side of the champion's headgear.

"Good shot," chuckled Corro through his mouthpiece. The champ drew himself down into a half crouch then darted out of it with a flurry of punches at Alejandro's head. The boy blocked the first two but the third landed smack on the tip of his nose, the only part of his face not protected by the padded leather helmet. It was not a hard punch, but it stung.

Alejandro backed off. He circled in half-skips off the balls of his feet.

"Good footwork," said Corro, advancing. The champ lashed out with a right that landed hard against Alejandro's bicep and sent a dull pain through his shoulder. Suddenly, the bout had ceased to be a joke. Alejandro bobbed and shuffled to his left and snapped a straight left arm into the center of Corro's face. The champ was surprised at the skill of the maneuver and his hands dropped for a split second. Alejandro saw the opening and hooked a right into Corro's ear.

"Fix!" shouted one of the players.

Corro was not the world titleholder for nothing. Fun was fun, but this kid was getting wise. "And you can't get wise if you leave your belly open like that," the champ said to himself and stepped forward. His low right hand swung like an axe and thudded into Ale's solar plexus. All his breath escaped him. He buckled and would have fallen if Corro had not clinched him in a cradling hug.

"Don't worry, kid," the champ whispered in Alejandro's ear. "I ain't so great at soccer neither."

Someone called out, "Ding!" and in a few seconds Alejandro, still in Corro's embrace, regained his wind and his humor. He separated himself from the champ, took Corro's wrist and raised his arm high to the cheers of the team.

CHAPTER 5

THE FLYING TRAIN CLATTERED ABOVE AND CRIES OF DELIGHT WHIRLED
AROUND THEM. DIEGO, ANA AND DANIEL STOOD BENEATH THE ROLLER
COASTER DEVOURING CORN ON THE COB. THE BUTTERY, SALTY CORN JUICE
glistened on their lips and chins. They tossed the naked cobs into a bin
and Ana took Diego's head between her hands, licking his lips and
sucking the drops from his beard.

"Me too!" cried Daniel, and his mother tongue-bathed his chin and
cheeks like a cat cleans her kitten.

It was Daniel's thirteenth birthday. They swooped and screamed and
laughed through the rides at Italpark on Libertador Avenue. Later on
they drove out along the Costanera Sur, where they stopped for a while
to sit on a wall and watch the river lap the shore.

Daniel got out first, running ahead, when they finally parked the car
in front of their home. The street was deserted. Diego shut his door and
walked around the car toward Ana, who was waiting on the sidewalk.
As he neared, she made a pirouette and in one swooping motion bent
over from the waist, tossing her ample skirt high in the air to expose a
scantily clad derriere.

Diego laughed.

Ana struck a tough-guy stance and set her jaw. She squinted at him.

"You have it good with your little Indian, eh? Cheap entertainment. But what happens when I run out of script?"

Later, after Daniel had gone to bed, Diego entered his room and sat on the bedside and stroked his son's hair.

"Dani, you're getting to be a big boy. So I'm going to stop coming in every night to make sure you're covered and give you a kiss. Is that all right?"

"*Está bien, papi.* Anyway sometimes you wake me up."

"I love you."

"I love you too."

Diego went down the hall, undressed and got into bed with Ana. They lay entwined in the darkness. The wind whistled through the space where the windowsash had settled out of plumb. Ana slept, her head on Diego's shoulder. Her breast rose and fell gently and her breath, the scent of fennel, bathed his face. He closed his eyes and a stream of hypnotic imagery carried him to sleep. When he bolted up at the crash of the door, he had the unsettling portrait of a smiling cyclops.

He and Ana threw off the covers and had not even reached their robes, draped over the footboard, when four shouting men stormed into the bedroom leveling automatic weapons and short pump-action shot-guns at them.

"Combined Forces!"

"Avert your eyes! Avert your eyes!"

But it was impossible not to behold the spectacle. A burly red-complexioned man stepped up to Diego and stuck a shotgun barrel under his chin.

"You heard the order. Avert your eyes."

But Diego could not lower his head because of the pressure of the cold metal tube. He had to look sharply aside so as not to stare the man in the face. The man moved his big ruddy head in front of Diego's averted eyes and pressed his bulbous nose against Diego's. Diego shifted his eyes left, but the man craned his head so as to be again in his prisoner's line of vision. Diego looked directly into the man's bottle-green eyes.

"Are you going to make it difficult?" the man said, and slammed the shotgun butt into Diego's groin. He crumpled onto the bed.

"Son of a whore!" shouted Ana, throwing herself atop Diego.

One of the intruders slipped a black hood over Ana's head from behind, shoved her off her husband and pressed her face into the mattress. He straddled her and handcuffed her wrists behind her as the big red-faced man handcuffed Diego.

"Look what a pretty ass she has," said the man sitting on Ana. "Let's see if it's intact or if she goes for a little buggering now and then." He spread Ana's buttocks but she heaved and twisted face up beneath him. She got one leg out from under and sent him tumbling backward with a kick in the chest.

The man sprawled on the floor. The others laughed. The man chuckled as he picked himself up off the floor then stepped to the bedside where Ana sat terrified, blinded by the hood. He pulled a .45-caliber pistol from a shoulder holster and crashed the butt of the weapon into the side of her face.

Daniel stood in the bedroom doorway in his pajamas. He lunged at his mother's attacker and hung from the man's neck, his legs flailing the air. The intruder snapped his elbow backward into the boy's ribs and Daniel fell to the floor in a ball.

"Don't be a little hero," the man snarled down at him.

Diego, numbed by the blow and stunned by the speed with which his haven had become a battlefield, struggled to his feet. He stared vacantly around him. As if through the wrong end of a telescope, he remotely saw his wife unconscious, hooded and naked on the bed, his son curled and groaning on the floor and four armed men standing there, just standing, like himself.

Two of the men grabbed the robes and covered Diego and Ana, knotting the fabric belts tightly chest-high. One threw Ana over his shoulder like a sack of grain and carried her out. The other hooded Diego and marched him out of the apartment past a fifth man guarding the door, an M-16 cradled at the ready, and down the flight of stairs to the street, where another sentry stood. The door to the street-level apartment opened and Diego heard the gravelly voice of Mr. DiNardo, the baker.

"What the hell is going on here?"

"Combined Forces Operation," answered the street guard. He shoved

Mr. DiNardo back into his house and pulled the door shut. "Don't bother calling the police," he said through the closed door.

Two Ford Falcons without license plates were parked in the street in front of the house. The man carrying the deadweight bundle of Ana dumped her in the trunk of one. Diego was hustled into the back seat of the same vehicle and shoved down onto the floor. A man got in the back with him and placed one booted foot on the small of his back and the other on the back of his head. When Diego stirred, the man pressed his face to the floor.

Four men ransacked the apartment. One man picked the crying Daniel up off the floor, slapped him sharply and said, "Don't be a pussy." He threw him into the bathroom and slammed the door. "Don't come out until you hear we've gone," he warned.

The men were disappointed in that they found nothing to indicate subversive affiliation. They stole two watches, a cassette player, a portable black-and-white television set and the cash they found in Diego's wallet and Ana's purse.

The car with the two prisoners in it left the scene.

"Target positive. Heading for roost. Lift no-go zone," said the driver into the microphone of a dash-mounted radio.

The tires ring. His ear to the rail, a far-off train. Someone's sniffles. His. Bare thighs against cold rubber floormat. The urge to pee. Don't cry. Don't give them cause to gloat. The promise (illusion?) that he could be a man if he acted like one. The scent of Ana. He's wrapped in Ana's robe. This could happen, you knew it could. Has it happened? Not to me. Not to Ana. Ana, Ana, Ana. A heel in the back of the head. The taste of rubber and dirt. A gunbarrel like a spear in the ribs. A spear in the ribs? A sponge of vinegar? He turns his head to the side for air. A fart. One says, "You're an animal, baldy." One sniffs. "What did you eat? The hand of Gardel?" The thick odor settles around his head, filters through the hood. He wretches. Where going? Just on and farther. Into the darkness of the hood. Deeper. Into the darkness of hate, the pitch of murderous rage. He groans and kills three men or more. Strains against the shackles, bites their throats, chomps cartilage and artery. A thumping from the trunk.

Ana! He weeps anew. Sobs and thanks a God he does not believe in. The ring of the tires, the motor's purr. Dani! Hurt? Call Santiago! The smell of gasoline. Torture. The torture of me. My flesh burned. The torture of Ana! I'll explain: I'm a doctor, work in the shantytown. Charitable activity among the poor, mistaken for subversive. Don't you see?

Please. Don't you see? Please. Don't you see?

Radio static. "Approaching roost. Open gate."

"These damn new shoes are biting my feet," said the larger of the two men as he and his partner changed ends of the Ping-Pong table after the second game of their best-of-five match. "My wife gave me them yesterday for my birthday, but they're too narrow. And if I take them back, she'll get all offended."

"So that's why you were off last night. Happy birthday," said the other, who dragged a lame leg.

The big man wore blue jeans pulled high on his ample girth, cinched with a fancy-stitched white rawhide belt. The sleeves of his beige shirt of heavy-duty cotton, the kind used by factory men, were rolled past the elbow to expose a crude and faded tattoo on each forearm. One was a Medusa bust, snakes swirling from the head of a woman the artist had intended as buxom and sensuous, but who had been ravaged to ugliness by the years of shifting tissues of her patron. The other was a dagger, over which was written the legend "*Patria o Muerte.*"

The smaller man wore a rumpled and wide-lapelled corduroy suit and an old bow tie. He reached stiffly to make his shots, but the bum leg did not greatly impair his game. He was quite good at Ping-Pong.

The clop-clop of the ball against paddle and table ricocheted hollowly off the walls. They had barely begun the game when a man in uniform stuck his head in the door.

"You got work."

The big man swore and they put down their paddles. The little man said, "Remember. Three to nothing. My serve."

They walked down a rust-colored hallway to an elevator, an old one with a hinged metal-grate door that opened like an accordion. They took it to the basement. They walked down a corridor of metal-doored cells and turned left at a hand-painted sign in the form of an arrow reading: THE PATH TO HAPPINESS.

They entered an office and were perfunctorily briefed by an officer. Then they crossed the hall to one of the torture chambers.

Diego was in the center of the harshly lit room, shackled by the wrists and ankles, face up, to a high metal table. His hood had been replaced by a tight blindfold of dirty, greasy cloth. He was naked. Vomit streaked his shoulder. The windowless gray room smelled of burned meat, sweat and excrement. Along one wall was a counter with a sink and a cabinet beneath the sink. Swatches of dried blood stained the walls. Painted (in blood?) on one wall was the legend: VIVA LA MUERTE!

The small man took a clipboard from a nail in the door. At the top of a ruled page it said: "Navy Mechanics School. Secret" Below that were various categories headed "Interrogator," "Group," "Case," "Time of Entry," "Time of Departure," "Condition of Prisoner." The names of the interrogators in the four cases registered on the sheet were the aliases Schnoz, The Shepherd, The Turk and Baldy.

The larger man walked over to the table where Diego lay bound.

"Hello," he said, and at the same time crashed his fist down from high into the center of Diego's abdomen. After a few seconds, when he was sure his words would be heard, he said, "I am Pumpkin. My associate here, we call him the Gimp. Because he limps. He has limped ever since he was shot in the back by a smelly Bolshevik like yourself." He leaned over and spoke, softly now, into Diego's ear.

"You are cowshit. A platter of dung. You're not even as well off as cowshit. Because cowshit dries up in a few days and when it rains it melts back into the earth. You'll wish you could melt into the earth. But we decide when to let you die. And you, my little red friend, are going to have to endure life, if you can call it that, for a few days or weeks more."

The Gimp took a device that looked like a two-pronged soldering iron, from the cabinet under the sink and plugged its long cord into a 220-volt outlet in the wall near the table. The cord coiled on the floor like a serpent.

The man called Pumpkin looped a wire over Diego's big toe to ground him. Diego felt the wire and recalled the tags on the toes of cadavers he had dissected in the medical school morgue. Pumpkin filled a plastic pail with water at the sink and emptied it on the prisoner.

"Telephone for you," said the Gimp, and touched the implement—"*la picana*"—into Diego's ear.

Diego wailed. He was convulsed by a chain reaction of miniature explosions, like cells bursting. He felt himself burst from his skin, as if his skin had split and popped like the skin of an overripe grape and he was left raw with flesh and nerves exposed and the raw flesh stroked with a stiff metal brush.

The torturer withdrew the *picana*. Diego stopped bucking and bouncing. He had bitten his tongue and blood dribbled from a corner of his mouth. He choked on the blood and turned his head to the side. As the blood ran out he heaved up from his convulsed belly but nothing was regurgitated.

The larger man clamped his hand on Diego's jaw and shook his head. "What brand of mayonnaise do you use?" The words penetrated the chaos of Diego's brain, but he did not comprehend. "What brand of mayonnaise do you use?" Pumpkin screamed hysterically. "Tell me! You putrid pile of shit!"

Diego's mouth and lips contorted and he fought to form a word. "Hellman's," he whispered.

"Wrong!" cried Pumpkin, and the Gimp jammed the *picana* to Diego's nipple.

When his howl subsided, the two torturers remained silent. Pumpkin cocked his head toward the far wall. "Now rest a minute and listen carefully," he said. A muffled scream seeped through the cinderblocks. Diego could not still his shaking, but above the cymbal-ring in his head he heard a faint and anguished wail.

"That is your wife," said Pumpkin.

Diego lurched and the shackles cut into his flesh. He pulled and the steel dug deeper into his wrists and ankles.

"Sons of whores!" he shouted. He repeated it, but the damnation deflated into a whimper.

The torturers did not move or speak and the three men listened to Ana's cries.

"Do you want me to tell them to stop?" asked Pumpkin.

"*Sí. Sí . . . por favor,*" pleaded Diego.

Pumpkin left the room and after a minute came back followed by two men supporting Ana, racked and ravaged, between them. Dried blood hid half her face. Her left eye was bright purple and swollen shut. She could not stand on her own, but when she recognized Diego she snapped upright and strained against the men to go to him.

As she struggled, the Gimp grasped Diego's penis and pressed the foreskin back to expose the glans. He touched the *picana* there and Diego bucked and cried out.

Ana sobbed and collapsed into a crouch. She was kept from falling to the floor by the grip of her tormentors. She wept.

"Now, now. Don't cry," Pumpkin said to Ana. "You can stop all this if you want." He unwound the blindfold from Diego's head. Diego blinked back the brightness and discerned the blurred image of his wife squatting between two men.

"Would you rather we continue stimulating your husband, or would you prefer to stimulate me?" asked Pumpkin. He moved toward Ana as he pulled down his zipper. He pulled out his half-hard penis and waved the organ in Ana's face.

"You decide. The prick or the *picana.*"

Diego summoned the strength to shout, "No! Ana, *cuore.* No, no."

The Gimp touched the prod to Diego's testicles and Diego screamed.

"All right, all right. Stop," whimpered Ana. She bowed her head. When she looked up again into Pumpkin's thick-lipped and lecherous face her eyes were clear and hard. She closed her eyes and opened her mouth. The torturer guided his penis into it. At the first touch of it Ana clamped her jaw shut and yanked her head back with a savage growl. Pumpkin loosed a fathomless scream. Snarling, Ana tugged and worried the thick gristle and pulled a chunk away. She spit it onto the floor.

The big man fell on his back on the floor, one hand squeezing the spurting wound. Ana's torturers shook her madly as if they thought she would cough up more meat. The Gimp dropped the *picana* to the floor.

"Diego, *mi vida!*" cried Ana, blood dripping from the corners of her mouth. Diego watched helplessly as the floundering Pumpkin reached behind him to draw a pistol from a holster at the small of his back. The mangled man struggled to his knees, still clamping the remainder of his penis in his left hand, and leveled the gun at Ana.

Ana's captors let go and lunged in opposite directions as Pumpkin shot her in the face and emptied his weapon into her spasm-racked corpse.

Eighty thousand people jammed the River Plate soccer stadium on the afternoon of Thursday, June 1. At a signal from inaugural-day pageant director José María Bravo, students in white jogging suits at the southern end of the stadium released hundreds of red, blue and yellow helium-filled balloons. The fans cheered as they floated up and away against the brilliant sky.

The flags of the 146 member nations of the International Soccer Federation formed a circle at the center of the manicured playing field. Rows of students like rays from a stylized sun extended out from the circle. All at once, the students fell onto their backs and stretched over themselves sheets of colored cloth to form the flags of the sixteen nations that had made it though their continental qualifying competition to the World Cup tournament. The countries were: Argentina, Italy, France and Hungary in Group 1; defending champion West Germany, Poland, Mexico and Tunisia in Group 2; Austria, Brazil, Sweden and Spain in Group 3; Holland, Peru, Scotland and Iran in Group 4.

Argentine President General Jorge Videla, junta member Admiral Emilio Massera, International Soccer Federation President João Havelange, and Alfredo Cantill, president of the Argentine Soccer Association, stood in the Stand of Honor, a midfield box.

Six hundred gradeschool children in white smocks ran onto the field and kneeled at rehearsal positions to spell out in giant letters ARGENTINA '78.

A hundred million people watched the ceremony broadcast live around the world. In an aerial shot of the stadium, television viewers were able to catch a glimpse of the grounds of the Navy Mechanics School one kilometer away.

The field was cleared. The West German and Polish teams lined up. At exactly three o'clock, Argentine referee Angel Coerezza raised his arm and blew his whistle. Klaus Fischer tapped the ball off his right foot to Heinz Flohe.

The tournament had begun.

Pumpkin, deep in shock, was taken to the infirmary. Ana's body was removed. Diego had swooned on the table and his torture was suspended. He was blindfolded, handcuffed and covered again with the robe. Two men dragged him down a corridor.

They reached a metal door and a guard opened it. The men dragged Diego inside, past prostrate bodies, some groaning, some silent, and deposited him in a compartment separated from the next by a meter-high concrete wall. It was not a cell, but a stall in a common cell where recent arrivals at the mechanics school spent their first days.

"Don't sit, stand or speak," ordered one of the soldiers. They left Diego lying on the cold floor.

An excruciating thirst possessed him. The lining of his mouth and throat shriveled and cracked. His guts felt like clods of dirt. He groaned and pressed his tongue against the floor damp with condensation and urine.

Minutes passed and hours passed. His capacity for sensation beyond thirst gradually returned. He saw Ana's head burst again. He saw her slump to the floor. Again the fount of blood rose from the hole between her eyes.

"It cannot be," he whispered, and repeated it, as if some miraculous power could reside in the fervor of his lament.

He lay in the darkness, his cheek against the floor. After a while he realized he was dying and was relieved. He confused himself in his mind with a pigeon that he, as a boy, had watched die in Congress Plaza. His bones hollowed and his back spread into a mantle of dirty feathers.

The pigeon he had watched die, the pigeon he was, had strutted into an overturned tar can left by a street repair crew. The fumes had dizzied it. Its legs buckled and it fell onto its breast in front of the can and extended its wings. Pressing the bones of its wings against the ground, it pulled itself centimeter by centimeter away from the can. It raised its tail like a signal of distress and beat its wings exhaustedly against the ground. But it could not regain its feet.

The young Diego, the boy who many years later was transformed by torture into a bird, had watched the agonized pigeon go around in circles. When the bird stopped moving, the boy Diego had been relieved that it was out of its misery. But then it had started moving again, its tail high and its beak striking the ground with each small lurch forward. It circled back to the can and crawled in. After a long while, the boy rose from the bench and walked to the can and tapped it with his foot. The bird was dead and Diego was astonished at the complexity of the process of death.

Diego the bird pressed his wings against the floor of the cell and wriggled forward, seeking the can. He came up against a barrier. He curled into a feathery ball. His beak, moistened by the blood on his knees, softened and spread, regained the form of lips. He touched his tongue to the sweet and viscous blood. He licked his wound, then slept.

Mikhail was feeling lazy lately. He drank red wine every day with lunch, then slept a long siesta.

His dream this rainy afternoon took place in the same living room where he lay. In the dream, he stepped outside himself and observed Mikhail lying on the sofa. Then a thunderclap fused him back into himself and he no longer watched what happened but felt it, experienced it. The lightning and simultaneous thunder, as only occurs at ground zero, killed him and everything stopped. Electricity surged through him and he had X-ray vision for a fleeting moment. Then everything began going backward in the netherworld of death. The rain fell up and the clock's secondhand swept counterclockwise. He saw his friend Isaac, who had recently died. Mikhail believed, in the portion of his mind that remained outside the dream, that he had truly, in reality, died, and he thought how strange it was that the world of the dead was so like that of the living, to the extent that one would have the lazy desire to continue sleeping, even though dead.

But he could not continue sleeping and he rose groggily and walked heavy-limbed to the kitchen. He sat down at the table where Angela was reading the newspaper.

"I've had a disturbing dream."

"Tell me." She looked up anxiously. She loved to interpret dreams.

"I was killed by lightning and I liked being dead. It was very relaxing and I could see through things."

Angela wanted to hear no more. "God forbid," she said, touching her left breast. "Touch your left testicle," she instructed Mikhail.

"You touch it." Mikhail moved his chair closer to Angela's. She reached into his groin, gently squeezed, then took her husband's mangled hand. The two old people sat at the table and the rain pattered on the roof.

"Giulina, would you say a man must leave a trail behind himself in this world? Something to mark his passage?"

She regarded him with a sad-eyed indulgence, but said nothing.

"I've never felt old and all of a sudden I feel ancient. I review my years, consider my life, and it seems to me I have left a trail of vapor that was for a while a slash across the sky, but then faded and disappeared as if I had never existed."

"Did you suppose you were going to build the pyramids? You've been—you are—a good father to your sons and a good husband to your wife. You've made fine things with your hands. You planted trees that bore fruit for your grandchildren."

He leaned to her and they hugged awkwardly, half twisted in their chairs.

"Thank you my dear heart," he whispered, his eyes closed.

A knock on the door startled them.

"Ma! Pa!" called Santiago as he crossed the front room. "It's me."

"In here," answered Mikhail, rising. Santiago entered and kissed his parents.

"Now don't get upset. I've got bad news." Santiago was nervous. "Diego and Ana were arrested last night. Daniel is safe, with us."

"Oh my God," Angela stood up, then sat back down.

"Arrested for what? On what charge?" asked Mikhail.

"We don't even know who has them. The police say they have no record of their arrest and there was no warrant for their capture. I'm trying to get an appointment with an air force intelligence officer. He may be able to find out something." Santiago sat down and cradled his head in his arms on the table. He had not slept in forty hours. He lifted his head.

"I'll find him. I swear I will," he said.

CAPTAIN GUILLERMO ROIG KNELT IN A PEW TOWARD THE BACK OF THE NEARLY EMPTY CHURCH. HIS FOLDED HANDS RESTED ON THE BACK OF THE PEW BEFORE HIM AND HIS FOREHEAD PRESSED AGAINST HIS HANDS. HIS EYES were closed. He was trying to pray but could not find a beginning. Then the first words of the Lord's Prayer came to him and he spoke in a hushed and desperate whisper.

Though he had recited it hundreds of times, the prayer seemed new to him now. He heard the momentous and mysterious words in his heart. "Thy will be done . . . our trespasses . . . from evil." He looked up, past the altar, at the sculpture of the tortured, emaciated Jew hanging from the cross. He licked his dry lips. On an impulse, he pushed himself up from his knees, stepped out of the pew and walked toward the front of the church. He entered a confessional. He touched a button that rang a buzzer in the sacristy and waited, scratching the back of his hands.

He heard the priest step into the other side of the shadowy closet. The wooden shutter of the wicker window separating the two men slid back. Roig saw only a latticed shadow.

"Hail Mary, full of grace," intoned the priest.

"Conceived without sin. It has been two years since my last confession."

"What are your sins?"

Roig hesitated. His breath came in short, insufficient swallows. "I have let myself drift away from the church. We were living abroad. I was busy with my work. I sense that whatever small measure of grace I once had has drained away. I try to recall my love for God, and nothing is there."

"God does not abandon his children, though they might abandon him. Seek and ye shall find."

Roig's heart pounded. The blood beat in his ears.

"What else, my son?"

"I have caused men to be tormented," he said, his voice cracking. But it was out. He exhaled deeply, audibly. His fingers tingled.

"Tormented in what way?"

"To be subjected to pain." His lips pursed around the word. "Tortured," he whispered.

"Why do you do this?"

Roig tasted salty sweat in his clipped mustache. "Because they have information I need." His whisper surged with harnessed hysteria. "They are subversives. They're trying to destroy our nation. I don't want to do it, but they leave me no choice."

"There is always a choice." The priest's voice was firm. "If there were no choice there would be no sin. You are endangering your soul, my son. No matter what means you have devised for agonizing your fellow man, they are infinitesimal compared to the eternal flames of hell. Such a sin cannot be purged lightly. You must repent genuinely and long and then, perhaps, you may still be saved."

"But *padre* . . . the Inquisition. The Church itself administered torture. Because the salvation of its doctrine came before all else. These dark forces we are fighting would make the nation godless." Roig wrung his hands.

"Please, Father," he pleaded. "I need absolution. I have terrible dreams."

The voice came stern and vengeful. "The human authorities of the Church have erred over the course of history. I can offer you no absolution. God, in his infinite mercy, may. But only after long and heartfelt remorse. I believe you shall be damned if, instead of beginning your penance for this horrible transgression, you repeat it. Go, and take inspiration from the suffering of the apostles. Suffer and you may be cleansed."

The window slid shut and Roig moved to claw through the screen, but stopped himself. He stepped out into the nave. He looked at the crucifix and his face twisted in terror. He turned and strode quickly out.

A tremendous, wildly ecstatic bellow arose and tons of confetti swirled through the chilled and electrified air the night of June 2, when the first sky-blue and white striped Argentine jersey appeared on the field from the tunnel leading from the locker room. The stands were a high and wind-whipped sea of sky-blue and white flags. The thunderous stomping and shouting overflowed the giant bowl of a stadium.

"Ar-gen-tina! Ar-gen-tina!" cried the eighty thousand. The stadium trembled.

The Argentine team and the red-shirted Hungarian team lined up along the sideline. The Hungarian national anthem was played over the loudspeakers, its conclusion greeted with polite applause. Then the adagio strains of the Argentine hymn swept over the multitude and all present erupted in powerful, patriotic song.

Alejandro's throat constricted. Tears came to his eyes. He wondered if his teammates standing in their sweatsuits along the quicklime were likewise choking back tears, but he did not look. He kept his gaze fixed ahead, up into the thundering grandstands.

> *Y los libres del mundo responden,*
> *Al gran pueblo Argentino, Salud!*
>
> *And the free peoples of the world respond,*
> *To the great Argentine people, Hail!*

When the anthem ended, the stadium exploded in another tumultuous cheer. The starting players stripped off their suits and ran in place, jumping and stretching to chase the chill. Then the team huddled around Menotti.

"This is what we've been working for. Whatever you've got inside you, leave it out there on the field tonight," said the coach.

The huddle broke and the teams took the field.

This was Menotti's lineup: Ubaldo "the Duck" Fillol in goal, captain Daniel Passarella, Luis Galvan, Alberto "the Rabbit" Tarantini and Jorge Olguin on defense, Americo Gallego, Osvaldo Ardiles and José Valencia in midfield, and Rene Houseman, Leopoldo Luque and Mario Kempes forward.

Hungarian coach Lajos Baroti put Sandor Gujdar in goal, and in front of him, Peter Torok, Istvan Kocsis, Zoltan Kereki, Joszef Toth, Sandor Pinter, Tibor Nyilasi, Sandor Zombori, Karoly Csapo, Andras Torocsik and Laslo Nagy.

The nervousness of both squads showed in the opening minutes. The ball bounded in cautious and imprecise passes among the awkward, wooden players. The tingling exhilaration of the game's commencement had barely faded when Nyilasi, deep in Argentine territory, lofted a centering pass from the right wing. Olguin jumped to head it away but the ball brushed his hair and fell to Zombori. The Hungarian let fly a violent left-footed shot on goal. Fillol dove to his right and blocked the shot. But the rebound rolled to Csapo, who sent it into the net over the sprawled goalie.

The Hungarian ambassador to Argentina and his staff of ten jumped up and shouted with delight. But the massive groan of eighty thousand others smothered their cheer. Desolation swept across the stadium like the shadow of a stormcloud.

But less than a minute passed before a rustle rose on scattered voices of the valiant. And, as others less staunch took heart, the chant swelled again, the voices multiplying like miraculous loaves, until it resounded louder than ever up into the starry sky.

"Ar-gen-tina!

"Ar-gen-tina!"

The team shook off its stupor and ran and passed. At fourteen minutes Portuguese referee Da Silva Garrido whistled play to a halt at the foul of a Hungarian defender just outside his penalty area. Ardiles positioned the ball for the free kick. He approached it determinedly, but instead of putting a shot on goal he tapped a short pass to Kempes. He fired a shot that was blocked by Gujdar. But the rebound rolled to

Luque, who, with Gujdar on the ground, sent the ball off his left instep into the goal.

The stadium erupted. A blizzard of confetti and a deafening roar engulfed the giant concrete basin. As the roar diminished to a rumble, the Hungarians put the ball back in play. But the game degenerated during the rest of the first half. Both sides dawdled and erred.

Baroti must have railed at his squad during the locker-room recess because, with the whistle that began the second period, the Magyars went wild. They crashed and tackled and kicked the Argentines and sent them tumbling. The players cursed each other unintelligibly.

Both teams were wary of the mistake that could decide the contest. The end approached and many fans resigned themselves to a tie; one point instead of two for a win. Menotti replaced Valencia with Norberto Alonso and Houseman with Daniel Bertoni.

But with six minutes remaining, Luque, just outside the Hungarian penalty area, directed a pass from Gallego off his chest to Alonso, who sent it back with a tap of the heel between two defenders to the charging Luque. The ball hung in the air, uncontrolled. Gujdar came out and collided with Luque and the ball dribbled slowly, agonizingly off to the right, toward the goal line.

Bertoni galloped in from the wing to nudge it over with the outside of his boot.

In the locker-room Passarella and Bertoni hugged and kissed each other on the cheek. Tarantini sat on a bench and stared at the wall as he ran a hand through his damp mop of curls. Ardiles, his legs battered and bruised, winced as he pulled off his socks and hobbled to his locker. Menotti huddled with a journalist and sucked in his hundredth cigarette of the day.

"These are the things that renew you, give you new hope," the coach was saying. Normally taciturn, he spoke rapidly, with feverish animation, into the reporter's microphone. "You feel that, thanks to soccer, you're alive. You get what I mean? Soccer brings you together with the people. And life is transmitted that way, heart to heart. When we left the training camp for the stadium and I saw all the people of José C. Paz in the street cheering, filling the route with affection for us, I had a terrible fear. For the first time I had a tremendous fear of losing. Victory became an obligation. How could we return defeated? Winning was the only way to pay back all their devotion. It was the same when we neared the stadium. It took an hour to go ten blocks. I swear, I want to win for them—the people. If it were possible I'd go to every house in the country and say, 'Thank you. This triumph is yours.' "

The locker-room door opened and in walked Videla, Massera, and Brigadier Orlando Agosti, the air force commander and third member of the junta. The grinning despots circulated among the players pumping hands and slapping backs.

Agosti approached Menotti, who saw him coming and cut short his interview. The coach stood up and reached for the brigadier's outstretched hand.

"Great job, Menotti. Great job."

"Thanks, Lieutenant," said the frazzled coach. He immediately realized his mistake and stammered an apology.

Agosti laughed. "That's okay, César. I'm whatever rank you say. You command in here."

Juan-Cruz awoke on the floor of a cell barely lit by a fuzzy yellow beam sifting through a square screen on the door. His head throbbed.

As with every awakening during the week he had spent, alone and virtually ignored, in this stinking cell, he started at the recollection of Roberto crumpled at his feet. When he moved to rise a bolt of pain shot from his head to his heels. He fell back to the floor. He paused and huffed, then wrestled himself to his knees. Pawing the wall, he gained his feet and stumbled to the metal door.

"Hey! Guard!" he shouted, his face pressed to the screen.

A gangly young soldier came running, his bootsteps echoing off the walls of the narrow corridor. "Shut up!" he ordered, and pounded his rifle butt against the door. The noise hurt Juan-Cruz's eyeballs.

"My son. Where is my son?"

"I said shut up!"

Juan-Cruz repeated his plea. The guard unbolted the door. He raised his rifle and was about to strike the prisoner when, from down the hall, came the shouted order: "Stop!"

An army officer approached. The guard lowered his rifle and stood at the ready.

"How have you found the accommodations, *viejo?*" The young lieutenant wore combat fatigues. His eyebrows joined at the bridge of his nose and his chin was a battlefield of shaved-over, decapitated pimples. "You must forgive us for not getting around to you sooner."

Juan-Cruz insisted about Roberto.

"You'd better worry about yourself," said the officer. He ordered the guard to take the prisoner to "the office."

The guard marched Juan-Cruz down the hall and shoved him into a windowless cinderblock room. Juan-Cruz staggered into a metal chair in the center of the room. There was a metal bed frame, a long counter along one wall, some basins and a big old bathtub, the kind with feet, filled with water. He was sitting slumped in the chair, his chin on his chest, when the door opened and the fatigue-clad officer entered with a clipboard in hand. On the board was a single sheet of paper. It was a mimeographed form that read:

STRICTLY CONFIDENTIAL AND SECRET

I   CASE:

      NAME:

      PSEUDONYM:

      DATE OF DETENTION:

      POLICE RECORD:

      CONTROL UNIT:

II   KNOWLEDGE OF WEAPONS

      KNOWLEDGE OF EXPLOSIVES

      SEIZURE OF FACTORIES

      SEIZURE OF UNIVERSITY

      PROVIDED REFUGE IN HIS HOME

      DISTRIBUTED PAMPHLETS

      GRAFITTI

      LED POLITICAL GROUP

      TOOK PART IN ATTACKS

      CONVERSION OF SUPPORTERS

      CONVERTED

"You have no police record, neither here nor in Córdoba," the officer said. "But you were accompanying your son when he killed an officer of the national security forces and you tried to abet him. That is sufficient. You are guilty. But the severity of your punishment depends on your cooperation or lack thereof. So begin. Tell me of your political activity and all you know about your son's activity."

"The only political activity I ever exercised is the casting of a ballot, and that precious few times." The effort of speaking made Juan-Cruz's head pulse with pain. "About my son's activities, I know nothing. He came to our home injured and we cared for him, as any parents would do. Now will you tell me what has happened to him?"

"You are to answer questions, not ask them," said the officer, emphasizing his words by rapping his pen against the clipboard. "Are you active in a labor union?"

"No."

"Did you have subversive propaganda in your home?"

"No."

"Do you own a weapon?"

"No."

"What is your political affiliation?"

"I am not formally affiliated, but I am a lifelong Peronist."

"Who are your son's companions?"

"I do not know a single one."

The officer exited. Juan-Cruz remained in the chair in the center of the room. After a moment, the officer returned with two men. One of the men took a coiled length of rope from the countertop. The other straightened Juan-Cruz in the chair. They wound the rope around his chest, pinning his arms to his sides. They tied his ankles to the chairlegs.

When they had finished, without a word, they lifted the chair and carried it to the edge of the tub and tipped it forward so that Juan-Cruz' head dunked under the water.

He was able to gulp a breath before going under, but the immersion unleashed in him a ferocious panic. He had never learned to swim and had always harbored a primordial fear of drowning. He twisted against the bonds and rocked violently in an effort to tip the chair onto the floor. The struggle consumed his small reserve of oxygen. His head swelled. He felt himself losing consciousness.

The two men pulled the chair back onto its feet. Juan-Cruz gasped and coughed. The rope around his chest kept him from sucking in all the sweet air he craved and in an instant his head was back underwater. The blood drained from his arms and legs. All the blood in his body coursed to his head and furious scarlet swirls scored his eyelids. A kaleidoscope of diamonds drained into the vortex at the point between his eyes, and he went limp.

They pulled him out. He vomited down his chest and, in his desperation to breathe, choked on the vomit. At a signal from the officer, one of the men squatted behind the chair, reached around the prisoner's chest and squeezed hard up and under the ribcage. The blockage spewed out and Juan-Cruz was convulsed by the spasm of his diaphragm. He gulped air like a dog snapping at a fly. Then his head lolled to the side.

The officer plugged in a *picana* and touched it to the back of the prisoner's neck. He bucked and the chair tipped over on its side. Juan-Cruz's eyes opened wide and his eyeballs rolled toward the top of his head. The lieutenant squatted over him and grabbed his chin.

"The names of your son's companions."

"Don't know," whispered Juan-Cruz.

They tortured him until he passed out, then dumped him back in his cell.

Daniel knelt on the sofa, resting his chin on his arms folded across the sofa back. He stared out through a big window. A black bird hopped in the grass, stopping every few hops to cock his head, look furtively both ways and peck the earth. He pulled round worms from the rain-soaked soil and slid them down his gullet.

Daniel watched the bird for a while. Then he watched drops fall from the leafless trees. He had been kneeling on the sofa, looking out the window for an hour. Before that he had spent two hours standing at the window, watching and waiting. He spent most of every day there at the window. At first, he had started when the mailman approached. Even now, after a week, if a car stopped and parked on the street nearby he would run to open the front door and stand in the doorway until Monica or Carmen, the maid, felt the draft and came to close it.

He hardly spoke. He had little appetite. Monica bought him toys; a rugby ball, even a new bicycle, but they drew no response. Santiago sat for hours in the evening with his arm around Daniel. They did not speak but both appeared to take some slight comfort from the confluence of their grief.

Dani's eyelids leadened and he slid down the sofa back and curled into a ball on the couch. He slept, but not for long. He bolted awake and jumped up at the sound of the front door opening.

"I brought a book for you, Dani," said Cristina. She wore her school uniform of plaid skirt, white shirt and blue blazer and carried a bookbag slung over her shoulder. A dark thick braid swung across her back.

Daniel stood motionless before her. She took his hand and led him up the stairs to her room. Daniel never came into this room alone. But it was the only room in the house, the only place where he found relief, however fleeting, from his torment. It was a room filled to the brim with silence, some of which they displaced upon entering.

Pale yellow curtains hung across the top of the window. Suspended from the curtain rod on a nylon string was an oval of polished agate. Daylight came through the stone wafer in blue lasers.

Cristina's guitar stood in its open case leaning against the wall, and an antique glass oil-burning lamp stood on the night table beside the headboard. Next to it was a woven wicker basket filled with silk flowers.

They sat next to each other on the bed, which was covered with a deep down comforter. Cristina took a book from her satchel. It was a picture book on the wildlife of Patagonia. She turned the big glossy pages slowly and Daniel studied the photographs of ostrich-like ñandus, wooly camel-faced guanacos, fearsome condors with regal white feather necklaces. There were the maras, perky-eared rodents that look like a cross between a rabbit and a small deer. Daniel smiled.

"Someday we can go on a trip to Patagonia and see all these animals," said Cristina. She brushed Daniel's wavy black hair with her fingers. "Would you like that?"

He nodded.

"Oh, Dani." She clutched his hand. "Don't worry. Daddy is going to find them. Everything will be like it was before."

Daniel looked at her and touched her flushed cheek with the back of his hand. Tears welled in her eyes. She blinked and they rolled out. He stopped the trickle of a tear down her face with a finger. Another drop overflowed and Daniel leaned forward as if to kiss her on the cheek but touched the glistening globule with his tongue and tasted it.

"I ran out of tears," he said without expression.

Cristina hugged his head to her shoulder. Daniel rested his head there for a moment, then slid it down the front of her sweater, pressing his face against her breast. She held his head and rocked gently.

El Grafico, Argentina's major sports magazine, published a special edition on June 6 with all the inauguration pageantry and reports on the first-round games. The edition sold 330,000 copies, a record. On the magazine's first page was an editorial beneath a picture of the school-children spelling out ARGENTINA on the playing field. The article was titled "Thanks to Soccer." This is what it said:

> *We now find ourselves in the vertigo produced by a World Cup tournament. And it is time to stop, to detain the ball like the good players do, and to reflect. But not coldly. We want to think with the head, but also with the heart. Because the emotional impact of what is taking place today in Argentina is too strong and too important to pretend we are not living it with passion.*
>
> *Our correspondents, in the country's interior and abroad, did not hesitate to confess that they viewed the inaugural festivities with eyes full of tears. They, like we, were living a dream come true. Something that six months, one year ago, seemed impossible to bring about: the World Cup in Argentina. And to see it like that, in that grand framework, with just the right amount of pomp, designed and presented with dignity. We know there are mistakes. There always are. But considering things overall, from the moment the children formed the word ARGENTINA on the playing field, this tournament is a success. We still feel the emotion of the first day of the Cup in these fingers that tremble as they strike the typewriter keys. We are still shaken*

*by the vibration from Argentina's first game. We still feel
flattered and proud of the way the fans and the whole
country responded to the call from this, the most popular of
sports. People who never cared about a ball rolling across a
playing field drew near to soccer and are living it, elbow-
to-elbow, with the same intensity of those who were always
there in the bleachers and stadiums. We are still moved to recall
the way in which the whole country received the visitors, and
the measured enthusiasm and well-mannered euphoria exhibited
by those who filled the stands.*

*For those outside the country, for the insidious and malicious
journalism that for months carried out a campaign of lies about
Argentina, this tournament is showing the world our country's
reality and its capacity to do important things well and with
responsibility.*

*To those inside the country, the unbelievers in our own
house, we are sure that the World Cup has served to shake them
up, move them, and make them proud. A country like ours, so
battered and fallen because of difficult past experiences, is
demonstrating to itself its enormous possibilities. And this has
nothing to do with the outcome of the games.* Argentina has
already won its World Cup.

All the hours were the steel-gray hours of predawn. The hint of day
never made good and the prisoner ebbed in the dim netherness of
self-pity and resignation.

Diego felt his spirit slipping away. He lay curled and bleeding from
the wrists and ankles where the skin had been scraped off by the
shackles. He was too weak to close his anus and watery feces leaked out
of him. He was crying and sweating and he knew that the fluids—the
blood and shit and tears and sweat—were his essence. He felt his
essence seep out onto the floor and trickle toward the putrid pool, the
remains of other men's essences, in the cell's lowest corner. He knew he
was going to end like a rotten walnut, with nothing inside but bitter
powder.

He had no notion of time. He lay on the floor of the cell and it was as if he had lain there five minutes or five years. The intermittent sessions of torment lasted until he was unable to withstand any more, until the torture doctor diagnosed the imminence of death, at which point he was dragged back to his cell to recover sufficiently for a later inquisition.

Diego's three-by-three meter cell was not square, but constructed at odd angles. The floor was out of level and the toilet hole had been made in the highest corner. Stains of urine and feces and blood strayed diagonally across the floor. It was difficult to sit or lie down anyplace but the angle where the lowest point of the floor met the wall.

Diego spent most of his time in the cell unconscious or delirious. He snatched moments of lucidity when awakened by the cold. But respite from torture was a kind of torture in itself. Because every second, even the unconscious and delirious seconds, was wrapped in the terror of anticipation, dread of the moment when the door would again be opened and he would again be dragged down the hall. When he dreamed, he dreamed he was being tortured.

He fought to marshal the remainder of his essence, to corral his sanity, to embrace it. Sometimes he could hear through the walls the sound, little more than a hum, of a diesel-powered electric generator. He latched onto the sound, clung to it. He envisioned the motor's component parts; the piston driving into the cylinder, the gas compressing, the sparkplug firing, the cylinder's withdrawal, expulsion of the burned gas. Sometimes through a vent he heard the sound of a Ping-Pong ball clopping against table and paddle. It was a cherished sound. When it came, he sat with his back against the wall and imagined the ball bounding to and fro. He saw the players reaching and swatting. He kept score in his head.

But his sustenance was the robe. He had not been given any clothing and remained wrapped in the same robe with which he had been hastily covered the night of the raid. That it was Ana's robe and that it was his only succor, his shield, the single element of his existence that gave him strength, was his sacred secret. They had not been able to break him by racking his body for hours and days. But, had they known the secret of the robe, they could have destroyed him by simply taking it from him. Without it, he was naked.

By now Ana's green corduroy bathrobe was crusted and filthy. But Diego snuggled into it and pressed his face against the fabric. He sniffed the cloth and through the fetidness found a trace of the smell of her. He buried his face in the robe. He opened his mouth and his tongue touched the cloth, as if he were trying to taste her presence. He felt a hair. His hand rose to his mouth and he took the hair between his fingers and examined it in the twilight. It was long and black. It was a strand of Ana's hair.

He slid the robe off his shoulders and spread it on the floor. Naked, his bony hollow haunches raised like those of a sick lion at the watering hole, he pressed his face to the robe and searched over it minutely. He found two more strands of her hair. Though his breath left him in puffs of vapor, he was not cold. He sat and stared at the three strands across the palm of his hand. After a while, he separated them and slowly, with the greatest delicacy, began braiding them into a single strand. He wrapped the long black thread again and again around the third finger of his left hand, where his wedding band had been long ago, in another age. He held up his hand and looked at it. He shuddered with a surge of strength, the fortitude born of love and hate.

Then he rested, warm and strong in the cold and stinking cell.

Captain Roig was convinced by Diego's capacity for resistance that he must be an important figure in the subversive hierarchy. He was determined to break him.

Diego appeared to have died during his fifth day of torture. One of the torturers had fetched the doctor on duty. The bald and bespectacled physician, who sometimes applied injections to revitalize prisoners so that the session could proceed, had found a faint pulse. He had lifted Diego's eyelids and peered into his eyes with a tiny flashlight and listened to his heart through a stethoscope.

"If you want him to live, take him to the infirmary immediately. Otherwise he will be dead within a half hour," the doctor had said.

Diego spent a week in the infirmary receiving intensive care. He was fed a vitamin-rich complex intravenously and an antibiotic salve was applied to his raw wrists and ankles, and to his swollen eyes infected by the dirty cloth that had been his blindfold. When he had recuperated sufficiently he was taken to a small office next to the torturers' lounge. Captain Roig sat behind a desk there. He told Diego to sit down.

"You have regained a semblance of health. You can choose to retain it, or to lose it again. It is up to you. If you cooperate you will survive. If not, you will die.

"I can't tell you what I don't know."

"But you know quite a bit that interests us. We know your political affiliation. We know you are not a terrorist. They have been wiped out. The few die-hard assassins remaining in the country are not our primary concern at this stage of the game. What concerns us now is the tumor represented by your ideology."

Roig fancied himself an astute analyst of Argentine history and politics, the intellectual equal of any Marxist theoretician. He liked to engage intelligent and lucid prisoners in debate.

He leaned across the desk. "Do you really imagine socialism could ever take root in this country? It cannot. Because Argentina is rich, and Argentina is devout. There is so much wealth in this land that the system must allow the citizenry to compete for it and to accumulate it according to the merits of the individual. Your scheme serves to redistribute poverty, not abundance. That's why it can appeal in a poor country like Cuba. But this is a middle-class country and, as you well know, drastic social change, revolution if you like, is anathema to the middle class. What's more, much of the middle class and a great majority of the working class is Peronist. That is a bulwark against Communism that will last for a century. The Montoneros are our enemy. But they are not Peronists. The Peronists may be our occasional antagonist. But they are not our enemy. For those of us like myself, who have seen firsthand and appreciated the European democracies, Peronism is an obstacle to the establishment of democracy here, because it is essentially anti-democratic. But it is virulently anti-Marxist. That makes Peronism, when the chips are down, our ally. Who do you think fingered most of the union Reds? So you see, you have no chance of converting either the comfortable middle class or Peronism. And where does that leave you? Stranded with the few thousand deluded dreamers you count as supporters." Roig sat back and folded his hands across his stomach. His voice softened.

"You know, though you people are my enemy and I am sworn to

destroy you, sometimes I feel sorry for you. Most of you are intelligent and idealistic. You could have made a positive contribution to the fatherland. But you are our worst enemy. You are the viper in the grass, the diseased sprout that may spoil the entire crop. So you must be yanked out by the roots. If you give me just two names, then all the trouble we have taken with you will have been worth it. It is up to you."

"I think that even if I did give you names, you would kill me anyway," said Diego calmly.

"I will be honest. If I did not believe that you had seen the error of your ways, that you had repented, it would be necessary to execute you. I am going to give you time to think about what I have said. When you want to talk, advise the guard." Roig reached out and tapped a fogged glass window giving onto the hallway. A soldier entered.

"Take him to unit four."

At intervals Diego could not calculate, because no sunlight entered and he never knew if it was day or night, a hatch at the bottom of the door to this more conventional cell would open and a hand would push in a bowl of watery cornmeal mush or soggy pasta, sometimes with tripe or brains, and a tin cup of water.

Diego rested and thought. He sat on the bunk in his cell and examined the glossy beginnings of a scar that had formed over the wounds on his ankles and wrists. It seemed to him that if there were a little more light, just a little more, he would be able to see himself, discern the imprecise image of part of his nearly forgotten face reflected in the shiny healing tissue.

He understood that betrayal was the only means of survival. He knew enough about perhaps a half dozen individuals to deliver them into the hands of his captors. But he could not. He could not aid the same people he loathed so intensely. In his grief-swollen heart he knew that collaboration would be betrayal of Ana. He had to be a husband worthy of his wife. And he had to be a father worthy of his son. Because he knew that if he survived by treachery, the love between his son and himself would, over long years of reproach and resentment, be poisoned.

As he strained his eyes to make out some shadowy hint of reflection in his wound, the bolt slammed back and the cell door opened.

A naval officer Diego had not yet seen stood in the doorway.

"Captain Roig asks if you want to talk to him."

"No."

"Then get up."

Diego rose. The officer motioned to two sailor guards in the hall to take him from the cell. Diego stepped into the corridor and the officer tied a blindfold around his head. The loss of his sight, recovered after interminable days of darkness during the early torture, terrorized Diego. He panicked and almost blurted to the officer to take him to Roig. But the moment passed.

The sailors flanking him grabbed his arms and marched him down the hall. Diego heard the officer following. He did not know far they walked, but it felt like kilometers to his creaky legs unused to exercise. They turned a few corners along the way, then opened a door to the outside. The wind and freshness of the air exhilarated Diego and he thought for an instant that he was going to be released.

Then he realized he was going to be shot.

They walked across what seemed to Diego, from the levelness of the ground and thickness of the grass, a playing field. They stopped.

"You have been sentenced to death for the crime of treason against the fatherland," said the officer. "You have two minutes to pray."

"I am an atheist."

"Then use them to put your mind at peace."

"My mind is at peace. Carry on."

"As you wish," said the officer. "Kneel down."

"I would prefer to stand."

"As you wish."

"You are very accommodating. Like a good waiter." Diego smiled, not at his incongruous levity, but at the sudden, staggering and intimate understanding of the commonness of death; that one's last words could be dedicated to the petty ridicule of one's executioner.

The officer drew a 9-mm pistol from his holster and stepped to Diego's side. He held the gun at arms length, the barrel centimeters from Diego's temple. He pulled back the hammer with his thumb and it locked in a loud click.

The officer squeezed the trigger and the hammer slammed against the chamber with a loud click.

Diego's legs melted and he fell. He sensed he was still alive. He struggled to his feet and stood up as straight as he could. "How many times do I have to die?" He did not know if he spoke or screamed or simply thought the words. And while he stood waiting for the gun to be cocked again his lifetime compressed itself into an endless instant. And the vivid hallucination that flashed behind his eyes was not just his past. It was also a vision, bright and crystalline, of what his life would have been. He saw Ana, Daniel and himself in an orchard. They were picking pears.

"To have been a grandfather!" he cried silently. And as the eternal, cruel moment refused to close, he damned life with the last remnant of his being; life that, but for the pitiless circumstance of a faulty pistol, he would have seen out strong, without the final and ultimate humiliation of regret.

But instead of the click of the pistol being cocked he heard the officer order: "Take him back."

THE OFFICER STOOD AND REACHED ACROSS HIS DESK TO SHAKE HANDS WITH SANTIAGO. "I'D ASK YOU HOW YOU'RE DOING, SANTI. BUT IT'S OBVIOUS YOU'RE NOT WELL," SAID COMMODORE JORGE SAAVEDRA, THE AIR force engineer in charge of the project Santiago had been working on for a year.

In 1968, the Argentine air force had told the directors of the Military Aircraft Factory in Córdoba to come up with a prototype of a reconnaissance and counterinsurgency airplane for domestic manufacture. The prototype flew in 1969 and a team of military and civilian engineers, mostly young men, worked for the better part of the next decade resolving problems and improving the craft. The first dozen IA-58 Pucarás built in the mid-1970s were used in the hills of Tucumán province in successful combat against the People's Revolutionary Army, a band of a thousand Trotskyist guerrillas.

The two-seat turboprop bimotor carries as standard armament two 20-mm cannons with 270 rounds each and four 7.62-caliber machine guns with 900 rounds each. It can carry fifteen hundred kilos of bombs, grenades of napalm to be dropped from three external stations, one under the fuselage and one under each wing.

The plane made its international debut in 1977 at the twenty-third

Aeronautical Fair at Le Bourget, France. It was favorably received by specialists for its simplicity, easy maintenance and reduced cost, and was advertised by the air force as "an Argentine plane for the world." Military authorities tried to stir interest in the IA-58 Pucará among underdeveloped countries with actual, eventual or imagined insurgencies, but had little export success.

Saavedra, director of development of the IA-60 jet-propelled Pucará, lowered himself into his chair and Santiago sat down opposite him.

"No. I'm not well," Santiago said. "I cannot concentrate on my work. I need time off to resolve a personal problem. A problem concerning my family."

The officer, in whom Santiago had always sensed a fundamental and un-military kindness, did not inquire. He remained silent and attentive.

"I've been contacting officers I worked with on the IA-58 because I'm in a desperate situation. They have not been able to help me. So I'm going to appeal to you. You and I have a professional relationship and I have no right to expect your help, but I have to try."

"Let me say something before you go on," Saavedra interrupted amiably, his crow's-feet crinkling. "I was not part of the IA-58 project, but I know it inside out. And I know your contribution was essential. I tell you this with no intention to flatter. You are very talented. I have heard officers, some of them my superiors, wish aloud that you were part of the force. For my own selfish reasons, I'm glad you're not. I enjoy the opportunity to work with you professionally, man to man. So, if I can be of help, I will try."

Santiago, who chafed at both praise and criticism, did not thank Saavedra. He knotted his hands in his lap and looked, in spite of himself, beseechingly at the commodore.

"My brother is a leftist. I know absolutely, and I swear to you by my children, that he is not and was never a guerrilla. He is a doctor. He cures people. He does not harm them. He and his wife were taken from their home in La Boca by a group of armed men. The neighbors say the men identified themselves as 'Combined Forces.' The police say they know nothing."

Saavedra lowered his eyes at the first sentence. When he raised them, he did not look at Santiago, but stared out the window.

"This is the most difficult matter you could bring up," he said, regarding Santiago a moment before returning his gaze to the hazy sky over the city center. "I thought, stupidly, that you wanted time off because of problems with your wife or because you got an offer from Boeing or Lockheed and were thinking about leaving the country. But this . . . This is very difficult."

Santiago was silent.

"I'm going to be more frank with you than I should," said Saavedra. "I am air force officer of considerable rank, that is true. But I am also an engineer and my entire career has been on the technical side of the branch's operations. These have been dark years for our country. The nation confronted a treacherous enemy and it fell to the armed forces to defeat that enemy. I am proud of my uniform. But I am also thankful that the air force, because of its nature and the nature of terrorism, had the least part in the repression. That reasoning may lack valor, I don't know. But I'm glad the dirty work did not fall to me."

He paused and studied Santiago. "Of course, the branch was not entirely independent of the campaign, especially on the intelligence level. That does not comprise many men. I know some of them. They are not going to be pleased by my inquiries. But I will make them nonetheless. You have done a great deal for the armed forces and for your country. The least you deserve is an honest answer to a simple question."

Santiago rose and reached his hand across the desk. "Thank you," he said, and turned and walked out of the room.

Santiago knew it was going to be hard to find a parking space, so he and Daniel left home two hours before the game was to begin. Traffic was already heavy southbound on Libertador Avenue in the direction of the stadium, and as soon as Santiago crossed the General Paz highway separating the province from the federal capital he began looking for a place to park. He cruised the blocks around the Rivadavia railroad station, but there was nothing. He circled back onto Libertador heading north, passed the National Atomic Energy Commission headquarters on the left and slowed as he approached a long empty space along the curb in front of the Navy Mechanics School. On posts embedded in the sidewalk were signs with the silhouette of a soldier taking aim. The signs said, NO STOPPING, MILITARY ZONE. But there was no guard in sight. Santiago pulled forward quickly and backed up against the bumper of the car in the last space abutting the no-parking zone. He eased out the clutch and pushed backward against the car, hoping to roll it back a meter so that at least his rear wheels would be in the legal area. His arm was thrown over the seatback and he was looking through the rear window when the soldier tapped the fender with the barrel of his FAL.

Santiago cut the engine and opened the door. By the time his feet touched the street the guard had his weapon leveled at him. Santiago raised his hands.

"Easy, soldier," he said.

"You've got five seconds to get back in and get out of here." The boy's jaw jutted forward and seemed to quiver a bit.

"I've got a security clearance credential," Santiago said. He took out his billfold and opened it to show the soldier a high-level air force ID. The card had been issued him to facilitate access to air force installations. Santiago did not like to use it in unofficial business, but the document brought special treatment in a wide variety of matters, speeding the repair of a telephone or reducing air fares by fifty percent.

The guard examined the card and handed it back as he lowered his rifle. Presuming that Santiago was an officer, he said, "Sorry, sir," and returned to his post.

Daniel got out on the curb side. He stood at the iron fence and wrapped his hands around the black bars. He leaned forward between two of them until they touched his temples and stared across the beautifully landscaped grounds of the school, at its columned and porticoed façade. Santiago placed a hand on his shoulder.

"Are you up to a hike?"

Daniel nodded.

People streamed like legions of ants toward the stadium. They flowed from the side streets onto the crowded avenues and transformed every access into a spillway of sky-blue and white flags.

When Santiago and Daniel finally reached their seats, a good location not too high between midfield and the goal Argentina would be defending in the first half, the boy appeared exhausted.

"Do you want a hot dog, or a Coke?" asked his uncle.

Daniel shook his head no.

"This stadium is a lot nicer than Boca's, huh?"

Santiago immediately regretted mentioning the stadium where Daniel had been dozens of times with his father. But the reference did not seem to register.

Daniel shifted suddenly, as if he had just realized where he was. He sat on the edge of his wooden slat seat and surveyed the field below, the packed and buzzing grandstands.

"What color jerseys does France use?" he asked.

"Blue," answered Santiago, surprised at the animation.

"Blue like Italy?"

"Almost the same. A little lighter I think." Santiago's heart pounded at Daniel's awakening.

"What happens when Italy plays France?"

"They already played, in Mar del Plata. France used white jerseys and Italy won two to one." Santiago was so transported by Daniel's voice that he would gladly have answered unending questions about the uniforms, flags or national anthems of all sixteen teams in the tournament.

But then Argentina took the field and there was nothing that could be said or shouted that could be heard above the roar. Daniel climbed onto the seat of his chair for a better view over the standing adults and raised his arms and shouted with the rest of the faithful:

"Ar-gen-tina!

"Ar-gen-tina!"

Santiago spotted Alejandro in the knot of Argentine players. "There's your cousin, number 20." He pointed and Daniel sighted down his arm. The boy cheered.

Menotti made no changes in the lineup he had used in the first game. French coach Michel Hidalgo started Jean-Paul Bertrand-Demanes in goal, Patrick Battison, Christian Lopez, Marius Tresor and Maxime Bossis on defense, Dominic Bathenay, Henri Michel and captain Michel Platini in midfield and Dominic Rocheteau, Bernard Lacombe and Didier Six forward.

France dominated the early play. Lacombe consistently eluded Galvan's man-to-man coverage. The Argentine defense was porous. There seemed to be more blue jerseys on the field than sky-blue and white striped ones. But France could not take advantage of its penetrations. It could not culminate attacks with good shots on goal. Passarella stopped several advances and Fillol made a pair of routine saves.

The Argentine midfielders and forwards passed sloppily, surrendering many balls to the French. The Argentine attackers ran up against an impenetrable wall in Tresor and Bossis.

The fans gasped, stomped and shouted through a first half of close calls and bungled opportunities. It looked like the teams would go to the locker rooms tied at zero. With less than a minute left in the first period, Kempes dribbled toward the French penalty area, went around Bathenay and lofted a short pass over Battison's head to Luque. The Argentine forward was inside the penalty area and had Tresor beaten by a step. Luque fired a powerful left-footed shot. Tresor lunged feet first but the speeding ball was past his legs and he slapped it with his hand, which was partially hidden below his back. The ball ricocheted wide of the goal.

Tresor's maneuver was cleverly disguised, but the more astute spectators noted it and shouted at the top of their lungs: *"Penal!"*

Swiss referee Jean Dubach consulted the linesman, who had had an unobstructed view of the play, then trotted to the penalty spot.

A mighty cheer arose. Then, as Passarella took his position a few steps behind the ball, the cheer fell to an electrified hush and eighty thousand people held their breath. The Argentine captain sized up Bertrand-Demanes and approached. At the impact of Passarella's left foot against the ball, the goalie dove to his right. His only hope was a guess that that was where the ball was headed. But Passarella sent it sailing to Bertrand-Demanes's left and the ball billowed the net. The stadium erupted, and the first half ended with Argentina ahead 1–0.

With fifteen minutes gone in the second half, French midfielder Michel sent a high pass from the right wing over Passarella to Lacombe. Lacombe tried to loft the ball over the charging Fillol and sent it arching high into the air. It fell and bounced off the crossbar, back into play just in front of the Argentine goal, into which Olguin, Galvan and Six had tumbled in their zeal to follow Lacombe's high shot. Lacombe controlled the bouncing rebound and passed the ball to Platini, uncovered at his right. The French captain booted it into the goal.

It had been inevitable. France was playing better and had not scored until then for lack of fortune. The very few detached observers in the stadium thought, "We don't deserve more than a tie and one point for this performance. Let's just see if we can hang on to that."

But center forward Leopoldo Jacinto Luque did not think that. At minute seventy-three, twenty-five meters from the French goal, he received on his chest a pass from Ardiles and in the second the ball took to fall to the ground he whirled and smashed it with a booted right foot that channeled all the power of eighty kilos of muscle and bone and tendon. Dominique Baratelli, who had replaced Bertrand-Demanes in goal, lunged to his right in a futile attempt to touch the round rocket passing just inside the far goal post.

Daniel, intent on the play, responded a split-second before the mass of spectators. In the course of an elongated instant he leapt with clenched fists raised and as the shout rose in him saw a wave of people surge like the heave of the earth in an underground explosion.

Santiago hugged Daniel and lifted him off his feet. They jumped up and down in embrace, Daniel howling in Santiago's ear in the manner of radio sportscasters.

"Gooooaaaaalllll! . . . Argentina!"

Strangers kissed each other in bleachers and boxes.

With two victories, Argentina was assured of classification for the next round.

Angela Maglione walked hesitantly down Uruguay Street toward Viamonte, glancing from a scrap of paper in her hand to the numbers on the doors of old apartment buildings and office supply stores. She stopped in front of a run-down building and looked up its scarred façade. She entered.

Francisca Otero stood at the black metal-grate door of the antiquated elevator. She had on her most presentable clothes, an old gray houndstooth suit noticeably altered to fit her, and despite the chill had foregone her ragged overcoat for the trip downtown. But the veneer did not hide either her poverty or her exhaustion of body and spirit. Francisca pushed the call button again and again, looking up the caged shaft.

"It doesn't work," she said to the just-arrived woman. "And I'm too tired to walk up the stairs."

"What floor are you going to?" asked Angela.

"Third."

"Las Madres?"

Francisca nodded.

"Me too." Angela offered her arm to Francisca and the two women made a slow ascent up white marble steps dished in the middle by the tread of many, many tired feet.

"I have not been here before," offered Francisca.

"Neither have I."

They reached the second-floor landing and stopped to rest.

"Did they take your son?" asked the Italian-accented woman.

Francisca nodded. "And my husband," she said.

"My son and daughter-in-law," said Angela. The women, beyond formality, beyond timidity, looked into each other's eyes. Their hands found their way together and joined in a press of communion. They stood like that, resting and sharing their sorrow, for a long moment.

When they reached the unmarked third-floor door Angela knocked. The door opened a crack and a woman peered out. She opened the door all the way.

"We've come for the first time," said Angela. The elderly señora, with a fuzzy llama-wool shawl settled around her shoulders, bade them in.

"The elevator does not work," panted Francisca.

"And the telephone and the heat and sometimes even the electricity," said the woman. "They do everything they can to make life difficult for us."

"And the neighbors?" asked Angela.

"That's part of the strategy. People blame their problems on the nearest evident cause. The neighbors damn us for their inconveniences instead of blaming those who create them."

In the center of the room, which would have been the living room of the old, high-ceilinged apartment, was a long table at which sat ten women between the ages of forty and sixty-five. Some read newpapers, some conversed and sipped strong coffee from small cups, some sat staring blankly ahead. On the walls were posters in Spanish, French and English: LOS DESAPARECIDOS. LES DISPARUS. THE DISAPPEARED. There was a bulletin board with the photographs of fifty women who had been kidnapped while pregnant or with babes in arms. Across the top of the board was written: "Where are the infants?"

The elderly woman escorted Francisca and Angela to a small office where Mabel, the secretary of the organization, sat writing in longhand on a yellow legal pad.

"These two señoras just arrived," said the woman with the shawl, and left Francisca and Angela with Mabel.

"The first thing is to get the facts down," said Mabel, skipping preliminaries. She pushed aside the papers in front of her and readied a fresh sheet. "Who, when, where, how."

Angela, then Francisca, provided the information they had concerning their relatives' disappearances.

"Have you checked with the police?"

The women nodded.

"Nothing. Right?"

"Nothing," they replied in unison.

"Would you like some tea?" Mabel regarded the women through thick-lensed glasses. She was short and stout and her feet barely reached the floor. Her graying brown hair was curled in a home permanent wave. It was easy to imagine her in an apron stirring the Sunday spaghetti sauce while grandchildren toddled through the kitchen.

Angela and Francisca accepted the offer and Mabel rose and stepped out. She returned with a kettle and three cups. She poured the tea through a strainer into the cups, then sat down again across from the women.

"We're not very many. A few hundred. What we are doing is difficult and dangerous. Just a few weeks ago eight Mothers and two nuns helping us were kidnapped from a church right downtown. We are constantly harassed. They hope to scare us into silence. They're afraid we might ruin their soccer tournament." She removed her glasses and massaged her temples. Her unmagnified eyes were soft and weary.

"Some of those women may be dead by now. Some bodies washed up on a beach in Uruguay last week. We've heard for quite some time now that one of the ways they get rid of bodies is to drop them in the Atlantic from airplanes. Not bodies really, because according to the reports we've received, they aren't dead yet when they're dropped. They inject them with Pentothal to knock them out. The bastards even joke about it. They call it 'Pento-naval.'

"Our friends in Europe demonstrated against the staging of the World Cup here. We agree with them that it is terribly cynical to play games alongside concentration camps. But the tournament serves our purposes as well. What we must do is inform the people, of Argentina and the world, about what is going on here. The dictatorship hides everything and discounts the truth as invention. We are up against the power of the state in its entirety. We need the support of our countrymen and sympathetic people everywhere. With all the journalists here for the Cup, they cannot beat us up and drag us from the plaza these Thursday afternoons as they have done in the past. The tournament puts Argentina in the eye of the world. And we old women, with our sorrow, our anger and our determination, are the most eloquent expression of what Argentina is today." She looked from Angela to Francisca and back to Angela. "Are you up to it?"

"*Sí,*" they replied together.

"There's nothing more to be done until Thursday. Come at two o'clock. You can meet more of the Mothers before we go to the plaza. We wear white kerchiefs embroidered with the name of our missing relatives and the date of disappearance."

They all stood. Angela moved toward the door but Francisca stood still beside her chair. "There is one more thing I have to tell you," she said to Mabel. "Maybe after hearing it, you will not want me."

"What?"

"My son is a Montonero."

"He is still your son, and he is still a human being. The sons or daughters of some of the Mothers were in *la guerrilla*. I believe most were not. Some Mothers deny it to themselves. Some know and don't say. It doesn't matter. We are trying to find the truth. Nothing more and nothing less. If our children were terrorists then they must be arrested, tried and, if guilty, punished. We must accept that. What we must not accept is kidnapping, torture and murder and the lies we receive in reply to our questions. You will find out soon enough that we are reviled and ridiculed by many of our own countrymen. But we persevere, simply because we cannot do otherwise."

The three women exchanged kisses on the cheek. "Until Thursday," they said.

Santiago kicked up dust with each booted footstep that fell on the dirt road leading to his parents' house from the railroad station. When he arrived, he found Mikhail sitting on the seat of an old bicycle raised off the ground on a triangular kickstand. A rubber thong like a fan belt stretched between a wheel concentric with the forward sprocket and a smaller wheel attached to the handlebars. Mikhail, his face shaded by a flattened black beret, pedaled and the belt drove two circular whetstones, one coarse and one fine, in front of him. Intent on his work, he did not notice the arrival of his son. He held the blade of a large knife against the coarse stone and guided it slowly back and forth. Sparks sprayed off in an arc. Mikhail's legs pumped gracefully, his knees rising high. He buffed and burnished the blade on the fine stone and when he was satisfied with the edge, he held it against the back of his left wrist and scraped a few centimeters toward the elbow. The coarse hairs ceded to the blade. Mikhail distractedly regarded the bald spot.

"Hi, Pa." Mikhail, back to pedaling, turned his head slowly, like an owl.

"Santi," said Mikhail, surprised at the apparition. Then his eyes opened wide and his face flushed, the beret rising on his brow. "Any news?"

"No. Not yet." The light in Mikhail's eyes flickered and extinguished. "I just wanted to see you and Mom. I thought we could watch the game together on TV."

"What game?"

"Argentina and Italy. At eight o'clock."

Mikhail got off the bike and the men walked around to the front of the house. Santiago had not been prepared to find his father like this. Mikhail had aged a decade in two weeks. His gait was a slow hunched waddle. He went in and called to Angela. She came into the living room and embraced her son. Her eyes were sunken and ringed by dark circles.

"How are you, Ma? You look tired."

"I can't sleep. I spend whole nights staring at the ceiling . . . imagining terrible things."

Santiago told them of his fruitless interviews and consultations. "It's like a maze. You take two steps and run into a wall and have to back up and try another alley. Then you run into another wall. You think it's the army, then the navy, then you think it must have been the police. All dead ends. Then you think it was the Interior Ministry or maybe vigilantes. The habeas corpus got nowhere. The judges have a form letter saying the person is not under arrest and there is no warrant out for his detention."

Angela covered her face with her hands and sighed. Mikhail picked at a callus on his hand. He peeled off a tiny swatch of parchmented skin, rolled it into a ball and shot it like a marble off his thumb into the pile of cinders in the fireplace.

"Sons of whores," he said.

The three were sitting together that evening, Santiago between his parents on the sofa in front of the large old black-and-white television set when Channel 7 began its broadcast of the game.

Angela smiled her first smile in a fortnight when she saw her grandson in the trotting file of sweatsuited players.

"There he is! There's Ale!" She sat forward and reached across Santiago to slap Mikhail on the knee. "Do you see him?" But Mikhail could not make him out and by the time he got up and stepped to the set the camera angle had changed and Alejandro was no longer on the screen.

Then the Italian squad made its entrance and Mikhail stepped back and stood up straight, his hands on his hips. He breathed in deeply, puffing his chest like a jay.

"*Forza* Italia! Let's show these fascist bastards how to play football!"

"What are you saying, you crazy old man?" demanded Angela. Then, incredulously: "Don't tell me you're going to root against your own grandson."

"It's my affair who I root for," he snapped. "*Vamos, Azurra!*"

He sat back down as the announcer read the Italian lineup. He thumped his fist against the sofa armrest. "But they're all from Juventus! The whole damn team is from Juventus! Aren't there any soccer teams in Italy these days? There's not a single Napoletano."

It was nearly as he said. Enzo Bearzot, the Italian coach, had fielded a team eight of whose eleven members—Dino Zoff, Gentile, Scires, Cabrini, Tardelli, Benetti, Causio and Bettega—were from Juventus. Bellugi of Bologna, Antognoni from Fiorentina and Paolo Rossi, the young star of Lanerosi, were the only ones not from Turin.

The announcer began to read the Argentine lineup and Santiago's pulse quickened. Luque and Houseman had been injured in the game with France and, though he was the youngest and most inexperienced member of the team, there was a better chance than ever that Alejandro might play.

But no. Menotti had chosen Bertoni to replace Houseman and had switched Kempes from left wing to Luque's spot at center forward. Ortiz started at Kempes's position on the left side.

There was a commercial break before play began. In an advertisement for a clothes dryer, two women ride in an elevator. The elevator stops and a third woman with a basket of wet clothes sidles in. One of the women asks with a wry and knowing smile, "To the roof?" The third woman, reduced to a scullery maid by her lack of domestic appliances, answers with resignation, "To the roof." The original two women get off at their floor—they will enjoy a leisurely tea—and snicker.

Then, right before transmission from the stadium resumed, a man seated at a desk like a newscaster appeared onscreen and looked out at the television audience with studied sincerity. "These are trying times for our nation," he said. "Being a parent is an even greater responsibility now. Young people can easily be misled. Do you know where your children are tonight?"

"I fuck you in the center of your soul," said Mikhail.

Italy played cautiously. A tie would be enough to classify them for the next round. So the blue-jerseyed Italians hung back and concentrated on blocking Argentina's attempts to advance. The home team had its share of play at midfield, but thirty meters from the opposing goal the Argentine attack was engulfed by the sturdy Italian defense.

With thirty minutes gone and the game degenerating into a monotony of midfield exchanges, Osvaldo Ardiles, the midfielder whose creativity was the generator of the Argentine offense but who had fizzled in the games to date, began to function. He assumed his role as conductor of the orchestra. He opened up the field. In constant motion, he created spaces among the Italian defenders, taking passes and putting them on the boot of his advancing teammates.

But the doors continued to slam in the face of the Argentine forwards. Ortiz would get by Cuccureddu (another player from Juventus who replaced the injured Bellugi in the opening minutes) but he would run right into Scirea. Cabrini had Bertoni blanketed on the right side. And Kempes was not working at center forward. Constantly surrounded by blue shirts, he could not find any patch of grass to build momentum, to use his strength and gain a clearing to let a shot fly.

The second half belonged to the Italians and Franco Causio. The mustachioed and wavy-haired forward, his broad nose flaring, came away in control of nearly every ball disputed on the right side of the Italian attack. He faked and feinted and dribbled around the Argentine defenders. Because of him, the ball spent most of the second period moving toward Fillol.

Midway through the second half, Bettega, ten meters outside the Argentine penalty area, lobbed a pass to Paolo Rossi in front of him. Rossi, with Galvan breathing on his neck, tapped the ball off his heel back to Bettega, who as soon as he had made the pass to Rossi had sprinted for the space between Passarella, in the center of the field, and Tarantini closing in from the right. The give-and-go worked perfectly, just like a coach draws it on a blackboard with circles and triangles and arrows, and Bettega took the ball on his foot a step inside the Argentine penalty area. Tarantini slid feet first in a desperate attempt to block the shot, but he was too late. Fillol advanced two steps to cut the angle and covered the short side to his left. But Bettega crossed a hard right-footed shot to the goalie's right and suddenly, Argentina was losing.

"Aaaayyyy!" Mikhail bolted off the edge of the sofa, his arms raised and fists clenched. He jumped up and down. "*Forza* Italia!" he shouted, and jumped and hollered until he was too winded to continue.

"Sit down, old man, before you have a heart attack," said Angela disgustedly.

Santiago, though the goal hurt him, was amused by his father's jubilation. He smiled. He had not seen Mikhail so thoroughly animated in years.

The Italians fell back and, in the remaining twenty minutes, stifled every Argentine advance. Israeli referee Abraham Klein blew a long blast on his whistle to end the game.

It was the final game of the first round. Italy classified first in Group 1, Argentina second. That put Argentina in Group B for the second round, with Poland, Brazil and Peru. Italy joined West Germany, Austria and Holland in Group A.

Mikhail brought out a bottle of wine. He set three glasses on the table and moved to pour some for Angela, but she covered the glass with her hand.

"What's the matter with you, Giulina? Are you Italian or not?"

She cocked her head and looked at him quizzically. "Since when are you so patriotic? Isn't it you who says countries don't matter? Come off it, *caro mio*. Argentina lost a soccer game. That is not going to get us our son back any faster."

Her reprimand toppled Mikhail from his rare and airy summit. It did not matter so much to him that it had been Italy that won. He had wanted to celebrate Argentina's defeat. He had wanted to go to the window, open it wide and shout into the cold black night: "See? You're not so goddamn great as you think you are! You think you're the best at everything and you're not the best at anything!"

But Angela was here by his side, to signal his folly.

"I am an old fool," he said, his face fallen. He poured himself and Santiago a glass of wine. But Mikhail did not drink his, and after a while he got up and went to the bedroom. He fell on the bed, face down, and his booted feet hung over the edge.

The Plaza de Mayo is grand and lovely in the heart of Buenos Aires. At one end of the two-hectare square sits Government House, more a clay color than pink, though it is called "La Casa Rosada." From its balconies Perón and Evita harangued the multitudes.

Atop a narrow pyramid at the center of the plaza stands a statue of a woman. She represents the republic.

The garden around the base of the central pyramid has soil from all the country's twenty-two provinces. Marigolds and snapdragons bloom from the federated soil. Antique gas lamps line the walkways. Towering palms, the tallest trees in the plaza, shoot up and burst in frond balls. Plane trees and jacarandas adorn the perimeter of the square. In late spring fuzzy white pods drop from the plane trees and gossamer fibers float through the air. Some people are allergic to the stuff. They breathe it and break out in hives.

On June 16, 1955, navy planes aiming for Government House bombed the plaza as part of an abortive revolution against Perón. More than a hundred civilians, among them a busload of schoolchildren, died in the air raid.

The cathedral, where repose the remains of San Martín, dominates the north side of the square. It harbors an eternal flame in honor of the nation's founder. A Peronist mob set fire to its administrative offices the night after the plaza was bombed. The Church (Roman Catholic) was an early supporter of Perón but turned against him after he formally separated church and state and legalized divorce. The Vatican excommunicated Perón, but pacted anew with him when he returned from exile.

The Social Welfare Ministry takes up most of the plaza's south side. It is a black granite-based monolith of a building, intimidating and overbearing. Perón began his rise to power from the Welfare Ministry.

At the far end of the plaza is the Cabildo. Originally an adjunct to the cathedral, the Cabildo later became a sort of town hall. It is the only vestige of colonial architecture on the plaza. It was outside the Cabildo that the citizens gathered in May of 1810 to debate the removal of the Spanish viceroy. At that time, only about two hundred residents of Buenos Aires had any say in things. But outside the then-walled square crowds of native-born, disenfranchised residents clamored for independence. They shouted: "The people want to know what's going on!" The phrase has endured, and Argentines have periodically flocked to the plaza to be informed, or misinformed and manipulated by those in power.

The late afternoon sun offered little warmth. The benches around the plaza's fountains and flowerbeds were vacant. Office and Ministry employees crossed the square on their way to a bus stop or rendezvous. A knot of blue uniformed police stood near the pyramid.

Groups of four and five middle-aged and elderly women converged on the center of the plaza from various directions and sat on the vacant benches. Undercover police circulated, obvious in their attempt to blend in. Foreign journalists scribbled in narrow notebooks and satchel-draped photographers talked in small groups. When the Cabildo clocktower struck 3:30, the women withdrew from their purses white kerchiefs and tied them around their heads. They walked to the pyramid and formed a stretched-out circle around it. They began walking slowly, silently, around the pyramid.

Some passersby stopped to stare.

"Look at them. It's scandalous," said a gray-haired business-suited man in a cashmere overcoat. "And the jounalists eating it up." His voice rose. "Imagine the image of our country they are sending to the world!" He stepped toward the women.

"You are a disgrace!" he shouted. Some bystanders seconded him with their own taunts. Others glared at the Mothers with eloquently silent reproach.

Angela Maglione happened to be at the point of the circle nearest the man. "The disgrace is that our children have been kidnapped by the armed forces and nobody tells us where they are," she told him.

"What do you expect if you raised your son to be a terrorist? You are as much to blame as he is. You're a bad mother!"

"You have no right to say that!" cried Angela. She moved to break ranks and confront the man, but Francisca restrained her.

"Don't let them provoke you," she whispered, and Angela relented.

From the plaza's east end, from the direction of Government House, came four tall young men in blue and yellow windbreakers. They were Bjorn Norqvist, Ronnie Hellstrom, Ralf Edstrom and Staffan Tapper, members of the Swedish national team. Norqvist, with his first appearance in this tournament, had set a world record by competing in his 118th international match.

The goalie Hellstrom filmed the Mothers with a super-8 movie camera and Edstrom and Tapper snapped photographs with still cameras. Then Hellstrom approached the circling file.

"Be careful," one of the Mothers told him in English. "There are lots of undercover agents around."

"We're from the Swedish team. They cannot harm us," said Hellstrom, falling into step alongside the woman. "We want to know more about what you are doing and what you're finding out. In particular, we're interested in the case of Dagmar Hagelin."

The Mothers knew Dagmar's case well. They knew how, on the afternoon of January 26, 1977, Navy intelligence officers arrested a young woman named Norma Burgos, who they suspected was a Montonera. Miss Burgos was taken to the Navy Mechanics School and interrogated under torture. That night, some officers went back to her house in El Palomar, outside the capital, to ransack it and wait for Maria Antonia Berger. After the third cigarette crater was burned into Miss Burgos's face, she had told her tormentors that Miss Berger was due at the house the next morning.

Miss Berger was blond.

That next morning, a blond girl knocked on the door of the Burgos house. She was about to leave on vacation with her parents and had come to say good-bye to her friend Norma. The door opened and the girl was confronted by the orifice of a .45-caliber pistol leveled at her face. Panic-stricken, she turned and ran.

The officer ran after her. The girl was young—seventeen years old— and an athlete. The officer couldn't catch her. He dropped to one knee, took aim and fired. The girl sprawled forward on the pavement, wounded in the head.

A neighbor, a taxi driver named Oscar Eles, was about to leave for work when the scene unfolded before him. Another member of the kidnap team ordered him, at gunpoint, to surrender his taxi. The officer drove the vehicle to where the wounded girl lay in the middle of the street. The two officers loaded the limp and bloody bundle into the trunk.

The girl was Dagmar Ingrid Hagelin. Her parents were Swedish immigrants to Argentina and Dagmar was a dual national. She was blond, like Maria Berger.

Miss Hagelin survived the wound and spent the following months in treatment in various naval institutions, including the Mechanics School. But she remained paralyzed, incontinent and mentally disabled. She became a disappeared person.

By the end of May, with the Swedish team already in Argentina for the World Cup, the Swedish Foreign Ministry began to demand answers regarding Dagmar's disappearance.

After receiving several diplomatic ultimatums from Stockholm, the Argentine authorities decided they could not simply hand the invalid girl over with their apologies. So Dagmar Hagelin was killed and her body disposed of in a manner that assured it would never be found.

CAPTAIN ROIG GRIMACED BEHIND HIS POLISHED AND UNCLUTTERED MAHOGANY DESK. HE SHIFTED IN THE CHAIR, LEANED FORWARD AND BACK, BUT THE RODENT GNAWING AT HIS GUTS WOULD NOT BE APPEASED. HE ROSE and walked hunched over to a richly grained and gleaming cabinet of jacaranda wood. He took a bottle of Chivas Regal Scotch whisky from the cabinet and poured a drink. He threw the liquor back down his throat in a single swallow.

The pain in his abdomen was so acute that, had he not known its cause, he would have thought it was appendicitis. But the cause was evident; he had not defecated in six days.

He had tried prunes, then laxatives, but nothing shifted his bowels. He felt his waste harden and stall. He had developed a strange and special sensitivity for that part of his body, he imagined, similar to the sensitivity a pregnant woman develops for her womb. He was ravenous, eating more than at any other stage of his life. He gained weight, but was not getting fat. He was certain that his weight was increasing exactly by the weight of the food he swallowed.

He read the entire newspaper each morning while sitting on the toilet. The previous night, in a fit of desperation, he had lubricated two fingers with his wife's face cream and probed his rectum in an attempt to loosen or extract the hard fecal ball. He strained and groaned, holding deep breaths and pushing like a woman in labor, but could not expel the plug of shit.

He lay down on his back on a thick beige and berry-colored carpet covering the oak parquet in front of his desk. The rug was a Persian Yamut worth twenty thousand dollars. It had been taken as booty from the home of a wealthy left-leaning Buenos Aires psychoanalyst, now disappeared.

The pain subsided.

Roig's intercom buzzed. He pulled himself to his feet with a groan and stumbled to his desk. He pushed the button.

"Yes?"

His secretary began, nervously and apologetically, to tell him something about officers Benitez and Vitale.

But before she could explain, the two men swept into the room with a hooded man between them. Benitez slammed the door.

"What is the meaning of this?" Roig winced with renewed pain.

When the junior officers saluted, the man they were supporting nearly fell to the floor. They grabbed him and Lieutenant Vitale said, "If you will sit down, we will explain."

"Who are you to tell me to sit down? I am your superior."

Lieutenant Benitez drew his sidearm and held it pointed at the floor. "You will do as we say. I would add, 'With all due respect, sir' but that is precisely what this is about: whether you in fact warrant our respect and obedience."

"This is mutiny," stammered Roig.

"Call it what you will," said Vitale. "Tremendous things are taking place these days. You are aware of that."

"This man is a subversive," said Benitez, indicating the prisoner. "He is to be executed. Lieutenant Vitale and myself, with the young officers of the other armed forces branches, have waged the dirtiest part of this dirty war. We have no regrets. We have served and saved the fatherland. But the armed forces will eventually hand power back to civilians and we want to be assured that there exists an unbreakable bond of allegiance among all of us who took part in this war. Together with our counterparts in the other branches, we demand a pact of blood.

"You will execute this man in our presence."

Roig's legs trembled. He leaned on his desk and felt his intestine shift. He closed his anus with all his strength, clenched his buttocks against the glacial pack of feces.

Benitez slipped a knapsack off his shoulder. He took from it a large bag of thick green polyurethene, a towel and a 9-mm MAG Marietta pistol equipped with a black burnished Power Spring silencer.

Vitale pressed the prisoner to his knees on the rug and, without removing the hood, wrapped the towel tightly around his head. He stepped back and drew his own sidearm. Benitez, holding the MAG by the silencer, extended it toward Roig. He held his own weapon in the other hand.

Roig looked from one officer to the other, then at the prisoner. "This is insane," he said.

"It's necessary," said Benitez.

Roig circled unsteadily to the front of his desk. He took the pistol from Benitez. His arm dropped to his side. The barrel pointed at the floor. He imagined he might try to kill the mutineers, but that self-flattering fantasy passed in an instant.

"And if I refuse?" he asked pitifully.

"You won't refuse," said Benitez.

Roig stepped to the prisoner, who had fallen forward in the posture of a Moslem praying. He raised the gun and pointed it at the turbaned head. He stared blankly beyond his target. His arm dropped again to his side and the two junior officers thought to themselves in disguised panic that he did not have the nerve to do it and they asked themselves what on God's holy earth would they do now.

"Move him off the carpet," instructed Roig hollowly.

Benitez stepped forward. "What?"

"The carpet. I don't want it stained."

"That's what the towel is for."

"Just in case."

The two officers dragged the condemned man off the rug onto the parquet.

Roig stepped to the prisoner. He leaned forward and placed the silencing cylinder against the crown of the man's swaddled head and squeezed the trigger. The report was the sound of a match striking. The bullet crashed silently into the man's brain and he bucked and was dead.

Benitez took the pistol from Roig's limp hand and the two men bundled the corpse into the plastic bag and closed it with a knot. Both men snapped to attention and saluted.

"Request permission to retire, sir," barked Benitez.

Roig was dazed.

"Request permission to retire, sir!"

Roig looked down at the floor. "Permission granted," he whispered.

Vitale hoisted the heavy bag over his shoulder and the officers withdrew.

Roig squatted. With his forefinger he wiped from the polished oak a single large drop of cherry-black blood. He touched it to his thumb and examined its consistency.

"Good thing I didn't listen to them," he said slowly to no one.

Kempes shaved off his mustache for his return to Rosario.

Maybe it will change my luck thought the lanky, long-haired forward as the bus made its way the night of June 14 to the Rosario Central stadium. He had played here in the capital of Santa Fe province for four years; here fame had found him and carried him off across the Atlantic to Valencia and the limelight and riches of European soccer.

He was the only member of the Argentine team Menotti had recalled from overseas and his individual performance was considered crucial to Argentina's success. But his first round showing had been a disappointment. He had hit the goalpost twice against France. Supposedly the team's paramount offensive threat, he had yet to score a goal.

Argentina's first rival in the second round was Poland. The Poles had been the revelation of the '74 Cup, finishing third, and were considered a good prospect for reaching the final of this tournament, mainly because the Polish squad, unlike West Germany and Holland, had not lost its protagonists from four years earlier. (Neither Beckenbauer nor Cryuff were playing this time around.)

Before the game, at midfield, a representative of the Polish National Soccer Association presented midfielder Kazimierz Deyna with a plaque commemorating this his hundredth game in international competition.

Veteran Jan Tomaszewski was in goal for the Poles. Coach Jack Gmoch put Henryk Maculewicz, Wladyslaw Zmuda, Antoni Szymanowski, Henryk Kasperczak, Zbigniew Boniek, Adam Nawalka, Deyna,

Bogdan Masztaler, Gregorz Lato and Andrej Szarmach on the field in front of him.

The fans hailed the introduction of each of the Argentine players with raucous ovation. But when the name Mario Alberto Kempes was announced the coliseum exploded in a thunderous frenzy of cheers and confetti.

The announcer informed the crowd of the presence of President Videla in the honor box at midfield. The general, in a broad-lapelled double-breasted brown pinstriped suit—recalling the attire of a Chicago bootleg gangster—stood to acknowledge the applause. He raised both thumbs and graced the multitude with a rare smile.

Argentina began play conservatively, using the same defense-oriented scheme of four defenders, four midfielders and two attackers that Italy had employed so effectively in the first round. The strategy relied on counterattack, on taking advantage of the opposition's errors for offensive opportunities.

But it was clear from the onset that the chinks in the Argentine defense, especially Tarantini and Olguin, had not been mended. The Poles played tedious journeyman soccer but they controlled the ball and advanced.

Then at the fifteen-minute mark Houseman, moving up the right side, found Ardiles in the center, who in turn passed to Bertoni, who had penetrated upfield on the left without going offside. Bertoni braked, wheeled and lofted a centering pass in the penalty area four meters in front of Tomaszewski, whose major fault has always been the tendency to stick to the goal line, unable to emerge to clear or catch this type of pass.

Kempes galloped across the penalty area, a step inside of Szymanowski. With a leap more forward than up, he put his head at the sailing sphere. The ball shot past the goalie just inside the near post.

Without breaking stride, Kempes raised high his arms and ran to the sideline bellowing triumph and vindication. Pandemonium reigned.

Twenty-two minutes later the Poles were awarded a free kick just outside the Argentine penalty area. Deyna put a shot on goal, which Fillol blocked but did not control. Maculewicz headed the ball up and Lato, from four meters out, headed the ball toward the goal. Fillol was out of position and the goal was wide open. Just before the ball sailed across the goal line, Kempes lunged to his right and, stretched out and suspended in the air like a goalie, knocked the ball away with his hand.

Referee Ulf Ericksson's whistle shrieked. The black-shirted Swede ran to the penalty-shot spot.

Lato's goal was thus converted into a probable goal.

The crowd hushed as Deyna approached to make the shot. Fillol hunched and compacted his springs. When the Pole's foot slammed into the ball, Fillol dove to his left. The ball thudded into his midriff. No goal.

Argentina took the 1–0 lead into the locker room at halftime. When the teams came out for the second half, Menotti replaced Valencia in midfield with Ricardo Villa. The switch proved provident. The bearded star of Racing Club became, with Ardiles, the instigator and spark of the Argentine counterattack.

But the Argentine defense remained porous. Lato repeatedly skirted Tarantini on the right, but the balding Slav was unable to conclude his gambits and put a good shot on goal. Midway through the second period Boniek made the play of the game. He dribbled around three Argentine defenders, drew Fillol out and put the ball on the boot of Lato, who had only to kick it into the unguarded goal. Lato erred the shot.

Then, at seventy-one minutes, with the Poles threatening, came a concert—a duet—of Cordobeses. Ardiles the playmaker made a beautiful play. He stole a pass at midfield and rushed the ball forward. Zmuda, Szymanowski and Kasperczak all converged on the little midfielder. Ardiles kept the ball until just before he was toppled by Zmuda, then sent a sharp pass to Kempes who was charging through the space cleared by the convergence of Polish defenders. Kempes balked, Maculewicz overshot him and the Argentine forward, a step beyond the penalty spot, let fly a left-footed blast that blurred past Tomaszewski and billowed the net.

The Polish frustration showed minutes later when Szarmach took an errant shot from a bad angle with Boniek free in the center, in a much better position to challenge Fillol. Boniek, his face as red as his flaming hair, shouted a curse at his teammate. Szarmach ran to Boniek and each started shoving and alluding loudly to the perversions of the other's mother. Deyna arrived running and separated them.

*   *   *

Alejandro sat crosslegged on the floor and spread the Polaroid photographs out before him on the coffee table. He tilted the shade of the lamp to better illuminate the pictures.

In one, he stood next to his mother, her arms draped around him in the moment before she planted a proud kiss on his cheek. He stood erect, indulgent, amused and shivering. (Monica had insisted he pose in his uniform.) The other pictures were of him individually with Santiago, Cristina, and Daniel, and there was a group shot.

Half the neighborhood had tramped through the house that day. "We could charge admission," Monica had jested. All the neighbors wanted a photograph of themselves or their children with Alejandro. They would later show it to their friends saying, "Yes, Ale is almost like a son to me. I've known him since he was a tyke."

It was Alejandro's first free day since the tournament began. It should have been a festive time, he thought as he studied the pictures. But the contented household he had left only three weeks ago was now shrouded in unspoken sorrows. Only his mother seemed immune. She, as ever, bounced through the day from morning until night.

Life with the team had been so hectic and emotional that Alejandro had lost touch with home. Santiago had told him over the phone about Diego and Ana. But he had used the word "arrested" and Alejandro had assumed the family at least knew where they were detained, and that some sort of legal proceeding was under way. Only today had he learned of their enigmatic status of "disappeared."

He examined the picture of himself with his father. He had his arm around Santiago's shoulder. He recalled how his father had at first raised his hand and placed it tentatively on his back, then reached around and pulled him tightly and urgently against him. Santiago's face showed a tight-lipped attempt at fortitude, but his eyes were frightened, those of a man who knows he's guilty awaiting announcement of the verdict.

He set that picture aside and picked up the one of him with Cristina. She was trying hard to smile, turning up the corners of her mouth and showing her teeth, and failing. Her smile had always been so ready and reflective of her nature. Here it was a charade. His mother had related the pageant disaster and said Cristina had not been quite herself since. But he had not expected to find her so withdrawn.

Daniel looked genuinely happy in his picture. But his delight at the chance to bask in his cousin's glory was so fleeting, captured by the camera in the moment it lasted, that it served only to underscore the child's despondency. When the house had finally cleared out in the afternoon, Alejandro had taken Daniel to the back yard to kick around a soccer ball. Dani had even laughed. But after five minutes he had booted the ball away and stalked off to resume his vigil at the front window.

"Want some tea, or something to eat?" Santiago stood in the doorway.

"I thought you were all having a siesta," said Alejandro, looking up from the photographs.

"Everybody except me. Dani and Cristina have been in hibernation lately. And you know your mother and her beauty rest." Santiago sat on the floor across the coffee table from Alejandro. "It hasn't been a very pleasant homecoming for you, son."

Alejandro pressed the knuckle of his index finger to the cutting edge of his front teeth. "It's strange. That things could have changed so quickly."

"It's like lightning struck and started a fire," said Santiago. "Only it burns very slowly. Like peat."

"And me in the center ring of the circus. Like nothing had happened."

"Don't feel bad about that. There's nothing you could do." Santiago rubbed his forehead with a slow, hard pressure. "What's it like, being on the team?"

"It's hard to describe. It's great, of course. But it's more than that. Much more. When you're standing out on the field before the game and they play the national anthem, I swear, it makes you want to cry. Your skin gets all prickly and you feel heat running up your backbone into your skull and you know this is the greatest moment of your life, even if you live a hundred years. And what's really amazing is you don't care; it's all right that nothing will ever be better, even though you've got your whole life in front of you. It is that magnificent.

"Then there's the team, the brotherhood. I sit the bench, but it doesn't matter. I'm one of the twenty-three, a member of the team that will make history. We're certain we'll do it, we want it that much."

"You're not disappointed about not playing?"

"Oh, I'd love to get in the game. Sure. And I may get to yet if the forwards keep getting hurt. But I'll still feel great even if I don't play a minute. This tournament is something bigger than all of us. Don't you feel it? Something is happening to the country. It's bringing us together. It's making us proud to be Argentines."

Santiago looked away. He was silent for what seemed like a full minute. Then he looked at his son.

"You know, Ale, it takes a long time to learn some things. Unless something terrible happens, something to make you stop and examine what is going on around you, you never realize some things at all. You just go through life, around in circles, turning a stone and grinding grist like a blind burro." He picked at the crumbs on the tray holding the empty cups of the after-lunch coffee. "Proud to be Argentine," he said. "I have always been proud to be Argentine. But what is Argentina? If it's not the people, it's just a parcel of earth. The people make its history, its institutions. We've had fifty years of coups and rigged elections and tyranny and corruption. A state of siege for thirty-two of the past fifty years. You have no rights. Neither do I, nor anyone else. The constitution is a joke. They wipe their asses with it. They can pick you up off the street, throw you in a hole until you die and rot and not even tell your family where you are. And there is nothing to be done about it. But you don't worry about it until it happens to you or to someone you love. And while that is the state of things, we're busy being proud to be Argentines because our team is kicking a ball into the other team's goal."

Alejandro did not want to hear this. This was not what he had come home for. Resentment stirred and swelled in him as he listened to Santiago.

You bitter bastard, he thought, and almost spoke the words. Because it occurred to Alejandro that Santiago wanted to belittle his achievement since he was still bitter—and always would be—at having been denied, long ago, his own moment of glory.

Santiago, though the middleweight amateur national champion in 1964, had lost his final bout of the Olympic qualifying tournament and did not make the team that represented Argentina in the Tokyo games. The lanky left-handed Tucumano he fought in the final had left more of himself—more guts and spirit—in the ring, and had won a unamimous decision. Santiago, though he damned the judges as the boy's arm was raised, had known that the other was the better man. And he had never fought again.

"I'm sorry, son," said Santiago after a wordless while. "This whole mess is not your fault. And the last thing I want to do is take the wind out of your sails. It's great you're on the team," he said desperately. "Really it is."

Marta Ramirez caressed her swollen belly and spoke softly to the child inside her.

"Stay put, my precious," she said. "It's warm in there and you are safe."

Marta knew that had it not been for her condition when she was arrested four months earlier she would have been treated like the rest of the captives at the Mechanics School. As it was, she and five other pregnant prisoners were held in a separate ward. They had individual cells, each with a bed, toilet and sink, and they ate the same food as the navy personnel.

Diego worked on the maternity ward. Roig had had another talk, a brief exchange with him a few days after the simulated execution. Diego's profession could be of use to the institution and Roig saw no reason for him to languish in a cell when he could be working. So Diego attended to the six women, applying the rudimentary gynecology and obstetrics training he had had in addition to a kind of general practitioner's daily ministration.

Diego, dressed in a physician's smock and navy dungarees, stopped at Marta's open door at the end of this morning's round.

"*Buenos días,*" he greeted her, interrupting the monologue with her unborn child.

"*Buen día,* Doctor."

The sight of Marta hurt him every time he entered her room. The first days on the ward had been almost unbearable because all the women, radiant with the wonder in their wombs, had reminded him of Ana and how she had been with Daniel. How he used to caress the curve of her stretched skin and kiss her senstitive, laden breasts. Now it was only Marta who, excruciatingly, reminded him of Ana. Something about her dark eyes looked like Ana and she sometimes smiled in that peaceful, confident, peculiar way of pregnancy, as Ana had smiled while carrying their son. Even so, despite the sadness he knew awaited him there, Diego was drawn to Marta's cell. He always visited her last so he could linger in the bittersweetness.

"How are you feeling today?" He sat on the foot of her bed. She lay propped against pillows, her knees drawn up, her hands resting on her risen belly.

"I'm worried, Diego."

"About what?"

"My son is restless and I think tired of confinement. I'm afraid he'll try to come out soon."

"You are just about due. Time, tide and babies wait for no one."

"It's just that I feel full now. And I know that when he is born I shall feel unbearably empty. I will be just me again. And I will have to face what I've done." Her eyes brimmed. She blinked and tears rolled down her cheeks. She did not whimper nor did she grab shortly for breath as crying people do, but sat and stared ahead as the tears left tracks on her skin. Diego moved forward on the bed and took her hand.

"Don't cry, Marta," he pleaded. "Melancholy is normal in your condition."

"That's a diagnosis for outside. For the normal world. None of that applies here. Nothing is normal here." Her tears subsided and a stony resolution took over her face.

"You don't know what I've done. They were going to torture me. They said they would put the *picana* up inside me and shock the baby. You know, they never laid a hand on me; not even a slap. They never had to. They showed me the *picana* and I broke. I gave them the names of four people, and I have spent these months imagining what they did to those people, and I think the pain they could have caused me would not have been as great as the anguish I have known for my betrayal. I wish I would have died when they first brought me here. But I was pregnant and I was Catholic. I believed in God. I told myself I had to save my son and ever since I have tried to convince myself that that was why I did it. But I don't really know. You see? What if I had not been pregnant? I was so terrified, Diego. I can't stand pain. I don't know what I would have done."

Diego squeezed her hand. He looked out through the small barred window at a patch of impossibly blue sky. And his own collaboration? He was, in effect, helping them run a concentration camp. Sometimes, in the worst moments, he considered himself the equal of those Auschwitz inmates who pried gold fillings from the stiff jaws of emaciated corpses and shaved sunken-eyed skulls for pillow stuffing. But he had found some solace, some justification in Hippocrates. He spoke to Marta: "All of us who have survived have collaborated to a greater or lesser degree. And we are all, except those who have completely lost their minds, tormented by it. When I became a doctor I took an oath to help the sick and injured, the wounded and weak regardless of everything. If a person needs medical attention, his mere condition as a human being demands that I attend him. It is my moral obligation."

Marta's grip on Diego's hand slackened. "You have your oath. I had my religion. Now I've lost that. I am barren, except for this child. I expect no redemption or salvation—or even damnation. None of that. All I want is to never give birth, ever." She stared past Diego through the open door. "I want to go around with this big belly for the rest of my life."

But the baby, as if he had heard and sought to advise of his dissent, gave a sharp kick. Her water broke. She yelped and clamped her hands in her groin but the liquid seeped through her fingers into the sheet and mattress.

Diego stuck his head into the hall and yelled for the guard. A sailor came running.

"Fetch Dr. Schneider, quickly," said Diego, and the sailor ran back down the hall to the office of the naval obstetrician in charge of the women's care.

The doctor, a tall man with hairy hands, arrived followed by a pair of orderlies wheeling a high metal bed. The doctor examined Marta quickly.

"She's ready," he said and the orderlies lifted her onto the stretcher and wheeled her out, down the hall, toward the makeshift delivery room off the infirmary.

"Come with me," said Schneider to Diego, and the two men followed in Marta's wake.

*   *   *

The baby was born two hours later. It was a boy, as she had known all along it would be. Diego stood by during the delivery, the first he had witnessed since the birth of Daniel.

Schneider cut and tied the umbilical cord, wrapped the infant in a towel and handed him to the nurse, who left the room. He stitched up the episiotomy. Then he left too.

Marta panted. After a few moments of pure and exclusive relief at the end of the ordeal, she regained her senses and looked around frantically. Her eyes found those of Diego and she was about to say something when another nurse entered.

"Where's my baby?" demanded Marta.

"They're washing him. Don't worry. He's a fine big boy. Ten fingers and ten toes." The nurse cleaned Marta and changed the sheets under her, gently shifting the new mother.

Just as she finished, the nurse who had helped with the delivery entered with the baby in her arms. She held him up for Marta to see, then placed him against his mother's breast. Marta cradled her son tenderly.

"He's ugly, but he's the most beautiful thing in the world," said Marta.

The nurses and Diego smiled.

"It's a tight squeeze and their little faces get squished," said one of the nurses. "Only the cesareans are pretty right off."

"I don't care if he stays ugly. I'll love him forever." Marta kissed the baby all over his red wrinkled head.

*   *   *

It was cold in Rosario. The damp wind pierced the Brazilian players' yellow and green nylon sweatsuits and chilled their bones as they stepped off the bus.

A crowd was already gathered in front of the Libertador Hotel where the Brazilians were to spend the night before their crucial game with Argentina. (Brazil, in its first game of the second round, had defeated Peru 3–0.)

A whistle shrieked from the banner-waving mob as the players made their way along a police line into the hotel lobby. Zico, the baby-faced blond who had, to the extent it was possible, replaced Pelé as Brazil's national soccer idol, waved and smiled at the jeering multitude. A burly Argentine fan shouted, "Take this!" and jutted his hips toward Zico, grabbing his genitals with a ham-sized hand. Zico laughed and entered the hotel lobby, where curious guests had come down from their rooms to witness the arrival.

Another fan shouted *"Macaco!"* ("Monkey!") as the ebony-skinned Mendoca filed past. The Brazilian player ignored the insult.

Renewed vigor suffused the mob. Now that the object of its demonstration was in place, its reasons for being was more tangible. New arrivals blended into the tumult. The crowd was an animal with its own radiating warmth, its own locomotion, language and instincts, and, as if to demonstrate that it was indeed alive, it grew. It expanded up and down the avenue and around the corner, clogging the flow of traffic through the city center.

The fans nearest the hotel began jumping and others followed suit. A wave swept over the mob from front to rear. The chant formed and rose in a roar.

"Ar-gen-tina! Ar-gen-tina!"

Some of the Brazilian players went to the windows of their rooms on the sixth and seventh floor and looked down, curious and amused. But after a few hours the amusement turned to anger. The chants and the jarring orchestration of the horns of a hundred cars assaulted the windows and walls of the players' rooms. They could not sleep.

Coutinho, the swarthy Brazilian coach, emerged from the elevator and, fuming, looked around the lobby. He strode to the reception desk. The young man behind it could not mask his awe and intimidation, his outright fear of the Brazilian. Coutinho slammed his open hand against the counter.

"Where is the manager? Where are the police?" he demanded in Portuguese, too incensed to employ his faultless Spanish.

The manager, a middle-aged affable Rosarino, interrupted his telephone conversation with the police chief, with whom he was pleading unsuccessfully for dispersement of the mob. He approached Coutinho. His wide eyes and trembling lips expressed genuine regret over the circumstances.

"If those people and automobiles are not cleared from the streets surrounding this building, there will be no game tomorrow. And I will make such a stink with Havelange that it will not be us who forfeit."

"I'm doing what I can, Mr. Coutinho. I'm doing everything I can," squealed the manager, wringing his hands. "I've been on the phone to the police all night, but they only tell me there's no law against enthusiasm."

"Get the police chief on the phone," ordered the coach.

The manager made for his office off the reception area, the coach on his heels. He dialed the police and got the chief on the line.

"You again?" asked the officer on the other end.

"The Brazilian coach wants to speak with you," said the manager hastily into the receiver and, without waiting for the commander's reply, passed it to Coutinho.

The Brazilian skipped introductory comment. "Get your men down here and these people dispersed in half an hour, or I assure you that on Monday morning you will not be police chief of Rosario." That was all he said. He did not listen to the commander's response, if there was one, and returned the telephone to the manager, who, too nerve-racked to converse further, hung up.

Ten minutes later, a hundred policemen turned the corner onto the avenue two blocks from the hotel. Backed by water cannons and paddy wagons, the column advanced a block, and the chief emerged from a squad car. He planted himself and spoke through a loudspeaker mounted on the roof.

"I order you to disband peacefully. Those who do not comply will be arrested."

"Ar-gen-tina!" chanted the mob. "Ar-gen-tina!"

But the demonstrators had some idea as to what they could expect at the police station, and by the time a water cannon had advanced ten meters they were streaming down the side streets and the avenue, away. Even the hard-core fans, those nearest the hotel, gave way without protest.

But as they retreated, their cry rose and resounded off the surrounding buildings:

> *Los brasileños*
> *Están de luto*
> *Son todos negros*
> *Son todos putos!*

The Brazilians
Are in mourning
They're all black
They're all faggots!

Argentina and Brazil tied 0–0 in a dull and disappointing game. The result meant that the finalist from Group B would be decided on the solstice, June 21, when Brazil played Poland in the afternoon in Mendoza and Argentina played Peru at night in Rosario. Argentina and Brazil each had a victory and a tie in the second round. So, if they both won their third games, the finalist from Group B would be decided by the advantage in goals: the team with the biggest difference between goals for and goals against would advance to the final.

Brazil beat Poland 3–1. That meant Argentina had to defeat Peru by a margin of at least four goals.

The Brazilians arrived back at their hotel, the San Francisco in Chacras de Coria outside Mendoza, just as the first half of the Argentina-Peru game was ending. Coutinho and the players hurried to their reserved lobby and hastily arranged couches and chairs around the television set already tuned to the contest. Zico limped in with his arm draped over Dirceu's shoulder. The World Cup had ended for him hours earlier, seven minutes into the game with Poland, when he tore a muscle in his right thigh.

The first period ended with Argentina leading 2–0 on goals by Kempes and Tarantini. Waiters brought in trays of cold cuts and hors d'oeuvres, beer, wine and mineral water for the Brazilians, who ate ravenously during the intermission.

The Brazilians greeted the reappearance of the Argentine team with a shrill chorus of whistles. When the red-shirted Peruvians trotted onto the field, the lounge erupted in cheers and applause.

"*Viva* Peru!" shouted Toninho Cerezo. Mendonca cried, "Come on Cubillas, you black son of a black mother. We want goals!"

Coutinho leaned forward and turned off the sound. Without the blather of the Argentine announcer it was just like another of the team's innumerable viewing sessions of videotaped games, their own or those of eventual opponents. Only this was not a replay. It was live, and unraveling before them on the screen was their fate in this tournament. Fingers drummed nervous rhythms on the furniture. Clipped cries escaped whenever either team threatened the other's goal.

With only three minutes gone in the second half, Kempes advanced through the center of the Peruvian defense and the Brazilians sat forward clenching their teeth and fists. The lanky forward passed to Bertoni who, as soon as the Peruvian defender Quezada moved from Kempes toward him, passed the ball back to Kempes, who blasted it past the goalie Quiroga for the third goal.

"Bastards!" shouted one of the Brazilians jumping from his seat.

"Pansies!" railed another

Play resumed. One of the Brazilians kneeled and prayed aloud in an unintelligible jumble of appeals to Roman Catholic saints and macumba spirits.

Two minutes transpired before Larrosa sent a centering pass across the front of the Peruvian goal. With Quiroga in front of him at the far goalpost, Passarella headed the ball back across the goalmouth and Luque launched himself—the maneuver is called *la paloma* (the dove)—and drove the hovering sphere off the top of his head into the unguarded net.

"Corruption! Corruption!" shouted the Brazilians, clutching their heads. Mendonca threw an orange that bounced off the screen and Amaral kicked a wastebasket across the room. Here was the four-goal difference.

But hope was not lost. If the Peruvians scored and Argentina did not, Brazil would still advance to the final.

Marco DeBrito, the team's masseur, strode out of the lobby. After a few minutes he returned from the hotel kitchen with a live hen. He stood behind the television set and, with the chicken pressed tightly beneath his sinewy black arm, whacked off its head with a swift stroke of his bare hand. Blood spurted from the severed neck and the animal convulsed against the masseur's ribs. When the bird stopped wriggling, DeBrito raised the dripping carcass toward the ceiling and uttered an ancient African plea. Then he placed the decapitated fowl on top of the TV.

But Houseman scored Argentina's fifth goal at sixty-six minutes and Luque added the sixth at seventy-two minutes. Peru did not score.

Brazil, the only undefeated team of the tournament, was eliminated.

* * *

Only a few people must know for sure if there was something rotten about Argentina's lopsided victory over Peru. In any case—whether or not the game was rigged—many Argentines, even loyal fans of the national team, speculate openly that Peru took the field disposed to lose.

The people who feel that way, even if they discount an outright bribe, ask this question: Which team would the Peruvian players have preferred to see in the final? Argentina or Brazil?

Peru and Argentina are closely bound historically and culturally. The rightist military regime of General Francisco Morales Bermudez was a staunch ally of the Argentine junta. The Peruvian armed forces hosted many Argentine military advisers. The Peruvian goalie, Ramon Quiroga, was Argentine.

Rodolfo Manzo played for Lima's Deportivo Municipal and was a member of the 1978 Peruvian national team. He traveled to Argentina with his club for a series in 1980 and made a thinly veiled public reference to a fix of the Cup contest. Suddenly, without explanation, he was scratched from the tour and put on a plane back to Lima.

MARTA RAMIREZ'S SON SUCKED SINGLEMINDEDLY AT HER BREAST, THE SOUND OF HIS SMALL EARNEST SUCKLING MINGLING WITH THE COMFORTING HISS AND PERK OF THE RADIATOR IN THE CORNER OF HER CELL. Reclined on clean cool sheets, Marta was thinking that, all in all, things had not gone so badly for her.

Her fear that the child's birth would leave her desolate and defenseless had proved unfounded. The tiny pink boy—Manuel, after his grandfather—outside her now, able to clutch at her breast and squeal and gurgle, was a more tangible and complete object of her adoration than he had been while growing in her womb. And, as a sort of bonus, the attention she and the baby were receiving was even more indulgent than her treatment before his birth.

She had begun to sense again the presence of God. The child, so wonderfully new and innocent, left Marta suffused with a feeling of grace.

Captain Roig appeared in the doorway. He entered, followed by Dr. Schneider and a nurse. The woman, whom Marta had never seen before, stepped to the bedside and asked, "Is he done with breakfast?" But without waiting for a reply she lifted the baby from his mother's side and took him out of the room.

"We have arranged for the transfer of you and the child to a more suitable institution," said Roig. "The facilities here are inadequate and you'll be more comfortable and better looked after where we are sending you. You will be transferred by bus and the journey is not a short one. So the doctor is going to give you an injection to relax you."

"But we're fine here, really, Captain," protested Marta, bolting upright. Her eyes were wide, jumping.

"Don't worry," Roig assured her. "It's for the good of the baby."

The doctor turned the palm of Marta's right hand upward and rubbed an alcohol-soaked cotton ball over the crease inside her elbow. He pointed the tip of the hypodermic at the ceiling and pushed the plunger of the syringe until a few drops squirted out. He slipped the needle beneath her skin. She did not feel a thing. Within minutes, she was asleep.

As soon as she drifted off a priest entered. His linty long black soutane swept the floor. He took a wooden-beaded rosary from his pocket and lifted the sleeping woman's hands to her breast, then wrapped the beaded string around them. He half closed his rheumy eyes as he mumbled a Latin incantation then sliced a cross over her to brand her soul.

Two sailors came in and lifted her from the bed to a high wheeled stretcher and rolled her out of the room, down the hall. They made their way down long corridors to an elevator, which took them to a basement garage and loading dock. A blue navy van was waiting there.

"Come on. Come on," an officer prodded the sailors. They lifted Marta from the rolling bed and placed her in the back of the van, where seven other sedated prisoners lay stacked like railroad ties.

The officer drove the van through the morning traffic to the nearby Jorge Newberry Municipal Airfield and went through three checkpoints to a hangar where a propeller-driven Fokker cargo transport stood waiting.

Machine-gun-wielding soldiers guarded the entrance to the hangar as a crew of enlisted men unloaded the unconscious passengers from the van. They carried them slung over the shoulder like sacks of flour, up a short flight of metal stairs into the hold of the Fokker.

Four men in olive-green uniforms, distinguished only by differing yellow stripes on their sleeves, sat at a table in a cinderblock room. Each held a hand of playing cards before him. One of the men shifted his eyes right, then left, and finding the men on either side engrossed in the study of their hands, caught the eye of his partner and raised his eyebrows twice quickly.

The partner played a card, which was followed by one from the next soldier in rotation.

"*Truco,*" said the brow-raiser.

"I want *retruco,*" said the following player, a captain.

"Make it worth four," said the bidder, and they spread their cards face up before them.

"Ha!" cried the brow-raiser. "That's five straight hands."

"The cunt of the parrot!" swore the captain, slamming his fist on the tabletop. He glared across at his partner, a lieutenant. "Were you born a jerk-weed, or did you study to become one?"

"Forgive me," said the fine-featured lieutenant. "I never played much *truco.*"

"It's not real big among the better class, is it, Lieutenant Martinez de Sevilla of the Cunt of the Widowed Cow? I'm sure you're better at bridge, or canasta."

Blood rose to the younger officer's cheeks. But he said nothing. It was his turn to deal and he gathered the cards before him and shuffled. As he was distributing the hands around the table the door opened brusquely.

"Do we have any vacancies?" asked a man in the doorway, cradling a sawed-off shotgun. "We have a guest."

The man stepped back and a black-hooded man, his hands cuffed behind him, was shoved into the room. The man with the shotgun and another man with an identical weapon followed him in.

"Who is he?" asked the captain.

"Name's Alberto Rosenblum. Uruguayan, Jew and Tupa. Got everything going for him. A real fucking prize."

"Take off the hood."

The other man untied the sheath and lifted it off the prisoner's head. The arrested man blinked back the light and surveyed his surroundings.

"We'll begin your interrogation in a few minutes, Albertito," said the captain congenially. "But first, I want to introduce you to a friend." The officer brought to his pursed lips a spent .45-caliber cartridge suspended from a gold chain around his neck. He blew into the shell to produce a piercing whistle.

In ten seconds, a hunched and lumbering man wearing baggy gray sweatpants, rope-soled cloth slippers and a T-shirt with the legend IT'S BETTER IN THE BAHAMAS, came through the door. He lifted his head slowly and smiled a crooked and idiotic smile at the captain. The expression registered on only half the man's face. The other half of his countenance was paralyzed and blank, encroached upon by the hollow in the side of his head.

"Maté?" asked Roberto Otero dully, employing a tenth of his vocabulary.

"No, *macho,*" answered the captain. "Show!"

Roberto plodded to the wall and stood with his back against it. Still half-smiling, he fumbled with the drawstring of his pants until he succeeded in untying the knot. He loosened the pants and let them drop to the floor. Somehow Roberto knew the exhibition was for the benefit of the Uruguayan and he fixed his dumb gaze on the prisoner as he took hold of his large dangling penis and lifted it to show the absence of testicles.

"See how docile even the most ardent revolutionaries become with the proper attention?" the captain asked the prisoner. He took a straight razor from one breast pocket and a cigar from the other. He flipped the blade open and deftly sliced off the tip of the cigar. He laid the open razor on the table. One of the soldiers struck a match and held it between cupped hands to the captain, who sucked audibly on the cheroot and puffed out a cloud of thick smoke.

The door opened and Monica swirled in with the wind that fleetingly invaded the foyer.

Cristina, just home from school, sat on the couch in the living room playing her guitar. Monica threw her coat over the back of a chair and greeted her daughter with a smacking buss perfumed by the snifters of cognac that had followed tea, cakes and gossip at the house of a friend.

"Where's Dani?"

"Sleeping."

"Play something for me," requested Monica, leaning forward in anticipation, her hands between her knees.

"I'm tired of playing." Cristina set the instrument aside.

"What shall we do then?"

"I'm going to lie down for a while."

"Oh, don't be a spoilsport. Let's do something fun."

"Like what?"

Monica pondered a moment. "I know! Let's call up old Mr. Pardo-Comas," and before she finished the sentence she was pushing the buttons on the telephone. She sat straight-backed and, for effect, curled her lips around her teeth as if she were an old lady without dentures.

"Hello," she said in a squeaky geriatric voice when a man answered. "Is that you, Ricardito? This is your honeybun. I thought you might like . . ." She held the phone up in front of her and looked at it perplexedly. "He hung up."

"You're ridiculous," said Cristina, rising.

"And who are you? Miss Maturity?" said Monica, indignant.

"You don't have the slightest idea who I am. You think because you carried me inside you that you know me. That was fourteen years ago." She turned and walked away.

"Come back here, young lady!" demanded Monica. But Cristina was up the stairs and into her room before her mother was out of her chair. Monica heard the key turn and the faint click of the lock, like a punctuation mark.

She went to the highly polished hardwood cabinet against the wall and opened one of the doors. She took out a bottle of Chivas Regal and searched for a glass. Finding none, she shouted in the direction of the maid's quarters off the kitchen, "Carmen! There's no damn glasses in the damn cabinet! What do we pay you for? To sleep the siesta?"

She disgustedly unscrewed the cap and, for the first time in her life, took a swig of liquor directly from the bottle. She saw the broken, faceted reflection of herself in the bevel-edged glass of the cabinet door. She watched her reflection as she took another gulp and the laugh that burst from her spewed whiskey in a fine spray against the glass, fogging her image.

Diego swung his legs off the bunk and set his bare feet on the cold concrete floor. He sat with his elbows on his knees, his chin resting on his hands. He stared at the dark outline of his thick feet, strangely foreign to him now. He knew, from the quality of the blackness around him and the depth of his desolation, that it was sometime between midnight and dawn, one of those difficult hours. Every night he started awake from his dreams. He dreamed of Ana or Daniel, or both, and they were always in some way appealing to him.

He pulled the gray blanket around his shoulders and stood. He paced the four steps of the cell's length, back and forth, feeling the cold rise like sap through the soles of his feet, past his ankles into his calves. He fell back onto the bunk and cuddled in his wrap.

Since he had been attending to the pregnant inmates his conditions of imprisonment had improved markedly. The food was almost decent and he was allowed each day an hour of fresh air and exercise in a small sunny courtyard. He had recovered his health and was convinced that, for a reason he did not understand, he was going to survive. But the conviction brought him no satisfaction, since he could not imagine ever sleeping through another night. The endless hours spent reviewing his humiliation were eroding him. Each day he was more aware of his weakness, more prey to it, more obsessed with his inability to emerge from the past and the illusion of what might have been. He knew, by means of an almost mystical intuition, he could not withstand a lifetime of his own recriminations. The numbed resignation to survival he saw in other inmates eluded him. If it had not been for Daniel, his increasingly tenuous link to the world, he would have found a way to end his life.

He lay there, his knees drawn up, watching his breath vaporize and disappear in the cold and indifferent air.

He stayed like that for hours. After a while, he slept.

When he awoke it was midmorning and he wondered why he had not been roused earlier to make his rounds. But the change in routine did not alarm him. He stretched out on his bunk, wrapped in the blanket and the narcotic of a blank mind.

When the door opened and the guard set his midday meal of macaroni with tomato sauce on the small table, Diego asked him, "How come I'm not working?"

"All prisoners are confined to their cells. We're on short staff. Everybody's off, for the game."

"What game?"

The guard quizzically knitted his brow. "You don't know? The final."

And when Diego appeared still not to understand, he explained. "The World Cup. Remember? We made it to the final. Against Holland. Today at three o'clock."

Diego ate his soggy pasta and tried to assimilate this piece of information. Argentina in the final of the World Cup, for the first time in history.

Rationally, he appreciated its immensity. But it did not move him, and he wondered why. In his thirty-three years he had dedicated thousands of hours to soccer; playing it, listening to it on the radio, watching it on television, discussing it with friends—almost as many hours as he had spent on politics. He remembered that Alejandro was on the team and he imagined how exhilarated his nephew must be. A spark of interest kindled. The image of Alejandro on the field was like a narrow bridge over the walls of the Mechanics School, and his mind grabbed at the chimerical opportunity to abandon the fog of grief and death for the world outside; a world of citizenship and nation, pride and triumph.

He swallowed the last macaroni and slurped the bit of watery red sauce in the bottom of the bowl. He set the bowl back on the floor, licked the spoon and tossed it into the bowl.

Diego lay back on the bunk, his hands behind his head. He was well disposed to pass the whole day that way, adrift in the idleness of purgatory. After a while he rolled onto his side and curled up under the blanket like a fetus. He recalled the desiccated, huddled corpses of Chilean Indians he had seen as a child on exhibit at the Natural History Museum in La Plata. He had stood a long time staring into a glass case where the body of a woman lay. Long braids of black hair enveloped her head just as she must have wrapped them the morning a thousand years ago when she died without knowing that the dry Atacama wind would cure and blacken her skin, stretch it tightly over her brittle bones and preserve her so that a young boy, the son of Italian immigrants to America, might later wonder at her repose.

He saw himself lying for centuries just like he was lying now. He saw his eyes rot and dissolve, their powder blow away in a hot wind. He saw his hair grow and his skin darken then crack and draw taut over his bones. He imagined that the future authorities of the Mechanics School, after a millennium had passed and the stench was gone, might remove the door to his cell and hook a chain across the doorway to prevent curious students on field day from following their sad and sympathetic astonishment into the cell to at least cover the empty eye sockets of the ancient Argentine mummy.

Diego did not know how long he had been lying like that when a thud of urgent footsteps roused him. Through the door he heard a fumbling of keys and a harried voice ordering the guard to hurry. The door swung open and Captain Roig stepped in.

"Get dressed and come with me," he ordered.

Diego did as commanded and followed Roig down the hall.

"What's going on?" he asked, nearly running to keep up with the striding officer.

"You'll see."

Roig, in a turtleneck sweater and slacks, obviously called in for some emergency on what was in effect a national holiday, led Diego to the infirmary. Three men in civilian clothes huddled around one of the beds. The men made way and Diego saw a large man lying face up, his eyes open wide, his torso covered with blood, a ragged bullet hole in his neck. The one nurse on duty had cut the jacket and shirt away from the wound. Plasma ran into the man's arm from a plastic bag hung on the hook of a metal stand.

"He has lost a lot of blood," the nurse told Diego.

"Where is the naval surgeon?"

"You're the only doctor in the whole damn place," said Roig nervously. "Now get to work."

Diego instructed the nurse to ready scalpel, tweezers, probes and clamps while he disinfected his hands and forearms and tied on a surgical mask. He stationed himself at the side of the man's head and cleaned the wound with cotton and alcohol. He tilted the head in search of an exit wound. There was none.

Coagulated blood clogged the tattered hole and the bleeding had almost stopped. The man was deep in shock, but conscious. He winced and swore when Diego probed.

Only at the sound of the man's voice did Diego take note of his face. It was an ugly red Celtic face. From it shone green eyes, like bottle glass. It was the face that, on a far-off night, had pressed against Diego's own and ordered him to avert his eyes.

Diego's arms dropped to his sides.

"What's the matter?" asked Roig.

Diego stood still and silent. Then he said, "Nothing."

He resumed work. He clamped the small vessels still leaking the man's life out onto his chest. He probed brusquely with short pokes and the wounded man groaned in pain.

Then a strange feeling, a feeling he had never known, crept over Diego. For the first time, a man's life was entirely in his hands. What he did in the next few minutes signified life or death. It was his decision.

He probed cautiously and skillfully, minutely separating the pink and white and red tissue, searching for the slug. He touched it and, keeping the route to the bullet open with his finger, traded the probe for a pincer. He inserted the implement, grasped the bullet and extracted it slowly.

"Way to go, Doc!" proclaimed one of the wounded man's companions.

Diego placed the tweezer with the bullet on the metal tray. He took a scalpel and trimmed small pieces of ragged skin and flesh around the wound. When it was trimmed and clean, he stitched together the flesh inside with soluble sutures, then sewed the skin closed with thicker thread.

The wounded man's blood pressure began to rise. He would survive.

Diego straightened up with a groan and walked away from the bedside. He took off the gauze mask and walked to a window. The clouds sailing across the sky were so brilliantly white that his eyes ached. A robin perched on the branch of a tree in front of the window. It looked this way and that, then chirped and flew away.

Diego turned from the window and returned to the bedside.

"One last thing," he said.

He lifted the scalpel from the metal tray and, with the same assured deliberateness he had shown in extracting the bullet, as Captain Roig and the nurse and the wounded man's companions watched, reached across the man's throat. He pressed the blade down hard into the flesh and pulled the knife toward him, slicing through the cartilage of the esophagus, through the veins and arteries, separating the head from the body with a ferocious slash.

* * *

It was hard work, the digging in the Mechanics School fields near the river, though the earth was soft and came up in rich dark chunks on the sharp spade.

Diego, his head heavy and throbbing from the pistol-butt blow he had been dealt in the infirmary, dug slowly, deliberately. He had struck a bargain with the sole trooper, one of the dead man's companions, assigned this detail. It was to their mutual advantage. The alcoholic, prematurely retired officer did not have to strain his back, and Diego got to listen to the game.

The officer had a protruding's Adam's apple and the face of a basset hound. He sat on a tarpaulin. By his side were a .38-caliber Smith and Wesson revolver, a hatchet and a portable radio blaring the voice of José María Muñoz commenting on the just-concluded first half.

Argentina was leading Holland 1–0 on a goal by Kempes at thirty-seven minutes.

"What's the hatchet for?" asked Diego, taking a break in his labor.

"Never mind." The officer, if seen in another context, could have appeared as harmless as a neighborhood greengrocer.

"I hope you're not going to kill me with the hatchet."

"Shut up and dig. I'm trying to listen."

But Diego continued. "Did you see the film *Paths of Glory,* by Stanley Kubrik? It's about World War I. A soldier asks his comrades if they would prefer to be shot or bayoneted. They all say 'shot,' and the guy says, 'See, it's not death we're afraid of, but pain.' "

"If you don't shut the fuck up I'm going to revoke your stay."

"The hatchet is disconcerting."

"Don't worry about the fucking hatchet. I'm not going to kill you with the hatchet."

When the home team came back onto the field for the beginning of the second half, the two men in the broad expanse of pasture behind the Mechanics School, and anyone who happened to be within five kilometers of River Plate Stadium, heard the roar of the fans inside. The entwinement of the radio broadcast and the live sound of the ovation from the nearby arena struck Diego as mysterious and grand.

He dug. He drove the spade into the ground and lifted spadefuls from the widening trough. The earth opened slowly. He studied a clod and marveled at the bugs and creepers residing in the soil. He saw he had chopped an earthworm in half. He sensed a wistful fellowship with the worm he had killed.

Diego's hands, unaccustomed to such labor, hurt. He stopped digging to examine them. They were red and blistered where the fingers joined the palms. He stared at his hands, opening and closing them. He turned them over and saw in them the hands of his father. They were heavy hands, like Mikhail's, thick through palm and finger. He thought how they would never again open a letter, touch the cheek of a feverish child, tie a suture. Never again would they envelop the tender hand of his son.

He gripped the spade in his stinging hands and went back to work.

Until the last, life surprises you, he thought. He never would have imagined himself so serene. He was not afraid. His capacity to comprehend the notion of tragedy had been exhausted. There was no self-pity or despair. He only felt tired. He wanted to sleep long and profoundly.

But, for some intricate reason, he wanted also to listen to the rest of the game. The prospect of dying without knowing if Argentina was world champion unsettled him.

A grave is not dug quickly. Diego thought he could stretch the task for the forty-five minutes left in the game.

The entire nation, and much of the world, was tuned to the contest. Holland, the "Clockwork Orange" led by Austrian trainer Ernst Hapel to its second consecutive World Cup final (they lost 1–0 to West Germany in 1974), took the field again with Jan Jongbloed in goal, Wilhelmus Jansen, Erny Brandts and Rudolf Krol defending, Jan Poortvliet, Rene Van de Kerkkhof, Johan Neeskens and Arend Han in midfield and Wily Van de Kerkkhof, Dirk Nanninga and Robert Rensenbrink forward.

Diego dug slowly. He threw small spadefuls of wet earth up out of the crater and stopped occasionally to lean on his implement and contemplate the walls and bottom of his tomb.

The officer sat crosslegged on the tarp, his head forward and his ears pricked so as not to miss a word of the blaring play-by-play.

Diego dug and listened, listened and dug. The game progressed and Muñoz signaled the passing of the eighty-minute mark. "Only ten minutes—six hundred seconds—separate Argentina from the World Championship!" ranted the sportscaster.

Diego stood chest-deep in the rectangular well and thought: "Six hundred seconds remain in my life." He was affected as if by a drug, a powerful hallucinogen. Everything around him—the sky, the soil, the grass, the man—appeared different, new and bright. Water seeped from the earth and formed cold puddles where he would lie.

Muñoz's voice rose urgently. "Haan sends a long cross . . . Rensenbrink controls and advances on the right . . . lifts a centering pass into the penalty area . . . Danger! Danger! Comes Nanninga, header . . .

"Goooaaalll! Goooaaalll! . . . Holanda!"

"Damn, shit, fuck, cunt, bitch!" raved the officer, pounding the ground with his fists. "I knew it! I knew we couldn't win!"

"The game is tied!" cried Muñoz. "Nanninga with a header on a perfect pass from Rensenbrink at eighty-two minutes. The final of the World Championship is tied with eight minutes left in the game!"

Diego lay the spade in the grass and pulled himself out of the hole and sat with his legs dangling in the grave.

Play resumed. Diego watched the navy man wring his slender alabaster hands desperately before him. He observed the suffering of his executioner through the dwindling minutes. The officer bit his lip and twisted his flabby face with every rise in the announcer's voice. When the ball was at either end of the field, he rocked catatonically back and forth, picturing the sphere moving toward the Argentine goal—catastrophe—or nearing the Dutch goal—glory.

With twenty seconds remaining in the ninety minutes of regulation time, a Dutch centering pass bounded into the Argentine penalty area between Olguin and Fillol. Both players hesitated a crucial split second and the orange-shirted winger Rensenbrink arrived at the bounding ball. Fillol came out to confront him and diminish the angle. Rensenbrink's leg came down and through in excruciatingly slow motion, and the ball came off his foot then floated past the crumpling Argentine goaltender, toward the goal slowly, toward the goal . . . and bounced off the near goalpost, out into the field of play to be cleared by Gallego.

Regulation time ended with the game tied 1–1.

The officer guarding Diego was so distraught by the harrowingly close call that his hands trembled as he reached beside him and grasped the revolver. His extended arms, one hand clamping the other wrist, swung in an unsteady arc as he brought the gun around and leveled it at the chest of the man sitting silently, attentively three meters opposite him. The only thing steady about the officer was his gaze, which fixed on a spot at the center of Diego's breast as he squeezed the trigger. The explosion blasted Diego backward, threw him against the earth and hurled before his eyes a sky shimmering pale blue and white, like the flag.

The officer moved quickly. He had to if he was going to bury Diego and get back in time to watch the thirty-minute overtime period on television with the others inside. He knelt beside Diego and raised the silver-headed hatchet. A beam of sunlight caught it at its apex.

THE PLAZA DE MAYO WAS DESERTED EXCEPT FOR FIVE ELDERLY MEN SITTING ON FIVE DIFFERENT BENCHES. THEY WERE LONELY MEN OF MEAGER RESOURCES. IF THEY HAD HAD A FAMILY THEY WOULD HAVE BEEN SPENDING this Sunday afternoon with loved ones. And if they had had a television set they would have been watching the World Cup final on it, like the rest of the 25 million inhabitants of the country. Three of the men pressed portable radios to their ears and were transported by the broadcast from their loneliness and poverty, like a child is transported by the sound of the sea in a shell.

Juan-Cruz Otero sat on a bench near the equestrian statue of General Manuel Belgrano, the father of the flag, at the Government House end of the plaza. His elbows pressed into the flesh above his knees and a tingling of incipient numbness caressed his calves. He stared at the battered shoes that had covered hundreds of kilometers in a futile search for his wife in the week since he was released, dumped blindfolded on a moonlit country roadside. Against a background buzz of crickets he had been warned that if he talked of his abduction, he would be killed.

He had located the barren terrain just over the boundary of the federal capital where the *villeros* had been unloaded and where they had erected anew their clapboard dwellings. He had spoken with neighbors who could only tell him that Francisca had returned from the city one day, retrieved a bundle of clothes, bequeathed her bed and pots and pans to friends, and left. She had said only that she was going "with the Mothers of the Plaza de Mayo." That had been his only clue, and he had spent the past three days in the plaza waiting for her to appear.

He was trying hard not to look like a vagabond. Shabbiness could only bring him problems with the police. He had spent the previous nights in an abandoned freight car in the Retiro yard. Each morning he washed in the station's lavatory, slicked back his hair, buttoned the top button of his shirt and smoothed his ragged suit coat. On his way to the plaza he would pick up a discarded newspaper and make a pretense of reading it as he sat long hours on the bench.

A simultaneous whoop from two old men on adjacent benches toward the center of the plaza startled Juan-Cruz. The oldtimers stood and moved toward each other with shaky steps and embraced. One hopped delightedly twice before feeling the effect on his brittle bones. His newfound companion led him huffingly to a bench and the two men sat there beaming newly toothless grins.

Juan-Cruz got up and walked over to them. "What is going on?" he inquired.

"Are you from Mars, *muchacho?*" retorted one. "We just beat Holland! We're the champions of the world!"

The few cars transiting the city center honked their horns. The fire station two blocks up Rivadavia blasted its siren in a long scream and the balconies up and down the surrounding streets and avenues filled with people shouting and banging kettles.

The commotion frightened Juan-Cruz and he walked toward the Cabildo. But when he reached the far end of the plaza a column of hundreds of people waving flags and shouting and singing approached down Avenida de Mayo. He looked up the northern and southern diagonal avenues emanating from the square and was met with the same sight. People were pouring out of buildings and merging in a flash flood of humanity bearing down on the plaza. It was obvious there was no going against the tide, so Juan-Cruz turned and strode as fast as he could toward the opposite end of the plaza. But by the time he reached the statue of Belgrano a contingent of two hundred policemen had formed a barrier in front of Government House. The cops stood behind an iron-bar barricade linked together in sections like scaffolding. They held billy clubs and tear gas launchers at the ready across their chests.

Most of the policemen smiled, happy their country had won and knowing there would be no trouble with the festive crowd. But some were incapable of altering their practiced stony visage. It might have been the happiest day in the history of Argentina. But they were the federal police, after all. It was a matter of pride.

Within an hour the plaza was filled with more than 100,000 people. Juan-Cruz was trapped among the revelers near Government House. He could not escape.

A chant rose from the crowd.

> *Oh-le-le, Oh-la-la*
> *Si este no es el pueblo*
> *El pueblo, donde está?*

> *If this is not the people*
> *Then where is the people?*

A big red and silver touring bus escorted by siren-blaring motorcycle police pulled up from Alem Avenue and a frenzy swept across the crowd. The bus parked on Balcarce, right in front of the main entrance to Government House.

Alejandro and the rest of the players on the Casa Rosada side of the bus stood in the aisle and leaned across their teammates seated on the other side. The players opened the windows and stuck out their heads and arms and waved to the frantic horde.

"Ar-gen-tina! Ar-gen-tina!"

The chant was thunderous. The players joined in and the bus shuddered with the refrain.

The players all wore blue blazers and gray slacks, a kind of uniform they had been issued by the Argentine Soccer Association for official appearances. They filed quickly out and past the grenadier guards in colonial-era uniforms and high feathered hats. One of the presidential sentries, his bared saber lifted in salute in front of his face, was overcome by the moment and, forsaking the corps's tradition of reserve, shouted, "*Vamos todavía,* Argentina!"

Inside, it seemed that all three hundred employees of Government House were assembled to greet the team. Every one of the players, stars and bench-sitters alike, was besieged by clerks and colonels and secretaries and janitors.

A pretty girl planted a smacking kiss on Alejandro's cheek. He caught a glimpse of her before she was lost in the swarm of people trying to slap his back and pump his hand.

"All right! All right! All team members follow me," shouted a robust officer. The players and coaches disentangled themselves from the mob and followed him up a curving marble staircase. Their ascent was hailed by raucous applause.

The officer led them to a majestic cream and gilt salon. Fresco angels and veiled bathing maidens played across the ceiling. Luxurious Chinese rugs covered the floor. The officer lined the team up along the far wall. Menotti stood at the head of the file.

The door opened and President Videla entered alone and aglow. The smile overflowed and distorted his falcon face.

He shook hands with Menotti and stood talking with him for nearly a minute before moving down the line to shake hands with each of the players. He paused with Kempes and Passarella. He expressed his congratulations and gratitude in the name of the Argentine people.

Alejandro was almost at the end of the line. Videla congratulated Paganini at Alejandro's left then stepped sideways and extended his hand. Alejandro was mesmerized by the moment and by the depth and impassivity of the president's black eyes. Videla spoke and Alejandro listened deafly, astonished at the firmness of the grasp of the moist and bony hand.

By his third drink, Alejandro had developed a taste for whiskey; at least for Johnny Walker Black Label twelve-year-old Scotch whisky. The bottle sat almost empty on the low glass table. He, two other national team members and two army officers who had collared them at Government House promising "the night of their lives" sat around the table in various stages of inebriation. The officers' club was chic, as elaborately appointed as Regine's or Mau Mau, the capital's premier night spots. Golden mirrors arrayed on the walls reflected imprecise images from scattered love seats upholstered in a smooth, zebra-pattern cloth. A sphere sheathed in tiny mirrors hung above the few huddled couples swaying on the dance floor. The rotating globe sent fine bright beams swirling like a Flamenco dancer's skirt.

"Where's the bathroom?" Alejandro asked one of the officers over Sinatra's croon. He rose and unsteadily skirted the dance floor then turned down a short hall past the bar. As he stood relieving himself at the urinal, there came from the toilet stall behind him the sound of short and heavy breathing. The pants became gasps and the gasps culminated in a groan of delight. Alejandro zipped up his fly and turned around and, squatting slightly, saw two pairs of feet in the stall. The door opened and a short bald major in uniform emerged. His face was a mask of contentment.

"What a dusting," he sighed, then noticed the young man.

The girl, young and lovely, came out and bent over to smooth her stockings. She gently tugged the sheer fabric up from her ankles to her thighs. She lifted her skirt unabashedly up around her waist. She wore a blue satin garter belt and no panties. She unfastened and reclipped the stockings tautly. She smiled at Alejandro, but he did not see her smile.

"She's the best kid in the house, son," said the officer to Alejandro. "Too bad for you she's taken for the night. Rank does have its privilege."

Alejandro, unused to more than a glass of wine or two with meals, felt the whisky swell his head and breast. "No one outranks us today," he said.

"And who the hell are you, boy," demanded the major in a jocular tone that nonetheless carried the weight of his authority.

"One of the world champions," said Alejandro, and walked out of the bathroom. He could not cross the floor back to his seat because of the bulge in his trousers so he stood against the bar to wait for his longing to subside. The barman asked him what he wanted and he ordered another Scotch.

The major appeared at the other end of the bar and signaled to the barman. They huddled a moment. The officer looked across at Alejandro admiringly. The girl stepped from the darkness to the side of the major. He whispered up into her ear then jutted his chin toward Alejandro, who was staring self-consciously into the eddy of whisky and ice in his glass.

"Are you really one of the players?" Alejandro heard from behind him as slender hands lit on his ribs. "I don't care much about soccer, but I was rooting for you. We all were."

Alejandro turned.

"The major told me to give you a special congratulations."

Ale looked down the bar. The officer raised his glass in toast.

"You go with anyone the major tells you to?"

"He never tells me to go with anyone else. But this is a special day. And you are a very special person." She leaned lightly against him, barely brushing his chest with pointed, silk-sheathed nipples.

Alejandro looked into her hazel eyes. He suddenly sensed that if he did not take hold of her now, she would fade away.

"You're not going to congratulate me in the bathroom?"

"Oh, no. That's just one of the major's quirks. Come." She led him to a door marked DO NOT ENTER. She pushed it open and started up a narrow stairway. Alejandro watched her ascend. The light played softly off the white curves beneath her short skirt. She stopped halfway up and turned.

"Come on *campéon*. We're going to celebrate."

A wavering blade of grass tickled Alejandro's nose. A cold wind blew across the small of his back bared by the hike of his shirt. He lay face down in the front yard of his house. It was dawning. An hour earlier he had been deposited at the curb with a hearty drunken, "Ciao, Ace!" and he had stumbled a few steps toward the door before acquiescing to the beckoning ground. Oblivion had turned to deep sleep and he shifted against the earth now in a futile attempt to recover comfort. The itch of his nose and the icy fingers playing up his spine brought him around.

Santiago, who had knocked on Alejandro's door and been surprised that his son had not yet returned, stood on the terrace looking out over the treetops toward the river. The mantle of darkness lifted slowly and

Santiago was startled by a movement on the ground. It looked like a waking tapir groggily gaining his feet.

Santiago ran back inside, down the stairs and out the door into the yard to meet his staggering son. He braced Alejandro and they entered the house beneath a draped bedsheet banner—WELCOME HOME CHAMP!—made by Cristina and Monica. Alejandro's head throbbed. He did not see the banner.

He slept most of the day. When he awoke in the late afternoon his head still hurt. He thought of the girl and her cool flat belly. He remembered a waterbed, a mirrored ceiling, champagne in a silver bucket at the bedside. But there was a point beyond which everything was foggy or forgotten; blank time. He closed his eyes and saw the inside of a toilet bowl. His abdomen ached from retching and he tasted the trace of his bile in a dry and bitter swallow.

He showered then dressed in jeans and a white cotton dress shirt. His footsteps on the stairs signaled his descent and his mother jumped up from the couch. She ran to embrace him at the foot of the stairway.

"I'm so proud, I could burst," she said between hugs and kisses. Cristina stood behind her, radiating her own simpler sentiment. Santiago sat in an armchair and smiled at his son, understanding. Daniel slept on the rug, curled like a cat.

"Tell us all about everything!" squealed Monica, leading him into the living room. "Just think! An audience with the president in the Casa Rosada! Did he greet you all personally? What did he say?"

"He shook hands with all of us. I was kind of at the end of the line, with the other guys who didn't play, so he didn't have much to say to us."

"But he must have said something," insisted Monica, beside herself with elation and pride. "Oh, try to remember. Word for word."

"He congratulated us. Then he said something about football being like war. That not everyone is on the front line fighting and that the reserves deserve credit too."

On June 30, four days after the World Cup tournament ended, President Videla granted *El Grafico* magazine a rare and exclusive interview in Government House.

Q: *Though it is a question that you have been asked before,* El Grafico *would like you to express for its readers what you think the World Cup tournament meant for Argentina.*

Videla: The World Cup has a multiple significance. Firstly, it represented, for all the countries of the world, an imposing demonstration of organizational capacity. All that was done, in such a short time and with such efficiency, is a sample of what Argentines can do, on both the technical and human sides, when they put their minds to it and do it together. Secondly, the entire poplulation, without exception, contributed its happiness and legitimate fervor to the spectacle, showing itself at the same time hospitable and friendly to the visitors. They (the visitors) will be, without doubt, the faithful witnesses before their countrymen to our true reality, without the intentional defor- mation of an international campaign of lies. Finally, I want to underscore the emotional and patriotic content of the commu- nion lived in the homes and the streets, to the shout of "Argentina!" Sport, in this instance, was the means to express as never before the sentiment of national union and common hope for peace, unity and fraternity.

Q: *Could you recall for us a phrase, a dialogue, or a detail from your visits to the Argentine locker room?*

Videla: Yes. Something that remains profoundly engraved in my spirit. It was before a game. Upon entering the locker room, I found all the players praying. That touched me very deeply and I, as just another individual, joined in the prayer.

Q: *When you were young, as a boy, did you play soccer? What position?*

Videla: When I was very young I liked to play soccer and I played a lot. But it wasn't something regular, rather a sporting exercise with friends and schoolmates. I didn't have a regular position, but I always preferred midfield.

Q: *Were you a fan of a particular club?*

Videla: Without prejudice to the other clubs, I must admit that I was a fan of Independiente. It's a preference I've had since childhood. In those days the names were Bello, Lecea, Coletta, Sastre, Erico and other stars who wore the good old jersey of "the Reds of Avellaneda."

Q: In the wake of the World Cup, will sports in general and soccer in particular be an activity to which the government will pay more attention?

Videla: The government pays attention to and supports all athletic manifestations. It considers that they constitute a real school of virtue and ability, where the physical and spiritual unite for the formation of healthy and gentlemanly men. Soccer, within that framework, plays a very important role. And it deserves, as the organization and result of the World Cup has shown, the continued attention of the authorities.

Q: Are you aware that many of the players you congratulated for being world champions will soon be playing in other countries because our soccer system does not offer them adequate conditions?

Videla: The phenomenon of the transfer of players is not exclusively Argentine. We see it in all the countries of the world. There is a constant bidding, which we read about almost every day in the papers. It's not a matter of good or bad conditions, but rather of greater incentives in the form of very high pay. In the final analysis, everything depends upon the free decision of the players, because there is no doubt that, in a system of liberty such as ours, each person looks for the opportunity that best suits him.

Q: Mr. President, we ask you for a final thought.

Videla: We have been, for weeks, the most important focus of the world's attention. The mass media, especially television, have projected an authentic and vigorous image of the country. We are glad about everything that happened and the results obtained. But more than anything, we are encouraged by the *universal demonstration of a mature citizenry, capable of the greatest enterprise on the basis of unity and shared effort.*

Let this unity and effort continue, from today on, in every instance of common endeavor that we Argentines set for ourselves.

A navy guard escorted Santiago into Captain Roig's office.

"Sit down," instructed Roig, indicating a chair in front of his desk. There was no pretense of etiquette, no introduction, no handshake. The guard withdrew, his heavy bootsteps muffled on the Persian carpet.

Roig sat down opposite Santiago. A first phase of recognition altered the officer's expression from cold formality to curiosity. "I have seen you before," he said.

"I can't imagine where," responded Santiago.

The picture of a man leaping onto a stage flashed in Roig's mind. "Your daughter and my daughter are classmates at Highlands. I saw you at the Caledonian."

The coincidence, in its magnitude, was nearly incomprehensible to Santiago. But he sensed an inkling of its awful implications: that the terror is flesh and blood; it is your neighbor, it sits in the other pew in church, in the next row at the cinema.

"Small world," said Roig, breaking the silence. "Your friends exercise considerable leverage. Generally these matters are strictly secret, for reasons of national security."

"Where is my brother?"

Roig sat up straight and stiff. "It is my duty to inform you that the terrorist eventually identified as Diego Americo Maglione died in an armed encounter while resisting arrest the night of June fourteenth in the district of the federal capital."

Santiago dropped his head. After a moment, he raised his eyes to meet those of the officer. "That is a lie. My brother never held a gun in his life."

"I remind you that you are in a military institution and that the armed forces do not tolerate impeachment of their honor."

"I repeat: What you have told me is a vile lie. But that was to be expected. I demand my brother's body."

"You are in no position to demand anything. Because of your patronage, your insolence will go unchastised. But do not overestimate your degree of impunity."

"I am not leaving here without the body. I also want to know what happened to his wife, Ana Suarez."

"I have no information about any person of that name. As far as the body of Diego Maglione, it was cremated and the ashes disposed of administratively. But if you will come with me, I will put to rest any doubt you may have."

Roig rose and Santiago accompanied him down long corridors. With every corner they turned, Santiago felt he was being led deeper into an inescapable maze. They went through a pair of heavy swinging doors into a large room with white tile walls. At a marble-topped counter stood a man in a white smock.

"Wait here," ordered Roig, who disappeared with the employee down rows of high shelves of files and heavy bound books. The men reappeared after a few minutes.

Roig placed on the counter a white plastic bag, a sort of pouch drawn closed at the top with a cord. He pushed a cream-colored folder across the counter to Santiago.

"Here you have the autopsy report."

Santiago lifted the cover of the folder.

"You will see that the cause of death is massive trauma to the aortic artery inflicted by a single large-caliber bullet that traversed the body. Note also the official entry in the margin."

Santiago read the annotation: "Armed confrontation" partially covered by a seal of the naval high command and ratified with an illegible signature.

"Diego Maglione was only identified after disposal of his body, by means of fingerprints," said Roig. He opened the plastic purse and reached inside. He took from the bag a large jar with a screw-on lid, like those used for preserves. The jar was filled with foggy liquid. "A minimal portion of the body was retained for identification purposes," said Roig, pushing the jar across the counter to Santiago.

Santiago lifted the jar and looked into it. In it was a hand.

Roig assigned a marine with trousers tucked into his boots to escort Santiago back through the long corridors of the Mechanics School and past the reception desk, where all packages carried in or out by civilians were searched and where an unseemly scene might have arisen if the plastic pouch clutched to the breast of the glassy-eyed man were to have been examined.

Santiago walked to his car and got in. He placed the plastic bag on the passenger seat. He started the engine and waited a minute, then backed up and pulled toward the exit. As he sat at the exit, waiting for a break in the traffic that would allow him to pull out onto Liberator Avenue, he reached over and picked up the jar in the plastic pouch and put it between his thighs so it would not tip over.

He turned right, northward, as if he were heading toward his house. But before he had gone a kilometer he knew that was not where he wanted to go. He didn't have a destination. He stopped at a red light. He leaned forward on the steering wheel and his breast heaved as tears flooded his eyes. He lifted his head at the sound of the horns of cars lined behind him and put the car in gear. He drove ahead along the blurred avenue.

He turned off the avenue and drove down a tranquil, affluent sub-urban street, much like his own street, until he came to the river. He pulled the car onto the shoulder of the road and got out and walked across a stretch of cracked, red mud to the water. He sat down a meter from the edge and watched the ripples follow one another in an endless siege of the shore. He took the jar out of the plastic sack and unscrewed the lid. He poured the formaldehyde onto the ground beside him and looked into the jar.

The hand was open, the slightly curled fingers touching the bottom and the severed wrist near the mouth. It seemed to Santiago smaller and more delicate than his brother's hand, it seemed more like the hand of a child. He thought suddenly, "How do I know this is my brother's hand?" He reached into the jar, took hold of it and pulled it out.

Once he held the hand in his own, there was no doubt. It was cold and gray and dead, but it was Diego's. It was the hand he had taught to tie a shoelace.

Santiago stood and stepped into the water, sinking a few centimeters into the muddy bottom. The river washed around his ankles. He squat-ted and rinsed Diego's hand in the river, turning it over, washing off the mossy smell. He stood up and put the wet and rigid hand into the pocket of his wool coat then walked out of the river, across the hard clay strand. The muddy water squished from his oxfords.

He got back into the car and drove south, through downtown, through La Boca, up over the cess-smelling Riachuelo, and rumbled over the granite-block surface of Pavon Avenue. The tires beat a monotonous litany like a dirge into his head. Out past Adrogue he turned down a road lined with bare eucalyptus trees. He rolled down the window halfway and listened to the whiff of the tires against pavement and above that, faintly, the song of the fat brown *hornero* birds building their hanging mud houses high in the naked branches.

When he arrived at his parents' house he parked in the road and shut the door softly. They would be sleeping the siesta and he did not want to wake them until after he had done what he was going to do.

He walked back behind the house to Mikhail's workshop. The door creaked open. Santiago scuffed through sawdust to the far wall, against which leaned the garden tools. He took a shovel, its staff worn smooth as an old saddle, and went back outside.

The small jacaranda stood in its dirt-filled can. Santiago leaned the shovel against the side of the house and picked up the tree. He carried it to the center of the back yard and set it down there, where it would have ample room to grow. He retrieved the shovel and stomped it into the cold earth. He pried up hearty pieces, cutting down through the roots of pampa grass. His breath shortened as he struggled against the earth, against the world, wounding it with the shovel's blade.

When the hole was a half meter deep he tossed the shovel aside and fell to his knees. He took clumps of earth and crumbled the dirt away from the roots of grass. He sifted the soil through his fingers, he brought it to his face and smelled its fertility.

He reached into his coat pocket and took out Diego's hand. He placed it palm up in his palms and lifted it slowly, kissed it then laid it on a bed of sifted soil in the bottom of the hole. He stood and pulled the tree from the can. The roots and earth formed a ball, which he placed upon the open hand. He knelt and filled the space around the ball of roots, tamping the dirt with his hands.

"Every time I see a jacaranda flower, Dieguito, I'll know it's you, trying to tell me something." He blinked and tears fell into the dirt he pressed around the base of the tree. He wiped his nose and his dirty hand left a trail of snot and soil across his cheek.

"I just wish I knew what it is you're trying to tell me." He fell forward and pressed his face into the earth covering the roots of the small tree. "Oh, Diego, Diego," he sobbed. "What did they do to you?"

BOOK TWO

1
9
8
2

Santiago and Daniel stood on the edge of a high mesa and surveyed the expanse of scrub below, puffs of sage dotting the brick-colored earth. The banks of the distant river were a deep green that contrasted with the pastel plain like the track of a laden brush across a new canvas. In a far-off corral made of stacked fieldstone stood short, thick-necked horses. Near the corral was a house protected by a line of poplars tilted by the wind all at the same angle.

A sudden whoosh of rushing wind, the sound of a swinging saber above and behind them made the two men crouch and hunch their shoulders. The diving hawk passed overhead by a meter then planed out away from the mesa. The bird, without once beating its wings, rose again, banked and soared in a widening gyre.

Away to the left of the men was a hill called El Cerro de Los Pinos. A large wooden cross atop it stood out against the sky. Two brothers, Pierre and André Alaminat, French immigrants to Patagonia, had in 1914 strapped timbers to their backs and climbed the hill before leaving for their native land to fight the war to end all wars. They had planted their crosses and vowed to return to take them down. André came back to dismantle his. Pierre died at Verdun.

Bolls of cumulus clouds sailed leisurely across the sky.

"Should be good thermals," said Daniel.

"With those clouds, definitely," concurred Santiago.

Daniel turned and walked anxiously across the flat crest of the mount to where the hang gliders rested nose down, the wind rippling their blue and yellow sails. Santiago followed Daniel and helped him hoist his sail frame. Daniel's brown and sinewy arms flexed as he harnessed himself into the big kite. His heartbeat quickened—and, clutching the bar, he felt himself growing lighter.

"You're coming right after me?" asked Daniel above the wind.

"I'll be right behind you."

Santiago started back toward the edge. Then he stopped and turned.

"Don't go too high!" he shouted.

Daniel nodded.

Santiago walked to the cliffside and watched the boy shift his weight anxiously from one leg to the other. Daniel came running in long strides. When he reached the edge he launched himself out and over into the emptiness. He threw his legs back and pulled himself forward on the bar. His heart stopped for the second that transpired between the moment his feet left the ground and the sound of the sail snapping full of air. The fabric billowed and strained and he was aloft.

"*Dále!*" bellowed Santiago from the cliffedge. But Daniel could hear nothing above the racing wind. He could see nothing but the lilac-washed rusty earth two hundred meters below.

He stretched away from the mesa in a straight line, losing altitude imperceptibly. He banked slightly to the right and, as soon as he leveled out again, caught a rising thermal draft that pressed up against the sail and lifted him like a leaf.

Santiago, enthralled by Daniel's flight, stood on the cliff watching.

Daniel banked steadily and wheeled in a wide vertiginous spiral. He climbed fifty meters and leveled, he soared out of the draft in an enormous figure-eight.

He was completing the slow eight when he caught another draft and rose again. He climbed and climbed, then began to feel the strain in his biceps. He debated between heaven and earth. He banked and sailed and imagined he might stay aloft forever.

A hawk, perhaps the same one that had dived on them on the mesa, plummeted across his line of flight. His wings were trimmed for velocity, and he passed so close that Daniel saw his eyes.

Daniel's arms grew leaden and, as they did, the earth's call grew louder. He floated downward in long tacks and kicked up a burst of red dust with his first footfall. He ran as fast as he could, but he was carried forward faster than he could run. The nose of the kite dipped and crashed against the earth in the inevitably ungainly landing.

The sound of the wind was replaced by the thump of his heart, then his own wild laughter ringing out over the scrub desert. He unharnessed himself from the kite and looked up. He shaded his eyes and descried Santiago soaring above him.

When she came downstairs, Cristina found Soledad on her hands and knees on the kitchen floor, a bucket of sudsy water at her side. The woman swept bright swatches across the blue and white tiles with a wet woven cloth. She swabbed an arc before her then straightened up beside the bucket to dip the cloth in and wring it out.

"I'll help," said Cristina, grabbing another mop cloth from the closet. She knelt next to the woman.

"Don't bother yourself, dear," said Soledad.

"The two of us will finish in a shake." Cristina dipped her rag. "And the sooner we finish, the more time we'll have to study."

They cleaned the floor in a matter of minutes and sat down at a heavy wooden table along the windowed wall of the big kitchen. The first big drops fell outside and splattered on the concrete patio. The women raised their heads from the copybook and watched the raindrops fall faster and harder, dark spots overwhelming the blanched grayness of the concrete. The summer-ending storm had swirled from out of nowhere up around the hilltop. The brightness fled. The oaks and willows swayed and shook their heads.

The storm's commencement distracted the women a long while.

"I've forgotten how to say 'rain,' " said Cristina after some minutes had passed.

"It depends. There's one word for wind-driven rain, another for rain in sunshine, another for rain out of season."

Soledad was a Mapuche Indian. She had been raised on the reservation on the opposite shore of Lake Lacar and had worked for more than thirty years as a maid, cook and nanny for a succession of families in San Martín de los Andes. Santiago had had the good fortune to contract her shortly after he, Cristina and Daniel had moved south, to the house above the lake. Reflecting the sky, the deep lake stretched westward toward the snow-capped mountains, toward Chile.

Soledad was a thick, strong woman of soft speech. Her round face was a nut-brown and her brow was furrowed. From any angle her eyes were gleaming black but they warmed when they met Cristina's.

"Sometimes I think I shall never speak Mapuche well," lamented Cristina.

"You are right. You will never speak well. I don't even speak well any more. I mix in Castilian words. Sometimes I even dream in Castilian."

The rain fell hard then slackened. Soledad instructed Cristina in her language for an hour. The rain had nearly stopped and rays were piercing the clouds when Cristina rose.

"I have to go downtown," she said. She stood behind Soledad with her hands resting on the Indian woman's shoulders. She lifted her hands and gently stroked Soledad's thick black hair before bending down and kissing her on the cheek. "Thank you for the lesson," she said, then went upstairs.

Cristina went to Daniel's room and found him at his desk. He was huddled over a shadowed page, his forehead almost touching it. He did not hear her enter.

"I'm going down to the town," she said.

Daniel started at her voice. He pulled out the desk drawer reflexively, then swept the page into it with his forearm and shut it. He turned his chair to face her.

"Do you need anything from town?" she asked.

"I was just finishing something and was going to look for you."

"What are you writing?"

"A poem."

"A love poem?" She moved toward him.

"Sort of." He held his arms open to her and she walked into them and sat on his lap. She kissed him on the neck and cheek and ear. "Don't go to town," he said. "Santiago won't be home for another hour."

"Is it for me?" she asked, tapping the drawer with her finger.

"No."

"For your mother?"

He nodded. "Don't go to town."

"I have to and I want to. They depend on me to be there, just like I depend on them. You can come if you want."

"Forget it. But I'll walk down the hill with you." Cristina rose from Daniel's lap. He stood awkwardly, leaning slightly forward, his thighs pressed together. She laughed as he shifted.

"He's restless," she nodded at his crotch.

"He's a divining rod and you're a subterranean lake in a desert. He's got a mind of his own and he thinks about you all the time."

"And what about you?"

"Just most of the time."

He followed her out of the two-story timber and fieldstone house, down a path worn through the long yellow end-of-summer grass. The path led to a sharply inclined track that wound down the hill through a forest of dripping elms and oaks and sycamores. Vines hung like unkempt locks down to the ground.

The walked down the trail hand in hand, but released their grip at the sound of a motor struggling up the hill. Santiago appeared in a jeep and pulled to a stop alongside. He was smiling.

"Hi kids." Then to Daniel he said, "I got orders for two more kites."

"Great," replied the boy.

"Where are you going?" Santiago asked.

"I'm going to Lucia's house for a while. Dani's just walking me down the hill."

"You and Lucia are getting tight. Why doesn't she come up to the house sometime?"

"She's teaching me how to sew and the machine is heavy."

"Well, try to be home for dinner." Santiago pushed the shift lever forward and lurched away, up toward the house.

"What are you and Lucia sewing?" asked Daniel. "A big red flag?"

There was disgust in his voice. "You don't know how to lie. If you're going to lie, make up a better one. Or ask me and I'll make one up for you."

"I can't tell him, and you know it. So don't be so harsh."

They walked, their steps pressing silently into the wet along the track.

"You can't tell him anything. Not that you're another world-changer. Not that we're in love."

"It won't be long before he catches on to us, if he hasn't already. He's not blind."

Then, not ten meters in front of them, a silent tawny beast leapt down from a granite boulder. A puma.

Daniel and Cristina froze and the cat did the same. He stood broadside across the path, the muscles tense and sculpted in his haunch and shoulder. His head was turned toward them and his ears stood pricked—One flickered, his sole movement. He was so close they could see the long white whiskers sprouting like an old Indian's mustache beneath the triangular nose. They stood transfixed by his amber eyes. The pupils shone. The puma closed his eyes and the lids descended slowly, unconcerned, then rose again as slowly. He took a long step and bounded up into the wood, disappearing in a swish of fronds.

Cristina released the breath she had been holding during the animal's presence. Daniel ran forward a few steps and looked up into the forest where the cat had vanished.

"He's gone," he said and hugged Cristina.

"How do you know it's a 'he?' " she asked, craning away.

"Didn't you see it in his eyes? The loneliness?"

*   *   *

Saul Ubaldini, the leader of the beer brewers' union and nominal head of the General Confederation of Labor (Confederación General de Trabajo, CGT), extended his broad forearms across the tabletop and opened his thick hands palm up in a gesture of supplication. He wore a black leather jacket, a kind of personal trademark, despite the heat of the late summer afternoon. Ubaldini looked as if he were about to cry, his big features set in a caricature of sincerity. He was trying to make a point to Lorenzo Miguel, the lord of the Union of Metallurgical Workers, the largest and most powerful in the country. Miguel had spent two years under comfortable house arrest following the coup, and the dictatorship had "disqualified" him for any formal post in the labor confederation. But he still ran things.

Miguel sat back in his chair, his stubby legs extended under the table and his hands folded across his ample belly. A mane of white hair and white porkchop whiskers set off his tan and framed his clear gray eyes. Above him on the wall were three large photographs.

Juan Domingo Perón in his general's uniform, his breast bedecked with ribbons commemorating unwaged campaigns, stood narrow-eyed and smiling in the center portrait. To his right, his widow Isabel—at the moment enjoying a sunny and luxurious exile in Spain—pressed thin lips in a straight line. To Perón's left, deserving the biggest portrait, was the ever-radiant Eva, golden hair gathered at the back of her head, eyes flashing with the indignation, ambition, hatred and love that made her great.

Downstairs in the street, at the corner of Brasil and Saenz Pena, a sparse crowd of union officials, delegates, thugs, bodyguards and journalists was waiting for Miguel and Ubaldini to finish their conclave and emerge from the CGT headquarters. The men milled on the sidewalks and in the blocked-off streets. Among them, in distinct minority, were some hungry, jobless workers whose kids' crying or wife's jibing—or their pride and frustration—had prompted their presence.

The men talked nervously in small groups, glancing occasionally up at the balcony of the headquarters building where every five minutes someone appeared with a sky-blue and white flag. Waving it, he would begin to sing the Peronist march, or he would chant: "Now you see! Now you see! It's a glorious CGT!" But it did not appear too glorious at the moment, the CGT, the knots of men readying themselves for the march, especially compared to what they were up against. Because while the marchers waited for Ubaldini and Miguel, five thousand police and riot troops waited for the marchers.

The deployment was not conspicuous there at the corner. Some high-ranking police officers with gold braids on their blue caps stood beside patrol cars and talked into radio mikes. They were waiting for Ubaldini to come out so they could elbow up and officially inform him that the march was illegal, was going to be repressed and that he and the convoking authorities would be held responsible for any and all consequences. Riot troops—young men from the provinces—waited in armored vans a block away. In light blue fatigues and helmets and cradling tear gas launchers in their laps, they chewed gum and talked about girls or the weekend's soccer games or how they were going to kick Porteño ass.

Twenty blocks away, the Plaza de Mayo—the destination of the march—was surreally vacant. Sawhorse barriers surrounded it and more than a thousand police guarded the wooden frontier. Traffic was cut off around the square. Armored cars, paddy wagons and water cannon lined the streets. A few officers stood at the base of Belgrano's statue surveying the vast empty space, and for the first time appreciated its beauty. They could appreciate something only when they had it all to themselves.

The rallying slogan of this March 30 protest was "Bread and Work." It was sponsored by the CGT and a coalition of five political parties— the Peronists, Radicals, Intransigents, Christian Democrats and Developmentalists, who together represented three-quarters of the electorate. The national economy had been thoroughly mismanaged by the generals and their economy minister, José Martinez de Hoz, and each passing month produced more factory closings, more bankruptcy petitions, more locked-out workers banging on the company gates. Real wages had fallen more than a third since the coup, unemployment was at a 50-year high and there was no unemployment insurance. Because of this, the regime was vulnerable. It was not yet on the ropes, because its force of arms remained intact and loyal to President Galtieri, who seized every opportunity to declare that "the ballot boxes are well guarded" and advise his compatriots that civilian rule was a long way off. The parties and unions had decided that now was the time to press their claims, and they had called on the people to march to the plaza to demand Bread and Work.

Juan-Cruz Otero had heeded the call. He was in the street outside the CGT headquarters when Ubaldini and Miguel, preceded and followed by large men, stepped out of the building. A police captain made his way through the swarm of journalists jabbing microphones in the union leaders' faces. The officer did his duty and asked Ubaldini if he understood.

"Yes, sir," replied the brewer and he and Miguel linked arms with other unionists and started walking down Brasil, toward Santiago del Estero. Bass drums, the kind used in marching bands and the heartbeat of any Peronist rally, sounded their defiance.

Juan-Cruz fell in near the tail of the column. They marched down Brasil to Salta, where their further advance was blocked by a pair of water cannons and a line of troops. They turned left on Salta. When they had covered another block, another police officer approached the head-men and ordered them to desist. But the column advanced, past grocers' shops with windows full of stacked *damajuana* wine bottles, past yard goods stores, rubber stamp and stationery stores closed and shuttered in anticipation of the march and trouble. Residents of the old apartment buildings along Salta leaned out from their windows and stepped out on their balconies to cheer the marchers. Some shouted obscenities at the police.

The marchers proceeded along Salta, then turned down Independencia and turned again after a block onto the sprawling Ninth of July Avenue, the main north-south artery through the city center. Other columns of demonstrators converged on the avenue. The chants and drums and pop of canisters filtered down the boulevard through the gauzy haze of tear gas ahead. The column headed by Ubaldini and Miguel approached the statue of Don Quixote at the intersection with Avenida de Mayo.

The cast-iron man of La Mancha, his pointed goatee lifted by the wind, charged headlong on faithful Rocinante as if to exhort the march-ers to advance. The spurred stallion bared his teeth.

A line of riot police, clubs ready across their chests, advanced down the avenue toward the demonstrators. A pair of Ford Falcons careened from a side street and screeched to a halt in the dwindling space between the line of troopers and the marchers. Four plainclothesmen brandishing submachine guns burst out of each one.

"*Hijos de puta!*" shouted one as he pulled back the hammer of his square and snub-nosed weapon. He fired a burst of flashing staccato into the air. Uniformed police closed on the column from all sides. Some marchers broke ranks and fled. Some tripped and fell to be clubbed and collared by the police. The cops twisted arms, grabbed handfuls of hair and pressed their billies against the base of their captives' skulls. They shoved and kicked and punched their prisoners into paddy wagons. Ubaldini and Miguel and about seventy others, including Juan-Cruz, were surrounded in a compact knot in the middle of the avenue.

Then, from the south, a pack of a dozen horsemen approached at a full gallop, their crops and short whips flailing the air and the lathering haunches of their mounts. Hooves pounded the pavement in a terrifying clatter and the knot of marchers pressed more tightly in on itself.

Ball bearings! thought Juan-Cruz desperately. Then he shouted, "Ball bearings! Who brought the ball bearings?" But no one had foreseen this or provisioned himself with the only efficient means, short of firearms, of countering cavalry. The horsemen advanced, slowing the gallop to a canter, to a trot, and when they were just meters away from the thick huddle of demonstrators the riders reined their snorting, frothing mounts to a halt. Then the soldiers whipped the horses sharply and the animals plunged into the cowering crowd. The riders lashed out with whips and crops at the cringing demonstrators.

Juan-Cruz ran. He stumbled and dodged and jumped the curbs of the narrow mid-avenue islands of grass and benches and trees. He ran, bent forward, into the settling fine-mesh net of tear gas. Through the fog of battle came shouted orders and screams and the snap of rubber bullets against stone walls. He pulled the front of his shirt up over his nose and mouth and stopped to survey through stinging tears the blurry streetscape. The gas burned his nostrils and a thread of searing mucus trickled down his throat.

He looked down, blinking out tears, burying his face in the fabric of his shirt. He was standing beneath the statue of Quixote, but did not realize it, so it was incomprehensible to him why there should be encrusted in the sidewalk at his feet a plaque reading:

> *Bewitchment begone!*
> *And may God help truth and reason.*

Then Cervantes's exhortation was covered by a pair of boots, round-toed, thick and black. Before Juan-Cruz could raise his head he was whirled around. A big hand grasped his hair and pressed him forward until he ran into a wall.

"Spread-eagle! Hands high!" ordered the trooper. "Move and you'll be shot."

Juan-Cruz stood, his burning head bowed, feet spread and palms against the wall. A chorus of coughing told him he was part of a row of people in that same posture along the wall. Next to him was a middle-aged woman, her multicolored woven nylon shopping basket on the sidewalk between her feet. Artichokes pointed their acorny heads out of the basket and spoiled in the settling gas.

There was a commotion on the sidewalk behind Juan-Cruz. He craned his neck and peeked over his shoulder.

"I am a businessman, an executive, and I assure you, *Señor agente,* that I have nothing to do with these people," protested an older char-coal-suited man to a young soldier.

"I don't give a fuck who you are," said the soldier, wincing back tears. "Shut your mouth and spread-eagle against the wall." He gave the man a strong shove against the chest with his horizontal nightstick. The businessman retreated from the blow, astonished. Blood flooded his pallid, tear-streaked face.

"Have you no shame?" shouted the man, his spit flying. He grabbed the soldier's club and tried to wrestle it away. The two men struggled. The height and righteous rage of the civilian were more than the soldier could handle. The businessman wrenched the club away and waved it menacingly.

"Now let's see what kind of *macho* you are," he challenged the trooper, who was already lifting the flap of his holster to extract his pistol.

Juan-Cruz, from the moment the hand had clenched his hair, was certain he was on his way again to the torture chamber. The suffocating, chest-pressing gas recalled the panic of immersion, of drowning. He was determined, as only a man who has experienced torture can be, not to be tortured again. The businessman's resistance provided the diversion he needed.

He bolted and ran in a zigzag, expecting a report and a hammer blow in the back. But it did not come and he rounded the corner onto Alsina.

He ran up Alsina, away from the avenue. His lungs hacked through the dissipating gas. His legs ached. He ran until he could run no more. He stopped and bent over, his hands on his knees, and panted violently.

He looked behind him and around. No one was after him. No one was on the street. He looked down into the eyes of a skinny, big-headed dog whose coat was worn to the skin in spots. He held in his jaw a glistening blue and white joint fresh from the butcher. The old dog looked inquisitively up at Juan-Cruz. He dropped the bone and hobbled a step forward to slobber on his shoes.

IN THE MAGLIONE HOUSEHOLD UP ON THE HILL, THEY DID NOT LISTEN TO THE EARLY MORNING RADIO. SO CHRISTINA AND DANIEL DID NOT KNOW WHAT ALL THE FUROR WAS ABOUT, WHEN, UPON APPROACHING THEIR school, they saw flags and banners dancing above a cheering crowd of students swarming around the entrance.

"Ar-gen-tina! Ar-gen-tina!" the students shouted in unison, and it occurred to Daniel that Passarella or Kempes or Fillol must be inside, that one of the stars of the national team (maybe Alejandro!) must be visiting the school on some kind of tour of Patagonia prior to the team's trip to Spain.

"*Qué pasa?*" asked Daniel, tugging the sleeve of one of the kids on the mob's fringe. The boy turned, his pimply face red with euphoria, his eyes wide and alight as if he had witnessed the Virgin Mary descend to earth before him.

"The Malvinas! We took the Malvinas back from the English!"

"What?" Cristina looked at the boy incredulously. "What do you mean we took them back?"

"Just what I said. Our marines landed and the English marines surrendered and we hauled down the pirate flag and ran up the blue and white. They're ours again! After a hundred fifty years!" The boy turned and pressed back into the crowd, which throbbed and heaved with adolescent intensity. The students jumped up and down, shouting in rhythm, "*El que no salta es un inglés!*" ("He who doesn't jump is an Englishman!")

It took the principal, Mr. Grosso, who had fought his way to the top step, a full minute of yelling through a megaphone to quiet the tumult.

"This is the most glorious day of the century!" he shouted. "*Viva la patria!*"

The crowd of three hundred responded with a scalp-tingling "*VIVA!*"

"Classes are suspended in recognition of this tremendous day," informed the principal. "But we are going to participate in our own way, and to that effect fourth- and fifth-year students are to gather in the auditorium for assembly."

The crowd thinned out with the reluctant withdrawal of the youngest pupils. More than a hundred of the older students made their way through the school's high arched entrance and down the hall to the auditorium. They sat down restlessly.

The aspiring politicians among them, those active in the youth branch of the provincial populist party—the Neuquén Popular Movement—or the Juventud Peronists, those who had experienced the electric thrill of ovation at rallies disguised as dances or debates, were already formulating speeches full of rhetoric they had memorized from their texts. When Mr. Grosso opened the assembly to the floor and invited comment on the significance of the moment, a dozen hands shot up and waved, stirring the buzz and hum. The principal, a lifelong stalwart of the NPM, called on Carlos Díaz, the son of one of the movement's biggest contributors.

The boy stood. "This heroic deed allows us as Argentines to hold our heads high again in the eyes of the world, because we have thrown off the yoke of an arrogant colonialism that has stained our national honor for generations. This day is comparable only to those glorious days of the past century when brave *criollos* fought to forge the nation that has given our lives meaning. It demonstrates the courage and indomitabil . . ."— he flushed and struggled with the word and spit it out—"indomitability of our national character, traits that we, as the youth of the fatherland, are charged with guarding for generations to come. *Viva la patria!*"

The hall shook with an explosive "*Viva!*"

Mr. Grosso recognized Matias Maranzano, a big jowly boy. At the age of eighteen his hair was receding and he laughed only when required to.

"*Compañeros*. I have nothing new to say. But in this moment when we have taken the clay of history into our hands I want to recall the words of General Perón, who taught us that the option is national liberation or dependence. This redemption of our birthright, claimed with the blood of patriots, must serve as the realization of the fatherland as a protagonist in world affairs, a standard-bearer for oppressed and exploited nations. Lastly, I cannot let pass this opportunity to salute and congratulate the armed forces of the nation, which though they have been our occasional opponent, have shown themselves once again, as in the era of San Martín and the era of Perón, a reserve of patriotism capable of achieving the grandest objectives by interpreting the essence of our national being. *Viva la patria!*"

Cristina twisted in her seat. Her heart thumped like that of a snared hare, her breath came in gulps. Her fingers and toes tingled. She had not spoken before so many people since that day, four years previous, of her disastrous recital of Yeats. She found it difficult even to express herself calmly in front of the dozen members of the socialist students' cell, and the idea of standing before this crowd terrified her. But what she had to say was greater than her fear and she raised a trembling hand. Daniel looked at her with astonishment.

Mr. Grosso was glad to give a girl a chance after the interventions of two boys.

Cristina stood and began hesitantly, her words clipped by the constriction of her chest and throat. "*Compañeros*," she began. "There is no doubt that this is an important day."

"Louder!" shouted a boy from the back. Cristina began again and her attempt at volume cracked the words and she thought for a moment she was going to sit down and cover her face. But the moment passed and her lungs finally filled and she called out, "*Compañeros*. This is an important day. But its importance resides not so much in what already has happened as in the promise the day holds. What I mean to say is that whether the day is great or not depends on what we make of it. Because this is obviously just the beginning of something. And it is up to the people, not the armed forces, to realize the potential of this day."

Daniel, when he heard the word *people,* sat forward on the edge of his seat and tapped Cristina's thigh. But she was just gaining momentum, like a bicycle going downhill when the rider stops pedaling, to feel the pull of a force much stronger than that in his legs.

"Because pears don't grow on elms!" she said, almost shouting now. There, she thought, that's what I wanted to say, and she paused to feel the strength of her pounding heart. During the pause she discovered she had more to say.

"There is every reason to be cynical. Just three days ago the capital was a battlefield. The police beat, gassed and arrested thousands of people demanding recognition of their dignity. The regime is anti-popular and pro-imperialist. It cannot become overnight anti-imperialist and the champion of the people. But if the people rise to this occasion and seize this opportunity, it is not going to work out as the generals imagine. It may well backfire on them. Because the people in its entirety is not easily fooled."

"Red!" shouted a boy to Cristina's right. She ignored him. The buzz above the students' heads had thinned and dissolved to a silence punctuating the spaces between her words.

"It is true that imperialism exists—or existed—in the Malvinas. But it exists to a much greater degree in the heart of our country, right there in Buenos Aires, in the form of foreign banks and corporations, ambassadors who tell us what we must and must not do. The junta, if it really wanted to deal a blow to imperialism, did not have to send a fleet all the way to the Malvinas to do it."

Daniel tugged at Cristina's elbow. The auditorium simmered in silent tension. The students glanced furtively at one another, many of them almost expecting the doors to burst open to admit machine-gun-wielding soldiers who, they had over the years been led to believe, were ever-present, even if unseen, and programmed to react at the pronunciation of words like those coming from this gesticulating girl.

Mr. Grosso hurried out from behind the podium and stood at the edge of the stage.

"That's enough! That's enough!" he boomed through the megaphone.

Daniel grabbed Cristina's arm and jerked her roughly down into her chair. The students in the rows in front of them all craned around, their elbows over the backs of their chairs, to watch Cristina and wait for her to say something else or do something. Those to either side leaned forward and looked down the row at her, those behind stretched up to watch her.

"All right. Who else?" Mr. Grosso shouted through the megaphone. "Who else wants to say something about the recovery of the Malvinas?"

Cristina looked down at her hands clamped over the hand of Daniel and pressed the three hands tightly between her knees.

The waiter was not a midget, but he was not far from it. He was the height of a grammar school boy but at least fifty years old, and formal. He called Daniel "gentleman" and Cristina "miss." His starched white apron was tied in a big bow at the back of his narrow waist and it swayed just centimeters above the floor as he walked, his thick black shoes darting out from beneath it. His cap was of folded brown paper in the design of those used by old-time movie ushers, the kind of cap that can be folded flat and stuck under an epaulet or in a pocket. A milky cataract clouded one of his eyes.

Daniel had pushed himself half out of his chair and was leaning across the table to kiss Cristina when the waiter approached with a bottle of mineral water. The little man swerved sharply, but as inconspicuously as possible, away from the table. The kiss was quick and the doll-like man turned back toward the couple and placed the bottle on the table.

Cristina laid her arm across the table palm up. Daniel took her hand and she squeezed it and gave a tired smile. Only now, in the evening, was she able to relax. All day the tension and exhilaration of the scene in the auditorium had coursed through her. Afterward, outside, had come the loud reproach of some classmates, the quiet congratulations of a few and the silent stares of most.

Daniel squeezed her hand. Looking at her now, it was hard for him to believe she was less than a year older than him, though it always had been difficult to think of her as being of any certain age.

But her face was changing. It had already changed some. It had slowed down. Her expressions took shape more gradually. Her eyes did not dart but glided to their object. She even seemed to blink slowly, like a lioness or an owl, not from fatigue but from some inner assuredness that she need not harry herself.

Daniel's study of her countenance was interrupted by the arrival of Virgilio Torlaschi, a classmate and friend of Cristina.

"May I sit down?" he asked excitedly, his eyes wide under a cascade of blond curls.

"Sure," said Cristina, lifting her bookbag from the chair next to her to make room.

"I called your house twice, but the señora who answered didn't know where you were or when you'd be home, and I was worried something had already happened."

"What do you mean, that something had happened?" asked Cristina.

"You really went overboard in school this morning. This is still a dictatorship, you know. Ramón drills caution into us. Now you have marked yourself. I've just come from talking to him and he says that at least for a few weeks you can't attend the meetings. He said the other teachers at the assembly talked of almost nothing but you afterward and that most of the comments weren't flattering. He thinks you're likely to be placed under some kind of surveillance."

Daniel clenched his fists under the table. A bilious clot rose in his throat.

"But what I said had nothing to do with Marx or socialism," she protested, her voice a strained, indignant whisper. "Every political party in this country condemns imperialism. What was so objectionable?"

"Lots of 'people' in your speech, compañera. That's a word they don't like. And you called the armed forces pro-imperialist. You got carried away."

Cristina's anger was invaded and diluted by the harbinger of fear. It was not fear yet, but she knew it would come and its intimation was enough to chase the serenity she had been feeling minutes earlier.

The waiter, his long apron swaying, waltzed to the table and set down a steaming plate of puchero; a stew of potatoes, carrots, cabbage, sausage and chicken.

"Is the gentleman going to dine?" he asked Virgilio.

The boy appraised the dish. "It looks good," he said.

"Here. Take this," said Cristina, passing him her plate and silverware. "I've lost my appetite."

*   *   *

The invasion of the islands saddened the fans of Tottenham Hotspur.

There was a clear state of belligerence between Britain and Argentina, diplomatic relations were severed, and that meant Osvaldo Ardiles, Tottenham's star midfielder and one of the team's most popular players since joining it three years earlier, had to go home.

Ardiles, a slight and gentle man, was extremely nervous before the beginning of the semifinal for the English Cup against Leicester on April 3, the day after the invasion and occupation of the Falklands. When he stepped onto the field and thousands of voices joined in a spontaneous rendition of "God Save the Queen" for his exclusive benefit, he doubted the wisdom of having appeared. But then, as soon as the song finished, a chant rose up on other voices and Ardiles could not believe his ears. At first he thought it must be a small but vocal and audacious contingent of his countrymen. But then he realized there could not be that many Argentines in all of Britain, or all of Europe for that matter. The chant was too strong and too loud. He looked up and around incredulously and when he realized what was happening, that thousands of Tottenham fans were chanting "Ar-gen-tina! Ar-gen-tina!" he had to cover his face with his hands. The Spurs, as the Tottenham fans call themselves, had draped a big banner from the grandstand reading, KEEP THE ISLANDS. JUST LEAVE US OSSIE.

During the game, every time Ardiles touched the ball the Leicester fans shouted "Eng-land! Eng-land!" only to be answered by a cheer for Argentina from the Spurs. Ardiles played as a man possessed. Tottenham won, 2–0.

The next day, before boarding a flight for home, Ardiles was interviewed by a British television team. He told the interviewer: "This is one of the saddest and most difficult moments of my life. I never talked about the Malvinas with my British friends and teammates, because I know you cannot understand how much the islands mean to us. We have right on our side, but I also do not want to offend you, the British people, who have been so overwhelmingly kind to me. I am very sad. But sometimes one has to make a choice, and in this case the choice is clear. I am an Argentine. Good-bye and thank you."

He tried to swallow, and coughed, then walked off to embark on his journey.

*　　*　　*

There were lots of changes to be made in the islands now that they were under Argentine jurisdiction. For one, the new authorities decreed that traffic would circulate on the right. Work details were supplied with buckets and brushes and the draftees painted big yellow arrows indicating the proper direction in each lane. But the islanders were a stubborn lot—stubborn as only the most insular men of an insular race, as headstrong as Orkneymen and Shetlanders—and some demonstrated their defiance by continuing to drive on the left. Thus head-on confrontations (not collisions; the islanders were obstinate but not stupid) between Kelpers and Argentine tanks, personnel carriers and jeeps were commonplace.

Some of the islanders commented that the issue of driving on the left or right was not of great importance, as the heavy tanks and half-tracks were quickly ruining the roads and there would be no driving at all before long.

Place names also posed a problem for the new authorities; the capital, Port Stanley, was a case in point. Of course it had to be changed. But to what?

First they named it Puerto Rivero, after Antonio Rivero, a gaucho who accompanied Luis Vernet, the Malvinas' first governor, to the islands with a group of Argentine settlers and a herd of livestock in 1829. But only a few days passed before a history student pointed out that Rivero, upon returning to the mainland after a few years on the islands, had dedicated himself to cattle rustling, and perhaps did not deserve the honor of having the town named for him.

So the town was named Puerto Giachino, after Corvette's Captain Pedro Giachino, the marine infantry officer who was the only soldier, Argentine or British, to die during the Argentine occupation of the Falklands. He died shortly after dawn on April 2, a casualty of the battle for the residence of British Governor Rex Hunt, where most of the forty British marines stationed on the islands had regrouped the previous night after London informed Hunt that invasion was imminent.

The Argentine high command had ordered that every effort be made to avoid the shedding of British blood, military or civilian, during the takeover. The idea was that if no British blood was spilled the British would be denied a significant and exploitable emotional pretext for reacting with undue force. It was a good idea, and it was carried out. No British soldier or civilian was harmed during the operation.

That was not because the British marines did not resist. They doggedly defended the governor's residence for nearly three hours. The defeat of dozens of soldiers determined to fight is no mean task if you are not allowed to shoot them.

With first light shrouding the horizon, Giachino and his four-man patrol had crawled, scrambled and run to the side of the Hunts' residence and entered. Lieutenant García Quiroga shouted in English that the building was surrounded, that resistance was futile and requested the marines' surrender. There was no answer. The patrol made its way cautiously down a corridor that gave onto a patio. When Giachino and García Quiroga stepped onto the patio they were struck by fire from a MAC machine gun. Giachino was wounded by a bullet that entered high on his right thigh.

The rest of the patrol retreated into the hall for cover. The two wounded officers lay on the patio. They shouted for the medic, and another brave Argentine soldier, corpsman corporal Ernesto Urbina, scrambled into the open to try to aid them. He too was fired upon and wounded in the abdomen, but not before he injected Giachino with morphine.

The British marines expended several thousand rounds of ammunition and did not surrender until more than two hours later, when other contingents of Argentine forces arrived at the residence and it became clear to Hunt that continued resistance would only cause useless bloodshed.

Most of Giachino's blood had already seeped from a severed femoral artery during the two hours he lay on the patio floor.

When fire ceased, Argentine troops recovered the three wounded men, loaded them in a jeep and rushed them to the Stanley Hospital. Navy Lieutenant Doctor Arturo Gatica and a British civilian doctor worked on the comatose Giachino for nearly an hour, but it was too late.

Back on the continent, Giachino was hailed as a hero. One of the most poignant photographs of the war was that of his angelic blond eight-year-old daughter Vanesa, her eyes heavy-lidded from weeping, in the pew next to her mother at the funeral mass in Puerto Belgrano on Saturday, April 3.

There was a footnote to the brief biography of Giachino published following his death. The fine print noted that, following the coup of March 24, 1976, he had provided "outstanding service in anti-subversive operations." Then, for nearly two years, he had been personal bodyguard and trusted confidant of Admiral Emilio Massera—navy commander, junta member, ideologue and strategist of the "dirty war."

For a reason never made public, someone decided after a few days that the name of the Malvinas' capital would not be Puerto Giachino. And it was decreed that the name of the town henceforth would be Puerto Argentino.

ALL THE PLAYERS HAD LEFT THE FIELD EXCEPT ALEJANDRO. HE STOOD NEAR THE PENALTY SHOT SPOT IN FRONT OF THE FAR GOAL WITH HIS BACK TO THE SETTING SUN. HIS LONG SOCKS WERE FALLEN IN DAMP BUNCHES around his cleat tops. His shadow stretched out before him and he remembered how as a child he used to stand like that in the late afternoon and imagine himself, as tall as his shadow was long. He had wanted to grow up fast. Now it seemed it had happened too fast.

Another shadow appeared next to his. It stretched out even further.

After a minute Menotti said, "There are lots of ways of fighting for your country."

Alejandro did not look at him. They both looked ahead and Ale smelled the pungent smoke of the coach's cigarette.

"This is soccer and the other is war. But both are for the country."

Alejandro did not say anything and the two stood side-by-side, looking across the field, past the steadfast line of eucalyptus, past the pastures and fenced plots, toward the near and invisible sea.

The team that was going to Spain in May to defend the World Cup had been gathered at the secluded training camp outside Mar del Plata since mid-March. Kempes, Passarella, Fillol, Ardiles (once he arrived from London) and the others from the 1978 team were there. Some from that squad were not on this one, and others who had not shared that glory were, like Maradona, Trossero and Van Tuyne.

Alejandro had been waiting for this for four years. He had been dreaming of this while playing for Boca, while taking courses at the university, while doing his year of obligatory military service. Waiting and dreaming; because this time he was going to play. And they were going to win again and his play would be part of the affirmation of Argentine soccer as the undisputed best in the world, like that of Brazil in the sixties.

"I appreciate it, César," said Alejandro finally. "I know you're trying to find a way to say you could arrange it so I don't have to go, and you can't find the way to say it. But there really is no choice. My unit got recalled and I'm part of it. We who just got out are the trained ones. I mean, they can't send the kids drafted two months ago." He wiped the chilled sweat off his face with the front of his sweatshirt. "Sometimes it's hard to keep things straight. The game is such a big part of our lives."

Menotti took a deep drag on his cigarette and kept staring ahead. When the knot in his throat loosened enough for him to talk he said, "With guys like you, how can we lose?" and put his hand on the younger man's shoulder and turned with him. The two men walked like that, toward the big Tudor chalet where the team slept and ate. And Menotti swore to himself: We will win the Cup again and when we do I'll dedicate it to the Argentine people and to him. He could picture himself with the reporters, holding the gold trophy aloft. "To a man who could not be here, but who is with us in spirit. For Ale Maglione, citizen, soldier and soccer player."

The light from the full moon was so bright it seemed to fall in pieces onto the lake. Dancing black wedges of water smashed the light into slivers that the wind snatched off the surface and extinguished, but not before they blinked their brightness skyward.

Daniel and Cristina sat on a big dished rock on the cliff edge and looked out over the lake. This was their spot. They had spent many hours together here. They had seen the lake like this before (not exactly like this, because the lake is like the desert in that it disposes of few elements but never arranges them in the same way twice). They had seen it frozen and purple and shining like polished stone. They had seen it calm and fathomless blue, gray and frothing and cruel.

Cristina rested her head on Daniel's shoulder. She rolled her head back and looked up into the sky.

"The Mapuches believe the moon is a window," she said.

Daniel looked up at the moon. He saw in it the suggestion of a face.

"When their god had made the earth, he made one of the spirits of the sky into man and put him on the earth. The mother of the spirit who had become man was very sad at her son's departure from the sky. She missed him so much that she cut a window in the heavens to look through at him."

"And so he could look up at her. She knew he missed her too," Daniel said.

They sat like that, her head on his shoulder, listening to the wind rush through the pines and cypresses above and behind them. It was only in these moments that Daniel could contemplate without horror the path that had brought him here. With Cristina here beside him he could step to the edge of the lake, look down and not be afraid of falling and not feel the urge like a heavy hand on his back to leap. Secure for the moment, he could not see down into the depths. He knew it was deep. He knew all that was below on the cold black mucky bottom of the lake. But he did not fear it. Not now.

A portion of Daniel's life was shrouded. He could not recall the disposition of his family's home in La Boca—what room one entered from the hall, where the kitchen or bathroom was in relation to the bedrooms—despite having spent his entire childhood there. He had wanted to remember, and the gaping hole in his past had added to his anguish during their first two years in the south. He had lain in his bed through the hours between midnight and dawn trying hard to conjure images from his short, shattered life.

The psychiatrists, the array of specialists to which he had been subjected for two years before finally, absolutely refusing to continue, had told Santiago not to worry about the partial amnesia, that it was normal in such cases, that the boy's memory would return someday. But Dani had wanted to remember, and the doctors could not help him.

Cristina could. She was able to help him, it seemed, without even trying. From that night nearly two years ago when he had risen from his bed in surrender to utter despair, and stolen into the quiet dark hall. He had not known if he was trying to go to Santiago's room, for the embrace and caress that did not really ease the pain but somehow made it fleetingly bearable. He had not known if he would walk out into the snowy night to lay down in a drift and wait for the stinging, fine powder to numb him forever.

But he had stopped at Cristina's open door. He went to her bedside and studied her peaceful head on the pillow, a strand of hair across her face. He touched her cheek. She roused and opened her eyes slowly, her expression not that of a wakened child, that turning down of the mouth in fright or petulance, but one of wonder, then recognition and, finally, understanding. She had smiled, barely, and lifted the covers, pushing herself back to make room. Since that night, they had spent few nights apart.

Maybe Santiago knew. Maybe not. Perhaps one night he had risen and, for some reason, gone to look in on Daniel and found the bed empty. Perhaps he had looked around the house, calling in a whisper his nephew's name, expecting to find him in the kitchen or maybe even sitting in the living room by the big window as if waiting for someone. Not finding him anywhere, maybe he had peeked into his daughter's room to see them entwined and serene. Maybe he had looked on them for a long moment of melancholy before being overcome by contentment, thankful that a measure of grace had finally befallen them.

Because of Cristina, Daniel had been able to pull himself up out of the hole and see the rest of his life spread before him in myriad paths. Because of her he was here now, sitting on a rock, looking down on the black and silver lake.

An owl hooted and launched itself from a cliff-rooted pine.

"Maybe Ana is looking down through the window at you right now," said Cristina quickly, but not quickly enough, for before she could finish a lump rose in her throat. She buried her face in Daniel's lap. She quivered and Daniel enveloped her.

"Don't cry, *mi vida, mi corazón,*" he pleaded, rocking her. "Don't cry for me. I'm all right now." He turned his face to the sky and saw a face in the moon. Even though he was all right now—really, finally all right—he cried now at feeling Ana so present, that she should be able to see him so in love.

"Come on, come on, *mi amor,*" he said, lifting Cristina's head. Seeing his tears renewed her sobs. Squeezing her he said, "Don't be a jerk." Then he held her at arms length and smiled. "Don't you see that I'm happy. It's because I'm happy that I'm crying." He pulled her to him tightly and hugged hard. Laughter came up from deep inside. It spilled out, shaking him and her. She began laughing too, first a sniffling cough of a laugh but then real laughter and both their heads turned toward the sky.

*   *   *

Galtieri was nervous but he tried not to show it. His tongue was dry and his palms were moist. But this was a grand moment, the grandest, and hadn't he always affirmed that "The best in me comes out in trying moments and adversity" and repeated it enough to make it true?

Nonetheless, he was nervous. But the half a million people outside, just outside, braced him with their chants and banners and flags. Only minutes ago he had stepped to an upper level window and, keeping himself hidden behind the curtain—they were calling for him but he would not give them that yet—had surveyed the multitude overflowing the plaza. Even so, even with their reinforcement, he was having second thoughts about the sword, the ceremonial dress saber that was part of his uniform as commander-in-chief. Now he fidgeted with it. It would have been a dashing touch if he were receiving a Latin American general, or even head of state. But Alexander Haig was a United States general, four stars, former supreme commander of Allied forces in Europe.

"And a combat veteran," Galtieri thought nervously. And he, Haig, was going to be in civilian clothes, stylish ones at that. No, the sword was too much.

The assembled protocol players, the officers and diplomats, surreptitiously studied the president as they waited in the foyer at the north end of Government House for the arrival of the limousine from the Foreign Ministry.

Galtieri unhooked the saber from the clip on his belt and handed it to his aide-de-camp. In an unspoken soliloquy, the president cursed his bad luck at not having met Haig during his last trip to Washington, the previous November, when he was army commander but not yet president (before he elbowed aside the baggy-eyed General Viola).

Now that had been a great trip, he recalled self-importantly. He had been feted and flattered. "A majestic personality," had opined National Security Council Chairman Richard Allen. "Very impressive," was the appraisal of Defense Secretary Caspar Weinberger. *Newsweek* had called him "Argentina's General Patton" and Galtieri had been hugely enthused at the comparison. Ever since seeing the film, he had found in his own craggy features a striking resemblance to George C. Scott.

And Galtieri (even as he reminisced he referred to himself in the third person) had fulfilled their expectations and responded in kind to their compliments.

"Argentina and the United States march side-by-side in the ideological war being waged in the world," he had said in his toast at a State Department gala. He could not remember what had prevented Haig's presence at the event. What a pity he hadn't been there.

He worked an English phrase over and over in his head. He had learned enough to get by during two courses with U.S. military instructors, one in the Canal Zone and another at Fort Belvoir, Virginia, but had forgotten most of it by now.

"Thank you for coming, General. I hope we will talk as one soldier to another," he repeated to himself in the midst of the pomp and anticipation, his lips moving slightly.

Then he heard the sirens. The motorcade wailed past the Central Post Office on Leandro Alem and veered up Rivadavia toward the plaza. Galtieri stepped out beneath the arched and columned portico. A blaring black Ford Fairlane carrying security men, and four ranks of motorcycle police—two abreast—preceded the limousine. Another Fairlane and a like number of motorcyclists followed.

The crowd between the north wing of the Casa Rosada and the National Bank parted. Haig's limo swept up the ramp to the entrance and stopped. The rear door opened and Costa Mendez's polished mahogany cane emerged. The bald, dapper, lame aristocrat stepped out. The foreign minister hobbled to one side to clear the path for Haig. The secretary of state got out and strode straight ahead, seemingly oblivious to the thunderous chant: "Ar-gen-tina! Ar-gen-tina!"

Galtieri snapped to attention. He checked an impulse to salute and extended his hand, as did the U.S. secretary. The president's tongue was thick and dry, but he unburdened himself of his phrase.

"That's what I am here for," replied Haig.

Galtieri wanted frankness. The secretary was only too disposed to provide it. As they ascended the white marble stairway to the presidential office on the second floor, Haig commented in an offhand, ice-breaking manner on the beauty of Buenos Aires, its architecture and parks and plazas. He said that what little he had seen reminded him of Paris.

"Thank you, General," replied Galtieri haltingly. "It is a lovely city. Only during these past years have we been able to enjoy it with tranquility, thanks to our victory in the war against subversion."

"War?" said Haig, mounting without pause the polished steps. "From what I hear, that was more like a witch hunt. You don't know the meaning of war. But if you don't come to your senses, you will soon find out."

Galtieri stopped and stared at Haig, a step above him. The Argentine could not find any words.

"Am I speaking too fast for you?" inquired the secretary, who, before Galtieri could respond, commanded the intervention of his interpreter, an attractive Cuban-American woman standing beside the dumbfounded president.

"It is not necessary," stammered Galtieri in a thick accent. "*Entendí. Entendí.*"

They resumed their ascent.

For the U.S. delegation, the first round of talks at Government House included Haig, Undersecretary for Latin American Affairs Thomas Enders and Special Ambassador General Vernon Walters, a former assistant director of the Central Intelligence Agency, fluent in Spanish and chummy with dozens of South American military commanders, especially those with political appetites. Present for the Argentines were Galtieri, Costa Mendez and the navy and air force commanders, Admiral Jorge Anaya and Brigadier Basilio Lami Dozo.

At one point during the first session, Anaya, in an attempt to impress upon Haig the dearness with which the Argentine people regarded the islands, told the U.S. mediator that his son was a marine helicopter pilot stationed in the Malvinas. "The day my son sacrifices his existence for the fatherland will be the proudest day of my life," declared the swarthy and composed admiral.

Haig regarded Anaya wearily. "It's different when they start shipping home the body bags."

The two delegations exchanged views for just over an hour. Haig, who had come directly from London and who had slept only five hours during the previous three days, wanted to return to the Sheraton Hotel in Retiro where he and his entourage were lodged.

But he could not leave Government House by car. The presidential palace was besieged. The multitude blocked every exit, waving banners, trampling flowerbeds and railing against the British Empire.

Haig knew the demonstration was for his benefit. The regime had begun broadcasting the call to the plaza twenty-four hours earlier. It had decreed free passage on trains and buses and subways. It had exhorted the populace to show the U.S. secretary that the occupation of the islands was not the desperate act of a foundering dictatorship but the fulfillment of the entire nation's most fervent desire. And the people had responded to the call. Haig had heard their chants throughout the session.

To ensure that the magnitude of the rally was not lost on the visitor, the army helicopter that lifted Haig off the roof of Government House banked over the horde before heading for the Sheraton ten blocks away.

When Haig and the others had gone, Galtieri poured himself a Scotch and tried to calm his nerves and collect his thoughts. This moment could change his destiny and the destiny of the nation.

Interior Minister General Alfredo Saint Jean and a half-dozen other high-ranking officers were already on the balcony. The microphones were in place and a flag was draped over a flowerbox in front of the microphones.

Galtieri emerged. The plaza erupted in a cataclysmic ovation. He stepped to the microphones and waited for the tumult to subside. In that sublime moment he savored the realization of a dream. It was dreamlike, but not at all unbelievable. He had been sure all along that someday this was going to happen, that he, as president of the Argentines, would address a clamoring multitude from the balcony of Government House.

He felt like Perón that other general-turned-president he had abhorred for decades. But in this moment his kinship with the populist demagogue was so tangible that he had to consciously restrain himself from raising both arms aloft in Perón's habitual gesture to the adoring throng. He locked his left arm at his side and lifted his right in awkward recognition. It looked like something between a wave and a fascist salute.

Galtieri did not know exactly what he was going to say. But the boiling primordial power of the people below surged in him and he was infused with their implacable will. He recalled Haig's arrogance on the stairway and he thought: "If I had that prick in front of me now I would strangle him with my bare hands and throw his limp and lifeless body to the crowd."

"PEOPLE OF ARGENTINA!" he roared, his hand raised to quiet the raging host. "People of Argentina!" His voice was a guttural rasp, exactly like that of Perón. "The people want to know what is going on. I repeat: The people want to know what is going on." The commotion subsided. "In May of 1810, in this plaza, the people of that era gathered in front of the Cabildo to ask what was going on. That was the birth of the fatherland. Today, as in that time, but with millions of Argentines in the Plaza de Mayo and in all the plazas of the nation, the people want to know what is going on."

The strained, hoarse baritone boomed from the loudspeakers out over the square, over the entire metropolis. "Circumstances are such that I exercise the presidency of the nation, in representation of you all. Be absolutely assured, every man, woman and youth of Argentina, that, representing all of you I feel the pride and satisfaction of having maintained the dignity and honor of the Argentine nation in this meeting with the representative of the United States. The dignity and honor of the Argentine nation are not negotiated by anyone. The government of Great Britain, Mrs. Thatcher and the people of Great Britain have not heard until now a single word of attack or a single word damaging their honor or reputation. Until now. But I ask the English government and people moderation in their words and deeds. The Argentine government and the Argentine people might well become infuriated and respond to offense with even greater offense.

"Workers, businessmen, intellectuals and all walks of national life are gathered here in national unity, in defense of the country's well-being and dignity."

Again he checked the upward movement of his arms. He leaned to the microphone and bellowed, "Let the world be advised that there exists a people with an ironbound will and that people is the Argentine people. If they want to come, let them come! We will do them battle!"

An expansive thunder like a mushrooming cloud rose from the heart of the city. When it waned, he finished his speech by asking the crowd to sing the national anthem.

The hymn is a hearty, pace-changing melody. It starts off slowly, alluding to camaraderie among nations, that the nations of the world toast Argentina and wish her the best. Halfway through it quickens with a flourish of horns and builds to an inspiring final chorus repeated three times:

> *Oh, Juremos con gloria morir!*
>   *(Oh, Let us swear to die with glory!)*
> *Oh, Juremos con gloria morir!*
> *Oh, Juremos con gloria morir!*

The oath on 500,000 voices reverberated off the buildings surrounding the square. Galtieri left the balcony, making his way through the generals and admirals and brigadiers, biting his lip, looking down at the floor. He went to his office and closed the door behind him. He poured himself a Johnnie Walker. Alone in the room, he held the glass aloft.

"*Al gran pueblo Argentino, salud!*" he hailed in a quavering voice, and tossed back the drink.

DANIEL STOOD BEFORE THE BIG WINDOW AND LOOKED OUT OVER THE LAKE TO THE WOODED HILLSIDE OF THE OPPOSITE SHORE. IT WAS EARLY AND THE SUN WAS LOW IN THE SKY BEHIND THE HOUSE. THE SUNLIGHT CRASHED against the far hillside and the leaves blazed gold, red and orange.

He was suffused with a sense of invulnerability. "I'm going to tell him today," he thought, and slapped himself on the thighs. He turned and went to the kitchen, where he found Soledad washing dishes.

"*Buen día,* she said.

"It's more than a good day. It's a great day."

Daniel served himself coffee and sat down with his cup at the wooden table. There was a newspaper there and he perused it.

After a few minutes, he looked up at Soledad. "What do you think of this Malvinas thing?" he asked.

"What do you mean, what do I think of it?"

"Do you think it's good or bad?"

"I think it is neither. It's simply what it is."

"You were raised in Patagonia. I suppose people in the south are more attached to the islands than they are in Buenos Aires."

"I suppose the people who live there are more attached to them than anyone."

"But they're ours. The British robbed them from us."

The Indian woman stood the last plate in the dish rack and dried her hands on her white apron. She carried a bowl of potatoes to the table. "Listen, *m'hijo*. I'll tell you a story." She spoke as she peeled the potatoes with a small sharp knife, its blade eroded from many whettings. "When I was a little girl, I used to sell bouquets of wild lavender to the tourists. The boat that took them to the hostel at the far end of the lake stopped near the reservation, because there is a lovely waterfall there. I used to go onto the boat. There was a guide on it who spoke into a microphone, explaining to the tourists how it was that Lake Lacar and the lands surrounding it came to be part of Argentina. Because, you know something? The waters of Lake Lacar empty into the Pacific Ocean, not the Atlantic. And that was the original criterion for the border with Chile. Lands drained by lakes and rivers emptying into the Pacific were to be Chilean and land drained by lakes and rivers emptying into the Atlantic were to be Argentine. Anyway, the guide would explain how Francisco Moreno convinced the Chileans to accept another dividing line, one defined by the mountain peaks, that afforded more land to Argentina. And the guide, I remember he always seemed pleased and proud when he reached the end of the explanation, he would say something like, 'So just think! It is thanks to Moreno that we who were born around this lake are Argentines.' And I even as a little girl, thought that man ridiculous. I felt like asking him, 'Don't you think that if you had been born Chilean you would be proud to be Chilean.' I never did ask him that. But I told my father about Francisco Moreno and how we came to be Argentines instead of Chileans. And he asked me, 'Who was this Moreno to divide the land of the Mapuches?'

"So, since you have asked me, that is what I think about this conflict of the Malvinas."

Soledad, throughout the recounting of her story, had continued peeling potatoes and kept her eyes on her work. Only now, upon pronouncing the last word, did she look up. She looked so steadily and intently at Daniel that he saw his reflection in her black eyes and was disquieted by it.

"Where's Santiago?" he asked.

"In the shop," she said, and went back to her work.

Daniel took an apple from a basket on the counter and walked out the door, munching it as he strode across the coarse dewy grass toward the shed. He opened the door. Santiago was cutting a long aluminum tube with a hack saw.

The shop where Santiago and Daniel constructed hang gliders was equipped with two large worktables, each with two vices. From a pegboard hung an array of saws, wire cutters, hammers, turnbuckles, clamps and files covering most of one wall. In a corner were stacked spools of various grades of wire. Bolts of brightly colored nylon sail fabric stood next to the wire. The fan of a windmill adorned another wall. It was a remnant of the family's first year in San Martín, before the glider construction turned lucrative, when Santiago had made a living, barely, fashioning and erecting water-pumping windmills for farmers and ranchers on the plain east of town. The big fan with its dull blades reminded Dani of a carnival wheel of fortune.

"Buenos días," he said. "Why didn't you wake me?"

"You looked very peaceful."

"What are we working on? The one for Gómez or the one for Terranova?"

"Gómez is coming down next weekend for his, so we'd better get that one finished."

"What do you want me to do?"

"Why don't you start the harness?"

"Anything you say, tío."

Daniel arranged leather, shears, awl, eyelets, wire and clamps on the workbench. After a while, he looked up from cutting a swatch of cowhide.

"Santiago," he said, and sensed a slight waver in his voice. Just as his uncle looked up from his own work to say "Sí," Soledad opened the door hurriedly.

"Telephone, señor," she said. "It's Alejandro calling from Buenos Aires."

Santiago moved quickly out the door and ran across the yard. Soledad followed him and Daniel was left alone in the shop, his heart pounding ferociously.

In ten minutes, Santiago returned.

"He got recalled," he said in a leaden voice. "They're sending him to the Malvinas."

Daniel cursed to himself; not for his cousin's, but for his own bad luck.

"He's all worked up," Santiago continued slowly. "He said at first he was angry and disappointed that it would keep him from going to Spain. But now that he's thought about it, he thinks he's lucky."

Daniel did not know what to think. Everything was mixed up: the eagerness to tell Santiago about himself and Cristina, concern and admiration for his cousin, and even a twinge of envy, a momentary jealousy that Alejandro should always find himself in the midst of grand events. Then the emotional jumble untangled and what remained most palpably was dread. Dani was young enough to entertain the notion of war as romantic, but he was wounded enough to sense that the real stuff of it was grief.

Santiago stood beside his worktable and stared at the windmill fan on the wall.

"I think they're going to work something out," said Daniel encouragingly. Indeed, he was inclined to believe that the negotiations he had read about would bear fruit. "The British aren't going to go to war over a few thousand sheep on some frozen rocks at the bottom of the world."

Ramón, high school history teacher and mentor of revolutionaries, was right. Cristina was placed under surveillance following the student assembly. The authorities' intention was to observe, but also to intimidate, and the procedure became markedly less discreet over the course of the first week.

Cristina noticed the man, lean and young with pomaded hair, a fleece-lined suede jacket and a turtleneck sweater, leaning against the counter in the café where she met with girlfriends for coffee after school. He wore dark glasses. After she realized he was following her, it was that aspect of him that most bothered Cristina. She asked herself disgustedly, incredulously if these people were really so brutish and unimaginative that they could only propagate state stereotypes ad nauseum. She wondered if the dark glasses were his or if they were issued him by the desk sergeant along with the brass knuckles, blackjack and .45.

One day, sometime during the second week, the lean young man was no longer behind her and she thought they had desisted. She was relieved.

To get home, Cristina had to walk over a rickety bridge separating the town proper from the poor section, then walk up a dirt road between rows of shanties—terraced into the hillside like layers of ruined wedding cake—to the foot of the path leading up to the house on the summit.

A few days after the lean man had stopped following her, she was on her way home and found a jeep parked at the foot of the hillside trail. The skinny man was behind the wheel and an older man sat beside him. The older man was hawk-nosed and swarthy, but not like an Indian. He reminded Cristina of the drawings of a sword-swinging Sinbad or Ali Baba in her childhood picture books.

The men watched her approach. She was afraid, but determined not to show it. She looked straight ahead, intending to pass them by as if they did not exist, and continue up the hill. But when she was alongside, the man in the passenger seat reached down between his feet and lifted out a burlap sack tied in a knot at the top. The bag was weighted with something heavy and hard-edged, like bricks or stones, at the bottom. Between the topknot and the hard, jagged contours the fabric shifted and bulged and from inside came the weak but steady, plaintive cry of a small animal.

"You know, _ché,_" said the dark man loudly and abruptly enough to stop Cristina in her tracks a few steps above them. "This is the second albino pup my bitch has borne in three years. She must have the recessive gene."

Cristina turned and looked at the men. They stepped down from the jeep and to the edge of the stream right below her. They stood where the stream dallied on its way down to the lake and formed a pool. Cristina and Daniel often knelt at the pool on their way to or from school to drink water.

"Yeah, she's got the gene, that bitch, even though it doesn't show in her," said the older man, holding the shifting and squealing sack in front of him as if it were a just-fished bass. "And the only way to get rid of the gene is to snuff it out before it has a chance to pass itself on. Isn't that right, _ché?_"

"That's right," answered the lean man, the subordinate, who, despite the fading light, wore his dark glasses. Then, to make sure the point was taken (he presumed the entire world as thick as himself) he added, "Yeah. You have to kill them while they're young."

And the pup (if in fact that was what was inside, for Cristina never saw anything but a tremulous sack and did not hear anything but a whimper that could have come from a puppy, a kitten or a newborn human being) seemed to realize he was bound for something dreadful and awesome, because as the Arab-faced man lowered the bundle, the animal's lament rose in volume and intensity. It clawed the fabric.

"Stop!" shrieked Cristina and took a step down the hill just as the sack touched the water. The Arab looked up at her and smiled, then let the bag plunge below the surface. The whine disappeared and the water churned. She could not help but watch. The splashing subsided until the only thing disturbing the smooth surface was a string of bubbles rising from the sack like pearls.

The man lifted the still, dripping bag from the water and tossed it into the back of the jeep. It landed with a soggy thud.

"*Chau,*" he said up to Cristina and climbed into the vehicle.

"*Chau,*" said the lean man, who climbed in beside him.

They drove off and left Cristina standing with a scream stuck in her throat and the small creature's dying breath in the pool where she used to kneel to drink.

Kids from the Chaco, or anywhere on the continent, of course were not as adept as the islanders at digging blocks of peat. It was equally understandable that the Kelpers were not going to lend the Argentines their long-bladed spades designed especially for the purpose, the ones the Falklanders had used the previous spring to slice out the blocks that had dried over the summer and would heat their homes through the long winter. So the soldiers had to dig blocks with their field shovels, those short-handled spades with the blade on a lock hinge that allows it to be used likewise as a pick or hoe.

At first the soldiers chopped out ragged blocks, but after about a thousand they got pretty good at it. They stacked neat blocks of peat around the anti-aircraft cannons, the machine-gun nests and mortars and command posts. They dug trenches and foxholes for weeks, and it seemed to the conscripts that digging was the essence of warfare.

After the trenches were dug there was little to do except wait on guard for the task force to arrive and attack. So the soldiers waited and shivered. They watched the sun set earlier each day and tried to figure out ways to fill their growling stomachs and dry out their feet without them freezing.

"A kid from the Forty-second shot a sheep with his FAL last night and they had a barbecue over there," said Raul, a copper-hued thin boy from Jujuy who shared a foxhole with Alejandro. The Jujeño jutted his chin to the east, farther out along the perimeter, toward the sea. "My fear of getting staked still outweighs the longing in my belly. But for how much longer I don't know."

"Your problem is you didn't bring any personal reserves. What do you eat in Jujuy? Lizards and cactus spines?" Ale sat on the ground outside the trench, his bare feet wrapped in a wool scarf. He was taking advantage of the rare afternoon sun to drape his soggy socks over his helmet and open his boots to the rays.

"I've always been skinny, though I eat like an animal. I must have a high metabolism." The Northerner sniffled, sucked a gob of mucus into his mouth, curled his tongue and sent a gleaming pellet sailing. "How are your feet?"

"Not bad. Yet."

"You must take care of your dogs, campeòn. They're your living."

"You don't have to remind me." Alejandro rubbed his feet briskly. "Yours all right?"

"Sí. Trenchfoot is not my problem. Hunger is my problem." He kicked an empty ration can. "Damn! I wish I had some coca leaves. If they planned on starving us, the least they could have done was ship over a few tons of coca leaves so we could bear it."

"If we could only get dry," lamented Alejandro. "If the sun would just stay out for two days straight."

"The sun could come out every day and we'd never get dry. There's still water in the trench and there's still the fog." Raul removed the helmet perched high on his head, on top of the hood of his jacket pulled over a knit wool cap, and sat on the helmet on the ground near Ale. "The fucking fog," he said.

The nightly fog was like none either young man had seen before. It creeped out of the darkness like a stealthy enemy and settled down into the trench around the soldiers as thickly as the vapor of dry ice. It settled into hollows, molding itself to the contours of the landscape, and rested on the soldiers trying to rest. Damp and clammy, they curled in their sodden sleeping bags and found a few hours' respite in fleeting dreams. They slept until their feet itched and tingled and woke rubbing one against the other. Sometimes they rubbed so hard and long that they rubbed the skin off, and that only made it worse.

But now the sun was out Alejandro was drying his socks, feet and boots and was, if not happy, relieved enough to feel something akin to happiness. Raul must not have been feeling too poorly either because he slipped off his mittens, the left one that had a thumb and pouch for the rest of the fingers and the right one that had a thumb, a sheath for the trigger finger and a wider sheath for the other three, and reached inside his jacket to pull out a wooden flute.

It was a *kena,* the flute of Andean melodies; age-old Indian melodies that cannot be transcribed on the European scale because they don't fit into it. Raul had been taught to play by his father, who had been taught by his father. There was no need to write the songs down. They were dispatched on the mountain wind and traveled town to town like Inca messengers along ancient cobble roads.

The brown boy curled his lip over the notch at the end of the instrument and coaxed out a plaintive strain. His breath filled the flute, escaping through uncovered holes only to be pressed back in to keep the cylinder fueled for the tune. The song was "El Condor Pasa." Alejandro had listened many times to the Simon and Garfunkel recording of the song, and the English lyrics came to him.

"I'd rather be a hammer than a nail," he sang softly. As he sang he wondered if the Indians had their own lyrics for the melody. He watched Raul, absorbed in his playing, and wondered what the song meant to him. He thought it was strange that he and Raul, whose great-great-great-grandfather probably fought the Spaniards with Tupac Amaru, should be sitting on an island with this tune swirling around them, enjoying this song that the British soldiers who were on their way to try to kill them probably liked too.

When the sad song ended the Indian boy flipped the *kena* into the air in front of him like a spinning baton and caught it as it fell.

"This is a great friend," he said. "A singing stick."

He pressed it again to the circular impression beneath his lip and filled his lungs, then launched another tune. The song gathered a festive force and Alejandro watched, incredulous that such an unimposing tube of wood could produce so strong a sound. The notes tripped and tumbled from the flute like children's laughter and Ale swept his socks off his helmet and began tapping the metal shell to the happy beat of the song. He tapped tentatively at first, then gave rein to the joyful spirit that moved his hands. He wanted to shout.

The music must have carried on the wind because a boy came running, heavily, clumsily in his boots. He ran hunched forward and clutched in one hand something Alejandro took at first to be a weapon— but then he realized, as the soldier neared, that it was a *charango*.

The *charango,* a small stringed instrument the soundbox of which is the shell of an armadillo, is the soul mate of the *kena.* They are a magical combination greater than the sum of the two component elements, like thunder and lightning. That is why if a *kena* player hears the strumming of a *charango,* or a *charango* strummer hears the lilt of a *kena,* he cannot be prevented from providing the complement.

The other boy stood by until Raul ended the song and looked up.

"Hello," said the boy, the instrument dangling at his side. "I heard you all the way over there." A sweep of his hand indicated his position across the field toward the sea.

"Shall we play something together?" asked Raul.

"I'd like to," said the soldier, who took off his helmet and sat down on it next to the flutist. "How about 'Pajaro Campana' ('Bell Bird')?"

"Great," said Raul and the other boy set his fingers on the frets and snapped his hand across the strings and the armadillo sacrificed to Euterpe came back to life and sent a ripple ringing across the heath. The flute joined in and the distinct sounds wound around one another. The musicians played off each other, spurred then reined in, teased and tested until they locked in a torrent of song that spurred Alejandro's heart. It was powerful and joyful and he kicked off the scarf swaddling his toes, leapt to his feet and jumped around in a wild dance. The *charango* player, without missing a stroke, laughed and yelled, "Yiiiiieeeeee!"

The cry fueled Alejandro's euphoria and he became a banshee, a dervish, a whirlwind, a mystic, and as he danced it came to him, not as a thought in words, that in this song resided the force and strength of America. For a moment it didn't matter that his name was Maglione or that his grandparents were Italian because he felt entirely, utterly American and was suffused, filled up with love for his land and the promise of something new and good, and he felt invincible. He danced and did not feel the freezing earth because his feet hardly lit. Then the song ended with a flourishing blur of fingers on strings and a crescendo of soul-piercing wood-borne wind and the three burst into wild and raucous laughter.

Alejandro stretched his arms to the sky and shouted with all his might: "The whore that bore you!" The cry rolled across the field and out over the sea like a dare to the British fleet. He stood like that with his arms in the air and was transported to the instant when the final whistle blew on June 25, 1978, in River Plate Stadium, when he had raised his clenched fists and bellowed his triumph.

Then the cold seeped through his feet and he came back to the Falkland Islands, to his trench on the outskirts of Port Stanley, to his comrade Raul and his unknown-but-loved comrade who played the best goddamn *charango* in the world. And he laughed again, but this time not like a lunatic, and hopped to his helmet and sat on it and pulled on his socks and boots.

The two Northerners had swapped instruments and each was trying out the other's when an officer, a machine gun slung across his back like a quiver, walked up. The three soldiers jumped up and saluted. The small and stocky lieutenant in charge of this section of the perimeter stood with his fists resting on his hips and looked from one soldier to the other. He knew Alejandro and Raul, they were part of his unit. But the other conscript was a stranger.

"I saw you jumping around like a *loco,*" he said to Alejandro.

"I was dancing," said Ale, and he smiled. "These guys are great musicians."

The officer stepped up to the *charango* player, who stood at attention. "Who are you?" he asked.

"Private Sergio Romero," the boy answered nervously, because he realized all of a sudden he was not where he was supposed to be.

"Where is your position?"

"Over there." He pointed across the field.

"Why aren't you there?"

"I heard music. I came without thinking."

The officer pressed his face closer to that of the soldier. "Where the fuck do you think you are? At a carnival? Did you come over here to play the flute or to defend the fatherland?"

"To defend the fatherland, sir."

"Every square meter?"

"Yes, sir."

"Do you love this land?" demanded the lieutenant, scraping the earth with his boot. He bent down and picked up a handful of soil and held it before the conscript's face. "Do you love it?"

"Yes, sir."

"You say you love it, but I don't think you love it enough. The attack could come at any time, and you abandon your post to sit around and play the flute like this was a Boy Scout camping trip."

"The *kena* is his, sir," the boy said nervously. "I play the *charango.*"

"What the fuck difference does it make?" exploded the officer. He pressed the dirt into the conscript's face and rubbed. "You don't love this land because you don't know it well enough. But you're going to get to know it. You're going to feel like you're almost part of it."

The officer grabbed the boy, who was spitting out dirt and fighting to hold back his tears, spun him around brusquely and gave him a shove. "Now march," he commanded, and the boy marched across the field biting his dirty lip and clutching Raul's *kena.*

* * *

The South Georgia Islands are one of the most lonely, desolate and inhospitable continuously inhabited places on earth. Gale-beaten mountains and glaciers rising absurdly from the middle of the frigid Atlantic, they have not a single tree, not a single bush. Mats of tussock grass and lichens are the only vegetation. A herd of reindeer, the descendants of stock imported by whalers and virtually the only species of land animal on the island, subsists on that.

Grytviken ("Bay of Kettles" in Norwegian) shelters the islands' population of twenty souls, members of the British Antarctic Survey meteorological and scientific team. At one time the town, an assembly of two dozen white and rusty corrugated metal buildings on the edge of the bay at the foot of snowy mountains, was home to more than a hundred seafarers. A church and a movie hall still stand, but are hardly ever used.

Norwegian whaling Captain C. A. Larsen named the town for the big iron pots the whalers used to reduce blubber to oil. Larsen was one of the founders of the Argentine Fishing Company that set up shop in Grytviken in 1904. The Norwegians had their whale-processing factory at Port Husvik, and the Scots butchered whales at Port Leith, just north of Husvik. It was good business for half a century. The advent of factory ships in the 1950s made the town obsolete.

Since the beginning of the century, the British have administered the Georgias as a dependency of the Falkland Islands, fifteen hundred kilometers to the west. The Argentines have claimed the Georgias as a dependency of the Malvinas.

On April 3, 1982, the day after the invasion and occupation of the Falklands, Argentine forces landed on San Pedro. A dozen British Royal Marines were stationed at Grytviken. They resisted the Argentine attack and killed three Argentine soldiers before surrendering.

The British retook the Georgias on April 25. Before dawn, amphibious commandos from the Special Boat Squadron attached to the destroyer *Antrium* landed on the rocky beach. They spent the morning in reconnaissance and reported back to *Antrium* by radio. The ship sent two helicopter gunships toward the island and, to the surprise of the pilots, they spotted the Argentine guppy-class submarine *Santa Fe* on the surface making for Grytviken wharf. The helicopters attacked the vessel with depth charges and cannon. The *Santa Fe* gushed oil, spewed smoke and ran aground on a shoal.

Given coordinates by the commandos, *Antrium* and the frigate Plymouth opened fire with 4½-inch guns on Argentine positions. The helicopters landed marines and British army troops. By the time they reached the Argentine marines' post in Grytviken, white flags were fluttering in the wind. A British detachment was sent to Port Leith, where another Argentine squad was posted, and obtained a similar surrender.

The British took the 137 Argentine marines on San Pedro prisoner. There were no casualties on either side, except for an Argentine sailor wounded on the *Santa Fe*. His leg was amputated by British surgeons aboard the *Antrium*.

The naval officer who commanded the Argentine position at Leith, and who surrendered it without a fight, without firing a single shot, was Lieutenant Alfredo Astiz. The rest of the prisoners were repatriated to Argentina via Uruguay. But Astiz was shipped to the British base at Ascension island in the mid-Atlantic and from there flown to Britain, where he spent the next two months comfortably detained while inter-rogated by intelligence officers. He spoke excellent English, having taken specialization courses with both the British and U.S. navies.

His unique treatment resulted from the fact that two of Britain's closest allies, France and Sweden, were desperately anxious to question Astiz about the disappearance in Argentina of French and Swedish citizens. Because it had been Astiz who, using the pseudonym of Gustavo Niño, had infiltrated the Mothers of the Plaza de Mayo and engineered the kidnap of Sisters Alice Domon and Leonie Duquet. And it had been Astiz who, as commander of the squad assigned the abduction of Maria Berger, had shot the fleeing Swedish girl Dagmar Hagelin.

The South Georgias fell without an exchange of fire. But back in Argentina, the media reported with a luxury of details on the inau-gural "battle" of the South Atlantic war. News magazines published fictitious final radio messages from the Argentine troops on San Pedro informing of heavy casualties on both sides and the destruction of one British helicopter and four landing craft. The magazines reported how, after destroying their radios and codes, the Argentine marines effected a strategic retreat into the mountains from which they would harass the invaders and continue the resistance "to the last man." The magazines identified the marines as members of an elite commando group called "the Lizards" trained in wilderness survival and guerrilla warfare.

On the afternoon of April 25, radio programs in Buenos Aires and throughout Argentina were interrupted by martial music. The Joint Chiefs of Staff, in their thirty-second communiqué since the Falklands were occupied, said: "The military junta informs the people of the Argentine nation that, for tactical reasons, communications with the naval forces defending the South Georgia Islands have been cut; that the apparent initial triumph of the British forces was due to their numerical superiority, but that does not mean they exercise unrestricted control of the island; that our forces have made a tactical retreat and continue fighting in the island's interior with an unbreakable spirit of combat based on the moral superiority of those who defend the fatherland; that, independent of the final result of the fierce struggle, the objectives fixed by the military junta regarding the recovery of the islands will be maintained, with it being understood that sovereignty will not be negotiated nor will national dignity be violated."

Britain eventually decided that the extradition of Astiz to France or Sweden would violate those articles of the Geneva convention regarding the treatment of prisoners of war. The ruddy-cheeked lieutenant was returned to Argentina via Brazil.

A year and a half after the war ended, during the southern hemisphere summer of 1983–84 that saw Argentina's return to democracy, Astiz found it impossible to relax on the beach at Mar del Plata. The same magazines which during the war had hailed the valor of the leader of the Lizards, the same magazines that had lauded the armed forces for wiping out subversion without ever asking how it was done, had suddenly become champions of democracy and human rights, because democracy and human rights were the order of the day. Reporters and photographers from the magazines bothered Astiz on the beach. The magazines published pictures of Astiz rejecting the reporters' advances.

"How can it be," the publications asked righteously, "that this abductor of nuns, this scourge of the rights of man, this spineless reptile who surrendered without a fight, sits tanning himself without a care, wiggling his toes in the sun-warmed sand?"

*   *   *

On December 7, 1941 the cruiser USS *Phoenix* was anchored in Pearl Harbor, Hawaii. Bombs fell around it into the blue-green water and onto other vessels. The ship's cannons of 125, 40 and 20 millimeters thundered and spat hot metal at the Japanese bombers. The *Phoenix* went unscathed and throughout the Pacific campaign and after was known as the *Lucky Phoenix*.

Forty-one years later, on May 2, 1982, the same cruiser, the most heavily armed ship in the Argentine navy, was displacing 13,500 tons of seawater 230 miles southwest of the Falkland Islands. The ship, now called the ARA *General Belgrano,* and its crew of 1,091 men were 30 miles outside the exclusion and free-fire zone declared a month earlier by the British.

At 1600 hours the changing of the watch had just been completed. The wind blew from the northwest at seventy kilometers per hour and four-meter-high waves broke against the *Belgrano's* heavy hull.

At 1600 hours on May 2, 1982, many crewmen not on duty were having tea with cakes or small sandwiches—*la merienda*—in the ship's canteen. Others were resting in their bunks below decks.

At 1601 hours there was an explosion. The sailors said later that it seemed weirdly far off. There was a long moment of fading thunder and the ship shuddered from bow to stern, seeming to lift out of the water. A few seconds later came a second explosion.

It was a historic moment. The impact of the two Mark 8 torpedoes, each containing four hundred kilograms of Torpex high explosive, fired by the Royal Navy's HMS *Conqueror,* constituted the first attack ever carried out by a nuclear-powered submarine. The first torpedo pierced the *Belgrano's* hull and exploded just to the stern of the rear engine room, directly below the first below-decks platform. Its detonation blew up six fuel tanks, the rear engine, sailors' quarters D-402-L, a diesel-powered electronic generator, the compass room, the dining area, the second radio room, the canteen, and the junior officers' quarters. The second torpedo penetrated the hull toward the bow between the twelfth and fifteenth beams and exploded almost at the keel.

The second explosion stopped the ship dead in the water. Twenty meters of bow fell from the vessel. The D boiler burst. The metal of the bulkheads, decks and walls glowed orange and balls of intense heat raced down the passageways and ventilation tubes. Fires broke out, some because of the fuel oil gassified by the explosion, others due to short circuits. The main forward circuit board exploded.

This transpired in a matter of seconds. When all motors, mechanisms and generators gagged and stopped, there was a strange dark silence. Then there were cries and whimpers. Above all, there was the sound of water—the steely South Atlantic invading the ship.

The forward engine room flooded and water filled the passageways from parts of the second and third below decks to the upper decks. Hundreds of sailors were trapped.

The ship listed. In the first seven minutes following the attack it listed fifteen degrees. Acrid smoke like tear gas filled below-decks passages and chambers, reeled and swirled in the wind above.

The rudder stuck at fifteen degrees to port.

The alarm gongs and loudspeakers were dead. The ship's commander, Captain Hector Bonzo, had been making his way from the radio room to the situation room in the admiral's chamber. After a moment of stupor he began shouting orders. The orders were passed by voice up and down ladders and along passageways and bulkheads.

Many men were burned by the steam. Blisters rose on their faces and arms and backs. They vomited and screamed making their way along corridors slippery with oil and vomit, with stinging eyes they looked through the smoke for ladders leading to air and the life rafts, ladders between death and life. The uninjured helped the burned and wounded up onto the deck inclined between the slate sky and the churning black sea.

Bonzo soon realized there was no saving the ship. He ordered the life rafts thrown into the water and within minutes sixty orange rubber rafts, each enclosed by an orange nylon superstructure, were bobbing alongside the ship. The captain went to the communications room, put the codes and ballast in canvas bags and threw the bags overboard.

By 1621 hours the ship was listing twenty degrees to port and the stern was sinking. The main deck was slick with spilled oil. At 1623 Captain Bonzo, on deck three, gave the order to abandon ship. The order was relayed by megaphone by his second-in-command, Frigate's Captain Pedro Galazi.

The sailors who could began jumping from the ship onto the roofs of the rafts, as they had been trained to do. Most jumped from the port side, which was approaching sea level as the vessel listed one degree per minute. Others climbed down nets draped over the rising starboard. The injured were passed from the port side to the rafts.

By 1635 the starboard side of the hull was so far out of the water the crustaceans affixed to it were showing. The high and violent sea made it difficult to get the rafts away from the side of the ship. The men pushed aside the walls of the nylon tents enclosing the rafts and used the oars to try to get clear. Officers in a motorized rubber launch towed some of the rafts away.

Some of the life rafts drifted toward the sectioned bow, where twisted claws of metal ripped the rubber and deflated the floats. The men in those rafts, those who could, jumped out and swam to others. The water temperature was one degree Centigrade.

At 1643, Bonzo and Junior Artillery Officer Ramón Barrionuevo were the only ones left on deck. Barrionuevo jumped, then Bonzo. They were pulled into a raft.

Bonzo wrote later: "The ship continued to list and sink, steadily but softly, as if it were waiting for everyone to get clear so as not to pull them down with it."

At 1701 hours, exactly one hour after it was struck by the torpedoes, the cruiser ARA *General Belgrano* disappeared from the surface, taking 272 trapped, dead or wounded men to the bottom. The sailors huddled and shivered in the rafts in the tenuous light. They bailed the water that washed over the floats and took turns manning the pumps to keep the floats inflated. In some rafts there were thirty men. In others there were three or four. The wind came up stronger at 1800 hours, to one hundred kilometers per hour, and the waves grew to six meters. The wind-chill factor was minus-ten degrees Centigrade.

Some of the rafts were lashed together, but the lashings had to be cut because of the violence of the sea. The rafts drifted apart and, separated by mountains of water, each became a solitary cork on the angry southern ocean.

The men took turns hugging the urine bag for warmth. Some sang or said prayers and some mentioned the names of companions they had not seen on deck, hoping that someone would say, "Yes, I saw him. He's in another raft." Sometimes that was the response and sometimes the response was silence and the aversion of eyes.

It stormed all night, abating the next morning. The rafts were drifting southeast, away from the continent.

At 1300 hours on May 3 an Argentine naval aviation Neptune observation plane flew overhead. It made several passes and the men knew they had been spotted.

In some of the rafts wounded men had died. Their bodies were kept on board, because the survivors knew they would be rescued soon. At 1700 hours the destroyers ARA *Piedrabuena* and *Bouchard,* and the cutter *Gurruchaga* began the rescue. It was hard to bring the rafts alongside the vessels because of the rough sea. Later, the Antarctic exploration ship *Bahía Paraiso* and the Chilean vessel *Piloto Pardo* joined in the rescue.

The survivors were looked after on board the rescue vessels. They were given dry clothing, coats and blankets, and hot food. The injured and wounded were treated. The ships reached Ushuaia, the world's southern-most city, on May 4. The healthy survivors fell into formation on the deck of the *Bouchard.* They walked down the gangplank by twos, some with an arm draped around their companion's shoulder. Someone among them yelled, "*Viva la patria!*" Everyone shouted it in unison. Someone yelled, "*VIVA EL BELGRANO!*" and they all shouted that strongly, together.

Seven hundred and seventy of the 819 men who abandoned ship survived. All told, 321 men died in the attack—65 more than the total of British soldiers who were to die in the six-week campaign to regain the Falklands.

British Prime Minister Margaret Thatcher told the House of Commons on May 4: "The naval task force in the South Atlantic is clearly under political control. The cruiser *General Belgrano* constituted a real threat to the Royal Navy and if we had waited any longer, it would have been too late."

Peruvian President Fernando Belaunde Terry, who had taken over the mediation effort after Haig gave up, believed at the moment the *Belgrano* was attacked that peace was near. The British had bombed Argentine positions at Port Stanley on May 1, but combat had not begun in earnest and, until the sinking of the cruiser, only five men had died in the conflict. The headline of the *London Daily Mirror* edition of May 5 read, PEACE SUNK WITH THE BELGRANO.

When the cruiser was attacked, the nearest British vessel other than the *Conqueror* was more than 250 miles away and the Belgrano was moving away from it, westward, toward the continent. Mrs. Thatcher lied to Parliament to conceal the real reason why the cold and bloated corpses of 321 young men bobbed on the choppy South Atlantic or lay on its dark bottom. Military victory in the Falklands was the greatest political boost conceivable to her administration. She was resoundingly reelected to another term in office on the tide of patriotic fervor provoked by her Falklands campaign.

At a mass for the *Belgrano* dead, Argentine armed forces chaplain Monsignor José Medina said in his homily, "Their death was magnificent. Because they died in fulfillment of their vow before God to serve the fatherland until their blood was spilled."

CRISTINA MISSED THE MEETINGS. SHE MISSED THE CAMARADERIE, THE DISCOURSE, THE LAUGHTER. THEY WERE FUN, BUT SHE NEVER WOULD HAVE USED THAT WORD TO DESCRIBE THEM BECAUSE SHE HAD NO DOUBTS ABOUT the seriousness of their purpose or illusions about their danger. She missed the other girls with whom she shared a barely bridled excitement about what could be done with the world, and she missed the books— the trading and discussion of camouflaged tracts. So, a week after the incident on the hillside, a week during which she had not been followed or bothered, she asked Ramón if she could resume attendance, and he consented.

Army Intelligence Lieutenant Elias Hadad missed the war. A grand chapter in his country's history was passing him by. His longed-for assignment to the islands did not materialize; and each passing week without orders increased his bitter resentment.

With the sinking of the *Belgrano* he was consumed by a furious impotence. His sole consolation was the knowledge that the British were not the only enemy. And if he was not to be on the front fighting the colonialists, he was going to do his part and then some against the nationless advocates of anarchy at hand.

Hadad and his young assistant walked out of the federal police station in San Martín de los Andes and got into a white Ford Falcon, the license plate of which was illegible, as more than half of it was shoved up under the bumper. They cruised the quiet lamplit evening streets and Hadad bummed black tobacco cigarettes off his subordinate, who had deferred to night and removed his dark glasses. A tic blinked his right eye every few seconds.

"Las Heras 558," instructed Hadad after a while. The driver proceeded to the address on the edge of town. He turned off the headlights before turning down the lane. The blocks in this part of town were sectioned into lots, some built upon, some with foundations dug, mostly empty.

"Here's good," said Hadad, and the driver pulled to a stop along the curb.

"What's up?" asked the younger man.

"The snot-nosed Reds' club is meeting in there tonight," said the officer, signaling an Alpine-style A-frame ahead on the right.

"I thought they were priority number ten on the list from one to ten," said the subordinate.

"No big deal. I just don't want them getting too big for their britches."

"Are we going in?" asked the younger man, reflexively touching the holstered pistol in his armpit.

"No. We'll wait. For the Maglione girl to come out. We'll take her for a ride."

"To where?"

"Around. No rough stuff. Shake her up, let her know we're on to them. We're not going to hurt her. Remember that. We'll give her the elevator treatment and send her home in messy undies."

Hadad had chosen Cristina as the object of his terror because he thought she was pretty. That was enough. He had liked her face and figure and what seemed to him that day on the hillside a measure of spunk, and he wanted a second encounter with her, not to paw or rape her, only to squeeze her for a moment.

The intelligence men talked about soccer while they waited in the darkness at the curb. Hadad, a fan of Independiente of Avellaneda, cursed Menotti for not selecting Ricardo Bochini for the national team. The other man damned Menotti too, but not for Bochini's or anyone else's absence from the squad. The younger man suspected Menotti of leftist sympathies.

"And I think he swallows the saber too," he said.

"What? Menotti a faggot? *Déjame de joder,*" said the lieutenant.

"That's right. Haven't you ever noticed how he sits with those skinny legs crossed one on top of the other? He must be happier than a dog with two tails there in the locker-room with all those big-dicked boys."

"How do you know they're big-dicked? You think you have to be *pijudo* to make the national team? If that was the case Bochini would be the captain. He has to fold it and strap it to his leg so it doesn't fall out of his shorts."

The conversation turned to speculation about the possible homosexuality of other prominent national figures. Then they hypothesized on the sexual inclinations of Margaret Thatcher, who, they maintained, even if she was a despicable bitch, had a healthy set of balls on her. They joked about her husband, who they said must spend most of his time at home in an apron and surely was always on the bottom when she wanted a roll.

They talked, waiting, and smoked the subordinate's cigarettes. They watched the A-frame until shortly after nine o'clock, when the door opened and two young people, a boy and a girl, appeared in the yellow light of the doorway, then stepped out and walked across the grass to the street.

"That's not her," said Hadad to the younger man peering through the windshield into the darkness. About ten minutes later the door opened again and Cristina emerged with another girl. They turned onto the sidewalk and walked toward the Falcon without realizing the car was occupied until they were almost upon it; even then only the mouths and chins of the men inside were visible, the upper half of their faces hidden in the shadow of the roof. The girls stopped short. Each uttered a quiet gasp.

"Just keep walking, like nothing," Cristina said to her friend. They continued along the sidewalk trying to appear relaxed and innocent. But they knew they were guilty and walked stiffly, as if on a tightrope, dreadfully certain that the slightest waver would send them plunging.

Hadad waited until they were alongside, and showed his face through the open window. "Hi girls. Can we give you a lift?" he asked.

They ignored him and kept walking. Then the car door banged like a starting pistol and they broke into a run. But Lucia tripped with her third step and fell. She screamed. Cristina stopped five meters ahead of her and turned, clutching her schoolbooks (and a copy of *What Is to Be Done?* wrapped in the dust jacket of *Wuthering Heights*) to her breast. As the lean man reached the fallen girl Cristina called out, "Lucia!" but by the time the word passed her lips Hadad was planted squarely in front of her. His hands were raised and spread in an absurdly conciliatory gesture that seemed to say, "Look, I'm not going to hurt you." He held his arms up like that, as if she were the one who was armed, and stepped toward Cristina. The hands swept down hard and fast like talons, and clamped her shoulders.

"You're coming with us," he said in not much more than a whisper. "Don't resist."

He pulled her to him and whipped around behind her, then pushed her toward the car. She screamed but the cry was suffocated by a strong bony paw. She dropped the books and struggled as the officer grabbed her wrist and twisted it behind her and he pressed it up against her spine until she thought her arm would snap. She stopped trying to scream and tried to say, "Okay, okay," but that too was stuffed back down her throat.

Hadad hustled Cristina to the car and sidled her across the front seat. His partner, who was hugging the breath from Lucia, waited until he was sure their prey was secure then whispered savagely into the girl's ear, "You're lucky tonight baby but you might not be lucky the next time." He slackened his embrace and she slumped to the sidewalk. The lean man bounded to the car, slipped behind the wheel, slammed the door and lurched off down the sleepy road.

Lights came on and curtains were pushed aside in the few nearby houses. After some minutes had passed, when it was evident the car had gone away and would not return, an old man—Abram Katzman—who had lived in San Martín de los Andes since reaching the shores of Argentina from Poland in 1947—hobbled out from his home and down his flagstone path to the street.

"Don't cry, little darling," he said, bending creakily over the weeping girl. His spotted alabaster hands reached under her arms. "It's never as bad as it seems." He tried to comfort her. He spared her what occurred to him with a wistful and wise melancholy: that it is always much worse.

For the first two blocks, Hadad kept his hand clamped over Cristina's mouth. He knew from experience she was in a state like that of a hooded bronco, incapable of struggle. She stared straight ahead with wide eyes and when he removed his hand her mouth remained open wide like a choirgirl's but no sound emerged. He released his grip on the back of her neck but she stayed rigid, her arms pressed tightly against her sides and her knees clamped tightly together. The only penetration of her senses was the strong sour odor of sweat not her own.

They drove out of town, along the lake road.

"Want to rape her first, then kill her? Or the other way around?" asked the driver.

"Let's fuck her first this time," said Hadad. "That way she'll have a final moment of pleasure."

"Why don't you fuck each other?" said Cristina, surprising herself.

Hadad slapped her sharply across the face. "Another word and I'll tear out your eyes," he hissed. Then to the driver he said, "To the station."

In a few minutes they reached the federal police headquarters, a two-story cube of stucco-covered concrete blocks. The driver turned down a ramp to the parking lot beneath the building and pulled the car into a slot in a row of Falcons. The men got out. Hadad reached in and grabbed Cristina's arm. "*Vamos, princesa,*" he said, and yanked her out.

The one-act drama was supposed to end here in the basement. There was no intention of taking her upstairs. The fewer faces she saw, the better. And until now she had only seen army faces, no policemen.

They marched her between them to the elevator, an old cage model with an outer door that opens like an accordion along a track. The elevator car was waiting there and the subordinate slid open the outer door, the one barring entrance to the shaft, then the door of the car. But instead of pushing Cristina into the car he reached in and pushed the second-floor button, then slid the inner door closed again. He closed the outer door and a prong at the top of the door clicked into a slot at the top of the frame. There was a sound like a bolt dropping into a bucket and the car rose before them.

Cristina was scared and confused. The cables whirred and the mechanism hummed as the elevator counterweights, greasy black ingots of iron, descended on the track on the back wall of the shaft. When the car reached the second floor the mechanical hum stopped and there was nothing but the sound of three people breathing hard.

"When children play with fire they burn their hands," said Hadad as he grabbed Cristina's right wrist and raised her hand to waist level and shoved it against the cage of the door. Cristina made a fist and the diamond-shaped space formed by the flat hinged pieces of metal was not big enough for her fist to pass. But Hadad forced the hand against the grill. He pressed, twisted and wrenched—scraped the skin off her knuckles—and the pain was such that she could not help but unclench her fist, so that her hand slid through the space. She tried to pull it back through but Hadad had both hands clamped around her forearm.

The lean man pushed the call button and there was the clank of a gear catching and the counterweights rose. The cables whirred and the shadow of the floor of the descending car appeared in the shaft above the struggling figures. Cristina screamed. As her scream echoed off the damp basement walls Hadad prepared to pull her hand back out through the cage at the last second. But at the very instant he began that motion, Cristina bent forward and sunk her teeth into the flesh of his hand. The man's cry drowned the echo of hers and he let go of her hand. The lean man watched all this taking place and saw Cristina was going to pull her hand free. Even though that had been the idea, that she was not to be hurt, it was different now because she was going to save herself and he knew it could not be like that, so he heaved against the handle of the outer door and though it was not supposed to open unless the car was there, it opened anyway because of its age and his strength. It opened halfway, until the folding grate bit into her wrist like a fox trap. She closed her eyes and fainted as the elevator car fell past her, and she did not hear the sound of her bones crunching or feel the thump of her head against the floor or see the thick blood spurt from the stump of her wrist.

Daniel twisted abruptly from his stomach onto his back. He kicked off the blanket and sheet and lay still and breathing hard until the cold crept over him. He sat up and pulled the covers back over himself and cursed.

He curled his sweat-sheened palms into fists. His jaw ached dully but he could not keep from clenching his teeth.

He would not go to her room when she got home, he thought. Let her wait, simmer, boil, even burn the rest of the night for him.

His imagination ran wildly through elaborate variations on a single theme. He imagined she had hit it off with one of the boys from the study group, that they had gone somewhere, to the dark romantic illicit plaza after the meeting and were panting and groping at each other, oblivious to, or worse, tacitly mocking his woe. Dani inventoried the array of horny young prospects among the world-redeemers. It could be an intellectual, a boy who saw in his sparse but carefully cultivated chin-whiskers and wire glasses the smoldering image of the young Lev Bronstein. Then he thought, no, it must be a working-class boy, the spawn of a long line of factory militants who told the others with haughty humility how he was going to finish high school, sure, but even so would work lifelong in the factory because that was where the revolution would kindle. He probably had his stumpy, gnawed, dirty fingers under her blouse right now. Or maybe it was Ramón, their dialectically materialist spiritual guide who with his benevolent conde-scending smile had explained how pair-bonding was bourgeois. That couples, even loving couples, could not be exclusive because one person could not be the private property of another and that repression of anything, including the urge a young emancipated woman might have to experience a knowing touch and technique, only served to stifle the bloom on the bush of life.

Daniel rolled on his bed and cursed her for leaving him alone. He would show her, show her she was sorely mistaken if she thought she could play that way, dabble and dawdle, get hot and save the best, the prize for him. He was not going to finish what he had not begun.

He threw back the blanket violently, shoved down his pajama trouser—he was naked from the waist up—and sat up on the side of the bed with his feet on the sheepskin rug. He looked down at his flaccid penis. He held his hand cupped before him and swabbed his mouth with his tongue, marshalling spit. He drooled a glistening glob into his palm and lifted his cock with the other hand and laid it across the gob of saliva and closed his hand around the thickening joint. He rubbed and spread the spit along the shaft and tugged back the foreskin to anoint the glans. He closed his eyes and stroked and conjured the image of Cristina's buttocks and breasts and downy mound but likewise pictured strange hands caressing them and he pumped furiously, as if he would pull it off. He gnashed his teeth and groaned.

When it was over, he hunched forward and his shoulders heaved in a single sob. Weeping silently, he slid off the pajama pants and with them wiped the dribble from the tip of his cock then crouched to wipe the gleaming spots of semen from the floor. He stood up, sniffled and blew his nose into the crumpled flannel, then pressed the fabric into a ball and threw it into the corner.

He climbed naked back into bed, where sleep delivered him from the siege of shame, desolation and betrayal, so that he did not even hear the police jeep pull up outside.

Santiago was also waiting for Cristina. She had told him not to wait up, that she would be home late. But he had been reading without heeding the hour and when he had looked up, it was midnight and she still was not home. He had begun to worry. He was sitting at the kitchen table, looking at the grained and knotted wood, when he heard the vehicle approach. At first he thought it must be one of Cristina's friends, a friend with a jeep, who had brought her home, but in the next instant he was certain something had happened, and his legs went weak as he rose.

When he opened the door to see the official vehicle and the uniformed man approaching, he buckled under and had to steady himself in the doorjamb.

"Are you Santiago Maglione?" asked the officer. "The father of Cristina Maglione?"

"Yes. What's wrong?"

"You'll have to accompany me to the station."

"What's wrong?"

The policeman looked blankly beyond him. "I don't know," he lied. "They only told me to bring you to the station."

Santiago stepped unsteadily back to the kitchen to fetch a wool jacket draped over the back of a chair. He followed the officer to the jeep and got in beside him. The policeman turned the vehicle around with difficulty, as the steep access to the house was little more than a track, and they made their way slowly, cautiously, down the hill. Santiago sat straight-backed and tautly still. Everything seemed infinitely fragile, so that sudden movement might shatter it and with it the crystal structure of love that was the remainder of his family. The jeep rocked, the wheels dipped reluctantly into ruts, the headlights shot crazily through the dangling vines, flashed haphazard past the sturdy elms.

They reached the road below and in a few minutes arrived at the station. They got out of the jeep and walked up the steps to the building's entrance.

Santiago felt flushed and hot. He was remotely aware of a dull ache at his temples but could not loosen the clench of his jaw. The policeman led him to the captain's office, a cubicle of formica panels and frosted glass. The captain sat at a gray metal desk with his hands folded on top of it. He stood as Santiago entered and indicated that he should take a chair. Santiago sat down and so did the officer.

The captain's face was tired and gray. It was the face of a man impossible to imagine ever having been young. The bald crown shone grayly. There was almost no space between his lower lip and the sorry promontory of a vanquished chin. His jowls hung heavily. He licked his small mouth.

"It is my sad duty to inform you that your daughter's body was found on the shoulder of the lake road two hours ago," he said hollowly.

Santiago's hands rose to his face. The icy white fluorescence assailed him. It was too bright and there were no shadows. He leaned forward, his head between his knees, and saw a bright white vortex and felt himself falling into it. He tumbled forward out of the chair, onto his knees on the floor, and pressed his forehead against it silently begging that his life should end.

"Come on, sir" implored the officer. "Don't lose control." He called for assistance and the man who had fetched Santiago entered. The two policemen lifted him back into the chair, then left the room. Santiago sat hunched with his hands covering his face, and wept. After a while he lowered his hands, opened his eyes, stood up and opened the door. The captain was waiting in the hall.

"Where is she?" Santiago's voice was thick.

"This way," said the captain, and walked down the hall. Santiago followed him into a room where Cristina, covered with a sheet, lay on a table. The officer stepped to the table and turned back the sheet. She looked severe, as if death had taught her cynicism. He reached out and softly touched the back of his hand to her cheek.

"My poor baby."

"She was murdered," said the captain, behind Santiago. "Please forgive the frankness I am obliged to employ, but the author of the crime was most assuredly a sexual psychopath. She had been raped."

The room, the voice, the wax likeness of his daughter became a dream. Santiago said to himself, "This cannot be." Because he knew such a thing was impossible, that he could not withstand such a thing, that he could not continue to exist if such a thing as this were happening. But he did not die or evaporate, and he saw and listened.

"It was without doubt a maniac," said the captain. "She is missing her right hand. A search was made of the area where the body was found, but the hand was not recovered. The killer may have taken it as a macabre trophy."

MONICA FLEW TO SAN MARTÍN FOR CRISTINA'S CREMATION. SANTIAGO MET HER AT THE SMALL AIRPORT OUTSIDE TOWN, NEAR THE SKI RESORT. ENVELOPED IN A LONG BLACK NUTRIA COAT AND AN AIR OF SORROW she walked slowly across the lobby toward him. She gave him a perfunctory kiss on the cheek before removing her dark glasses.

Monica had turned forty. But she looked, despite her grief, younger than when Santiago had last seen her, almost four years ago. Her crying was over. Her eyes were shadowed and outlined and slightly changed, slightly Oriental. The skin that had barely begun to sag during their final year together had been tucked and hemmed and anointed. He thought she looked like another person, like a stranger whom a plastic surgeon had tried his best to make look like Monica, without completely succeeding.

"You've changed," she said to Santiago, and set her mouth in a line. She waited for his response, as if she had thrown down a gauntlet. But he said nothing, so she continued. "You were never petty and cruel. You refused to agree to the transfer of her body to Buenos Aires just to hurt me. She could have rested in my family crypt in La Recoleta. I want my baby near me." She looked for a moment as if she might lose her studied composure.

Santiago felt nothing but a leaden, tired disgust. He could not be moved enough by Monica to argue. "Cristina would have wanted to stay here," he said calmly. "She loved it here. She wouldn't have wanted to rot in a marble vault."

Monica flinched. "Part of the ashes are rightfully mine. I'm taking them with me. And I'm going to have a mass said for her, whether you like it or not. Thank God you weren't able to make an atheist of her too."

Santiago walked away from her, to the conveyor where luggage from her flight, the only arrival, was slowly circulating. He retrieved her suitcase, part of a set he had given her, and she followed him out to the jeep. He drove her to the town's best hotel, which in another month would be filled with skiers, and left her there.

He did not see her again until the next day. When Monica saw Cristina, who appeared to her impossibly old, like a middle-aged woman, in the pine coffin, she broke down. She buried her face in Santiago's breast and wept.

"Why? Why?" she sobbed. "We had it so good, Santi. If we had stayed together this would not have happened."

Santiago did not love her and he did not hate her. But neither did he feel indifferent toward her now. What he felt had much more to do with Cristina than with Monica, a sort of transitivity. She warranted tenderness because she was Cristina's mother. So he did not say what he was thinking—that if they had stayed together she would not finally have had all the things she wanted out of life: the wealth and status, the leisure and recognition she had acquired with her new husband, a widowed retired army general and director of Fabricaciones Militares, the state's mammoth arms manufacturer. So instead of reproaching her, instead of asking why she was so concerned now, now that Cristina was dead, about having her near when she had not come to visit her once in nearly four years, he offered his shoulder in silence, held the back of her head gently and stroked her hair.

Cristina's body was consumed by fire and her ashes gathered in two vases. The son of the crematorium's owner handed them to the father and mother.

They drove up the hill (Daniel could see the jeep from where he sat, absolutely alone, on a dished boulder on the cliff) to Santiago's home and went inside. Monica sat down at the kitchen table and Santiago put a kettle on the stove for tea. The urns stood on a narrow table in the foyer, as if Cristina had been left out of earshot of her parents' impending discussion.

But there was nothing confidential or personal she would have heard. Santiago and Monica sat silently at the table sipping hot tea, each wrapped in thought, each staring at some faraway point inside themselves. Then Santiago said, "I got a letter from Alejandro. You might like to read it, and take it back for your husband to read. I'm sure he would find it interesting."

He went upstairs. In a minute he returned and placed the envelope on the table in front of Monica. A twinge of jealousy, that Santiago should have received a letter, coursed fleetingly through her sadness. But the missive also thrilled her. She took it from the envelope and held it before her. Santiago noticed her hands, loose-fleshed and spotted, like the hands of another, much older person. Monica read to herself:

Dear Father,

I'm sure you'll be surprised by this letter. You're probably thinking "It takes a war for him to sit down and write me," and I can't blame you. I haven't been much of a correspondent.

Anyway, we have a lot of time on our hands over here. Time to write letters and time to think about things. That's what makes us want to write, I guess, because you think about a lot of things and you think that maybe you won't be going home. I don't mean to be morbid or anything and chances are I'll come through all right, but the possibility exists and there are always things you want to say that you never said. So I want to tell you that I love you and have missed you these past years. I think I'm just beginning to understand now how wounded you were by what happened to Diego, and if I ever seemed uncaring or cold about it, please forgive me. It was only because I wasn't capable of understanding.

That said, I'll tell you some about what's going on over here. I may be jeopardizing the delivery of the letter with some of the stuff (everyone assumes there's censorship of the letters, but I can't believe they read every line of every one) but I'm going to tell you anyway so, if something does happen, I'll at least have made the effort to bear witness.

First of all, don't believe the shit you read in the magazines. Some copies of Gente and Le Semana and Siete Días have made their way over and they're quite cherished for their comic value. But it's black humor, most of it.

The first few weeks weren't bad. We had almost enough food and the clothing held up all right for a while and if we weren't exactly comfortable, well, what the hell, we didn't come over here on vacation. For the first weeks the morale was really high, like the magazines said. The kids were all excited about being a part of it. But then the days dragged on and nothing happened and food got scarce and you were always cold and your feet were always wet and you stunk because you hadn't had a shower in a month. I tell you, that all would not be so bad if you saw that it was unavoidable and that everyone was suffering together. But you can't hide things on these islands and everyone knows the warehouses in the port are full of rations and there are thousands of sheep out here and they don't let you shoot them. We all know that the officers eat plenty, and wash and change their uniforms and sleep in beds with sheets and blankets. I was talking to a kid the other day, a conscript, and his job is serving lunch and dinner to the officers of the general staff in Stanley. He serves them roast lamb and steaks flown over from the continent. In fucking white gloves! Can you believe that? There is a black market in cigarettes and chocolate, and if you look behind the guys selling, you're likely to find an officer making a profit. Every week you hear about a few guys getting staked for some offense or other. They tie you spread-eagle to pegs in the ground and leave you out all night, and it's freezing fucking cold over here. Some of the guys punished like that got frostbitten and had to have their feet or hands amputated.

So all that has made for a great decline in morale, especially among the younger kids, the last batch: They're eighteen or nineteen years old and most of them had just two months training before coming over. I talked with a kid the other day, a Formoseño, who had fired just four live rounds during his training. He said he hopes if he gets killed he goes to hell, so at least he'll be warm.

But you know, along with all the shit, you see some inspiring things too, things that make you proud in spite of all and make you feel honored to be here. The little things, like the way some guys don't complain and don't brag either about how many Englishmen they're going to kill, but just take it all and shut up. If they say something it's a word of encouragement and a reminder that we're here defending what is ours, and nobody said it was going to be easy or fun. They're the guys who keep us going, and mostly they're just conscripts like the rest of us.

Well, my turn on guard is about to begin, so I'm going to end this. Let's see if it gets through. Don't worry about me. I'm doing all right.

I think that when the time comes, all these kids are going to forget about everything except the fact that the enemy wants to take over a piece of our country, and they're going to fight well and we'll win.

The first thing I'm going to do when I get home and get discharged is visit you and Cristina and Dani. Give them hugs and kisses from me. To you, I send a strong hug and kiss.

Your son,
Alejandro

Monica bit her lip and folded the letter slowly then put it back in the envelope. She pushed it across the tabletop to Santiago.

"Tell the armchair hero all about it," said Santiago. "Our generals are good at fighting dirty wars, 'cause they're dirty bastards. When it comes to fighting a real war, they're incompetent."

"I'm not going to tell him anything. And if you care about protecting your son, I would advise you to burn that letter. It could be very compromising."

Santiago looked at her and it seemed to him he was looking at someone he didn't know. The facelift helped. "You're a model citizen," he said. "You're exactly what they want us all to be."

"I'm just concerned about the only child left me. And if you can't understand that, then our daughter's tragedy becomes incomprehensible."

Santiago bolted from his chair. He felt for an instant capable of striking the taut and tampered face, capable of shattering the mask. Monica stifled a gasp. But Santiago checked himself, the rage burned out, smothered again by the overwhelming indifference toward this woman with whom—it was utterly incredible to him—he had spent twenty years of his life.

"Come on," he said. "I'm taking you back to the hotel."

She rose, watching him warily. She put on her fur then went to the foyer and picked up one of the vases. Santiago walked past her out to the jeep. She followed, stepping awkwardly in her heels over the long, leaf-strewn grass.

When they reached the hotel, before opening the door, she leaned toward him to buss him with the touch of lips to cheek, as a sort of seal on this encounter. But Santiago, who had not said a word during the ride, caught her face in his big hand and clamped her jaw, holding her away.

"Uhhh!" she muttered, alarmed, through pursed crimson lips.

He let go and she fumbled for the door handle to let herself out and, clutching the urn against her, hurried up the stairs into the hotel.

Santiago and Daniel sat sunk into overstuffed armchairs in the living room. A tenuous moonlight filtered through the big window, barely diluting the chamber's darkness. They had been sitting silently there for two hours.

The telephone rang. It sounded four times before Daniel rose and answered it.

"Hello," he said. The caller spoke and Daniel stood listening blankly.

Then, after a few seconds, his features twitched back to life and he asked, "Where are you?"

The telephone bell tinkled curtly, the sound of the connection being cut. Dani held the receiver away and looked at it as if it were the most foreign object in the world. He hung it up, and sat back down.

Some minutes passed in silence before he said matter-of-factly, "That was Lucia. She was with her. It was the cops."

Daniel moved mechanically and hummed a monotone, or little more than one. He moved between the dresser and his bed, and stuffed a few pairs of underwear, some socks, an extra pair of trousers and a sweatshirt into a canvas knapsack. His eyes barely registered the objects around him. Instead of thinking more clearly with the passing days, he was sinking deeper.

Soledad appeared in the doorway. "I know you are going," she said. "Your uncle has gone. Before you go, you must come with me. To look for something. Something that will help you."

Daniel followed her outside, across the yard and into the wood. Soledad seemed to glide over the bed of fallen leaves, deeper into the shadow of the forest.

She stopped and turned to Daniel. "*Lemunantu,*" she said. " 'Ray of sunshine that penetrates the forest.' It is the name I gave your woman. Look there where the sunshine falls." She pointed to a tall oak illuminated by a golden chute from above. The tree had been split by lightning. The bolt had struck in the crotch where the trunk divided six meters above the ground. It was as if a wedge had been placed there and struck by an enormous hammer. The main trunk was split through the white wood into the red-brown core.

"*Rehue,*" said Soledad. "The tree of the world. Struck by the ax of Pillán. We must dig."

She went to the base of the oak and knelt. She cleared away the moist earth between two big roots, then stood and searched until she found a short hard branch, which she used to pry and dig the more solid earth below. Daniel found his own piece of wood and began digging next to her, not knowing what for. But he dug earnestly.

They dug, scraped and chiseled the ground until Daniel struck a rock.

"That is it," said Soledad, leaning into the hollow. She scraped around the edges of the rock and pried under it with her stick. She lifted it out. It was a fist-sized chunk of black granite. She wiped it with her hands and rubbed it on her skirt until it shone. "A piece of Pillán's ax," she said.

They walked back to the house, Soledad leading Daniel. When they were inside she said to him, "You must stay the night. In the morning I will give you something."

Daniel could do nothing but obey. He pulled himself heavily up the stairs and collapsed on his bed.

Soledad took the stone to the basement, to the workbench where Santiago made models of gliders.

"What form do you harbor?" she asked the stone, examining it. She clamped it in a vice and assembled a small hammer, chisels and files. She tapped and chipped and chiseled the rock, changing its position in the vise as she progressed.

It was dawn when the Indian woman went up the stairs to Daniel's room. She sat beside him on the bed and touched his shoulder.

He stirred and she said, "Now you may go." Daniel sat up. She held out a small gleaming black sculpture of a condor. He received it from her.

"You have shared with him the heights. He will protect you. You have separated yourself from the earth to soar in the currents that bathe the summits and the hearts of men. You are his kin, and you will meet in Wenulentu, the River of Heaven that you call the Milky Way. There too you will be reunited with Cristina, who now is a silver vapor. When you join her, your spirits will fuse in a star."

Daniel slipped the talisman into his breast pocket and buttoned the pocket closed.

"Thank you," he said, and kissed Soledad on the cheek. Rested, he had emerged from the previous day's stupor. His eyes were clear. He stood and slung the knapsack over his shoulder.

"I dreamed about Cristina and you, together," he said. "You were carrying her piggyback across a shallow river. But you stopped in the middle, unable to continue, and shouted to me on the shore. I could see you gesturing and your mouth open wide, but I couldn't hear you. You must have been shouting for me to come into the river to get her. Then Cristina's shoulders arched forward over your head and she grew giant wings and rose and lifted you in her talons, like and eagle with a hare, and carried you to shore."

"Perhaps that is why the bird in the stone revealed itself," said Soledad.

Daniel took her hand between his. "You loved her too. I know that now. I thought I claimed all her love. Now I see it wasn't like that, that she had too much love for just one person."

"Sit down," said Soledad. "A minute more." She sat on the bed, pulling him down beside her.

"I think I know what kind of thing it is you will do. It is what I would do if I were able.

"The Christians speak against revenge. But even they in their hearts know that vengeance is pure, like the tear of a warrior. It is the only emotion as strong as love, because it is the child of love. The soul rejoices in vengeance, may even be redeemed by it."

Daniel walked out of the house, down the hill to town, and took a bus that skirted seven azure lakes on its way to Bariloche.

The mesa hunkered on the horizon like a beached whale, driven by a mysterious compulsion to fight its way onto the land and across the red dust desert. And this looming mountain was the biggest behemoth in all the oceans and his determination to die was as gigantic as himself.

Santiago drove along a straight and solitary road toward the mesa, a familiar and foreboding promontory from which he used to launch himself to soar above the sage. The tires rang against the road and drummed a deadening, hypnotic rhythm against the joints in the concrete slabs.

The cliff had not been his destination, at least not his conscious destination, when he left his home. He had simply left because he could not stay there any longer. He had bent over the bathroom sink and splashed water onto his face. The impossibility of staying struck him in the instant he lifted his head, saw his dripping face in the mirror and did not recognize himself. He saw only a vaguely familiar visage, like that of a man whose path he had crossed years ago. So he had dressed and gone out of the house, leaving the door open. He climbed into the jeep and drove down the hill out of town.

He pulled off the road where the highway began a gradual curve away from the butte and left the jeep on the shoulder. He struck out across the brush. When he reached the foot of the bluff he looked up at it silhouetted against the blue sky.

A nearly vertical high quadrant of the face of the hill was pocked with caves. The caves were like those inhabited by Greek monk-hermits who pull their sustenance up in buckets filled by novices aspiring to the dank and lonesome air of the hollows. Santiago knew the caves guarded secrets. So he climbed the hill, following a route more direct than the one he and Daniel used when they came to fly. He climbed like a baboon, scrambling on all fours. His feet slid out from under him because of the grade and he scratched for handholds in the scrub and rock to pull himself upward. He was sweating and paused to listen closely to the wind.

His fingers were bloody and his muscles knotted when he hoisted himself to the lip of one of the high caves. Without stopping to look back on the plain, he crawled into the dark maw and kept crawling. Dust and blood formed a paste on his hands and he crawled until the last ray of daylight was smothered by the blackness. He rolled over on his back and lay in the absolute darkness, his eyes open, his breath labored.

After a while a chill stole over him. He shivered and his teeth chattered. He could not move. He lay paralyzed on the floor of the dark cave.

Later, he stopped shivering but was still cold. He was hard and heavy, pinned to the floor by the weight of his hands and feet and heart. He lay on the bottom of a deep sea. Billows and waves of water passed over him, long matted fingers of seaweed wrapped around his head. The depths closed in on him, the only person in the universe.

He did not move and he did not sleep but was swept over by the black billows and waves, the eddying ether of desolation. It swirled and lapped over him in the entrails of the mountain. The earth surrounded him like a tomb. The ether dissolved him. It eroded flesh and bone but something of him remained beneath the billows and the waves. He sensed the essence of himself, his spirit or his soul. When all the worldliness and corporal trappings, the experience and grief were stripped away, his essence was like a pearl in a pool, and the water in the pool was not water but the revelation, liquid and pure, that nothing is so abominable as vanity, and the vain forsake all mercy.

Diego appeared. He stopped a few steps off and declined to come nearer, to enter Santiago's ethereal embrace. His face showed a trace of vexation.

"Come, *hermanito,*" said Santiago.

But Diego stood still. "Why did you stop making windmills? You should have kept making windmills," he said, then stepped backward into the darkness.

Santiago lay in the cave for three days. He roused with the feeling of having come back into his body. He bent his legs and his knees cracked loudly. He pushed himself up to a squat and saw in the darkness a flickering whorl of tiny comets tail out and away. He stayed crouched for a minute to get used to his head being above the rest of his body, then straightened up to a hunch and took tentative blind steps forward. After a few steps the darkness ceded and he walked toward the light until he was struck in the eyes by a searing blaze. He retreated a step and covered his eyes with his forearm. He waited for his eyes to adjust, then walked to the mouth of the cave. Still shielding his eyes, he looked down and across the valley. The sage glistened purple, silver and green, and a black thunderhead sailed away to the north.

He looked westward, toward the mountains. The sky was bright and light cascaded over the plain between the bluff and the first rise of the cordillera. Beyond the foothills, far off, rose the Andes. The snowy peaks confounded themselves in brilliant white clouds, so that Santiago could not tell where the mountains ended and the clouds began. It looked like the mountains reached to heaven.

When he returned home, Santiago found Soledad sitting at the heavy wooden table drinking tea. He sat down across from her. They did not speak at first and she examined his haggard face, sunken-eyed, ascetic, illuminated. She served him a cup of tea. He loaded it with sugar and sucked up the hot sweet brew. After a few minutes she said, "A man has called from Buenos Aires three times. A military man. He said it was a matter of urgency. The number is beside the telephone."

The mention of urgency did not have an immediate effect on Santiago because it seemed to him that nothing in the world, no possible event or circumstance, could be of any transcendence. Then it struck; that it was a military man who called, that his son was a soldier at war. The single numb nerve alive inside him twitched. He thought, "Oh, God, no."

He went to the telephone in the living room. On a notepad was a number and the name Brigadier Cosentino, Santiago's former boss, ex-director of the Pucará project. He dialed the number and looked out the big window across the lake below and waited as the connections clicked across a thousand kilometers of pampa. The receptionist at air force headquarters answered and Santiago asked for Cosentino. He was connected with the brigadier's secretary. She told him the brigadier was in a meeting.

"Tell him it's Santiago Maglione," he said.

In a few seconds Cosentino came on the line. "I've been trying like the devil to reach you," he said.

"Is it Alejandro?" Santiago asked hollowly.

"Alejandro who?"

"My son Alejandro. He's on the islands."

"Oh. I didn't know that. No, no, it's not about him. Though it occurs to me that his being there may weigh in your decision. I have a proposition of the utmost importance. Your country needs you, your skill and ingenuity. I can't tell you what it's all about over the phone, but if you still love this land, our *patria,* I will have a plane pick you up at the San Martín airport today. Just tell me yes or no."

Santiago paused for a moment, but not to reflect on anything. He was incapable of reflection or rationalization. Without knowing why, he said yes.

DANIEL SAT BY THE WINDOW IN A TRAIN SCURRYING ACROSS THE VAST PLAIN. THE RHYTHMIC ROCKING, THE EVENLY-SPACED CLACKING OF THE HURTLING COACH AND THE MONOTONY OF THE LANDSCAPE HAD LULLED HIM into a trance. He did not notice the arrival of the small bent old man.

The man wore a battered fedora and a gray wool overcoat too large for him. He carried an old black leather satchel. He lifted it above his head in an effort to put it on the luggage rack, but he was too short. He climbed unsteadily up on the leather seat. But, because of the motion of the train, he could not keep his balance when he tried to straighten up. He stepped down and nudged Daniel.

The boy started from his reverie.

"Would you be so kind as to put this on the rack for me?" he asked. "I cannot reach it."

Daniel got up and stored the bag. He sat back down and the old man sat opposite him, in the window seat that afforded a backward view of landscape whipping away toward the horizon. The man removed his hat but not his coat. His hair was thick and gray.

After a while he took a notebook from one of the big pockets of his coat and began scratching numbers on the page with the stub of a pencil. He looked up from his calculations and held the pencil vertically before his eye like a sight. He fixed the pencil-sight on a distant solitary ombu and followed the giant tree, sighting down the line of the pencil, across the prairie until it was no more than a dark spot.

"If the earth's circumference is forty-two thousand kilometers and it makes a complete rotation every twenty-four hours, then we're traveling right now at about eighteen hundred kilometers per hour. Ever think of that?" he asked Daniel.

"No," answered the boy.

The little man, suddenly animated, leaned forward. "That's because the velocity of anything depends on where it's measured from. When you're standing on the street corner, you think you're standing still, but you're really rocketing through space. You don't realize it because the lamppost and the mailbox and the buildings are all rocketing through space with you at the same speed." He sat back and clapped his hands once and smiled. His teeth were white and straight.

"That's Sir Isaac Newton," he said.

Daniel was strangely amused. He remembered something attached to that name. "Rate times time equals distance," he recited.

"*Muy bien, muchacho!*" exclaimed the man, leaning forward again to slap Daniel on the knee. "A star in your copybook!" He sat back and both passengers resumed their contemplation of the countryside. They had not gone much farther when the old man, his face serious now, again addressed his traveling companion.

"Light," he said.

"Pardon me?" said Daniel.

"Light," the man repeated. "It is light that refutes Newton."

"Refutes him?"

"Yes. His theories are not correct. Rate times time does not equal distance."

"I don't understand."

"Newton assumed space and time are constant, and they are not."

Daniel regarded the man quizzically.

"Let me explain." The man held up clasped hands as if in prayer. "It all works well enough in our world, on ground level shall we say. Rate times time equals distance at any speed man has ever attained and can ever hope to attain. The problem is the speed of light. It is not relative to anything."

266 CHAMPIONS OF THE WORLD

"How's that?"

"See that tree out there?" The man pointed to a scraggly poplar. "Relative to that tree, we're moving at about seventy kilometers per hour. But imagine you're in a car driving on a road parallel to the train tracks. If you were doing sixty in the car and measured the speed of the train from the car, the train, relative to you, would be going ten kilometers per hour. If you were going a hundred, the train would be going thirty kilometers per hour in the other direction. Understand?"

"Yes," replied Daniel, suddenly interested.

"That all goes down the drain with light. Because light, no matter where you measure it from, always travels at two hundred and ninety-nine thousand kilometers per second." He held his hands up and out, next to each other. "If you're in a spaceship going two hundred and ninety thousand kilometers per second and they shoot a beam of light past you from behind, you measure the speed of that light from inside the spaceship thinking it's going to be nine thousand kilometers per second and you're astonished to find out that the light went past you at two hundred and ninety-nine thousand kilometers per second." He stopped, tired by the emotion of his discourse.

"What does that mean?" he asked after catching his breath. "It means time and space are not constant. They are mutable. Time slows down and space shrinks. Light is the only constant. It is as incredibly simple as that."

The old man sat back, exhausted. He soon fell asleep and his head bobbed and bumped gently against the window. Daniel stared out over the pampa. He had read a creation myth somewhere and remembered that it began with the appearance of light. "God is light," the book had said. That was logical, he thought. That must be right, if light is the only constant thing, the only unchangeable thing in the universe. But as he stared across the weary plain it occurred to him that if old constants like time and space had been knocked down, this constant would likewise eventually be dethroned. He thought they would find out sooner or later that the only immutable thing, the only constant everlasting ever-enduring god of a thing was darkness, which, after all, was there before light.

*   *   *

Angela carried a sign nailed to a piece of crate wood. It was block-lettered in her own hand with a thick black marking pen. The sign said: LAS MALVINAS SON ARGENTINAS. LOS DESAPARECIDOS TAMBIEN. ("THE MALVINAS ARE ARGENTINE. THE DISAPPEARED ARE TOO.")

The phrase, honed and simply eloquent, had come to her upon awakening and she had roused Mikhail to tell him. "What do you think?" she had asked.

"I think we should paint it on the door of La Casa Rosada," he had answered.

About three hundred people, mostly Mothers, some accompanied by husbands, daughters or sons, formed a slowly rotating circle in the middle of the Plaza de Mayo. Some of the women carried placards with large photographs of a son or daughter with the question WHERE IS SHE?

Since joining the Mothers four years ago Angela had walked with her companions more than a thousand kilometers in a circle around the narrow pyramid in the center of the square. They had walked another thousand kilometers over the course of hundreds of trips to the Interior Ministry and the Federal Courthouse, the armed forces branch headquarters, offices of military chaplains, embassies and press conferences. All their walking had gotten them nowhere, these inexorable women—stout and lean, firm and fragile, rich and poor, brilliant and brutish women—who refused to accept the proposition that their sons and daughters could have been snatched away as if by specters, degraded and murdered, and that no one would ever have to answer for it. Their relentlessness had earned them the loathing of the government and the aversion of much of the populace. They were commonly known as Las Locas de la Plaza de Mayo.

But these madwomen kept marching every Thursday in the front yard of Government House, and their numbers increased. Participation had become physically less dangerous, as the regime could no longer afford the spectacle of its agents clubbing old women and dragging them off to paddy wagons, though plainclothesmen were still on hand, observing with disguised malevolence. Citizens paused on their way from work to the bus stop or subway to regard the procession, slow and silent like a vigil. Some surely felt sorry for the women. But most had been too thoroughly programmed by the dictatorship's propaganda to see them as anything but pawns, subversives, witches.

Angela Maglione, Francisca Otero and Juan-Cruz Otero walked side by side, as they did every week. The two women had become more than friends.

Angela did not know that Ana was dead. She harbored the hope that she was alive, but at times despaired of seeing her again. Then Francisca would renew her. Because Francisca was a fortress of faith.

She worked in the Mothers' office five days a week. She scrubbed floors, washed windows, filed papers and peckingly transcribed letters and communiqués on the old Remington. She was a stalwart companion to all the Mothers, her unfaltering conviction an example to them. Her days and dreams were consumed by the quest for Roberto, whom she knew to be alive. She knew because of the recurring pain in her loins. It was the same pain she had felt in bearing him and she knew that as long as Roberto was alive yet beyond her reach she would suffer this pain. Sometimes days would pass without her being doubled by a stitch. Only then would she grow despondent; and when the longed-for contraction finally racked her anew she rejoiced.

Shortly before this day's demonstration was to disband, a column of women surrounded by some forty young men arrived at the plaza from Diagonal Norte. The Mothers stopped walking and watched the group's advance from the direction of the cathedral. The young men, their hair close-cropped and their eyes flashing, chanted:

> *Madres de la plaza, el pueblo las rechaza!*
> *Estas son las madres que quieren a la patria!"*

> *Mothers of the plaza, the people reject you!*
> *These are the mothers who love the fatherland!*

The women, a dozen middle-aged matrons, advanced amid the boisterous escort, their heads high in a caricature of pride. All of them held a swatch of knitting and a pair of big needles that did not pause as the column progressed, but kept crisscrossing, hooking, purling, devouring yarn from the plastic bags dangling at their elbow.

As they neared the center of the plaza, one of the young men, whose blond hair was bushy on top but nearly shaved at the sides, rushed forward.

"These are the true mothers of the Argentine nation!" he cried. "These are the mothers whose sons are defending the Malvinas, the mothers we can be proud of! But do the foreign journalists go to the obelisk where they sit day after day making scarves and socks and caps for the soldiers? No! They come here to photograph and interview these sellouts, these traitors who continue trying to undermine the nation even when we are at war!"

(It was no coincidence this group should appear in the plaza this particular Thursday. There was a dearth of foreign press because of a news conference by the *Belgrano's* Captain Bonzo.)

The young man was working himself into a frenzy. He threw up his hands and looked defiantly around at the people who had stopped to observe him. "Want to see something? Something that will demonstrate just what I mean?" He made a signal and from the midst of his comrades emerged a shiny new green plastic bin, just like the scores of bins donated by the municipal sanitation corporation for use as receptacles for donations to the war effort. This one, like the ones along Calle Florida and Lavalle and Santa Fe, had a sign on it reading, "Fondo Patriotico." Two of the young turks carried it forward and placed it at the perimeter of the Mothers' circle.

"Good and loyal citizens like you," said the orator with a sweep of his arm to encompass the bystanders, "have filled dozens of these bins with cash, rings, jewelry, all kinds of things in the measure you have been able to give, and some have given far beyond their means. Let us see what these ladies, if the term may be so loosely construed, are willing to part with for the sake of their country."

The Mothers' gyre had stalled at the arrival of these people. The kerchiefed women looked at one another and murmured, some looked down at the ground. Hundreds of people had gathered around. Their eyes bore into the Mothers, accused them, dared them.

"See!" shouted the provocateur. "What more proof do you need?" His scream was barely past his lips when the shout, deep and resonant as if from the bottom of a well, burst from Angela.

"Hold on, you little snot!" she bellowed and broke ranks with three strides to stand square in the face of the young man, her placard resting on the stick over her shoulder like a rifle at ease. "My grandson is over there freezing his butt off waiting to fight the British while you and your thugs are here picking on old women," she berated him, her Italian accent thickened with ire. "Some of us have sons and grandsons on the islands and that is one thing. But another thing is that we have already lost a child to the junta's kidnappers, and we're here defending them the only way we can." She glared at the women surrounded by the youths. "Only if they send you your son back in a box, God forbid, will you understand. Only then may you presume to judge us."

"You see? You see?" railed the blond youth, his fists clenched, his face swollen with blood and fury. "She's not even Argentine! And she dares speak!" He turned to Angela. "Why don't you get back on the boat and go back to the hole you crawled out of?"

The placard snapped forward like the hammer that strikes the boxing bell and smacked the young man squarely on the nose.

The blow ignited bedlam. The ruffian entourage of the soldiers' mothers, or those posing as soldiers' mothers, flew against the circle of Mothers. The young men punched, flailed and ripped kerchiefs and handfuls of hair from gray heads. They waved the scarves as trophies and whooped and aimed kicks at the rears of the fleeing Mothers. The women the men had escorted withdrew. At the moment the fighting started, uniformed and undercover police appeared as if from nowhere and joined the fray, laying on their own blows. The husbands, sons and brothers accompanying the Mothers, and not a few of the Mothers themselves, fought the thugs and police. But it was only a matter of minutes before a hundred people were under arrest and on their way to various downtown police stations.

Both Angela and Francisca were arrested. Angela's eye was coming up purple when they found each other in a jammed cell. Francisca's right hand was swollen from the punches she had applied to one zealot's ear.

They and two dozen other Mothers were held for a few hours, then released with threats and insults.

The men were held longer. Juan-Cruz was in a cell in another precinct with a score of men from the plaza. The cell, a sort of holding pen, had a concrete floor, a urine hole in the corner and curses scratched on the walls. After a few hours an officer came every quarter hour, opened the door of metal bars, stepped in, grabbed someone by the shoulder and shoved him out. The prisoner thus summoned did not return, and Juan-Cruz crouched in the corner tasting his fear mixed with beads of sweat that rolled down from his brow. He looked skittishly around the cell at the men, some milling, some seated on the floor, some standing at the door with their foreheads pressed forlornly against the bars. His eyes fell on a lean, sharp-featured, curly-haired young man wearing a suit and tie. He had seen him before at the Thursday marches. The man had always greeted Francisca with a handshake and formal yet genuine affection.

He pushed himself up out of the crouch and went to the suited man's side.

"Excuse me, sir," Juan-Cruz addressed the man hesitantly.

"Yes?"

"You are the CELS lawyer, true?"

"That's right."

"I am the husband of Francisca Otero," said Juan-Cruz, extending his hand. They shook and Juan-Cruz took the lawyer lightly by the elbow. "Please come over here a minute," he said. "I have something to tell you."

Juan-Cruz led Leon Zanela, a lawyer for the Centro de Estudios Legales y Sociales, to the more sparsely occupied wall and began speaking in a whisper. He explained nervously, rapidly how he had been detained before and how he knew he could not again withstand what it was they were going to do to him, so he wanted to tell the lawyer, so it could be documented, revealed, punished, of his experience in the graveyard in Córdoba. Insisting politely, preventing Zanela from interrupting, Juan-Cruz related the secret burials in the "no name" section.

"I'm glad you told me all this, Mr. Otero," said the lawyer when Juan-Cruz had finished. "But I assure you that when they take you from this cell they are not going to do anything but note your name and document number and let you go. This is 1982, not 1978. What is important is that, when we get out of here, you come to CELS. We will talk about this cemetery business in greater detail."

The cell door opened and an officer entered. He stepped over to Juan-Cruz, grabbed a fistful of his sweater and shoved him out the door.

CHAPTER 8

THE BRIGADIER SAT AMPLY AT HIS DESK IN HIS OFFICE AT THE AIR FORCE BASE OUTSIDE RIO GALLEGOS, PROVINCE OF SANTA CRUZ. THE BASE WAS THE FORCE'S MOST SOUTHERLY, DUE WEST OF THE FALKLANDS ON THE ATLANTIC coast, and also the command center for air operations against the British task force.

A fierce Patagonian night wind rattled the windows. The officer, the base commander, was hatless and balding and wore a shiny green nylon flyer's jacket with a single insignia on his left breast. He smoked cigarettes one after the other. A straight-line salt-and-pepper mustache adorned his lip. On the wall behind him was a large map of the islands, a standard topographical chart, not a military operations map. Taped to the wall were sheets of white paper with the black silhouettes and specifications of the warships in the task force. The sheets pertaining to the Royal Navy destroyers *Sheffield* and *Coventry,* and the frigates *Antelope* and *Ardent* were stenciled with the word HUNDIDO ("SUNK") and a date.

The brigadier regarded Santiago from beneath graying, bushy brows. "You come highly recommended," he said amiably. His face was pallid and creased, especially around his dark-ringed eyes, from worry and fatigue.

"I haven't really practiced during the past years. I've been living in the country."

"Still, they speak highly of your resourcefulness."

"That's nice to know, I suppose." Santiago was already doubting the wisdom of having come. It was another place, another time, entirely different circumstances. But it was the first time he had spoken face-to-face with a military officer since he confronted his brother's killer. And this man's mustache was just like Roig's.

"We need someone resourceful," said the officer. "Precisely because we are running out of resources. We have sunk or damaged a third of the task force. It has been a damn good showing, but we have paid a high price in planes and pilots. The enemy's position is consolidated. Goose Green has fallen. They will soon advance on Puerto Argentino. They are professional soldiers and their commanders are combat veterans. Let me be frank. We in the air force believe that if the British ground troops can count on substantial support from the fleet—air cover from the carriers and artillery from the other vessels—our ground forces will not be able to stand up to them."

"My son is there. In the sixth regiment of Patricios."

"Officer?"

"Conscript."

"That increases your stake in this. We believe we have a single chance, a last chance to turn the tide of the war. Our only hope resides in dealing a devastating blow to the task force. We must put at least one of the carriers out of commission and sink four more gunships."

The brigadier rose and stood beside the map. He ran his finger down Falkland Sound, which separated the two main islands of the archipelago. "The strait is six hundred kilometers from here. That is the limit of the operational radius of our aircraft, even sacrificing armament for extra fuel tanks. The fleet has retreated more than one hundred kilometers out of range, some fifty kilometers off Puerto Argentino." He traced his finger eastward. "We must increase the operational radius of our aircraft to allow them to strike a lethal blow and make it back.

"Now, the only fighter-bombers in the Argentine armed forces with the capacity for in-flight refueling are the Navy's Super Etendards. But without Exocets, they are a weapon without ammunition. The last Exocet was used to sink the *Atlantic Conveyor* and we have been unable to acquire more on the international market. The British know this and consequently feel quite secure.

"What they do not know is that we have acquired seven Gabriel III air-to-surface missiles. The Gabriel is an Israeli version of the Exocet. The Israelis, it seems, are very adept at copying French arms, the Dagger being the most notable example. And they are anxious to demonstrate the efficiency of their weapons. I don't have to tell you that the Exocet has been the star of this conflict. Aerospatiale has doubled their price and still has more orders than it can handle. The Israelis depend on arms exports and would like the Gabriel to be as dramatically publicized. In short, we have the Daggers, the Gabriels and some guest technicians to connect the latter to the former. What the aircraft lack is range. That is where you come in. You will be working with two branch engineers— I believe you know one of them, Gibaja—on the adaptation of seven Daggers for in-flight refueling. And the work must be completed in five days."

Santiago scanned the map of the islands from the strait to Stanley and wondered where in that expanse was his son and what he was doing at this moment. He felt suddenly cold. He looked at the point in the ocean off Stanley where most of the British fleet was riding the waves and he imagined bombing and burning vessels slipping beneath the surface. The vision caused him neither joy nor sadness. He, required as a principal artifice of such death and destruction, was indifferent to it.

He got up tiredly. "Where do I sleep?" he asked.

"We have a room prepared for you in the officers' quarters. I hope you'll be comfortable there," said the commander. They walked down the hall and outside. Santiago buttoned his coat and raised his collar against the gale. They walked past sandbagged sentry posts manned by smooth-faced soldiers.

When they reached Santiago's room the brigadier unzipped his jacket and took a plastic-covered credential from an inside pocket.

"You're the only civilian on the base. Security is extreme. You must wear this tag at all times. Gibaja will come for you in the morning. Try to rest." He extended his hand and Santiago shook it. "Thanks for coming," said the officer. "Your country appreciates it."

Santiago had no response for that. He went in and closed the door behind him, then stood for a moment in the dark. He sat down heavily on the bed without removing his coat. Mechanically, he turned on the radio on the night table. Galtieri's gruff voice rasped from the box.

". . . against the depredations of anachronistic colonialism."

"Mr. President," said the reporter, "according to figures provided by the distinct armed forces branches, more than four hundred Argentine soldiers have died in the South Atlantic. How many men is the nation prepared to lose in the revindication of our right to the Malvinas?"

"Mr. Journalist, we, of course profoundly lament the death of each and every young man who has made the ultimate sacrifice on behalf of his country. But I affirm without the slightest reservation that though the price be four hundred, four thousand or forty thousand loyal and brave sons of the fatherland, it is not too high a price to pay for the defense of our sovereignty and dignity. And I am certain the nation in its totality agrees."

Santiago turned off the radio. He sat on the bed and listened to the moaning wind.

Daniel arrived at his grandparents' house on a Thursday afternoon. On his way to the workshop behind the house he saw Mikhail sleeping in the sun in a canvas chair. Next to him was a young jacaranda that, despite the imminence of winter, clung to most of its leaves. Daniel walked across the yard and stood over the peaceful old man with the white stubble beard. Mikhail's head was thrown back, his mouth open wide, and he snored loudly. Daniel had a sudden strong impulse to walk away and leave him with his measure of peace; to leave, rather than this parcel of grief, nothing more than footprints pressed into the yellow autumn grass. If the old man slept long enough, even the footprints would be gone when he woke. It would be as if Daniel had not come. And for a while longer, until Santiago's letter reached them, it would be for Mikhail and Angela as if Cristina had not died.

He left Mikhail sleeping there and walked to the shop and entered. He went to the workbench beneath the two square windows and opened the drawer. He opened the cigar box. The Orbea was not even dusty. It appeared to have been cleaned and oiled not long before. He lifted out the gun and a box of cartridges, replacing them with a letter. He closed the box and the drawer, then put the revolver and bullets in his coat pocket. He stepped out and looked across the yard at Mikhail.

He walked back across the grass and reached down and touched his grandfather's shoulder. Mikhail roused with a grumble and shaded his eyes against the sun.

"Dani, *m'hijo,*" he sputtered. He pushed himself out of the chair and they embraced tightly. Then Mikhail held him at arm's length to look at him and realized something was wrong.

"What?" he asked.

"Cristina is dead."

Mikhail wavered and dropped back into the chair. He did not say anything and neither did Daniel for a minute. They looked across the pasture, through the barbed wire, past the grazing red cattle with white birds on their backs, past the ombu to the horizon.

"How?"

"Murdered. By *milicos.*"

Mikhail sat and Daniel stood silently by his side.

"Where's Grandma?" the boy asked finally.

"In the city. With the Mothers." He spoke slowly, with great effort. "They walk around in circles in the Plaza de Mayo." He rose and took Dani by the hand and they walked hand-in-hand into the house. Daniel sat at the kitchen table. A *damajuana* of wine sat in front of him. Mikhail took two glasses from the cupboard and poured the wine. He sat down across from Dani. Each took a sip.

"Yours?"

"No. The grapes went bitter." Mikhail rubbed his eye. "I planted new vines, but it will be a few years before they bear." They stared into their glasses of wine. Then Mikhail said, "Santiago?"

"I don't know. He went off somewhere."

The old man, his skewed eyes glimmering, looked at Daniel. "Dani, won't you stay here with your grandmother and me? We miss you so."

Daniel did not answer. He was very tired. He hardly heard what Mikhail said.

The old man reached across the table and clamped his strong right hand across his grandson's forearm. Daniel looked up and was almost frightened by the panic in Mikhail's eyes.

"The main thing, son, is to keep on. Keep up the fight. It claws you and rips at your guts, but you can't let it defeat you. You must load it on your shoulder with all the rest and carry it along."

It occurred to Daniel that he could say, "Yes, that is so," joining his meager force to what was left of Mikhail's and maybe the confluence of their miseries would afford some respite, some slight hope or its illusion. But he could not second or sustain Mikhail. He could only ask, "Carry it where?"

Mikhail released his grip on the boy's arm.

"Where else? To your tomb."

Daniel looked down. Then he loosed a short clipped laugh and looked up again with a face incapable of laughter, a face so barren that no laugh could have crossed it in ages. But he had laughed.

"That should be a short trip," he said, and wished he had left Mikhail sleeping.

There was no more use in talking. Neither found anything more to say. Daniel stood up, stepped to the other side of the table and bent over to kiss Mikhail. The old man stared straight ahead. He allowed himself to be kissed but did not reciprocate. Then, as Daniel was drawing away, Mikhail reached up quickly with his left hand, like a cat darting his paw at a fly, and pulled Dani's head back down to his chest. He pressed Daniel's head to his heart and Daniel heard it pound. He felt the fingers dig into the nape of his neck and felt the absence of the middle fingers in the space not scratched.

The sun spilled over the top of Government House. The cold shadow of the presidential palace crept centimeter by centimeter back toward the building, like a blanket pulled imperceptibly toward the foot of the bed until the sleeper awakes to find himself uncovered and cold. But this rising sun pulled the chilled blanket of darkness off the plaza and Daniel, sitting asleep on a bench near the center of the square. He awoke when the shadow retreated from his face. He rubbed his eyelids with dirty fingers and stretched his arms above his head. He twisted and craned, groaning. He leaned forward and rested his elbows on his knees. He was staring at the pale brick-colored paving tiles between his feet when an ant, likewise stirred by the sunlight, crossed the ridged tile with a particle of something, food or building material, nearly as large as himself.

The insect moved unfalteringly across the tile fifty times longer than his own length, descending into the valleys that were the furrows only to climb the high mesa of the succeeding flat ridge, and down, and up and across, and down, without pause.

The ant's progress fascinated Daniel. He could not understand how the ant knew where he was going. When he was in the valleys he could not see anything ahead and even when he traversed the high flat crests the particle he carried blocked his view. Then the insect got lost. He turned down one of the furrows and proceeded for what in ant's terms would have been a few blocks, then stopped and turned in a full circle. He about-faced and headed back whence he had come, but overshot his original path. He seemed to realize that and turned ninety degrees and climbed out of the valley and continued in his original direction until he began meeting up with other ants. He would stop and appear to exchange information with some of them before continuing his journey. He passed a mass of his companions swarming over a dead beetle and was not distracted by their feast. Daniel kept track of the ant as long as he could from the bench, then got up and walked a few steps bent over so as not to lose him. He stood like that, bent over, stepping absurdly slowly in the first minutes of day in the Plaza de Mayo, watching an ant and never once thinking his strange behavior and shabby appearance might draw the attention of police. It was as if he were immune. In fact, no policeman bothered him and he was able to follow the ant to the tiny burrow at the edge of the walkway where he and his fellows lived.

When he looked up, Beto was almost upon him. Daniel froze frantically at the recognition of his childhood playmate and had an impulse to run.

"I don't believe it!" cried Beto, smiling broadly, approaching with open arms. Dani allowed himself to be embraced and raised his own hands to Beto's shoulders, setting them there like lighted pigeons.

The grinning Beto held Daniel at arm's length to examine him. Then, his happiness turning to concern, he asked, "What's the matter, Dani? Have you taken to sleeping in the plaza?"

"No. I'm waiting for the ceremony to begin."

"What ceremony?"

"The twenty-fifth of May. They're going to raise the flag and Galtieri is going to make a speech."

"I haven't got time for holidays. I got married. To Sara, you remember, the Polish girl who lived on Brandsen Street. I'm going to be a father in four months and I'm working my ass off trying to get a little saved up. I'm on my way to work, but I've got time for a coffee. Come on."

They walked toward the Cabildo, crossed Hipolito Yrigoyen and entered the café on the corner. They sat at a table by the window. An employee, an old thin man wearing a yellow apron over khaki work clothes, spilled sudsy water onto the floor on the far side of the room, where the chairs were still upside down on the tabletops. He looked up in annoyance when Beto called to him. When he brought the tray with the coffee and milk he slid the cups brusquely onto the table and sloshed in the rich coffee, then the steaming milk.

"I haven't seen you since the day my grandfather died. Remember? You never came back to the neighborhood," said Beto without reproach. "I heard you went south with your uncle."

"To Neuquén."

"You know, everybody talked about your folks for weeks, months after they were taken away."

"And that's all they did: talk." A fettered and muzzled beast stirred in Daniel's belly. "Everybody talked and talked, and talked and talked and talked. In whispers after dinner when the kids had gone to bed. They said 'What a shame, they were such good people' or 'They must have been mixed up in something' or 'I always thought they were strange. You never saw them at Mass.' We're great talkers. All bark and no bite. Galtieri thinks he can beat the British by talking up a storm from the balcony of Government House."

"What can I say, Dani?" Beto stared into his coffee. Then he looked up. "The only thing I can say is that you were and are my friend and if there's anything I can do for you, I'm right where I've always been, still in the Boca, still on Rocha. You know where to find me." He reached across the table, placing his hand on Daniel's, and squeezed.

Daniel looked into the eyes of his childhood companion and saw nothing in them, no compassion or affection or tenderness, and he felt the knot in his gut tug tighter. Because he understood, an understanding beyond mere perception, that the affection and tenderness were there in Beto's eyes and heart, because Beto was still the same person, but that he, Daniel, had changed so thoroughly as to be blind to those qualities. He tasted this wisdom on the back of his tongue like sour milk. Daniel longed to be reminded of what he had been, way back when he could cry and laugh. But those days with Beto were like something he had read about or seen pictures of, not something he had lived. So he looked back into his old friend's eyes and saw nothing.

"You can't do anything for me, Beto. But I'm going to do something for you. For you and for your kid. For the whole shitty country and the shitty country's shitty kids."

"Don't talk like that, Dani. You never used to swear."

"I learned."

Beto let go of Dani's hand. "I've got to go," he said, standing. He took a bill from his pocket and laid it by his cup.

"I'm sorry to see you like this, Dani. But I'm glad I saw you. Remember what I said."

He turned and left Daniel sitting there with that last phrase in his head. Daniel closed his eyes tightly and tried with all his might to remember what it was Beto had said, but he could not.

There was a canteen, a sort of lounge, in the officers' quarters. In addition to a bar, it was furnished with a couple of tables and a pair of sofas, two armchairs and a half-dozen straight-back chairs arrayed before a television on a stand against the wall. These days the canteen almost always harbored a few pilots playing cards or watching television, hunkered down in the overstuffed chairs, which were a good place for a man who had made it back one more time to appreciate the company, the mere presence, of other men and savor his extended sojourn in the land of the quick.

The lounge was right next to the mess hall, which in this case more closely resembled an expensive restaurant. Santiago sat at a table in the mess with Commodore Nilo Gibaja, one of the engineers with whom he had been working on the Daggers. After five twenty-hour days, the modifications were complete. The system had been tested with a C-130 Hercules as the tanker, and it worked. Santiago and Gibaja were exhausted, wrung by amphetamines, but also suffused with the special professional contentment that comes with resolution of a difficult problem. They were eating steaks and salads.

"Just think," mused Gibaja, smiling. "The Jews bail us out."

"It's not all that strange," said Santiago. "Their prime minister was blowing up British imperialists when you and I were in short pants."

"Still, old man Rudel must be turning over in his grave."

"I never had the pleasure."

"Mean old coot. Drank a lot of beer. I think he had a tube that drained into his wooden leg."

Hans-Ulrich Rudel, the most decorated German officer of World War II, was the single most influential factor in the formation, technical and ideological, of the Argentine air force. Rudel flew more than two thousand missions in Stuka dive bombers and was credited with destroying five hundred tanks, one battleship, one cruiser, one destroyer and seventy landing craft. He lost a leg in one of his many crashes but learned how to manage the aircraft with one foot and a prosthesis, and was soon back to bombing the Allies. He emigrated to Argentina after the war and passed on his skill and fascism to the nascent elite corps of aviators. He also wrote a book, an apologia for Nazism called *In Spite of Everything.*

The waiter had just placed demitasse cups of coffee before Santiago and Gibaja when an officer stuck his head in from the corridor.

"They tried to kill Galtieri! It's on TV!" he shouted, and disappeared.

The dozen diners moved as one, chairs screeching. The men rushed for the door and crammed through it into the hall, through the next door into the canteen. In all, about twenty men huddled in front of the television. One stepped forward and turned up the volume. They listened and watched, rapt, as a harried announcer related the news.

The footage appeared. Galtieri emerged from the Case Rosada and strode across Balcarce Street to the plaza. Around the flagpole next to the statue of Belgrano was formed the squad of Grenadiers that would raise the standard. Groups of schoolchildren invited to attend the National Day ceremony lined the walkways leading to the center of the plaza.

The white-smocked children shifted anxiously and craned their necks, almost breaking ranks, when the president appeared at the base of the equestrian statue of the father of the flag. A crowd of onlookers surrounded the scene, trampling flowerbeds and straining for a glimpse of the tall white-haired general.

Galtieri saluted and stood erect as the flag was hoisted up the pole. The TV camera followed the unfurling banner up and framed it against the sky. An army band struck up the national anthem and the people sang heartily. When they reached the first refrain of *"Oh, juremos con gloria morir!"* a man (or was it a boy?) stepped from the crowd and raised a revolver at the president. Galtieri, with his back against the granite base of the monument, looked like a man about to be executed by firing squad. The president and the assailant were both in the foreground of the television image. Galtieri's hand came down from the brim of his hat and he buckled slightly, bending forward in expectation of impact. The scene was so perfectly recorded by the camera crew that the flex in the assassin's hand was clearly visible as he squeezed the trigger.

But there was no report. And as the assailant stared with stark incredulity at the treacherous weapon, he was lifted off his feet and hurled backward by the force of two .45-caliber dum-dum slugs from separate pistols striking him simultaneously in the chest.

At the explosion of the rounds, the camera jiggled and dropped and the stunned television viewers had the sensation of tumbling with it as jumbled images of feet and sky and sidewalk swept across the screen.

Then the studio newscaster reappeared. He reported that President Galtieri had not been injured, that the weapon, a vintage Spanish Orbea revolver, had misfired and that the would-be assassin was killed by security agents. He reported that the assailant, a youth between sixteen and eighteen years old, carried no documents and had not yet been identified.

What the announcer did not report, because he had no way of knowing, was this: In the moment he saw he was about to be shot, Galtieri had lost control of his sphincter. He had been immediately surrounded by bodyguards who, advised by the odor, realized the president's predicament. The only one who did not realize it was Galtieri himself. The president, though cowed and quivering, was reciting lines from a script he had read or heard or composed himself about a situation such as this. Oblivious to everything, he mouthed remote-control bravado.

"Let the ceremony continue!" he blathered. "I will not withdraw! I will not retreat!"

But the commander of the security detail, Captain Armando Pasucci, was in control. He had seen many men and women shit themselves; in the back seats of cars, stretched out on bedframes, on their knees before him begging for mercy. This did not faze him. He knew Galtieri was incapable of resistance and he took hold of the president firmly by the arm and wheeled him around, ordering the other men to keep him encircled. They escorted the president, who walked with a curious and hesitant short-stepped gait, back across Balcarce through the high portal into Government House. The grenadiers guarding the door raised their sabers vertically in salute, but Galtieri did not salute back.

SANTIAGO HAD RECOGNIZED DANIEL THE INSTANT HE APPEARED ON THE TELEVISION SCREEN. IN THE SECONDS COMMENCING WITH THE SHOUTED ADVISORY OF AN ASSASSINATION ATTEMPT, HIS MIND—SO INTENT THE PRE-VIOUS days on resolving a technical problem that virtually nothing else, mercifully, had entered it—flew back to San Martín, to Daniel, and he suffered the terrible knowledge of his negligence and guilt; that grief had confounded him, defeated him.

It was not that he had believed Dani had gone off to mourn alone and would be back when his mourning was done. It was simply that, upon his return from the cave, Daniel's absence was another fact, registered and accepted as such, along with myriad and bewildering absences and presences in Santiago's physical and emotional surroundings.

When the news bulletin ended, Santiago, his face gray-white, had made his way through the crowd of murmuring men and gone to his room. Only when locked safely inside, face-up flat on the bed, did he realize his devastation was the product of fear as much as the result of having seen the nephew he loved like a son shot dead on television. Lying there on the bed he could not deny that, from the second he recognized Daniel, he had been terrified that the other men would somehow know, would turn on him and tear him apart. Only now was the fog of fear dispersing. Only now was the loss settling over him.

But it was different from his previous moments of knowing loss. He thought: Perhaps the heart is like the ball of the foot or the palm of the hand, in that if it is chafed and rubbed and battered enough, it forms a thick callus around itself. He wondered that he did not cry. Then he remembered a scribbled crumpled scrap of paper he had found more than a year ago on the workbench of the shop. He took his wallet from his pocket and pulled out the piece of page, then unfolded it. He read:

> Would that I could cry again
> That sad salt water bathe my heart,
> Drown the pain
> And carry it off to the sea of sorrow.

> But tear like woman's seed is fixed
> And mine all spent in so few years
> In vain,
> In vanity and heartlessness.

And he sobbed for Daniel. But the immensity of his impotence pressed down on him and he struggled to raise his chest, to expand his lungs against it. His breath came short and dilated. He was suffocating. He was void of strength and the exhaustion was painful, as it had been in the last round of his last fight. And now, like then, he wished for the bell, not caring if he lost, wanting only that the round should end.

Santiago's eyes opened slowly. He lay for a moment in his jacket and boots and tried to recall something from the dense sleep. He sat up on the side of the bed, his elbows on his knees, his face in his hands. Then he got up and went out the door. He walked down the corridor and out the front door of the building, across a wide grassy clearing toward the airfield.

It was before dawn, clear and cold. The sky was immense and jeweled with thousands of stars. He stopped to look up.

The sentry snapped to attention when Santiago reached the gate to the hangar area. He and the other engineers and technicians had been working so continuously on the Daggers that his appearance at this hour was not odd or noteworthy. There were other sentries at the gaping maw of the largest hangar.

He entered the huge garage and looked down the length of it. It was silent; nothing stirred. The seven Daggers, their delta wings fanned out like glider sails, stood all in a row, forty-five degrees to the wall, their noses pointing outward, toward the open door at the other end of the hangar, wing tips nearly touching. The Gabriels clung one to each plane beneath the starboard wings.

He walked to the bright red upright chests where the mechanics kept their tools. He opened a drawer, took a wrench and walked across the cement floor, his footsteps echoing through the enormous hall. He stopped beneath the fuel pod under the port wing of the first Dagger. He reached up and loosened the big nut capping the hose access to the pontoon-shaped pod. He unscrewed the cap and, as it came away, the jet fuel spilled out, over his hands, onto the floor.

He walked to the next plane and did the same. He went down the line of aircraft unscrewing the caps of the fuel pods to let the fuel cascade to the floor. When he finished with the last plane—it took less than three minutes—he looked back up the row. Beneath each plane spread a dark pool. He breathed the dizzying fumes. The separate pools flowed one into the other, and the perimeter of the puddle beneath the last aircraft crept toward the toe of his boot.

He took a box of wooden matches from his jacket pocket. He opened it and struck one. He held it a moment between his fingers, until the sulfurous smoke curled away and the flame flickered clean. Then he tossed it out in front of him.

The flames leapt with a whoosh and Santiago backed off, steadily but unhurried. He watched the fire race and the yellow and orange and blue tongues lick the bellies of the jets, the paint peeling. He stepped backward, intent on the flames. The first explosion threw him back and down, washing him in a wave of heat. He rolled over and pushed himself up and ran. Another explosion shoved him from behind. He ran toward the hangar door. The sentries from that end ran toward him.

At the third explosion he stopped and turned to watch the chain of detonations—one so close to the next that it seemed like a long

continuous explosion—erupt through the high arching roof in a con-
flagration of color, flash and blinding power. The guards pulled up
short and watched, their mouths agape, as the jets disintegrated in the
inferno.

Alejandro pushed back his helmet and raised the night-vision goggles
to his eyes. He looked down the hillside across the plain to the west.
Shells from the 155-mm guns three kilometers behind him whistled high
over him and dropped in thunderous puffs on the flatland toward the
horizon. He could not see what effect the rounds were having, if any, on
the enemy. But he hoped they were extracting as fearful a toll as the
British bombardment of Mount Longdon had taken on its defenders.

Alejandro, who with two other soldiers manned a ½-inch machine
gun near the crest of the hundred-meter-high hill, wondered what the
lull in the British shelling meant. Until an hour earlier, Longdon and the
neighboring heights had been subjected to near continuous bombardment from the 4½-inch guns of the HMS *Avenger, Glamorgan* and
Yarmouth offshore.

Ale and all the troops defending the horseshoe-shaped perimeter
along the high ground—Wireless Ridge, Mount Longdon, Two Sisters,
Mount Tumbledown and Sapper Hill—around Stanley had been expecting the British advance for forty-eight hours. They did not need to
be told that the war had been reduced to the battle for the hills.

Alejandro was surveying the terrain below and his trenchmates were
taking advantage of the halt in the shelling to sleep when a call, "Friend
approaching!" came from off to his left. And before he could grab his
gun a soldier was crouching on the edge of the trench. Alejandro raked
the elastic-held goggles down his face. The boy's white teeth shone in
the center of his grease-painted face.

"Good thing I'm not a Gurkha," he chuckled. "You'd be hamburger."

"Get down, *boludo!*" whispered Alejandro harshly.

The boy climbed into the hole.

"What the hell are you doing, roaming around out there?"

"Retreating. Like everyone else from Mount Kent. The live ones, I
mean." Mount Kent was the most exposed hill of the perimeter.

"It's over over there?" asked Ale. The other two boys in the nest
roused groggily.

"Yeah. But we hung on longer than they bargained for, I bet. It was hot. Lots of casualties on both sides."

"What happened? What did they hit you with?"

The new arrival took off his helmet and sat on it. He wore a knit wool cap beneath. "Who's got a cigarette?" he asked.

One of the awakened soldiers gave him one and struck his lighter to it. The black-faced boy inhaled deeply and sighed as the smoke flowed out.

"First, they creamed us with 105-millimeter artillery for a few hours. Airburst shrapnel and white phosphorous. The phosphorous falls like wet snow and sticks to you. Burns through your jacket, shirt, even boots. The only way to keep it from burning right down to the bone is to cut the skin away with your bayonet. The fucking screams, man . . ." He paused and smoked. "Then they sent the Harriers. They've got these bombs they guide with lasers. They hit the ground and roll and explode for a hundred meters, wipes out everything in its path."

"What about the ground forces?"

"They come behind light tanks. And they use anti-tank rockets against dug-in positions"—he looked around—"like this. It's weird, a foxhole hit by one of them. The guys are dead, but it looks like they're sleeping. They're not blown apart or anything, like with an artillery shell. There's just a little blood running out of their ears. It's the concussion. Shatters your insides, but leaves the outside intact."

The boy took the last drag off the cigarette, sucking the tobacco into ash down to the filter. He dropped the stub on the frozen ground, stood up and put on his helmet.

"This ain't my unit," he said, and clambered up out of the trench. "Good luck," he bade back over his shoulder, and disappeared into the darkness.

Alejandro checked the machine gun for the hundredth time, that the ammunition belt fed in correctly and that other belts were at hand. The other two soldiers took hold of their FALs and hefted and cradled them.

Then a mortar-fired flare burst high overhead and bathed the hill in eye-aching white light. The two soldiers jumped to the front of the position beside Alejandro and the three looked down across the plain. Tanks and columns of soldiers had already advanced considerably and would soon reach the foot of the hill. The flare burned out as it fell and the advance continued beneath a blanket of fearsome darkness.

"Why doesn't one of our fucking genius officers call in some artillery?" asked one of the boys. And as if someone had heard him, points on the plain heaved up amid thunder.

The hill was strongly reinforced and before long the enemy was pinned down not far above its base. Alejandro manned the machine gun, spraying fire down the hill at whatever moved among the vanguard as one of the others fed the belt into the port. The acrid smell of gunpowder stung their noses. The third soldier peered through his goggles down the barrel of his FAL, occasionally squeezing off a round at some ill-defined target.

Then artillery fell again on the hilltop and time slowed down. The shells sang and the boys dove into the corners of the hole, their hands reflexively covering their ears against the clap. The rounds burst deafeningly around their hole and Alejandro imagined himself boring into the hard earth with his mittened paws.

When the shelling lulled he went back to the gun. He adjusted his goggles and surveyed the scene. He saw crouched soldiers darting from rock to rock, pausing at each protected point to choose the next objective meters away. Fire sprayed from a position to Ale's right and he followed suit strafing the rocks below. He continued firing until the barrel of his weapon glowed a dull orange. He paused and, only then, thought of his trenchmates. He looked behind him and there was no one.

The position to his right resumed firing. Seconds later a fizzle-tailed projectile that seemed to travel in slow motion whistled up the hill and exploded. The neighboring gun's staccato ceased. Alejandro again looked down the barrel of his weapon and squeezed the trigger. It spat a dozen rounds and jammed. He grabbed his FAL and sighted down it. Nothing moved below. A weird silence enveloped the hilltop and suddenly Alejandro had the overwhelming sensation he was the only defender left. The eerie scarlet scene he saw through the night goggles brightened and he lifted them to see it was dawning. A thick white mist rolled across the plain and tumbled up the hillside. Ale thought for a moment that it must be a new technological warfare technique developed by NATO; remote controlled cover-providing fog. Then he recognized it as the same fog of all the Malvinas dawns. The only difference was there were men hidden in this fog, men moving forward, bent over, running with rifles slung beneath them, rifles they would use to kill him.

"Hey!" he shouted to his right. Then to his left, "Who's there? Anybody there?" A bullet rang off a rock in front of him.

He scrambled out of the trench and ran like a spider toward the summit. He dove over and rolled down a ways. Sliding on his belly, he stopped himself. Still clutching his rifle, he pushed himself up and looked around. Above him and to either side was nothing but an empty hillside. He turned around and looked down and saw for off, where the hill spread onto the plain to Stanley, scores of men running clumsily. Some carried rifles. The arms of others pumped unencumbered.

Alejandro took off down the hill. He stumbled and tripped in long leaping strides. He fell a number of times but did not feel the smart of the rocks on his knees and elbows and chin. The only thing that mattered was that life lay across the narrow plain and death was here on the hill.

The officers' mess was serving steak these days for breakfast, lunch, tea and dinner. They were thick juicy grilled sirloins flown over from the continent during the weeks before the arrival of the task force. Captain Roig sneered at the white-gloved conscript-cum-waiter who set the slab of broiled beef in front of him this early morning.

"Isn't there anything else to eat around here besides steak? No *media lunas,* or anything?" he asked peevishly.

"No sir," replied the boy.

But Roig did not believe him. He surmised that it had been decided that the officers be fed a steady diet of steak to fuel their valor. It was common knowledge that red meat nourished the savage in a man. Then another explanation sneaked into his consciousness: that the high command had already given up the cause for lost, conceded the battle and simply did not want to leave all these fine Argentine steaks to be savored by the enemy.

Alone at the table in the nearly empty mess, Roig was chewing his beef and chasing defeatist speculation when an army officer in a down overjacket entered. He pulled the hood off his unhelmeted head and stomped to the bar, opened a bottle of Scotch whisky and poured half a glass. He gulped it greedily.

"Go have a look," said the officer sardonically to the few men regarding him. "It's like the Boston Marathon, with the finish line at the center of Stanley."

Roig rose and went to the window. He rubbed off the condensation and peered out. Scores of soldiers filed past in hunched and heavy-footed procession. Some supported comrades too weak or wounded to walk unassisted. Some clung feebly to the barrels of their weapons and dragged then along the scarred pavement.

"By all the saints!" swore Roig. He walked quickly back to the table, took his coat from the back of the chair, donned it and stalked out. He strode into the middle of the street and stood facing the parade of stragglers. He blocked the path of a bare-headed, red-faced conscript. The boy looked at him blankly with dull eyes and raised a raw red hand to rub the whiskers on his chin.

"Where are you going?" demanded Roig.

"Town," answered the boy, who, having stopped, wavered and seemed about to fall.

"Where is your commanding officer?"

"Don't know," the conscript mustered the strength to respond.

"You're a disgrace to your uniform and to the fatherland," snarled Roig as he grabbed the strap of the boy's FAL and snatched it from his shoulder. The officer cradled the weapon and marched up Ross Road, against the tide of weary soldiers. The farther he went along the road, the thicker the retreating column grew.

Intermittent explosions sounded far off up the road. They seemed to come from beyond the high ground where the pavement ended. But the sound was not that of a battle raging, something that could explain the massive retreat. Roig scanned the oncoming soldiers in search of an officer, someone who could tell him what was going on, but all the tired and bloodied faces were those of schoolboys.

Roig strode resolutely, faster now. He looked straight ahead, beyond the faces of the lesser men, these cowards who had betrayed their oath to lay down their lives. His jaw was hard and fixed forward. He said to himself, "I'll take some pirate bastards with me," and thought with satisfaction how appropriate that would be as an epitaph. He wished there were a comrade warrior at his side to whom he could say it, that it might be remembered and recorded.

He reached the end of the paved road and struck out across the rising heath. Ahead, men streamed and stumbled down the grade. The explosions grew louder and more frequent. Roig broke into a run. He scrambled up the first hill, dodging soldiers descending in headlong abandonment, and topped the rise. On the plain stretching out below, enemy soldiers advanced alongside and behind small tanks spitting puffs of smoke. Roig went forth into battle.

He scrambled from abandoned foxhole to machine-gun emplacement to artillery shell crater. A round screamed at him and he dove into a trench. He pushed himself onto all fours and turned quickly in a full circle like a dog chasing his tail, as if he were looking for another way out. But he was surrounded by walls of earth. Another shell, then another exploded around his refuge and rained on him a deluge of rocks and dirt.

He looked frantically again around his close quarters and remembered what he had read in a counterinsurgency course about the Vietcong, their network of tunnels that allowed them to attack here and emerge there, to hit and escape like moles.

"That's why they were able to beat the Yanquis," he said. "Because they had tunnels."

The only other thing in the foxhole was a boot. It stood upright in the corner and Roig wondered, in the midst of bombs pocking the hillside, why anyone would take off his boots in this abominable cold. To be able to run faster?

Then, because it was the only thing in the hole with him, he reached for it. And in the instant he grabbed it with his gloved hand he realized it was not an empty boot. He dropped it and it fell over on its side, the top toward him, and thick black blood oozed out onto the frozen ground. The shinbone gleamed blue and white.

Roig regurgitated his breakfast steak, tasting it anew. He choked and coughed over the small mound of vomit. Thick threads of saliva hung from his chin.

He threw himself backward against the earthen wall farthest from the heavy boot and, his eyes fixed on it, yanked off his gloves and clawed at his chest as if he were swarming with ants. He found the zipper of his overjacket, tugged it down and ripped open the front of his tunic. He tore at the buttons of his shirt. He peeled the overjacket, tunic and shirt off together, tugging furiously to free his hand from the cuff's constriction. He stripped off his undershirt—beside his drawers the only white article of clothing he wore—and raised his hand above ground level and waved the T-shirt wildly. He knelt like that in the hole against the forward wall, the side of his head and his bare upper body pressed against the frigid earth, with nothing but his hand above the edge, and waved the undershirt for minutes or hours.

He eventually heard a voice not far away call out in thickly accented Spanish, "*Salga con las manos arriba!*"

"Don't shoot! Don't shoot!" squealed Roig in English. He rose shakily.

The British soldier advanced. His face was painted black. He stood over the trembling man in the hole.

"Put your bloody clothes on," he ordered.

THE WEIGHT OF THE METAL-DETECTING DEVICE ON HIS BACK AND THE DISC-TIPPED POLE MADE ALEJANDRO SINK INTO THE SOGGY PEAT THAWED BY THE WINTER SUN. HE STEPPED SLOWLY, EXTRACTING THE REAR BOOT FROM the softly sucking earth to put it down, timorously, resignedly in front of him. He described with the sweeper a broad arc over the murderous sod and listened for the beep.

Most of the soldiers from his unit watched as Ale, two other conscripts and a British officer swept the field. The prisoners of war stood in ragged file outside a warehouse on the southern edge of Stanley. The two hundred or so POWS stamped the earth to chase the chill. Black-bereted soldiers, their faces smudged like coal miners, guarded them idly, their FALs, the same standard-issue weapon surrendered by the vanquished troops, pointing at the ground.

Some of the British soldiers doubted the valor of the Argentines. Some of them had commented openly, thinking the prisoners did not understand or hoping some of them did. Alejandro had understood. And he had volunteered for the mine-clearing detail.

"There must be three brave lads in the lot of you," the enemy captain had said after mustering these prisoners and calling for volunteers. "The Geneva convention prevents us from obliging you. But I'll be damned if

I'm going to risk my men because your officers, in violation of that same convention, sowed mines at random without any record or chart. So let's have 'em. Three Argies with balls."

Alejandro had stepped forward, along with Ramiro Estevez and Gustavo Sosa, a Chaqueño who had fought like a demon and was alive now because a bullet had struck his helmet and knocked him out. He had cried inconsolably upon awakening a prisoner, and through his tears composed inspired epithets regarding the Argentine officers, their ancestry and progeny. He had vowed not to return to the continent, where, in any case, he had no family and few friends. He had been the first to volunteer for the detail.

"I'm going to ask them to send me to Australia or one of their other colonies," he had confided to Alejandro when they were being instructed in the use of the equipment.

Alejandro's beeper sounded and he turned to stone. "Here's one!" he called frailly to the British captain ahead and to his right. But before the officer could respond, a muffled explosion convulsed the earth directly to Alejandro's right and vibrated through the soles of his boots. He looked and saw Sosa hurled backward. The boy landed spread-eagle on his back. Ale dropped his sweeper and took a step toward his comrade before freezing in terror, precariously balanced over his spread legs. Sosa rolled over and struggled to push himself up on all fours. His blue-pink intestines hung in the shreds of his jacket and belt. Alejandro was close enough to hear him groan and he watched with rapt horror as the Chaqueño gathered in his guts with his right arm and pushed himself up with his left. He staggered to his feet and plunged forward madly, blind. His fourth step triggered another mine. The explosion lifted him off the ground and propelled him forward in the air. He landed face-down within reach of the British officer's sweeper. The stumps of his calves stuck up behind him, the jagged bone protruding from tattered flesh. But he was not dead, nor even unconscious. He raised and turned his head and his glass eyes found those of the enemy officer.

"*Por favor,*" whispered the Argentine.

The captain laid his sweeper on the ground and stretched the one long stride separating them. He knelt beside the boy and rolled him over and he spilled out onto the tawny earth.

"*Por favor.*"

The officer reached to his holster and drew his pistol. *"Vaya con Dios,"* he said softly to the boy, and placed the barrel against his temple and fired.

The white-helmeted guard, a machine pistol slung across his torso, spoke with the driver, then signaled to the other sentries at the gate. The heavy doors of iron bars swung open inward and the car pulled forward. Juan-Cruz, sitting with Francisca in the back seat, squeezed her hand.

The car rolled slowly down the long driveway to the José T. Borda National Neuropsychiatric Hospital. Futile buds fooled by a few days of sun strove to break from the twigs and gave the elms and lindens a dreamy green halo. Francisca surveyed the tranquil, wooded grounds and thought madness perhaps not so dire.

They parked near the entrance to the main building. Juan-Cruz, Francisca and Zanela, the CELS lawyer, got out of the car.

"Wait for us here," the gray-suited lawyer instructed the driver. "We don't know how long we'll be."

The three walked up the stairs and entered. They inquired and were escorted down a broad, shadowless, fluorescent-lit hallway to the office of the institution's administrator, Colonel (retired) Claudio Elizondo.

Elizondo, a short, paunchy man, stood as the three entered. He had been expecting them with annoyance and apprehension.

"The court order," demanded the administrator without preliminaries. Zanela produced the document from his inside breast pocket and watched Elizondo peruse it. The colonel's jaw twitched. A fly perched on an oily strand of thin hair combed horizontally across his crown in an effort to cover his pate.

"I repeat, as I reported in the deposition, there is no patient by this name on these premises."

"We are going to see for ourselves just the same," replied the lawyer curtly.

"As you wish, but I refuse to waste my time escorting you on a wild goose chase." Elizondo lifted the telephone on his desk. He spoke sharply to his secretary and within seconds there appeared in the doorway a doctor in a white smock. The physician, not caring for introductions, said, "Follow me."

He led them along a labyrinth of corridors. They passed through a wing of bedridden idiots, the air thick with the smell of excrement and sweat. They walked through a sticky-floored ward of babblers and squawkers. They looked into the bovine eyes of the drugged and dazed.

In some sections the patient-inmates seemed to have free rein and wandered aimlessly in faded green nightshirts or tattered clothing and slippers. They smiled and drooled.

"Where are the doctors and maintenance personnel?" inquired Zanela.

"We are grossly understaffed," responded the doctor without looking at the lawyer.

They passed along a corridor of cells for the criminally and dangerously insane and peered through visors in the solid metal doors. Inside the concrete boxes raving or placid psychopaths fondled their genitals, smeared the walls with feces or lay straitjacketed on the floor.

Juan-Cruz gripped Francisca's hand tightly as they followed the doctor. Years of tending a flickering flame of hope through endless frustrations and rejections had brought them to this infernal place. Now, within this macabre world of terrifying and incomprehensible beings, he was agonized by the juxtaposition of longing and dread. He wanted to find Roberto, and he did not want to find him here.

In his moment of vacillation, Francisca saw her son. He sat in the corner of a large barren room. A few inmates milled about or stood staring out the windows. Roberto sat with his back to the wall, his legs stretched out before him. She clenched Juan-Cruz's hand and pointed to the corner. They moved toward him.

A Persian blind sliced the afternoon light that fell across him into jagged stripes, hardening the contours of his angular body. They reached him and Francisca knelt by his side. She placed her hand beneath his chin and gently lifted his misshapen head.

A thread of silken spittle strung across his chin. She wiped it away with her hand and as she did, Roberto saw her face. The corners of his mouth lifted ever so slightly. The lips closed softly, touching each other in the beginning of the formation of a sound or a word.

"Mm . . ."

She leaned forward, holding his heavy lolling head tenderly, and kissed him.

*   *   *

Alejandro walked down the dim tunnel next to the guard. He could not swallow. Their synchronized step drummed off the walls and pounded his ears. He shuffled to foil the cadence. The four separate footfalls harried him more. His arms hung hollow and heavy at his sides, as if they were tied to his shoulders with string.

The guard threw the latch of the cell door. Its hinges creaked. Santiago stood in the middle of the cell, directly in front of the door. Ale's first impression was of his father's composure. He seemed as calm, as maddeningly tranquil as the rare cold air of the cinderblock cell.

The guard said nothing, not how long they would have together or what was prohibited and what was allowed, and closed the solid metal door.

Santiago raised his arms and moved toward his son. Alejandro, stiff-armed, clutched him by the shoulders and held him off.

"Why?" His face twisted with disgust. "Why?"

"Let me hug you."

He shoved his father back, away. The violence of the gesture left Santiago rigid and mute.

"You're a traitor!" Alejandro rasped, repeating, "A traitor!" He stepped forward and grabbed his father by the front of the shirt. "Why don't you kill me right here, now? Why don't you smash my head against the wall!" His face flamed, his eyes swelled and his spit flew in Santiago's face. "They were trying to kill me, and you helped them!"

He spent his rage. The reproach trailed off in a groan. He slumped to his knees, his hands clawing down his father's breast, and hugged Santiago around the thighs.

"Kill me if you want, Father," he wept. "That would be better than what you did."

Santiago placed his hands on his son's head and stroked his soft, childlike hair. There came to him the vivid memory of a bruised toddler, this same boy hugging his father's knees in search of succor.

He stooped and helped his son to his feet. He guided Alejandro to the narrow bed and sat the boy down next to him. He hugged his son tightly and kissed him a hard kiss. The wounded and desolate warrior disappeared and Ale's arms rose of their own to wrap around his father's broad back. The two men held each other desperately.

After a minute, they separated. Santiago stood and went to the barred window.

"I've been thinking a lot about you. And about Cristina and Daniel, even about your mother. Jail is good for thinking," he said, looking out.

He could see a barn across a pasture. Its foundation was of jagged fieldstone, gray and hazel, and the white mortar described a single convoluted line dipping and winding around the rocks in an indecipherable script. One of the rusted zinc roof sheets had blown off and left a stretch of gray rafters exposed like the ribs of a decaying beast.

He turned and faced his son. "I wish I would have made more effort along the line to talk, really talk seriously, man to man, with you about the things you were going through; about the things I was thinking about, too. That's all history now." He sighed. "Anyway, I'm thankful for this chance to talk."

But he did not talk. Neither did Alejandro. They remained silent, quietly wrestling with specters in the still and heavy doldrum of the cell.

Then Santiago said in a far-off voice: "I think there's a kind of lonely contemplative hermit, a sad fairy who lives in the shadow of our hearts; at least one lives in me. And all he does throughout one's life is try to get one ready to face death. For some reason I don't understand I've always felt more or less consciously the palpable presence of death. Deep down, it always seemed to me a short and uneventful journey from womb to grave; that a man plays away his childhood, stumbles through his youth and works away his manhood, gets old and plays dominos, drinks vermouth and dies, and that's it, chau.

"But then when I was grown and well along that road I got some knocks and they kind of jarred me into the discovery that everything is not inconsequential, that something matters. And that what matters is beyond men and nations. That there is a realm of ideas and ideals, and only ideals can truly and compellingly claim a good man's allegiance.

"I understood, in a crystal instant of wisdom like recompense for all my grief, that we should not win the war.

"See, son. If any land, any nation would be great and good, it must revere the greater and farther and more difficult realm of ideals. You love your country. I love her too, difficult though that may be for you to comprehend. But in that moment of lucidity it became clear to me that if we won the war, we would lose the country. We would lose

Argentina herself. Because we would have bequeathed her to the same men who raped and ravaged her and, still bloody from that carnage, had the shamelessness to present themselves as her redeemers and champions.

"I know no one will understand this. I don't care if they do. It doesn't matter. That's why I present no defense in the court-martial. It only matters that you try to understand. It will take time, maybe a long time. I want my father and mother to hear this too, and it will have to be by way of you, so just listen.

"I did it for you. And for all the kids like you over there. Because you had to have a country to come back to. And a triumphant Argentina that because of a vile dictator's dream of glory, might, with great fortune, have been able to give a decrepit empire a kick in the ass—that's not a country. Taking back something that's yours from the thief who stole it could be something to be proud of. But it could not be like they designed it. It could not be that the *milicos* become heroes like that. They killed my brother and my daughter and your sister and the brothers and daughters and sisters of thousands more. But who would have remembered that? Had we won, the murder and torture and pillage would have been a footnote in history, reduced to insignificance by the nation-redeeming conquest of the Malvinas.

"Now that you kids are back and can tell the story, it's clear we never could have won. Not with officers who are brave when it comes to knocking down doors at dawn but not so valiant when it comes to facing soldiers across a battlefield. No. We would not have won even if we sank half the fleet. We would have lost sooner or later, and it would have been that many more lives wasted."

Santiago placed his hand on his son's shoulder. "You'll have a lot of time to think about these things and you'll judge me according to your own standards. But there is one more thing I want to say and it is something I want you to hold close, very close, when you learn that I have been shot.

"I can do it, son. I am stronger than I have ever been. My step will not falter."

Alejandro stood and the corners of his mouth twitched. He blinked and a fat tear overflowed his eye and rolled down his cheek.

"Now that's the one thing that could fuck me up, *hijo mio.*" Santiago brushed away the tear. "Please don't cry."

Alejandro composed himself.

"Go on now," said the father.

Santiago walked him to the door. He knocked and the soldier opened it. The two men hugged once more, quickly and strongly, and Alejandro broke from his father and said, "I'll tell Grandma and Grandpa."

He stepped out of the cell and the guard closed the door and threw the bolt.

Alejandro began to walk away.

"Ale!" Santiago pressed his face to the window in the door. "I forgot to ask you. What happened in Spain?"

"We got eliminated yesterday by Brazil. Didn't even make it through the second round."

"That's because you weren't there."

His father's face in the small barred square was a blur. "Adiós, *padre.*"

"Adiós, *hijo.*"

The war was lost. The cup was lost.

Galtieri was deposed. The dictatorship crumbled. When he left Government House for the last time, two days after the fall of Stanley, the disgraced despot carried with him in his briefcase confidential documents he planned to use to incriminate others if they tried to make a scapegoat of him. He also carried the British flag captured by Argentine forces when they had invaded the islands ten weeks earlier.

Galtieri hid the flag in a closet of his high-rise apartment, where he spent his days secluded like a leper, imagining what might have been and being startled by the reflection in the mirror of the sagging, dull-eyed face that each morning seemed a year older than the day before.

Often, when his wife was out and he was alone, he would pour himself a whiskey and reach back into the closet in his study and take out the carefully folded Union Jack. He would sit and spread it out over his lap like a steamer blanket, then lightly stroke the diagonals of red and white running through the blue.

One day, he took his wife's sewing kit into the study and cut a square of fabric from the corner of the banner. He carefully stitched a hem in the angle cut into the flag so the cloth would not fray, then did the same around the edges of the sectioned square. He folded the standard and put it back in the closet. He took a blue blazer from the closet and put it on. Then he folded the piece he had cut and pushed it into the breast pocket of the blazer, leaving a point sticking out. He walked into the master bedroom and stood before the full-length mirror admiring himself and the flair of the hankie.

"Yes, Mrs. Thatcher," he said in an imaginary dialogue, as if at a cocktail party with the British prime minister, "you have gained a transitory victory. But our inalienable right shall be vindicated." Casually he pulled the handkerchief from his pocket, blew his nose loudly into it, and burst into raucous laughter.

Mikhail's ship sailed at night. The night of the first day of spring. The night before the dawn of Santiago's execution by firing squad for the crime of high treason.

He stood with Angela on the dock, delaying his ascent of the steel stairway. The night was clear. Mikhail looked up at the sky.

"I think I shall not look at the night sky during the voyage," he said. "At least until we cross the equator and that"—he signaled the four brilliant points of the Southern Cross with his chin—"has sunk forever below the horizon."

"I remember when we came. Once past the Cape Verdes, on deck scanning the sky every night, you were so anxious to see it for the first time."

Mikhail lowered his gaze and looked around him slowly. The big cranes reared like the skeletons of Trojan horses. The black water murmured against the hull.

"How can you remain here?"

Angela saw the infinite sadness in her husband's eyes. "You were a young man," she said. "You were going to Spain and I thought my heart would break. I asked you why you had to go. Do you remember?"

Mikhail reached back and found the moment. It seemed so long ago. Another lifetime.

"Yes."

"That is why I have to stay."

After a moment he said, "But you will come."

"I will come. When what must be done here is done." She took his hands in hers. "It's no longer a matter of a mother's grief. The disappeared are all my children. They are all our children; Argentina's children. But she would turn her back on them, disown them, forget them. And if that happens, nothing in the world shall prevent it happening again. Remember what Alejandro told us? How Santi wanted his son to have a country to be a man in? I want that for Ale too. For all the young ones."

Mikhail picked up the two suitcases on either side of him, then set them down. He stepped to Angela and they hugged.

"I'm so tired, *cuore mio,*" he whispered. "Too tired."

He stepped back and again hoisted the bags. He went up the stairs. Angela walked down the pier without looking back.

At the bus stop a little while later she heard the long hollow howl of the ship's horn and imagined it pulling away from shore with Mikhail aft, watching the city and its lights recede, watching the frothy wake widen, the wave smooth to a ripple, the ripple to a purl, until no trace of the vessel's passing adorned the shallow sea.

Douglas Mine graduated from Cornell University in 1976 with a degree in anthropology. Subject to fits of wanderlust, he spent eight months backpacking from Cape Town to Cairo through the eastern half of Africa, and another eight months backpacking from California to Ecuador. In 1979, he joined the Associated Press as a journalist. He spent five years reporting from Argentina, Uruguay and Paraguay, with special assignments in Cuba and Venezuela. He is currently stationed in El Salvador.